FLYING WITH EYES CLOSED

A.O. NORRIS

AuthorHouse™ LLC
1663 Liberty Drive
Bloomington, IN 47403
www.authorhouse.com
Phone: 1-800-839-8640

Published by AuthorHouse 03/05/2014

ISBN: 978-1-4918-5153-1 (sc)
ISBN: 978-1-4918-5154-8 (hc)
ISBN: 978-1-4918-5155-5 (e)

Library of Congress Control Number: 2014900681

For all those I left behind at that airline.
Thank you for the times together,
I will never forget them.

Contents

An important message regarding all new hire flight attendants:

Hello,

This message is going out to all applicants that are attending UPside Airs new hire training class. UPside Air will set up and take care of all hotel reservations at the Airport hotel outside of ORD. All information about check in time is in your packet. Please remember that class starts promptly on Wednesday June 23, 2009 at 8:00 AM. Late arrivals will be dismissed from training. The address to the hotel as well as directions to get from the hotel to the training facility is located in the training packet.

Before coming to class we ask that you please familiarize yourself with the following airline terms that will be mentioned throughout your time with us:

Air sick bag—A bag found in a seat back pocket for passengers to vomit in.

Baggage handler—An employee dealing in the baggage department of the airline. Can work out on the ramp or lost luggage department.

Bases—Main airports of operation for an airline. UPside Air currently operates out of four bases: PHL, ORF, DCA, and ORD (To be closed in January 2010)

Block time—The time you will be paid as a working crew member. Begins when the door to the aircraft closes to the time the door to the aircraft re-opens.

Bulkhead—The space in front of the first row of seats on an aircraft. Usually a built in wall. (Note: NO luggage may be stored in the Bulkhead area.)

Captain—The pilot in command of the aircraft.

Commute—Meaning to fly to or from your domicile base to where you live on your off time.

Catering—An employee dealing in bringing all beverages, spinzels, napkins, etc. to the aircraft.

Crew member—General term to address pilots and flight attendants.

Crew room—This is a room found in each base that UPside Air operates out of for crew members to spend between flights. There is access to computers, printers, internet and your V-file. In addition, there are also couches, tables, and a television with a VCR. (Note: Crew members may NOT utilize the crew room as a hotel.)

Crew scheduling—The department that operates from company headquarters in Chicago assigning trips to crew members as well routing and re-routing aircrafts.

Deadhead—To fly on an aircraft as a revenue passenger from one airport to another. (Note: All deadheading crew members MUST be in uniform as they are still being paid block time.)

Domicile base—The base crew members must report to at the beginning of a trip. Crew members will finish their trip in their domicile base as well.

Express carrier—A separate airline that a mainline carrier hires to fly shorter flights. STRATA Airlines currently has three express carriers operating for them, including UPside Air.

Ferry—To fly on an empty aircraft from one airport to another. (Note: All ferrying crew members MUST be in uniform as they are still being paid block time.)

First Officer—FO for short. The second pilot in command of an aicraft.

Flight deck—Where the aircraft is operated from. (Note: due to changes in equal rights laws, the flight deck may no longer be referred to as the 'cockpit')

Flighties—Short term coined for 'Flight attendants'.

Fuelers—Ground personnel in charge of adding fuel to an aircraft.

Gate agent—The airline employee that operates the gate to the aircraft.

Ground stop—When all aircraft at an airport have halted from taking off or landing due to weather, emergency in the airport, etc.

Hanger—Where aircraft are kept when on maintenance or between operating flights at night.

Holding pattern—When an aircraft must circle above an airport until gaining clearance to land. Could be due to weather, heavy traffic flow, etc.

Inflight department—Refers to jobs dealing with the flight attendant side of the airline industry.

Inflight manager—The manager in charge of the inflight department from domicile to domicile. (Note: DCA based flight attendants will report directly to Mikey Panasosky who is the current inflight manager in DCA.)

Interphone—The phone at the front of the aircraft. The three main functions of this phone are:
FLT: Calls the flight deck.
PA: Addresses the passengers over the PA.
EMR: Calls the flight deck in an emergency.

Jet bridge—The bridge between a terminal and the aircraft. (Note: Jet bridges are to only be operated by qualified gate agents.)

Jump seat—The seat at the front of the aircraft for working crew members to sit in during take off and landing.

Leg—A single flight from one airport to another.

Mainline carrier—A major airline.

Mechanic—An employee that handles all mechanical issues on an aircraft. (Note: Crew members are NOT qualified to use the mechanics vehicle for transport within an airport.)

Mechanical—When an aircraft has an issue that would prevent it from operating correctly.

Mono—The nickname Corazon has given to Chuck. When translating from Spanish 'Mono' means monkey and 'Monito' means little monkey.

Non-rev—Crew members may fly for free, or 'Jump seat' on STRATA Airlines and all of their express carriers/partners. (Note: Crew members may only fly for free should there be an available seat on the aircraft. This does not always include the actual jump seat.)

Over night—The time spent at a hotel over night when on a trip. (Note: UPside Air will provide a hotel on each trip so long as a crew member is OUT of their domicile base.)

Passenger loads—How full a flight is. Passenger loads are counted in three different zones on an UPside aircraft for weight and balance purposes.

Ramper—An employee that deals with the ground operations of an aircraft. Managing the baggage handlers, fuelers, weight and balance, caterers, etc.

Regional Jet—RJ for short. A smaller aircraft. UPside Air currently operates a fleet of Canadair CL65 Regional jets.

Reserve—RSV for short. A day in a crew members schedule in which they can be called to operate any flight. RSV flights are given to flight attendants based on operational needs.

Robot—Term coined for a business professional that wakes up and does the same 9-5 job every day until they are either retired or dead.

Routing—The path that an aircraft or crew member follows on a day to day basis.

Seat back pocket—A pouch hanging on the back of the seat in front of a passengers seat. Contains an inflight magazine, safety information card, and air sick bag. On bulk head seats, the seat back pocket will be found on the wall directly in front of the seat. (Note: It is important to check every seat back pocket at the end of each flight for trash.)

Sign in book—A book found in each crew room to be signed by all crew members at the start of each trip. Please include your name, the time you arrived at the airport and the routing number of your trip.

Slam clicker—Term coined for an unsociable crew member who arrives on an overnight, goes to their room and locks themselves in it until their flight the next day.

Slow descent—The portion of a flight when a plane has been cleared for landing at an airport.

Soma Air—Another express carrier of STRATA Airlines. UPside Airs main competition and rival.

Spinzels—Small twisted pretzel snacks to be handed out on a flight. (Note: Only one bag of Spinzels PER PASSENGER. Not to be handed out before 11:00 AM Local time.)

STRATA Airlines—The mainline carrier that UPside airlines operates for.

Taxi—When an aircraft moves on the ground at an airport.

Ticket agents—Airline employees who issue tickets when checking in for a flight.

Trip—A flight to be flown, given to a crew member that will begin and end in their domicile base. Trips can be between one and five days with a chance of being held out an extra day based on operational needs.

Turnaround flight—A flight that leaves and returns to it's domicile base in the same day.

Up and away certificate—Awarded to flight attendants by STRATA Airlines frequent fliers for performing exceptionally inflight.

UPside Air—Your current express carrier. Company headquarters are located in Chicago. Operating to destinations up and down the east coast, certain destinations in the mid-west, and parts of Canada.

V-file—A flight attendants file in their domicile base to be checked at the beginning and end of each trip for news regarding the company or messages from your inflight department.

<<<<<<<<<<<<<<<<<<<<<<<—Denotes a flash back in the story.

>>>>>>>>>>>>>>>>>>>>>>>—Denotes a flash forward in the story.

~~~~~~~~~~~~~~~~~~~~~~~~~—Denotes an imagination sequence in the story.

We also ask that you please take a moment to review and familiarize yourself with the structure of the interior of our aircraft as well.
~~~~~~~~~~~~~~~~~~~~~~~~~

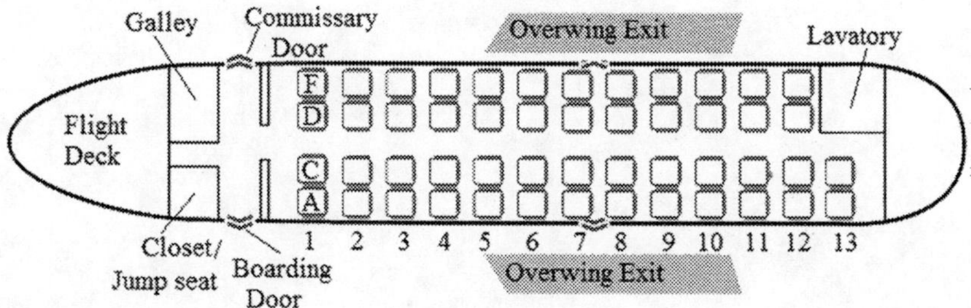

Thank you, we look forward to meeting you in class.

Janie Sanders
Inflight training manager

Camden DePonce
Assistant inflight training manager

Part I

Bad flight attendant

For a good cup of coffee in Raleigh, North Carolina

May 6th, 2010

The alarm blares.
Wake up. *Wake up.*
The sun is peeking
through the curtains
and into my eyes.

What time is it?
One in the afternoon?
I have three hours
before I have to be
on the plane
and at work.
I love late show times.
I hate the hangovers
they usually bring.

I rise from my coffin
of a bed
and toss on
my white tee-shirt
from yesterday.
Dirty jeans
I've worn for the last
three days of the trip.
Stupid white sunglasses
I found on the plane.

I put on my sandals,
shuffle my feet
out of the hotel room
(Key in the back pocket),
and down the hall
like a man on a mission.

That mission was the same today
as it was yesterday.
The same as it will
more than likely
be tomorrow.
The mission:
find
some
coffee.
Without it,
I'm dead to the world.

I'm blinded by the afternoon sun
as I leave our hotel
devoid of any fashion sense.
The glasses do nothing
to protect my eyes.

What do I care?
I'm not likely
to run into anyone
in Raleigh I know
with the exception of
my fellow flighties
or pilots.

They'll be out themselves
looking for restaurants,
book stores,
Wal-marts . . .

Our hotel used to be
in the middle of nowhere,
down a winding road,
surrounded by forest.
The rooms were large and nice,
but considering
we got in to the hotel
at eleven in the morning
and didn't leave
until four
the next afternoon,
it left little to do
apart from sleeping
the time away.

The next overnight we have
will surely be
only nine hours,
so I can forgive myself
if I lay around all day
when the opportunity
is there.

The new hotel we stay at
doesn't have as many
nice amenities as we'd like,
but it's within walking distance
of the Duke campus,
the bars,
and the dangers
of a long overnight
somewhere decent.

I'm hung over.
I only have myself to blame,
but it eases the pain
to blame John instead.
Whatever, he's a good guy
and it'd be downright rude
to refuse a free beer
or six
from him.
He's how all pilots should be.

We get a deal at Charlie's pub anyway
since the owner is currently dating
one of our flight attendants.

Where can I find
a good cup of coffee?

I can be sneaky about it
if I don't want to pay
for it.
Find an oil changing center,
maybe an office building,
something of the sort
with a lobby
or a waiting area.

Walk in,
and stand around
for a few moments
as if I'm waiting
for someone
or something . . .
maybe check my watch
and cell phone.

Then casually stroll
over to the free coffee stand
and pour myself a cup.
Make eye contact
and smile
at the receptionist
as I do so.

But wait—what's this?
Only powdered cream?
You cheap bastards
couldn't spring
for the tiny cups of milk?
The problem
with the powder
is that it twists my intestines,
gives me stomach pains,
and ultimately
makes me gassy.
And a gassy flight attendant
is not
a happy flight attendant.

So what's it going to be today?
Cheap route for a free cup?
Or a happily owned
local joint-
diner, coffee house,
or maybe kiosk
in a super market . . .
the hell with it.
I get paid tomorrow.
I'm treating myself
to a cup today.

It will make the difference
between a bad day
and a good day.

The last thing I'd do
is settle for the coffee
in the hotel room.
That stuff
tastes like mud.
Mud flavored coffee
is the worse.
And I happen to know
for a fact
those coffee pots
haven't been cleaned
in ten thousand years.

The only thing dirtier
than a hotel coffee pot
is an airplane coffee pot.

One good thing
about the coffee makers
in the rooms
is that they sometimes
come with a decent
coffee cup.
And if I like it enough,
it's mine.

"Hello, front desk,
how may I help you?"

"Hi, sorry to bother you,
but it seems that house keeping
didn't bring me any new
coffee cups
while cleaning my room . . ."

"Oh, we're so sorry,
we'll have someone
send one up right away."

Suckers.
One stylish,
new coffee mug
on the way.
It's only karma
when the cup breaks
in my suitcase
the next day.

The phone rings
in my pocket
as I make my way
into town.

Damn it,
I bet it's scheduling.
I can see it now:
"Hi, is this Charles?
This is Katie in scheduling.
We've added another
two days to your trip,
with six legs a day.
Enjoy your weekend
spent in boring hotels
while passing blurs of faces,
early morning show times,
long days, and best of all,
nowhere to find
a good cup of coffee."

I almost dread
looking at the phone.
It could be scheduling,
but it's not.

My heart
is brought to life faster
than the rest of my dead,
coffee-less body
to hear Corazon's voice
on the other end.

"Good morning
my little Monito!
How are you today?
What's the time difference
between there and home?
You know you called me
drunk last night,
and I couldn't stop laughing!
I hope you're
enjoying your trip . . ."

The frivolous banter
we make
between each other
as I pass through
the town
is enough
to make the world around me
become more alive
than it really is.

I hang up
from my happy
little conversation
as I enter the empty
coffee shop.

"Hi, how are you today?"
Smiles the cute girl
behind the counter.

"Hung over.
Can I have a medium
cup of coffee?"

She laughs
at my stupid joke
that harbors truth
within it
and I exchange
my hard-earned two dollars
for coffee.

She points to the table behind me
when I inquire
as to where I can find
cream and sugar.

I place a napkin
on the table
and my lid on the napkin
and smile with delight
as I look down.
Ah yes!
The liquid creamer!
Victory for Chuck!

I come to the conclusion
that today
is going to be a good day
as I make my concoction:
two creams,
three sugars,
a stir stick inside,
and the lid back on.

I wave goodbye to Mrs.
-I'm-working-at-the-coffee-joint-to-pay-for-college
as I make my way
out the door,
back through town,
up the hill,
and into my hotel.

I return to my cave
of a room
and swing open
the curtains
to let the day in.

I slowly drink my coffee
as I pull on my uniform
and get ready for work.

I take one last look
around the room
to make sure
I haven't forgotten anything.

I roll my suitcase down
to the lobby.

John is sitting
on a couch there
and smiles
when he sees me.

"Good morning man!"
He says
with a hangover-free voice
"Did you know
that when Chuck Norris
does a push up,
he doesn't push himself up,
he pushes the earth down?"

We both chuckle
as the phone
in my pocket rings.

His eyes widen
as an "Uh-oh."
escapes his lips.

I look at the phone
with a smile
on my face.

"It's crew scheduling."
I say.

"So what
are you smiling about?"
he asks.

". . . today
is going to be
a good day."
I reply,
taking my last
sip of coffee
from my cup.

Henry

July 7th 2009

I met Henry my first day
of flight attendant training
in Chicago.

To save money on hotel rooms,
our company stuck us
with a roommate
when we began training.

I guess they figured
that if you could last
a month
without picking a fight
with your roommate,
you would be fine
getting along
on the plane
with passengers.

I had never
had a roommate before,
but he seemed
like a nice enough guy.

You learn a lot
about someone
sleeping in a bed
five feet away
from theirs
in a hotel room.

He was in his mid-thirties
and had worked
for our mainline carrier
STRATA Airlines
as a baggage handler
for several years.

He was married,
and kept a photo
of him and his wife
on top of the television
in a metal
four by six frame.

He had a two year old daughter,
but he never really
said much else
about her.

His laid back
'I don't give a care'
attitude
made him easy
to get along with.

If I was tired at night
and asked him
to turn the television off,
he would have
no problem doing it.

He would tell me stories
about when he used to be
a ramper,
and how he would be outside
at six in the morning,
tossing those damn suitcases
on to the plane.

It didn't matter
if it was a hundred degrees
in the blazing hot sun
or there was snow
up to his ankles,
those passengers bags
had to be loaded
onto the plane
and he
was the one doing it.

He told me how
he would toss them
from a large rusted trolley
onto a conveyer belt
that went up into the plane
when the flight
was going somewhere,
and the opposite way around
when the plane landed.

Six hour shifts.
Hundred pound bags . . .
I could never do it.
My hands are too soft.

He would drop the bags
and know something
expensive inside of it broke.
But he didn't care.
He would look up
at the plane
to see passengers faces
peering out of the round
windows at him.

And then he would just
smile and wave,
before picking up the bag
and carrying on
as if nothing
had happened.

Because he worked
for STRATA Airlines,
he got all of the free
flight benefits,
but he never
got to use them
because he worked
all the time.

So that's when he decided
he didn't want to be
the man handling bags
on the ground outside
of the plane anymore,
but rather
the man handling
the sodas and pretzels
inside the plane
instead.

The most interesting part
of his stories
were about how
when he worked
underneath the airport
in the mess
and tangle
of conveyer belts
taking bags every which way.

Sometimes a bag would
'fall and get busted open'
(He explained this
by making air quotations
with his fingers.)
The rampers would then
split the booty
between each other
like blood thirsty pirates
and chock it up to
a destroyed baggage loss.

It's got to suck
for the poor old Grandmother
whose bag
happened to wind up
jumping
off the belt that day.

After spending eight hours
in a training class together
with someone,
and then the entire night
in the same hotel room,
you start to realize
all the little things
they begin to do
that bother you.

It was always stupid stuff
like leaving
the bathroom towel
on the floor,
or his clothes
strewn about,
but the first real incident
happened about two weeks
into training.

We had to buy our own food
and since sandwiches
and ramen noodles
were pretty cheap
that seemed to be
the menu for me.

After coming back to the room
that evening from studying
with some of my class mates,
I went to make a sandwich,
and the bread was all gone.

"Dude, what happened
to my bread?" I asked.

"Oh, sorry man,
I got hungry
and made a sandwich.
I'll pay you back,
don't worry about it."

After two weeks
with the guy
I knew
he wouldn't pay me back
for a couple
of slices of bread,
so I just shrugged it off.

Then one weekend
I had gone to bed early
when I wasn't feeling well
after an evening
with Corazon,
when I heard Henry
come into the room
making all kinds of ruckus.

He reeked of alcohol
and had his arm
around some woman
who clearly
wasn't his wife
in the photo.

"Oh, sorry man . . .
I thought
you were still out
with Corazon."
He said.

"No, I came back early."
I replied
and rolled over.
He left the room
immediately after that.

I was more upset
that he had woken me up
than anything
but I said nothing of the incident.

Two days later
we began our aircraft
familiarization class,
which was taught at night
(That's when the airplanes
were sleeping
at the hanger in Chicago.)

Not even five minutes
into the class,
our instructors
Janie and Camden
asked Henry
to come with him.

When you get called
into the office
at the beginning of class,
it was never for anything good,
and you usually
didn't come back.

We all talked amongst ourselves
for ten minutes
while they were gone,
wondering
what Henry could have done.

He scored good grades
on his test.
He was an easy
to get along with
kind of guy.

Apart from bringing someone
back to our hotel room
(Which I never
told anyone about),
he never broke
any of our training rules.

They then returned
and asked me
to come with them
as well.

Now I was getting nervous.
I wondered
what kind of shit
I was caught up in.

They took me into their office
and told me
that the baggage handler manager
at STRATA Airlines
had gone to clean out Henry's locker
at the airport
since he was transferring
from the baggage handling department
to be a flight attendant,
and what they found
shocked them.

Portable DVD players,
laptop computers,
mini alcohol bottles
from the plane (empty).
All kinds of goods
that had been deemed
'destroyed baggage loss'.

I was somewhat surprised,
and couldn't believe
that he was stupid enough
to have left that stuff
in his locker.

They then asked me
if I knew anything about it,
but I just shook my head
and said no.
I began to worry
if he had ratted me out
about knowing,
and thought that maybe
he was trying
to drag me down with him,
but it turned out he hadn't.

They said the reason
that they called me
into the office
was because he was asked
to leave training
and was sent back to the hotel
to pack up and leave.

They were worried,
however,
that if I had any valuables
in the room,
they might be leaving
with him.

They told me
I could leave training early
and go back to the hotel
to make sure
he didn't steal anything
that belonged to me,
but I told them I trusted him
and that he wouldn't
have stolen anything of mine
(I also didn't want
to have to make up
a class over the weekend.)

As class went on though,
it began
to worry me more and more.
I didn't *really* know this guy.
He was just someone
I shared a room with.
Hell, he ate my bread
without asking,
and now that thief
was alone
cleaning out his side of the room,
and quite possibly
mine as well.

I told Corazon about it,
even though my instructors
told me not to say anything
to my class mates
about the situation.

She told me not to worry.
Easy enough
for her to say,
she wasn't the one
that was sharing a room
with the pink panther.

When we got back
to the hotel
at three in the morning,
after a long night
of aircraft familiarization,
Corazon and I
went straight up
to my room.

I was shocked.
It looked as though
a tornado had blown through.
His pillows
were on the floor.
His sheets
were strewn across the bed.
The picture
of him and his wife
was face down
on top of the television.

I started to freak out.
Corazon told me
to calm down
and check my stuff.
Much to my surprise,
nothing of mine was touched.

My laptop was still there.
My iPod
was still on my nightstand.
Even the emergency money
I kept hidden in my suitcase,
that I know
he had seen me take out,
was still where I left it.

The gears in my head
began turning, and within moments,
it made sense.
The photo of his wife
was turned facing down
and his bed was a mess
because obviously,
he wanted to take advantage
of a hotel room our company
had paid for with his lady friend
he had brought over
the weekend before.

It seemed as though
he went out
with a bang.
Literally.

"Monito. Come here,
there's a note on the counter!"
Corazon explained.

The note simply stated
"Thanks for not ratting me out.
I owed you one.
—Henry."
It was left
on top
of a new loaf of bread.

The Zorro of practical jokes

August 2nd, 2009

The phone rings.
Wake up *Wake up*
I reach over to the night stand, blindly feel around for it.

"Hello?"

"Hi, is this Charles?"

My first call from crew scheduling. The beginning of what would be a long and tiresome road of sleepless nights and early show times for trips. Three days after graduation from our flight attendant training, I found myself right back where I left off at the hotel. My home in Chicago.

Being on reserve can be no fun at all. When you begin a reserve sequence it will last a time span of anywhere from one to six days, during which time you become the company's personal bitch. That means, anytime between Five AM of the day you begin, and midnight of the day you finish, the company owns you.

Being on reserve is very self-explanatory. If another flight attendant calls out you need to be ready to take their place in two hours. Why would another flight attendant call out? Maybe they're sick. Maybe their plane's broke down somewhere else and requires maintenance. Maybe they didn't get that day off that they wanted and so they're making you pick up the slack. Damn senior flight attendants.

So what does that mean for people like me on reserve? People that have just started this career? Unfortunately, it means we don't get much say in the matter.

It means you have to have your phone on you at all times in case scheduling needs to reach you. And when they do reach you, you have two hours to get your ass to the airport.

This would serve as a bit of a problem to someone like me, being so that my domicile base is Chicago, and my actual home is in Maryland. I would prefer to be based in DC, but like I said before, when you're as low as I am in seniority, you don't get much say in the matters. So for the month of August, I took up residence in a hotel not far from Chicago O'Hare.

In case you're wondering what happens when you don't answer your phone or make it to the airport in the span of two hours . . . well, that's another story that I'll get into later.

"Hi Charles, this is Katie in scheduling. We've got a two day trip for you . . ."

I should really keep a pen and paper on my night stand. ". . . It's a two hour call out . . ." Terrific. ". . . And you'll be over nighting in Milwaukee."

"Got it. Airport in two hours, Milwaukee tonight. Can you fax that schedule to my hotel?" I asked.

"Yea, no problem, it's on the way." She said.

I rolled out of bed. Pulled my uniform out of the closet. I'm quietly fixing my tie in the mirror when I hear Corazon moving around in bed. She stretches, wipes her eyes, and yawns.

"They call you for a trip?" She asked.

"Yea . . . I'll be back tomorrow though." I replied.

My tie was done. My bags were ready. I kneel at the foot of the bed. Brush her hair away from her face.

"If they don't call me . . . I'll have something made for us to eat when you get back." She says. I smile, kiss her forehead. That will be nice.

Rocco was working at the front desk when I got downstairs.

"I need the shuttle to the airport. I also had a fax sent here." I tell him. He hands me my schedule and I take the shuttle to the airport. I was a little bit nervous since this was my first official trip since I graduated. I found my way to the crew room and checked the sign in book for my trip. The pilots had already been there and signed in, so I just went straight to the plane.

The captain was a guy named Pablo. He was a big fellow from Argentina currently residing in Canada and commuting to Chicago. The FO was a fairly new cute girl in her late twenties named Christie. It didn't take Pablo long to figure out that I was new. I was fumbling around on the plane like an idiot trying my hardest to remember what the hell I was doing before the flight boarded.

"Hey man, just relax. We're not here to grade you or anything . . . just do your own thing." He told me. It calmed me down, and I went on with the first flight. Just after I closed the aircraft door Pablo came on the PA and made an announcement to the passengers:

"Folks, this is your captain speaking, try to be nice to our flight attendant today, it's his first trip since training." I was so damn embarrassed, I knew my face was red. But the passengers laughed and applauded for me. My nerves were calmed.

I thanked him after the flight, although he said it was no big deal, he just wanted to have fun on this trip. Then he told me that I needed to 'swab the deck' before we went to lunch. Now, with what little attention I had paid in training, I certainly don't remember 'swabbing the deck' as part of my in flight regime.

"Yea, you know all those newspapers that are always left behind . . . you're supposed to wet them, and put those on the floor . . . and clean . . . the . . ." He was barely able to finish his sentence without laughing. Christie came out of the flight deck and defended me. I couldn't believe that after only one leg of our trip he was already messing with me. But I figured he was someone I could have fun with on this trip. I told him that if he wanted me to do such a thing, then on the next flight he would have to come out of the flight deck, newspaper under his arm, and greet every passenger on the way to the bathroom. Pablo smiled and shook his head no.

"See? You can't fool me. I'm like the . . . Zorro of practical jokes. I won't fall for child's play." I gloated.

The next leg wasn't a long flight, but much to my surprise, the red call light lit up from the flight deck. I answered it.

"Hey, it's Pablo. I need to use the bathroom." He said from the other end. I was silent for a moment. "That means . . . you need to come up here." He said.

"Yea, no problem . . ." I hung up the phone. He couldn't. He wouldn't. I opened the door and watched with eyes wide open as my pilot passed through the aisle, newspaper under his arm, greeting passengers as he made his way to the bathroom. I could hear some passengers laughing as I closed the flight deck door behind me. He did it. He actually did it.

After the flight was over, he came up to the front of the plane once more to say goodbye with me to all of our passengers. He said nothing, as he nodded his head in the direction of the floor. He was really serious. He wanted me to get down on my hands and knees and clean that dirty floor with the newspapers that passengers left behind. I told him that I never agreed to such a thing. There was no contract, no handshake. He looked to Christie for validation. She told him she had no idea what he was talking about. I later learned he had pranked her way worse than I got it when she started flying though.

<<<<<<<<<<<<<<<<<<<<<<<<

When Christie first started flying for UPside Air, he had poured white powdered coffee creamer into a plastic bag, taped it up, and then snuck it into her in-flight bag. He then proceeded to convince her that someone had smuggled cocaine into her bags and that she had become a drug mule. He even went so far as to have TSA come on board and play along with it. A funny prank I'll admit, but she told me she was nearly in tears before they let up.

>>>>>>>>>>>>>>>>>>>>>>>>

"So I get to look like a fool in front of everyone for nothing?"

He asked with a grin on his face. I smiled back. He nodded and said that we would see who had the last laugh, but I reminded him who was the Zorro of pranks.

When we took the shuttle to the hotel, he filled out the sign in sheet with our names, room keys, and wake up calls on it.

"We have a 6:45 AM show time at the plane tomorrow . . . How much time do you need to get ready in the morning?" He asked me.

"Just a half hour." I replied.

"So is 6 AM alright with you then?" He asked. I said sure, and he filled out the hotel's sign in sheet before handing it back to the van driver. It was already late when we arrived at the hotel so I decided to just get to bed early. I set my alarm for 5:30 AM so that I could have at least a half hour to get ready.

5:30 AM comes early for a guy like me, and needless to say, I was in a rush to get ready. I should probably set my alarm to give myself forty-five minutes to get ready but an extra fifteen minutes of sleep can mean a world of difference.

I was out the room by 5:55 AM and rushed to the front desk. What I didn't realize was that at this particular hotel, the front desk wasn't where the van takes you to the airport, it was the back door. And this hotel was built like a labyrinth. I rushed through the hotel's maze of hallways trying to find the pick up point for my ride. I showed up five minutes late. Pablo and Christie were nowhere to be found. I wondered if they had already left. I started to freak out. Was Pablo playing one of his tricks?

There was no way Christie would let him get away with something like making me late.

At 6:10 the van pulled up.

"Did you just take a crew to the airport?" I asked the driver.

"I take a lot of crews to the airport" He replied sarcastically. I guess because he hated his life, he had to make me hate mine as well.

I was at the airport by 6:15 AM. I rushed through security, checking my watch over and over again along the way. I arrived at the gate. Much to my surprise, neither of my pilots were there.

"Have you seen my pilots for this flight?" I asked the gate agent, out of breath. She shook her head no.

"Would you like me to let you out to the aircraft?" She asked. I didn't know what else to do, so I said yes. She swiped her badge and opened the door to the taxi way.

The plane was shut down, pitch black. Now I was really losing it. I wondered where they could be. He said 6 AM! I looked up at the closed door of the aircraft. I told myself, I could do this. I saw the door opened a lot of times during training. I reached up to the release handle of the door and pulled. It weighed a ton and it didn't budge. I used my other hand and reached up pulling with all my might.

"Open! Open!" I swore under my breath, pulling the handle. I turned my head to see a huge plane taxiing to my right. People were staring and pointing at me through their windows. I must have looked ridiculous dangling on the side of the plane. I gave up and stumbled off. I was so frustrated. I'm such a loser sometimes. Pablo and Christie casually approached with coffee in their hands from the gate.

"Hey man, why'd you come here so early?" He asked.

"Where the hell have you been?! You told me 6 AM this morning!" I shouted. I was frustrated as hell. Pablo chuckled as he sipped his coffee.

"Yea . . . I meant 6 AM for a wake up call. What did you think I meant, 6 AM for a van time?" He asked. I stared blankly at him.

"Wait . . . No, you said on the van yesterday 6 AM . . ."

"Yea, I meant for a wake up call. You said you only needed a half hour in the morning to get ready, so I gave you a wake up call of 6 AM. So we could take a 6:30 van and be here at 6:45. Our show time." I looked at my watch. It was 6:45 AM. Our show time.

I looked at Christie, who shrugged her shoulders and sympathetically said: "I didn't know."

"Oh, I made this for you also." He said, handing me a complimentary sleeping mask from the hotel. It had two holes cut out of it for eyes. "I thought you might want this . . . Zorro." He said laughing. He reached up to the handle of the plane that I was struggling with, and with one hand, twisted it clockwise, pulling it open.

". . . Well played sir. Well played." I said.

>>>>>>>>>>>>>>>>>>>>>>>

It was late when I got back to Chicago that night. I greeted Rocco at the desk as I took the elevator back up to the room.

"Hey . . . I'm back." I called out to Corazon as I entered the room. The bathroom was empty. The bed had been made and unused. The TV was off in both rooms. Only the lamp on the desk was turned on. There was a note on the desk:

'Mono, They called me for a trip. See you soon.

-Corazon'

I heated up a cold pizza that was in the mini fridge and ate it alone on the side of the bed in silence.

You didn't say the magic word

April 19th, 2010

"Would you like something
to drink sir?"
"Yea, give me a diet coke."

Oh, now you've done it.
'*Give me* a diet coke'?
If there's one thing
that pushes my buttons,
that's it.

It's bad enough
he demands
that I have to give him a drink.
It's bad enough
that he doesn't look up
from his newspaper
to respond to me.
But the worse part . . .
is that he doesn't
even add a 'please'
on at the end.

I would expect
a little politeness in return
after being nice myself
to begin with,
but that's not always the case
in a lot of my scenarios.

8 AM flight from DC to Detroit
on a Monday morning
isn't always
the happiest in the world.

What happened to
the loud college kids
I had on my flight last night
from DC to Rochester?
What happened to
the polite old grandma
that just smiled and nodded,
even though she couldn't hear
half of what I was saying?

I don't mind giving the college
kids a free drink.
I don't mind repeating myself
to the elderly woman four times.

But this fifty year old
Robot in a suit
won't even look up
from his newspaper
to demand his diet coke.

Shake it off man.
Just keep going.
"Ok . . . And would you like
ice with that sir?"

"No, just give me the whole can."
Eyes still fixated
on his morning paper.

What did I do wrong?
We boarded on time.
We left on time.
We're going to arrive early.
Hell, I was even
handing out spinzels
and it wasn't even
11 AM yet.

But the best part
was that he still didn't
say 'please'.

"Sorry sir . . .
I can't give away the entire can
until everyone's been served.
That's STRATA Air's policy,
not mine."

That got his attention.
Now he's looking up at me
from his newspaper.
"I don't care.
Give me
the whole can."

All right, he's getting louder.
Some people around him
are watching us.

Play it cool man.
Stand your ground.
"Sorry sir . . . if I gave a whole can
of diet coke away to everyone . . .
there would only be enough
for ten people.
And then
all the other people
that wanted diet coke
won't be able to have any."

I've cracked open the can
and the cup's
already half full.

The look on his face
is priceless.
His hands crinkle his newspaper.
"I don't care!
Now you are going
to give me
that whole can!"

Hey, maybe if you yell at me
louder, you'll get the can!
The can
will find it's way
to you.
Maybe that's how it will work.
The can will magically
jump out of the cart
and onto your tray,
all out of fear
of the angry Robot.

Not today buddy.
You want to pick a fight,
you got it.
Kill him with kindness.
"I'm so sorry sir.
If there's any diet coke left
after the service is done-"

"I don't give a shit,
give me the can!"

Silence.

I couldn't believe it.
Not only
was he verbally threatening me
(A big no-no on an airplane)
but he had just turned
my family friendly flight
into a PG-13 rated drama.
Possibly comedy
from the other passengers
point of view.
In fact, the man sitting behind him
is smiling.
He obviously finds this amusing.
I smile back.

He's on my side.
The winning side.

"Well sir,
imagine if we have
to make an emergency diversion
somewhere and land suddenly.
We could be stuck
on the ground for hours.
Then I would be
more than happy
to hand out all the beverages
that we have on board
to keep everyone happy."
I said smiling.

He was so mad,
the top of his bald head
was turning red.

"In fact, that will be the case
in a few moments
when we have to divert
to the nearest airport.
Then everyone on board
can have all the soda they want
to make up for their lost time.
Everyone except the one passenger
that we had to divert to that airport for
so that the police
could escort him away.
Can you guess who that is sir?
. . . Can you guess who that is?"
I asked.

I was trying to remain calm.
Stand your ground man.
Stare him down.
Show him you mean business.

His silence was all I needed to hear
in order to push my cart
to the next row
and to the smiling passenger
behind him.

Deep sigh.
The worst is over.

"Would you like something to drink sir?"

"Can I have a sprite please?
-With ice if you have some."

"Yes sir . . ." I said smiling.
"*. . . and would you like
the whole can this morning?*"

The now infamous juice can races!

December 7th 2009

I arrived in DC and headed to the crew room as normal at the end of my trip. Surprise, surprise . . . another email from my in-flight manager Mikey.

"Charles, we need to have another meeting to discuss an issue you had on your flight . . . blah blah blah . . ."

God, what did I do this time? My life's like a freakin' television show. Every week there's some new problem or issue that arises. Gets me all worked up and worried: "Shit, this is the end . . . I know it is this time. I'm going to be fired." I always think the worse, even if it's not. This isn't the end. This is just another email from Mikey for another meeting. For another mistake. I wondered what it could be. No wait—I knew what it was.

When I went to her office for the meeting she had me close the door as always.

Take a seat in the chair in front of her nice little office desk. I was smiling, although inside I was a bit nervous. Don't let her see that, keep your cool. Stand your ground man. Keep it together.

She speaks so pleasant and understanding "Charles . . . do you know why you're here?" There's really only two people in the world that call me Charles: My mother, and Mikey. And they both only do it when they're displeased with me. I tried playing dumb. I shook my head no. "Well . . . apparently we had an incident on your flight a few days ago and it needs to be addressed." Oh yea, I knew it. "Why don't you tell me your side of the story first?" She asked. I stared dumfounded. "About the juice cans." She said. I smiled. "Charles, I trust you, I know you wouldn't lie to me. So why don't you just start at the beginning."

<<<<<<<<<<<<<<<<<<<<<<<<

We were working a flight from . . . you know I don't even remember, it all blends together eventually. Any ways, it was a short taxi on the runway. Some of these pilots taxi the plane like it's in a damn

Nascar race. Slow down! It was causing me to be in a hurry. Safety announcements, walk through, one quick look to see if everything is secure . . . Yea, it looks secure. OK, call to the flight deck "Hey, it's Chuck. The cabin's secure." Pull out the jump seat. Sit down, wait for take-off.

The engines power up, we pick up speed. Take-off. As soon as I heard it begin to shift, I knew. I could hear the cans of juice slide down the container, hitting the inside wall, and bursting out of the cabinet. I don't believe this, what a newbie move.

I could imagine Camden telling us in training: "This happens to everyone at least once. It doesn't matter if I tell you or not, sooner or later, you're gonna forget to lock something . . . and it's going to fly out during take-off. No matter how short or long you do this for . . . it'll happen to you once. After that, believe me, it *never* happens again."

Fifty cans of juice fell to the floor. Have you ever seen fifty cans of juice fall out of a cabinet during a takeoff? There was nothing I could do about it. Since the plane takes off at an angle and not directly straight up, when they hit the floor they just slid down the aisle quickly. People had surprised looks on their faces. Heads poked out from their seats, a few people chuckled. I was paralyzed. I knew my face was red. I reached up for the phone and slowly took it off the hook.

Breathe.
Just breathe.
Keep it together.

". . . Ladies and gentlemen, that was your beverage service . . . if you'll clear the way; your pretzels will be following down the aisle shortly." Everyone was laughing and clapping for me . . .
>>>>>>>>>>>>>>>>>>>>>>>>

I stopped my story there. Maybe that's all that Mikey knew. Maybe, but not likely.

"It's OK Charles, as Camden told you in training, that's normal. It happens to everyone. Once I forgot to lock the coffee maker in its place and when we took off, the coffee pot flew out and hot coffee spilled all over a passenger in the first row!" She said. I smiled. I guess Camden was right after all. "So why don't you continue on with your story then?" She asked.

Dammit, I knew I wasn't off the hook that easily.

<<<<<<<<<<<<<<<<<<<<<<<

. . . As soon as it was safe to stand again, I walked down the aisle with a plastic bag collecting all the juice cans. Surprisingly, none had burst open. Just a few dents here and there. All were recovered and accounted for. A few passengers even asked to take a can home with them as a memento of this hilarious event after the flight was over.

Well, afterward, that got me thinking how to turn this into a fun little game. I contemplated all the ways to go about it, and on the next flight I had it all figured out. It was a full flight: young kids, old business men . . . and to be honest, I was starting to have second thoughts.

"What the hell am I doing? I'll never get away with this. I'm gonna be so screwed if I get caught." I told myself. "You know what? To hell with it, you only live once."

I thought.

Same routine as before. I made double sure that the cabinet with the juice cans was properly locked this time, but not until after I took a can of orange juice and a can of apple juice out of it. I set them on the counter. I picked up the phone. My heart was racing.

Breathe.
Just breathe.
Keep it together.

"OK . . . here's the deal . . . on the last flight coming in here, I forgot to lock this cabinet here where we keep all the cans of juice. Honest mistake, happens to everyone. So during takeoff, fifty cans of juice fell out of the cabinet, and slid down the aisle." A few people were smiling. I had everyone's attention, that's for sure. "Well everyone was so amused by this, that it got me thinking: 'If apple juice and orange juice were to have a race against each other, who would win?' So I happen to have two cans here . . ." I took my jump seat with the two cans. ". . . I'm going to place a can of apple juice and a can of orange juice at my feet here. And when we take off, the two cans will slide down the aisle. Whichever can reaches the end of the aisle first, wins. So . . . with that said, how many people think that orange juice is going to win?" Some people raised their hands. "How many people think that apple juice is going to win? Come on now, don't be shy." Some more people raised their hands. "OK, keep the aisles clear, is everyone ready?"

We were next for takeoff.

"I'm gonna get so busted. One of these old business men are gonna rat me out, I know it. They look so serious, they must think I'm nuts." I thought. ". . . To hell with it. I want to have fun. I want these people to have fun. For the rest of their lives, they're going to remember the flight attendant that raced cans of juice down the aisle."

The plane took off.

The two cans began to slide.

>>>>>>>>>>>>>>>>>>>>>>>>

Mikeys hands were cupped over her mouth. Her eyes were wide.

"Charles . . . what do you have to say in your defense?" she asked me.

I sighed. What could I say? "You know . . . I was just having a good time. I know it could have caused a safety issue, but look at it like this: if I had used soda instead, it could have burst open and sprayed everywhere. Juice would just dribble onto the floor. Also, I made sure the aisle was clear. And everyone's reaction . . ." I had to stop talking when her facial expression failed to change. I was caught at a loss for words. She didn't look pleased at all. She placed her hands over her mouth again and took a deep breath as she always did before giving me pearls of wisdom.

"Charles . . . I don't know what to say. I'm glad you're here. I'm glad you love your job and you want to have a good time with the passengers. But that's not UPside Airs way. We fly an express jet for STRATA Airlines and they're the mainline that signs our checks. So we have to abide by their rules and not make up our own. You have to be professional. Safety has to come first. You understand this . . . right?"

I nodded while looking past her at a poster of a kitten dangling from a rope by its claws with the caption 'Hang in there' written beneath. I smiled to myself.

"I'm going to have you sign a piece of paper. Now I know this is December, and you only have 2 weeks left before your probation is over, but this is your second offense. One more before December 19th . . . and I'm going to let you go. Do you understand?" she asked.

My focus moved from the kittens problem back to my own. I nodded.

"I guess you can't tell me who it was? That reported me?" I asked her out of my own curiosity. She shook her head no, and told me it was confidential. I had a feeling I knew who it was though. I'm so damn lucky I wasn't fired, but she knew my intentions were good. I didn't mean any harm. That great race never took place again.

Conclusions?

<<<<<<<<<<<<<<<<<<<<<<<

The plane took off. The two cans began to slide. Slow at first . . . then picking up speed. People began clapping. Then cheering. Then hollering. I couldn't believe it. Young kids, and even old business men—especially old business men! The ones I thought would rat me out, were getting into it the most. One serious looking business tike was holding up money: "Come on!!! I got 20 riding on you, Orange!"

The emergency call chimed from the front, it was my captain. He didn't seem like a nice fellow from the start. And he certainly wasn't happy with my shenanigans.

"What the hell is going on back there!? All we can hear are passengers screaming! We're about ready to divert!" He shouted. I told him not to, and explained the situation. He was pissed.

>>>>>>>>>>>>>>>>>>>>>>>

It turns out that it was him that ratted me out. I knew it had to have been, it was just never confirmed until almost seven months later. I asked Mikey to take a look in my in-flight file, just for the sake of looking through it. There were so many mixed papers in it, medical documents, up and away certificates, letters, notes . . . and there it was. The report of my juice can races, signed by the captain himself. He blew it way out of proportion saying I had people screaming in the back of the plane like we were under attack or something. Mikey was a bit flustered, realizing at that moment when we had our conversation in December she couldn't tell me who it was that turned me in. But it had to be documented, signed, and placed in my in-flight file. A file that I much later discovered we had every right to look through. I smiled and looked at Mikey, neither of us said anything about the incident, as I shuffled the paper to the back and continued going through the file.

"If it's any consolation to your own curiosity . . . about what happened with those cans of juice . . ." I said, still looking through the file ". . . apple juice was the winner of the race. I guess it's because it didn't have all that pulp to slow it down."

When the sunlight beams

October 19th 2009

It was a rough afternoon
in October.
You know the kind
when the wind is so cold outside
that it stings your face
to the point that it's red.

I had been separated
from my crew in Allentown, PA
when I missed
my dead head flight
back home.

I can't believe they didn't wait for me.
But it was the last flight of the day,
as well as our trip,
and I'm sure all they wanted to do
was get back to Philadelphia
as much as me.

Crew scheduling wanted
to put me back up in a hotel,
but I was ready
to get back home already.

So I wound up at the nearest bus station
and purchased a ticket
to ride the bus
from Allentown to Philadelphia
with a promise
to be reimbursed from payroll.

Although I knew
with all the paper work
I would have to fill out,
and the time it would take
to see the money again,
it really wasn't worth the trouble.

I had to wait at the bus station
for almost a half hour
before the bus arrived
from its previous destination.
I was thrilled to get out
of that urine smelling bus station.

Despite the fact
that it was a large
gray hound bus,
most of the seats were full
except one near the back
on the right side.

This was where I met Mel.
She was also twenty one,
and on her way to the airport.
Her family was Russian,
and had only been in the U.S.
for about fifteen years or so.

She smiled when I stopped
in front of the seat beside her
and asked if it was taken.
She said I could have it,
although there really wasn't
much of a choice,
since it was the only seat left.

Her blonde hair
was in a pony-tail,
and she was wearing sweatpants
and some random College sweater.
She had a book in her hand
that I can't recall,
and headphones on.

At first, I immediately
calculated I would fail.
(Which I think I still should have.)
This girl wouldn't want anything
to do with me.

I was a nervous wreck,
whose only real life experience
revolved around a year abroad.
And she was a cheerleader
or held some sort of
social position of power
back in high school.

I wasn't an idiot, or even bad
at talking to girls,
but she was way out of my league.

Luckily, I saw
that she was listening to
Alexisonfire on her iPod.

"Preppy girls don't listen
to Alexisonfire!" I thought.
Maybe I got her all wrong.
Maybe she was the cute but smart girl
who gets into non-mainstream music
and is attracted
to walking contradictions.

Turns out she was.

Now that things were over
with Corazon
(for the first time around),
I figured it wouldn't hurt
to give it a shot.

I started a conversation with her
"Hey you like Alexisonfire too?"
I asked.

"Oh yea, I'm a much bigger fan
of Dallas Green though.
I think he's incredible
as a solo artist."

No way.

I couldn't believe she shared
the exact same perspective as me.
And we continued talking
for the entire two hour bus ride.

She was on the way
to catch a flight to Florida
for a funeral of a friend
of the family or something
that she really didn't seem
all that upset about.

We shared each others stories,
talked about our lives,
pointed out
all the weird people
on the bus.
I cried internally every time
she bit her lower lip.

We sat together
as the afternoon sun moved
slowly down the window
warming our arms.
Despite the cold weather outside,
the temperature
was perfect on the bus.

I swear every time
she touched my hand,
I thought I was gonna have to go
into that cell they called a bathroom
on the bus,
and use it for more
than its intentional purposes.

So the bus ride ended
at the airport
and I walked with her
all the way through security
and to her STRATA Airlines gate
to say goodbye.

We exchanged numbers,
and made plans to call each other
the next night
and then go out to lunch
when she returned
to Philly in a week.

It was a long wait
until the next night,
but when you live in an airport,
time goes much slower than normal.

When we finally did speak,
we were crazy for each other.
We spoke for hours on the phone . . .
which drove her parents mad.
We talked about
absolutely nothing.

There was such a connection.
Every time I made her laugh,
it reminded me of the sun
moving from the bus window
slowly up my arm.

I had a bouquet of flowers
that I purchased for ten dollars
in a vending machine
by baggage claim for her
when she arrived back
at the airport again.

"Hey I know a nice little place
to eat here called the Jet rock café."
I told her, even though
their food was horrible.

I took her to the F terminal
where I was currently residing
and to the food joint
that was slowly killing me
day by day.

She thought it was hilarious
when we arrived in the terminal
and I said "Home sweet home!"
She had a lame kind of giggle that
in turn made me smile.
I didn't want her to see me,
for fear she may not do it again.

After we ate,
I waited outside with her
for her brother to arrive
to pick her up from the airport.
We made plans to meet
the following week in Allentown
so that she could show me around.

We shared a kiss,
nothing heavy or special,
but it left the both of us
with smiles on our faces.

I watched as her and her brother
drove off in his little black Mercedes
into the cold.

I didn't hear from her
the next day.
Or the day after that.
I called her parents house
and got no answer.

On Wednesday morning,
at about 10:00 her number
popped up on my phone.
It was her mother
on the other end however.
She told me in mostly broken English,
through more tears than I have,
that Mel had been killed.

Somewhere between
Philadelphia and Allentown
a bus had blown a tire
and flipped over on the high way.
Her brother was in the hospital
still in critical condition
but Mel however
had been crushed,
literally,
by a Gray hound bus.

Her mother was going through
her daughters phone
to let all of her friends know
and give directions
to the funeral home.

I was beside myself.
I asked for directions
from the bus station
to the funeral,
even though I didn't think
I was going to go.

But the next day, I found myself
on a bus towards Allentown.
I didn't imagine my trip
back to Allentown
would be for this purpose.

I took a twenty minute taxi ride
from the bus station
to the funeral parlor.

It was extremely sad,
I felt like I didn't belong there.
There were so many
of her friends,
family,
class mates.
So many tears.
And there I was, alone.

Who were these people?
Who were they to her?
Who was I to her?
I guess that everyone had assumed
I was just a classmate or something.
The only person I might have recognized
would have been her brother,
had he not been in the hospital
as her mother said.

I sat alone during the service.
I spoke to no one.
I waited in line
to approach the closed casket.

All I did was place my hand
on top and think a moment.
I thought of the brief time
we spent together.
The bus ride.
Our conversations.
Our lunch.
Our kiss.

I couldn't cry.
There are sometimes
when you are beyond tears.

It wasn't very long
before I was back on the bus
to the airport again.
It wasn't a very full bus ride,
so I took the seat
that Mel and I had sat in
when what seemed like
an eternity ago
by myself.

At least,
I think it was the seat.

I stared out the window
at the passing Pennsylvania
country side.

To this day,
sitting at a window
while the sun warms me
brings back those memories
that I will never be able
to capture again.

But I still think of her sometimes
when staring out of car windows,
with the sun
beaming down on my arm,
warming me
until I reach my destination.

I hated that bed in Chicago when it was empty.

August 12th 2009

The phone rings.
Wake up *Wake up*
Corazon reaches over
to the night stand
and blindly feels around for it.

"Hello? . . . Oh no, two hours?
OK, no, it's no problem.
I'll be there."
She says.

She rolls out of bed.
I hear her hurry
into the bathroom
and turn on the shower.
She pulls her uniform
out of the closet.

"They call you for a trip?"
I ask.

"Yes . . . I have a lot
to get ready for,
I don't think I will make it
to the airport in two hours!
I told you
we shouldn't have stayed up
late last night."

"No you didn't . . ."
I smile.

I check my phone.
No missed calls.
No news is good news
(for me).
Not so much for Corazon.

I hated that bed
in Chicago
when it was empty.
I pull myself out of bed
and toss on the first
decent pair of clothes
I can find.

Corazon is rushing
to get her stuff together
as I turn on the morning news.

What day is it?
Wednesday? Thursday?
It doesn't matter.
What time is it?
I look at the bottom
right hand side of the television.
6:13 AM.
It's too early to be depressed
by what the news
has to tell me.
I turn on cartoons instead.

Corazon has her uniform on
and her bags packed.
She straightens herself
out in the mirror.
She's so gorgeous.

She smiles at me
"You're coming to the airport with me?"
She asks.

"Of course."
I reply.

"Looking like that?"
She asks with eyebrows raised.
I guess she doesn't
want to be seen with me
if I look like a bum.

I change into a white button shirt instead
and we make our way
for the lobby.
Rocco is working the front desk
when we go downstairs
and we ask him for the shuttle
to the airport.

I grab a muffin
from the breakfast area
and take it back to Corazon.

"You need to eat too, Mono."
She tells to me.

"I'll wait until I get back
to have a real breakfast."
I smile.

We hold hands
on the hotel shuttle
as the sun slowly
rises up over the city.

She shares some of her muffin with me.
I don't take a lot
despite being hungry by then.

We arrive at the airport
and show our ID badges
in the crew line at security.
A small chain attached to my wallet
sets off the metal detector
and she laughs at me.

With thirty minutes to spare,
we stop at a coffee kiosk.
I talk her into letting me
buy her a tea.
We sit at a dirty table
and watch passengers
order their drinks
and hurry on their busy way.

I walk with her to her gate
that her Denver flight
is departing out of.
The gate is crowded,
it's going to be a full flight.
She sighs.
I hug her.

"If they don't call me for a trip . . .
I'll have something made for us
when you get back.
Promise." I say.

"That's a lie . . . we both know
you can't cook."
She replies.

"I know . . . but I can microwave."
I say.

We kiss and I hold her
for a few more moments.
This was always the hardest part.
I let her go
and she walks through
a crowd of passengers
and down the jet bridge
before disappearing out of sight.

I had planned on going back
to the hotel then,
but instead I took a seat
on the chairs in front of
the giant glass window
facing the plane.

I stayed there with my coffee
and watched
as the passengers boarded.
I watched as the plane
pushed back from the gate.
I watched as it traveled
down the taxi way.
And I watched as it carried Corazon
up into the clouds.

Then I left.

>>>>>>>>>>>>>>>>>>>>>>>

I was called for a two day trip
a few hours later
and didn't get back to Chicago
until late the following night.
"Hey . . . I'm back."
I called out to Corazon
as I entered the room.

The bathroom was empty.
The bed had been made
and unused.
The TV was off
in both rooms.
Only the lamp on the desk
was turned on.

I heated up two cold pizzas
that were in the mini fridge
and put hers
in the microwave
when she hadn't come back.
I laid in bed and shut my eyes.

I felt her shake me awake
around midnight.
"I'm so sorry Monito,
my flight was delayed,
so I was late coming back."
she said.

"It's OK . . . your dinner's
in the microwave for you
like I promised."

"Take that! . . . bitch."

May 3rd 2010

I don't think I've described our plane yet. I fly on a regional jet (Or RJ for short) for a company called UPside Airlines. It's not the big kind of plane that carries you across the ocean to exotic and beautiful places. That's the job of a mainline carrier we fly for called STRATA Airlines. We're what's called an 'express carrier'. They pay us to make the little hops from places like Rochester, Raleigh, Bangor, and Charleston to places like Chicago, New York, and Atlanta. The express carrier carries out the short BS flights that the mainline is too cheap to run with their big fancy planes.

Our aircraft has fifty seats. The flight deck is in the front (obviously) with a seat that pulls out of a cubby hole to the left that I sit in called a jump seat. From a passengers point of view facing the front of the plane, the left side of it is called air craft left, and the right side is called air craft right.

At the front of the plane on aircraft right is the galley. It has a coffee maker, a trash can, a beverage cart and various little cabinets and drawers filled with ice, cups, spinzels, etc. There is a door on aircraft right called a commissary door that caterers bring us our stock to.

Directly across from that is the boarding door. When opened, it falls downwards and becomes a pair of steps. It weighs roughly about one hundred fifty pounds. It's closed electronically by a button above my jump seat. Not all airports use a jet bridge, so sometimes people have to walk down the airplane stairs and then into the terminal. Sometimes it's raining. Sometimes it's raining and it's cold. And when there's no jet bridge and people have to walk outside in the cold rain, they're unhappy.

But the worse part is that the cold rain sits on the steps, so when I close the door,

the cold rain tends to all come down on me at once. I've been drenched a few times and I still have yet to learn my lesson.

I hate when passengers board our plane and say "Oh, it's one of these little planes." It kind of hurts my pride.

I used to respond to that by saying: "Small planes mean small crashes." But one woman took serious offense to it, and now I just say:

"Small planes mean small problems." That's not much more reassuring, but it's still better than dropping the big bad 'C' word on board. There are smaller planes

out there though.

There are two seats on each side of the air craft. Twelve rows of seats on air craft right, and thirteen rows of seats on aircraft left. Across from the last row of seats on air craft right is a tiny, disgusting bathroom. If all this of this airplane talk seems boring or confusing to you, you can imagine how I felt listening to it for a month in training.

>>>>>>>>>>>>>>>>>>>>>>>>

I dreaded the first time I worked
the longest day
we have in our schedules.

The day went something like this:

DAY	FLTNO	DPS-ARS	DEPL	ARRL	BLKT	GRNT
WE	3723	DCA-PHL	700	722	22	38
WE	4231	PHL-DCA	800	821	21	39
WE	3614	DCA-PHL	900	922	22	38
WE	4163	PHL-DCA	1000	1021	21	354
WE	3122	DCA-ORF	215	247	32	43
WE	4122	ORF-DCA	330	400	30	46
WE	3562	DCA-RDU	446	546	101	

So despite all those flights
being relatively short,
it's still about
an eleven hour day,
and that's not including
the forty five minutes prior
to the first flight
that we have to be on the aircraft
to do our safety stuff.

If we catch a delay
somewhere in there,
all it does is shorten the time
between flights.
UPside Air *never*
cancels a flight.
There would have to be
fire falling from the sky
for that to happen.

Now, assuming there are no delays
(Bad weather,
thunder storms,
maintenance,
dinosaurs on the runway, etc.)
we tend to make it through
the day alive.
Exhausted in the end, but alive.

The first day I did that trip
my pilots told me
we'd be keeping
the air craft all day.

That's good news,
especially with a nearly four hour break
in DC from ten in the morning
until two in the afternoon.
That meant I wouldn't have to
drag my suitcase with me
to another plane,
losing precious time
eating and napping.

At the start of the day
I brewed coffee
for my pilots and me.
Since the flight to Philadelphia
is so short
I only do a beverage service
upon request,
but usually people sleep
on those early flights.

So there's not a lot for me to do
except drink coffee
and write songs
on napkins about Corazon.

Now, technically
we're supposed to brew
a fresh pot of coffee every flight,
and empty the trash,
and replace the ice,
amongst other little
tedious things.

But since my pilots and I
were the only ones drinking coffee,
and my passengers barely
had anything to throw away,
and no one was using the ice . . .
I figured I could let that stuff slide.

And since no one
would be taking the plane
over from us,
I didn't have to worry about
getting in trouble for it.
Or so I thought.
(Cue foreshadowing music.)

After the fourth flight
of the day we arrived in DC
right on time
at 10:20 in the morning.
Much to my surprise,
I opened the air craft door
to see a flight attendant
and two pilots waiting
at the bottom of the steps.

I poked my head into
the flight deck door
as it opened.

"Hey . . . are we swapping planes?"
I asked my pilots.

"Stand by."
Said the captain
as he got on the radio.

I hate when pilots use their
flight terminology with me.
Just say
"Let me find out"
or
"Give me a second."
Not
"Stand by."
Freaking aviation nerds.

The passenger bus pulled up
to the air craft and the bus driver
gave me the thumbs up
to let my passengers
off the plane.

People deplaned
and boarded the bus.
As the last few passengers
were leaving,
the captain called out to me
"Yea, looks like
we're swapping air crafts.
Theirs is on maintenance."

Shit, I had to give my plane
to another flight attendant
and I hadn't done anything
I was technically supposed to.

No point in trying
to get it all done now,
may as well just
start picking up trash
in the aisles first.

She was an old flight attendant.
So I figured she would be
sweet and understanding
and grandmotherly.

I was halfway through the plane
pulling newspapers out
of seat backs when I heard
an unfriendly "Excuse me!!"

Dammit.
I turned around to see
that old bat standing
at the front of the plane
with her arms folded
in a disapproving way.

"Oh, hey."
I said casually in a friendly tone.

"Is there a reason that the trash
hasn't been emptied?
Or the ice drawer
is full of half melted ice?"
She asked.

I approached her
with several newspapers
under my arm.
I smiled
"And there's hot coffee
still on the pot."
I said jokingly.

She didn't find it funny.

Ok, time for the excuse
"Sorry, we were supposed
to keep this plane all day . . .
and there haven't been
any services yet,
so I just thought-"

"How long have you been here?"
She interrupted.

"Sorry?"

"How long . . .
have you been flying . . .
for this airline?"
She said slower
as if I were stupid.

"About ten months."

"Then you should know better!
You can expect me
to be writing an email
to Mikey about this.
Now take care of your duties,
my passengers are on the way!"
She said and waddled off
to the back of the plane.

I was speechless.
I said nothing
as I opened the commissary door
and dropped my large trash bag
(consisting of three cups
and a couple of news papers)
to the pavement below.

I then poured the melted
ice water out the same door
along with the unused ice
I tied up in a small white trash bag
like I was supposed to.

I suddenly stopped for a moment
and developed one of the most
evil smiles I've ever formed
in my life.

I looked to the aft of the air craft.
That old monster
was no where in sight.
She must have been in the bathroom.
Either that, or looking for children
to shove into her gingerbread oven.

I took the piping hot coffee
and rather than
dump it into the toilet
like was supposed to,
I carefully poured it
all over the stairs,
making sure not to let any
escape on to the pavement.
I was the only one
that had a cup on that flight,
so the pot was pretty full.

I then plucked a can of apple juice
from the galley.
I pulled my bags
out of the over head.

I waved good bye
to the crypt keeper
as she was coming out
of the bathroom.

"Goodbye, I'm so sorry again.
Have a good day!"
I said with the biggest smile
on my face.

"Whatever."
She replied,
waving her hand
in a 'shoo' motion.

Oh, I've got your whatever.

My pilots were waiting
at the bottom of the aircraft
by the bus full of passengers
that had just arrived.

About thirty people
got off the bus
and on to the plane.
My pilots boarded the empty bus
"Hey, are you going to ride
to the airport with us?"
My captain asked me.

"No thanks . . .
I'm going to stay here
and watch the plane leave."
I answered.

They both had confused looks
on their faces,
but went on ahead without me.

I laid my suitcase down
in the middle of the taxi way
and created
a makeshift seat out of it.

I cracked open my can
of apple juice and took a sip.
And then I waited.

About fifteen minutes later,
the old flight attendant
approached the top of the stairs
to close the air craft door.
She had a puzzled look
when she found me sitting there
in the middle of the taxi way
staring at the plane
as if it were a drive in movie.

She scowled at me
as I waved and said
"Have a nice flight! . . . Bitch."
It was so loud from the engines,
I doubt she could hear me.
But I could hear her.
I couldn't see her,
but oh boy,
could I hear her.

As she pressed the button
to close the door,
it raised the stairs upwards
taking the hot coffee with it,
and just as it reached
it's last position
before closing,
I could hear an audible shriek
that came with it.

I smiled to myself
as I finished the last
of my apple juice
and made my way
for the terminal.

And sure enough
the following day:
Surprise, surprise . . .
another email from my
in flight manager Mikey.

"Charles we need to have
another meeting
to discuss an issue
you had on your flight . . ."

Every passenger sucks (with the exception of those that bought this book.)

After about a year of careful observation, I have made several notes about particular passengers that, to be honest, I just can't stand. These are the passengers that ultimately make my life, as well as everyone's around me, ten times harder than it already is.

Passenger "can you hear me now?"

This is a pretty bad one. This passenger has their cell phone glued to their ear the moment they get on the plane. They manage to get their bag in to the over head bin, their jacket off, and their seat belt on, all with the use of just one hand. The other hand is holding their phone up to their ear as they describe, in loud detail, just what it is that they're doing.

"YEA, ONE MOMENT BILL, I'M PUTTING MY BAG UP. UH-HUH. NO I'M ON AN AIRPLANE . . . YEA, JUST A SECOND, I'M TAKING MY JACKET OFF . . ."

Once he's completed his step by step description of what it's like to board a plane (I can only assume the person on the other end has never been on one before) he continues talking about that important business meeting that he has to make.

"THAT'S RIGHT, I'LL BE MEETING THE CHAUFFER AT THE AIRPORT AT ELEVEN . . . . NO, THE FLIGHT WAS DELAYED SO WE HAD TO RE-SCHEDULE THE MEETING WITH THE CLIENTS AND THEN DO LUNCH . . . . DID YOU GET THAT E-MAIL I SENT YOU . . . ?"

The best part is that this is usually going on as I'm trying to do my announcements. And asking them to turn off their cell phone is like asking them to turn off their pace-maker. I asked you to turn your phone off. Not put it in 'Stubborn passenger mode' or as you call it 'Airplane mode'. Oh, but it doesn't end there. Because once the talking has stopped, the texting begins.

Passenger "I'm running behind schedule!"

This passenger arrives at the plane sweating profusely. Their last flight JUST came in, or our flights late for whatever reason, and so they're sweating like a polar bear in the Sahara desert. There wasn't enough time for them to blame the ticket agent, or the gate agent, oh no. They were in too much of a rush for that. So the blame falls on your poor flight attendant. The blame isn't necessarily directed at me though. Just the anger.

Their watch is their best friend, and worst enemy. When we're boarding, they're constantly checking it while stating: "It's about time we got this flight under way!" As we're taxiing, they're checking it, while sighing loud enough for everyone to hear their frustration. And when our plane's in the air, not moving at warp speed, they're checking it, shaking their head in disappointment as they announce: "This is the worse airline EVER! I'm never flying this carrier AGAIN!"

Look buddy, it's an airplane. Not a rocket ship. But you're right though. It's one hundred percent our fault. No airline has ever been behind schedule or late in the history of ever. Maybe next time you want things to run perfectly, you'll hire your own private plane so that you can bitch to the owner themselves. Until then, shut the hell up and eat your spinzels. We'll get there when we get there.

The "everything bothers me" Passenger

Self-explanatory. Goes a little something like this-
DING (Call button lights up)

Chuck: Yes sir, may I help you?

The everything bothers me passenger: These over head bins are too small. And there's not enough room under the seat in front of me. And I don't like the passenger next to me. And your PA is too loud, it's giving me a headache. And it's too cold on this plane. And the blanket's too thin. And the bathroom smells like it's never been cleaned. And the baby behind me is kicking my seat. And it's too bright in the cabin for me to sleep. And there's not enough pretzels in this bag.

Chuck: I'm so sorry sir. Perhaps I can offer you a complimentary beer?

The everything bothers me passenger: Yea . . . I suppose that's alright. What do you have?

Chuck: Budweiser and bud light.

The everything bothers me passenger: UNNACCEPTABLE!

The robot

I've complained about this passenger plenty. And here comes some more! They wake up and do the same job Monday-Friday, 9-5, until they're either retired or dead. They usually have one or more of the aforementioned personalities, but what sets them apart is that they're dressed in a suit. And it's because of that suit they're more important than everyone else in the world. I don't have much else to say about them, as I've already previously described them and the certain personalities they can carry.

(For more info on The Robot read: *You didn't say the magic word*)

The out of control kids

Usually fly in groups of two or more. Usually more. And these pack rats have turned your quiet flight into an afternoon at Chuck-e-cheeses. They're climbing over the seats. They're climbing under the seats. They're jumping on the seats. They're coloring on their tray table. They're fighting each other. And where's the mother in all this chaotic nonsense? She's sitting across the aisle from them, with her face buried in an issue of '*Better Homes & Gardens*', or '*Oprah*', or '*How to Ignore What Your Kids Are Doing Monthly*'.

The only time their mother actually speaks up, is when I ask the children what they want to drink. The children will then stare at me as though I were speaking Martian. It is at this time—and this time only, the mother intervenes with: "Apple juice for the little ones. But only half a cup. Can you fill the other half with water? I don't want the kids having too much sugar and getting rowdy."

The screaming baby

Closely related to the out of control kids. This baby is not happy to be on an airplane. And they'll scream from takeoff to landing to make sure you know it, all while kicking the seat of the poor passenger in front of them. And what does the parent do? Nothing. To be perfectly honest, I'm not even sure the parent's on board. There is a baby screaming bloody murder at the top of its lungs, and no one takes claim for it. The baby just wails and wails away. Probably the reason why the parent dropped the baby off and ran like hell in the opposite direction

I've dealt with so many of them on the plane that I can tune it out at this point. It's unfortunate for everyone else on board, rolling their eyes and covering their ears in order to keep their heads from exploding due to the high frequency pitch of the baby's howl. And what's my response to:

"Can't you do something about that crying baby?!"

"It's a baby. Babies cry."

The 'tell me every thing about the plane' passenger

This one really pushes my buttons. Literally. That call button is chimed every chance they get to ask me the same questions I would expect from a five year old that's never been on a plane before.

"What river is this we're passing over?"

What am I a geographer?

"How fast is this plane moving?"

I don't know. A bazillion miles per hour maybe.

"Can I look in the cockpit?"

What are you, a terrorist?

"What altitude are we flying at?"
Above tree level, aren't we?

"How will I be able to track my bag if it gets lost?"
Look, I'm here to serve you pretzels and a soda. Everything else is really out of my jurisdiction. If you have a question about your pretzels or your soda, then maybe—just maybe, I might be able to help you out. Any thing else however, forget about it.

Old passenger-

This one isn't too bad, but I'm not talking about your average sixty five year old, sweet Grand mother. I mean the decrepit old passenger that's pushing ninety seven. This is the one we have to wait to be wheel chaired on and off the plane, and then moves slower than molasses when they get up to use the bathroom.

When I serve them, the conversation usually goes a little something like this-

Chuck: Would you like something to drink sir?

Old geezer: What?

Chuck: Would you like something to drink sir?

Old geezer: Huh?

Chuck: WOULD YOU LIKE SOMETHING TO DRINK SIR?

Old geezer: You know, back when I used to fly on the aero planes all of the stewardesses were nurses!"

. . . Wow. What an amazing story old timer. And while I'd love to stay here and reminisce about what the airline industry was like back when you were hanging out with the Wright brothers, I have to be moving on.

By the way, shouldn't there be a certain point in your old age in which everyone else should have to come to where you are? Not the other way around? Unless I'm working their flight with a non-stop service to the pearly gates, these old folks really shouldn't be on a plane to begin with.

Drunk passenger-

This can go either way. For the most part, the drunks just get on, slouch down in their seats, and then pass out. However, there are some exceptions to the rule. The drunk passenger has to constantly use the bathroom. That seal was broke about eight bloody Mary's ago. And the parties not over yet.

"Tommy! I need—*hic* I need another drink!"

Not only are they getting my name wrong, but they're loud and obnoxious when it comes to getting my attention. They would press the call button, but by this point they're seeing double, and aren't particularly sure which button is the right one to push.

It's kind of like the drunk girl at a party who's spilling her drink everywhere and everyone wants to toss out the back door. If only the back door wasn't 30,000 feet in the air. And telling them they've had enough is like telling them they're not allowed to breathe for the rest of the flight.

The last straw though is when they vomit. They can make it to the bathroom to piss every five minutes, but when it's time to toss their cookies—or in this case, their spinzels, believe me that's like a paraplegic running the fifty yard dash with the bathroom as the finish line. They don't quite make it to their destination, and grab for the nearest sick bag, if I'm lucky. Unfortunately, one sick bag is never quite enough, and the poor passengers they're standing over wind up with a little extra service on their flight.

However, they're not all bad.

Here's a short list of awesome passengers that I've had, or would love to one day have on board:

—Passengers that get on and just go to sleep.

—Passengers that give me tips for being awesome.

—Passengers that give me 'Up and away' certificates to rub in Mikeys face and prove to her that I'm doing a good job after all.

—Passenger's that bring food/snacks/drinks for me.

—Passengers that want to hang out and party with me on an overnight.

—Passengers that don't ask me for anything.

—No passengers at all.

—The band Blue October.

—The Kansas City teachers convention. (For more info read: *The Kansas city teachers convention*)

—Renee Zellwegger.

—The Chinese Olympic gymnast team.

—Someone that wants to give me a record label/movie deal for being awesome.

—The red power ranger.

—My Mother.

—An astronaut.

—Your Mother.

—Every hot girl.

—Big foot.

Apologies to the North

May 6th 2010

The only international flying we ever seem to really do is to Canada, which has easily become one of my favorite destinations to go to. The only down side is that in Toronto, we get put up at some lame hotel that's not situated around anything else except a south western style restaurant and a semi-decent bar.

My crew and I were fortunate enough however to be over nighting with one of our company's other crews at the same time. Their flight attendant was a girl named Kylie, whom I had met shortly after graduating training in the Chicago crew room. After striking up a conversation, I found out that she was the same age as me, and shared a lot of the same tastes in music as I did. So when I discovered that she was over nighting in Toronto the same night that I was, we decided to get our crews together for dinner.

6:05 PM-
I meet in the hotel lobby with Kylie, my pilots, and her pilots (I do not remember their names, as they are irrelevant to this story.)

6:08-
We leave our hotel and wander into the cold Canadian air (Despite it being May, it was still freezing outside.) We walk through the hotel parking lot, between a row of trees and into the south western style bar.

6:10-
We take a seat at a table for six in the barely occupied restaurant. Everyone that works there is dressed in cow boy attire (blue jeans, plaid shirts, cowboy boots, and a cow boy hat.)

6:13-
The waiter comes and takes our drink orders. I get the usual tequila and tonic. Kylie orders two beers. When I inquire as to why, she says it's

because she hates waiting on her next beer once she's finished the first. Understandable.

6:16-
I look over my menu while stealing glances at Kylie. Kind of cute.

6:20-
The waiter comes back with our drinks. Kylie wastes no time in diving into her first beer head first. I make a joke by saying,
"Wow, you must have had a really hard day at work handing out sodas and pretzels while pretending to like people."

Kylie sets down her beer and looks oddly at me
"No . . . I only had two flights today."

6:26-
The waiter comes back to take our food order. Kylie is just about done with her first beer.
"I'll have another one."
She says.

"You haven't finished your first one."
I say.

She quickly chugs the rest of her beer and slams the glass down.
"There . . . now I'll have another one."
We place our food orders and the waiter leaves.

6:28-
Kylie eyes my drink condescendingly
"What are you sipping on, princess?"
She asks.

"Tequila and tonic water."
I reply.

"You gay?"
She asks.

I frown at her
"You're funny. No, I'm not."

"Well, you better learn to drink if you're gonna be flying at UPside Airlines!"
She chugs half of her beer as her pilots give me the "Oooohhhhh!"

I hate being challenged. I finish the rest of my tequila and tonic and slam the glass down on the table in the manner that she had prior to me.

"You shoulda ordered two, you wouldn't have to wait."

"No need, I know where the bar is."

6:33-
I approach the bar and order a Canadian beer.
"You have your ID?"
asks the bartender. I show it to him.
"Oh, from the states, eh? What brings you up to Toronto?"

"Just here on business. Can you make it two, actually?"

6:39-
I approach the table again to a sarcastic:
"Oh! Look who's come back with two beers! Biiiiig man!"
from Kylie who has magically materialized two new beers in front of her.

6:46-
The waiter arrives with our dinner. Kylie alternates between stuffing a burger into her mouth and chugging her beer. I get a stomach ache from trying to keep up with her drink-wise, while eating my food at the same time. I was never good at multitasking.

6:55-
The waiter comes and asks if we are alright. Kylie asks if she can have his cowboy hat. He says no. She then asks if she can try it on. He laughs and walks away, although it's the same laugh I give to passengers when they say something stupid and think it's funny.

7:09-
The waiter comes back and collects our emptied dinner plates. He asks if we would like any desert. Kylie clangs her spoon on her glass and says "Liquid desert!" referring to her beer. He gives her the same laugh as before and walks off. I can tell he is becoming annoyed.

7:11-
Kylie fishes around in her purse looking for something. She turns to me "Hey, bitch. Go ask someone for a cigarette for me."

"You keep insulting me. Why should I?"

"Come on, please! I promise to behave!"

I groan and go to the bar.

7:13-
I approach the bar tender who I had seen step outside for a cigarette earlier when his last customer left the bar.
"Hey, my cute friend over there was wondering if you had a cigarette she could bum off of you."

He looks over my shoulder at Kylie who is pounding beers and making gestures similar to that of a cave man.
"Then why doesn't she ask me herself?"
He asks.

"Because she's . . . shy."
I get a cigarette and return to the table with it in my mouth.

7:15-
Kylie asks where her cigarette is. I tell her the one in my mouth is mine and if she wants it, I'll sell it to her for a dollar. She snatches the cigarette from my mouth and tells me I'll have to take an IOU.

7:16-
She steps outside with her cigarette and beer. The pilots hold a boring conversation about air planes.

7:23-
Kylie comes back in and says she wants to go to the bar next door. My two pilots and her first officer say that they're just going to retire back to their rooms. She calls them bitches and laughs like a hyena. No one else laughs.

7:29-
We pay our bill and leave the restaurant. Three of the four pilots leave and go back to the hotel.

7:31-
Kylie, her captain, and I enter the bar next to the restaurant. It's just as empty and lame as the restaurant, minus the stupid cowboy theme. Kylie loudly announces:
"What the hell?! Is this where the party is in Canada on a Monday night?!"
One lone bar patron chuckles.

7:32-
We take seats at the bar. Kylie is to my left and her captain is to my right.

7:33-
The bartender sets down some napkins in front of us and asks what we'll have. Kylie pounds her fists onto the bar and chants
"Beer! Beer! Beer! Beer!"
The captain rolls his eyes and orders us a pitcher.

7:36-
The bartender returns with three glasses and a pitcher. Kylie wastes no time pouring the beer from the pitcher into the glass, and then from the glass into her head.

7:39-
I jokingly ask if it would be easier to just pour from the pitcher directly into her mouth and cut out the middle man. She takes my suggestion to heart and does just that, chugging at least half a glass worth, and slamming the pitcher back down.

7:40-
Kylie loudly shouts (in a ridiculous pirate voice)
"Barkeep! Another round of ye' olde Canadian ale for me and my mates!"
The bartender chuckles and pours another.

7:44-
Kylie rests her elbows on the bar, folds her hands, and rests her head on them. She leans over to me and drunkenly asks
"So . . . Chuck. You have—you have a girlfriend?"
Her breath reeks of beer.

"Yea . . . I'm kinda seeing one of our flighties."

Kylie is extremely confused by this.
"What? No way! I thought you were gay!"

"No, we . . . already established that I'm not."

"Well who is it? Do I know her?"
I decide not to take the chance of ratting out mine and Corazon's secret relationship and shake my head no.
"No way . . . you're lying. Come on, stop lying . . ."
She leans across from me and motions to her captain who is wrapped up in the hockey game on T.V.
"Hey . . . Tom! This flight attendant here is straight!"

"So what? We have other straight flight attendants. And my name is Tim."
Kylie is confused again, although I'm not sure if it's from the sudden revelation of her pilots name or the fact that not all male flight attendants are gay.

7:56-
A guy in his mid-twenties comes into the bar and takes a seat next to Kylie. She is not pleased by this in the least bit and stares at him as though he just spit in her beer. She turns to me.
"Hey . . . who is this guy?"

I just shrug. He obviously hears this and introduces himself
"Oh, hi. I'm Rick."
Kylie stares blankly at him in the manner which she had been previously doing.

8:03-
Rick tries to make small talk with us after ordering his beer and several moments of silence.
"So, where you folks from?"

Kylie makes the same 'why are you talking to me' face once more before retaliating with:
"If you want me to talk to you, buy me a pitcher of beer."

He looks confused.
"But you already have a pitcher."

I speak up:
"What do we have to get you if we want you to *stop* talking?"
This gets a laugh out of her pilot.

"Quiet, gay boy. You heard me, Rick. Buy me a pitcher of beer."
Kylie says.

8:05-
Rick sits with a baffled look on his face, before actually ordering her a pitcher of beer. Kylie is giddy. I roll my eyes.

8:08-
The bartender brings Kylie and her new friend a pitcher of beer and she continues drinking. I am casually just sipping on mine now and have decided I've had enough.

8:34-
Rick has been talking non-stop about some trip he was on in which he back packed across Europe. The best part is, Kylie isn't even listening, nor is she responding. She's just nodding her head every now and again and looking at me while rolling her eyes.

8:42-
The captain has had enough of this, pays for our first pitcher and leaves. I'm tired as well and get up to join him. When I stand up, Kylie grabs my arm and pulls me back down into the seat.
"Oh no you don't. You're not leaving me alone with this loser!"
She protests loud enough for him to hear her.

9:03-
The bar is empty with the exception of the three of us. There is still half a pitcher left and nothing of interest worth writing about has happened. Rick is still telling his stupid back packing story.

9:14-
Kylie turns to me and states (rather loudly):
"I hope this isn't the way Canadian men pick up women at a bar! Are all guys in this country as much of a loser as him? How do they continue to populate? Or are Canadian women just so desperate that they *have* to sleep with the men here?!" The bar tender does not find this amusing.

9:20-
The bar tender makes last call. Kylie is not happy about this
"What? It's not even ten o'clock yet! And I still have half a pitcher of beer! This place SUCKS!"

The bar tender stares at her a moment the way she had stared at Rick when he first sat next to her. He then responds politely in the same tone I do when a passenger is screaming at me:
"I didn't say we were closing . . . I said it was last call."

Kylie stares back for a moment before retaliating with:
"This place still sucks."

9:24-
The bar tender leans towards me and discreetly whispers
"Hey man, you need to pay your tab and then take your friend and leave."

Before I can respond with a 'way ahead of you', Kylie erupts.
"What the hell?! I haven't done anything wrong! You can't throw me out, I have diplomatic immunity!"

I take her by the arm.
"Sorry, it's no problem. We'll pay and go."
I say.

"Hey, we can all go back to my place and have some drinks there."
suggests Rick.

"Only if you pay for our second pitcher we had."
Kylie replies.

I can't believe she's doing this. And the craziest part is, he agrees!
"Fine, we'll be waiting for you outside. Chuck, let's go! I need a cigarette."
She says.

As Kylie storms outside I reach in to my wallet. I only have a ten dollar bill, and it's in US dollars, but I leave it for the bar tender any way. I apologize again for Kylies behavior and thank Rick for paying for our second pitcher, although I really didn't want to go back to his place to continue this charade.

9:29-
I step outside and Kylie is nowhere to be found. I almost freak out for a moment before spotting her half way to our hotel. I look through the window of the bar doors to see Rick still paying our tab, before turning and running to catch up with Kylie.

9:32-
I catch up with Kylie just as she is walking into our hotel.
"Hey, I thought we were going to that guys place?"
I ask.

"What are you stupid? I'm not going anywhere with that loser. You have a lot to learn working here, starting with my first lesson of the night: 'how to get drinks from losers for free when you are a poor flight attendant'. Did you want to go home with that creep?"
I figure she has a point, as loud and obnoxious as she may be when making it.

9:34:
We step in to the elevator and press the buttons for our individual floors. Kylie is on the 5th, and I'm on the 7th. She is leaning against the wall, swaying back and forth, and does not look good.
"Hey . . . hey, do you know how they came up with the name Canada? Some Canadians got together when they . . . built the country . . . and were trying to decide what to name it. So they picked the letters C, N, and D. And . . . and they said: 'C' eh? 'N' eh? . . ."
She stopped right there. I thought it was the end of the joke, but the punch line was still on the way. She proceeded to vomit all over the floor. I stepped back a little, but some still splashed on my pants and shoes. She finished, wiped her mouth and said
". . . 'D' eh? You . . . you get it?"
Just then the elevator doors opened and she looked at me.
"Well . . . good night."
She said, and walked off the elevator as if nothing had happened.

9:35-
The elevator smells of vomit and south western style food when it reaches my floor. I hurry off and dart to my room.

The next morning there was a note from her under my door that just said: 'Sorry about last night. See you in DC. I.O.U. $1 for the cigarette.'

It's cold in Eerie

February 2nd 2010

The plane lands.
Passengers march off
like ants moving
toward the terminal.
Toward the out stretched
open arms of loved ones,
family members,
friends . . .

People say goodbye
and thank you,
although I'm not sure
how many of them mean it.
I respond the same,
but to be honest,
I don't always mean it.

Their flight is over
and they're at their destination
or at least a bit closer to it,
as am I to mine as well.

I doubt they'll remember me
for long whether I did
a good job or not.

Maybe they'll tell
someone they know
about a joke I told
or something funny I did.

Maybe I'll be a fleeting moment
in a conversation
about air travel
six months from now
when one of my passengers
will say something like:
"I had this flight attendant
on my way to Eerie once . . ."
And then on with their story
about whatever I did.

They probably won't
remember my name
so I'll get to be just
'the flight attendant'.
I wonder how many times
that's been my name
in a story someone's told
about me.

I pass through the empty plane
collecting trash, newspapers,
empty cups.
Throw them away,
and clean up for the next crew
that comes to the plane.

I take my bags and leave
with the pilots through the terminal
and outside the airport
to wait for the hotel van
to pick us up.
I'll see a few passengers,
some will smile and wave.

It's cold outside,
and all I have to wear
is that lame suit.
I refuse to wear the overcoat,
it looks ridiculous.

The pilots I'm with
don't say much,
they're not very social
about their plans
for when we get to the hotel.

It's 4 in the afternoon
and I know
that all they plan on doing
is nothing for the rest of the evening.
We call those crew members
'slam clickers',
meaning that when they get
to their hotel room
they slam their room door
and click it to the locked position.

I don't mind flying with them,
and I actually save money
when I'm with the anti-social types
since they don't want to go out
and party at all.

But the down side is
that I find myself
walking the streets alone.
I walk through the snow
in the cold
for five minutes
to the nearest McDonald's
for another dollar menu dinner.

I'll sit at the table alone
and eat quietly
as I watch the people
come and go.
Then I return
to my hotel room
once more.

This job's not always fun.
It's not always joking
and partying and going out.
Sometimes it's cold
and lonely in Eerie.

Mile high club

November 6th 2009

It seems as though ever since I've been working at this job, my friends all ask me the same damn question: "So . . . you join the mile high club yet?" What the hell? I actually think it's funny. I fail to see how this is possible for numerous reasons.

For starters: I'm actually at work. Now, despite the fact that it is the all American dream to knock out a quickie while being paid, it's a bit difficult when your office is 30,000 feet in the air and full of screaming babies, complaining old people, and a business Robot that needs another diet coke every ten minutes.

Secondly: I have to get past the dreaded assumption that all male flight attendants are gay. Find a good looking girl, flirt with her long enough, I'm sure she'll get the point.

>>>>>>>>>>>>>>>>>>>>>>>>

I once had a young woman on a flight of mine from DC to Cape cod. She had to have been around twenty five or so, traveling with her younger sister who was at least half her age. They were sitting in row 5. She had the aisle seat, and her sister the window. When we took off, she was leaning over her sister and pointing at things out the window, while at the same time extending her smooth right leg out to the aisle to keep her balance.

She was wearing one of those long white skirts that extended all the way down to her ankles and had taken off her heels.

". . . Nice." I thought, watching from my jump seat. "Does she know what she's doing?" I asked myself as she reached her right hand around to her leg and began caressing it. After a few moments, she was poking her head out from around the corner, playing a game of hide and peek with me. She knew what she was doing.

She wasn't even super attractive, she just had that overall 'girl next door' quality to her, much like the Playboy girls of days gone by. She wasn't *trying* too hard to look gorgeous, and that was what worked for her. When she got up to use the bathroom, she wiggled her behind back and forth. And I don't mean just a little bump from here to there. I had never seen anything like this. It was like being hypnotized by a damn lava lamp that could belly dance.

Breathe.
Just breathe.
Keep it together.

I couldn't believe this. I was there for these passenger's safety on a fifty three minute flight and I couldn't stop myself from staring at some hottie with a nice bottom. I rolled my eyes around the plane frantically trying to think of something—anything other than following her into the bathroom.

<<<<<<<<<<<<<<<<<<<<<<<<<<

And even if that had happened, if by some miracle daddy's little rich girl had reached the back of the plane and seductively motioned for me to join her, we come to the third point of why this is a difficult task to complete: The bathroom. For whatever reason, whoever designed these bathrooms on a plane that was built to hold fifty passengers must have assumed that all fifty passengers would be little people.

I can barely move around in these bathrooms, and I'm not that big of a big guy. I have no idea how these giant business travelers get in and out of there, and they're usually the ones stinking up the bathrooms to begin with.

You're probably thinking: well, a tiny bathroom must mean it's easier to clean right? Because it's so small, right?

HAHAHAHAHAHA!

Don't make me laugh!

STRATA Airlines hires cleaners to take care of their big fancy planes. UPside Airline flight attendants are responsible for cleaning *their* planes. Guess how many of us *actually* clean the bathrooms? (I'll give you a hint: NONE.) The people who designed the bathroom probably had the idea in mind that they didn't want more than one passenger in there at a time any longer than they had to be.

A friend of mine whose name I will not mention for her protection (It was Nicole.) once told me that she had in fact joined this discreet club, before she was hired here. She described in detail just how she was able to pull this off in flight. I won't get into the details, but I will say she was creative, and it can be done.

In November, I was working a flight from Montreal to Philly. The flight was a little more than half full. After I was finished setting up my beverage cart, I turned around from the galley to see a woman in seat 13 C laughing. This wasn't your everyday laugh. Her face was red, she was covering her mouth with her hand, I mean this woman was practically in tears.

"What's wrong with her? Is she high or something?" I wondered. Maybe she thought my announcements were just really funny. But then, why would she still be laughing fifteen minutes after takeoff?

I was half way through the plane with my service when a passenger leaned up to me and discreetly said: "Excuse me . . . the man that was sitting in front of me went to use the bathroom several minutes ago . . ."

So? What's your point? People always say the dumbest things to me.

". . . Alright." I said, before preparing to move my beverage cart.

"Oh, wait. The woman that he was sitting next to got up a few moments later and went into the bathroom also . . ."

Oh
my
God.

I looked up from my beverage cart and in the direction of the bathroom. I suddenly pieced together why the woman across from the bathroom was laughing so hard.

She must have known that I figured things out by the look on my face, and she began laughing again. I rolled my cart back up to the front of the plane and walked swiftly to the back again. I studied the door to see that it was locked. I listened closely for a moment. There was definitely *something* going on in there.

I hurried back to the front of the plane. Pretty much every head on board was turned and following me as I paced back and forth.

I made a call to my pilots. "Hey . . . there's two passengers in the bathroom . . ."

It was quiet a moment before the Captain spoke up: "Is it a parent and their child?" he asked.

What are they stupid? Do I have to spell it out? "No . . . There are two GROWN passengers in the bathroom . . ."

"Is one of them sick? Do they need medical attention?"

"No . . ." I replied again. I was getting frustrated.

They were starting to snicker by this point. They knew what was going on.

They just wanted to hear it straight from the horse's mouth. Dammit, they never taught us what to do about this type of situation in training.

"No . . . they're in the bathroom . . . and they're . . . fornicating . . ." I heard the both of them burst into laughter. "It's not funny! What do you want me to do?"

"Well . . . technically we should land the plane and have them removed for having relations in a public place . . . but here's the thing. We're already running late. And they're not really a threat to anyone. So we'll leave this one up to you." They told me.

I didn't want to go out of my way. "I . . . I don't know what I should do." I stated.

"I'll tell you what. We'll teach them a lesson. Park your beverage cart in front of the door so that they can't open it. And then come back to your jump seat and call me." Said the captain. I wondered just where they were going with this. But I was thankful to be flying with a good crew.

I rolled my beverage cart back to the bathroom and locked it in place. I think passengers had started figuring out what was happening as a few of them were laughing when I parked the cart in the back. The woman in 13 C didn't seem to understand what was happening until the cart was parked, and I walked back up to the front and took my jump seat. I called the pilots and told them it was parked. Just as 13 C peered over the cart the captain turned on the fasten seat belt sign. She began laughing again.

"Folks this is your captain speaking . . . we're coming up to some pretty rough clouds ahead, a lot of turbulence . . . that sort of stuff. We're going to need everyone to return to their seats, it's not very safe to be up now, especially if you're in the bathroom."

I smiled as I waited. The bathroom door began to open as it was suddenly stopped by the beverage cart. Thump. Thump. People were laughing now; they knew what was going on. I stood up after a moment and walked back to the bathroom. "Is everything OK in there sir?" I asked.

". . . We're stuck in here." He replied.

"I'm sorry sir . . . did you say 'we?'" Silence.

". . . Yea, we're stuck in here." He finally repeated.

"Are you in there with your child? Are they alright?" I asked.

"No . . . My girlfriend and I are stuck in here." He said hesitantly.

"Does she need medical attention? Is she sick?" I was playing the same game as my pilots had with me at this point.

"No . . . we're stuck." He said.

"I know that sir, but what are you doing in there?"

"We're . . . we're just stuck."

This went on for several minutes back and forth before I finally moved the beverage cart. "Alright, it should be fine, you guys can come out now." I said and returned to my jump seat.

The captain called from the front: "Did we get them?" He asked.

"Yea, but they're still not out of the bathroom yet." I replied.

"Well, we're going to be landing in about twenty minutes here, so you need to get these people out now. And point this guy out to me when he's getting off the plane, I'd like to have a word with him." He sounded like the school principal calling children into his office.

I went back to the bathroom and banged on the door "Hey, you guys really need to come out of there now. We're going to be landing soon." I called out.

This time it was the woman that spoke up: "I don't want to! I'm embarrassed!" She cried out.

"Just go, everyone knows!" The man responded.

Just as I took my jump seat again, the couple came out to a plane full of cheering passengers. The woman, beet red, wasn't at all bad looking. I wondered what she was doing with the goofy looking guy she emerged from the bathroom with.

They were the last two off the plane, and passengers were patting the man on his shoulder as they passed by. The captain was waiting at the flight deck door for the couple to deplane. I thought that he was going to yell at them or something. He stopped the man, motioned for him to come in a little closer, shook his hand, and told him to get the hell off our plane.

All your crimes (The dotted line . . .)

August 27th 2009

The phone rings.
Wake up *Wake up*
Corazon reaches over
to the night stand
and blindly feels around for it.

She looks at the name on the phone
before placing it back
on the night stand
and rolling over
to face me.
"It's just him again."
She says.

The bags under my eyes
were proof
of the previous nights crime.
Young and stupid.

Not even quite sure
what I was still doing
hanging around at that hotel room
in Chicago with her.

I guess I was in love at the time.
Like I said before,
young and stupid.

We caught the L
into the city that day
to the mall.

I had no idea of her intentions.
You can imagine
the look of shock
on my face
when she lead me
into the drugstore,
to the aisle with
the home pregnancy tests.

How could we have let this happen.
"Maybe it's a good thing?
Maybe this could work?"
I tried suggesting.

"You know why it can't."
She replied,
ignoring another phone call.

The look on the store clerk's face
was priceless
when Corazon asked
to use the bathroom,
after purchasing
a home pregnancy test.

The five minutes I waited for her
outside that bathroom
seemed like an eternity.

And when she finally came out-
"It's a dotted line.
I'm not pregnant."

What a relief.
A relief?
No, I'm not sure
what the word
for the feeling was.

I wasn't ready
to have a kid
at the age of twenty one,
but she could still sense
a bit of disappointment in the air
from me
on that walk back
to our hotel room.

We sat by the fountain
and watched the children
run about and play
as the sun went down,
holding hands with each other.

Then—then came the heart break.
Underneath Chicago's
crushing lights,
she told me
that we couldn't keep doing this.
We couldn't
keep seeing each other.

She had to try
and make her failing marriage
work back home
for her daughters sake.
That I would understand one day.

We stayed friends
for a few more years after that,
at least I lied to her
and said that we were.
Maybe I was lying to myself too.

I'll give you three guesses why I'm here, but it should only take you one.

January 28th 2010

He's one of those
southern preppy first officers
I'm flying with:
wears his cap backwards
and his Abercrombie button shirt
with the sleeves rolled up
and his collar popped
when we're out for a drink.

Put your collar down,
you look like Dracula.

He always manages
to make me feel
poorer than I really am,
but I don't mind
putting up with him
for four days.

I put away the last
of the commissary
when he comes out
from the flight deck
and asks
for a bottle of water.

"I've never heard
so many passengers
smile and say
thank you
to any of our other
flight attendants.
You obviously
have a great personality-
so what are you doing
working for a mid-size
regional airline like
UPside Air?"
He asks.

I hand him the bottle
of water and smile.

"Oh, I get it . . .
you like bein' around
all the other
hot flight attendants
and passengers, don't you?
Probably hook up with them
all the time, right?"

I laugh as I reach
into the cabinet
to the far right
for a small silver bag.

"That's a good one . . .
but I rarely get to see
any other
hot flight attendants,
and most passengers
automatically assume
that since I'm a male
flight attendant I'm gay,
so . . . meeting hot girls
is just the third reason
I'm here.
Definitely
not top priority."
I say as I open up
the bag and take the coffee
from its pouch.

I place it in the coffee maker
and hit the Brew button.

"That's cool.
So you like
all the free travel then right?
You said you just came back
from a vacation in Brazil,
so I'm guessing
you're only in this
for the flight benefits then?"

"Close second . . .
but not the reason
why I'm still here."
I say as I pour myself
a cup of coffee.

"So what is it then?
Why put up with all
the annoying passengers,
long hours,
and underpay?"
He asks.

"Hey-" I say,
"If you had a job
where you could get
all the free coffee
and pretzels you want,
you'd hang around too."

An entry from Captain Amazing's diary

March 13th 2010

Every airline has . . . this guy. He thinks he's the Pilot all women want, and all men want to be. His muscles are the size of my head, and he makes sure the world knows this by wearing shirts that are three sizes smaller than he should be wearing. He proudly parades through the airport with his chest sticking out as if to announce: "Out of the way everyone, there's a PILOT coming through!"

When I first met the man, I was waiting at our boarding gate in Chicago with Corazon. He approached with a First officer who later explained that the only reason he was stuck in the flight deck next to that douche bag for the next four days was because *two* other pilots already called out sick when they discovered that they would be working with him.

When I kissed Corazon goodbye and boarded the plane, he literally said to me on our way down the jet bridge "This is a surprise! A male flight attendant who's neither gay, black, or old!" And then proceeded to laugh maniacally. The FO rolled his eyes and later revealed to me that while he was being forced to do all the work in the flight deck, he noticed Captain Amazing carries a small, leather bound journal that he is constantly writing in.

Well, that evening at the hotel we devised a plan to get our hands on his diary and share his . . . pearls of wisdom with the world. We left several issues of his favorite magazines littered throughout the hall way: '*Sexy Girl Magazine*', '*Hunting and Killing Animals Monthly*', '*Sexy Girls on Top of Classic Cars Magazine*', and '*Work Out, Drink Muscle Milk, and Work Out Some More*'. We knocked on his door and when he came out and began collecting the magazines, we took our chances sneaking into his room, stealing his diary, and then running like hell. The following, is a day in the life of Captain Amazing.

Side note: He has no idea everyone calls him Captain Amazing, so please don't tell him.

Second side note: He has no idea I stole his diary, so please don't tell him that either.

3/13/2010:

Dear diary,

Today sure was freakin' sweet! I woke up around eleven this morning in SYR next to some smokin' hot chick that I brought back to my room from the hotel bar last night. For some reason she got mad when I called her Carol. Probably because that's not her name. But her name's not important, because she's just some hussy I picked up at the bar. Then I told her to go downstairs and fetch me my breakfast. She got mad again so I told that hussy to get the hell out of my room; I had to get ready for work.

I put on my uniform and went downstairs to the breakfast area so everyone could see how good I looked. But the only people down there were a couple snot nosed kids and their mom. And she wasn't even a MILF. She was uuuuuuugly! I guess that's upstate New York for ya. The kids were using that do-it-yourself waffle maker, but I wanted my waffles immediately, so I pushed them out of the way and took theirs. They started crying because it was the last of the waffle batter, and then their ogre of a mother started telling me I was a bad person for taking her kids breakfast. So I knocked her plate on the ground and stepped on her eggs and told her that none of them got breakfast now. She took her crying kids and left saying that she was going to have a word with the hotel manager. The second she left, I dumped all the cereal in the trash, poured all the coffee, juice, and milk out in the sink, and ate seventy-six strips of bacon and the last two hard boiled eggs. Then when the hotel manager came in demanding to know why I ruined that families breakfast, I asked "What breakfast? I don't see any breakfast here." Then I told him to pick up the mess of eggs on the floor before I wrote a strongly worded letter to the hotel chain.

I rode the hotel shuttle to the airport with my lame FO Raphael, and our sexy flight attendant Kylie. I sighed really loudly on the ride to the airport and announced how much I missed my jag, and wished it was in New york for me to drive around, but I don't think my two loser co-workers heard me, because they didn't respond. So I told them that I named my Jag Janice after the super model I lost my virginity to at the age of fourteen. That must have got their attention, because after I said that, they looked at each other and smiled. They think I'm totally rad.

When Raphael was doing his walk around for the plane, I told Kylie I'd be treating her to a romantic dinner in Paris this weekend. When she asked how we'd get there, I told her "We'll fly, stupid!" Then I told her to go get me my coffee. That's why I make the big bucks and she's just a stewardess. When Raphael came back from his walk around I locked the cockpit door and told him he couldn't come in until he admitted that I was the best pilot in the world and chicks totally want me and dudes totally want to be me, especially gay dudes because then they can get all the chicks too. He said he wasn't going to repeat any of that, so I told him to go run twenty laps around the plane and think about what he's done. He said he wasn't going to do that either, so I told him to make it fifty. That guy has no sense of humor. He thinks John is funny, and John is always telling those stupid Chuck Norris facts. Chuck Norris isn't funny! I know because I beat him up in 1971 and again in '93. I opened the door any way because Kylie said my coffee was done. And the best part is, she fixed the cappuccino button on the coffee maker, so it was extra frothy at the top, just the way I like it.

When we flew to PHL, there was heavy traffic and air traffic control told me we'd have to circle in a holding pattern for at least twenty minutes before landing. But I reminded them who I was and they immediately cleared a path for me. I told them if it happened again, I'd run them over in my airplane.

When we flew from Philly to DC I decided to take a nap. Raphael didn't like that, but I don't see what his problem was, the plane had an auto pilot button. He said that I needed to turn the auto pilot on in order for it to work. I told him that wasn't necessary because I can fly our plane with my eyes closed. Then he started saying something about the FAA and me being a safety hazard, but it bored me to sleep again.

We had two hours on the ground in DC, which I spent productively. I did five hundred push-ups in the crew room, learned Japanese, beat up seven terrorists, did five hundred more push-ups (with my shirt off), and ate a chicken sandwich for lunch.

When we got back to the plane I asked Kylie what time I should pick her up for dinner on Saturday. She said she never agreed to dinner, and then I reminded her who I was and that put her in her place because she got quiet after that. She knows the deal. Raphael came back to the airplane with a cup of coffee, and gave me a suspicious look after setting it down in the galley. Then he went outside to do his walk around, and I heard him specifically tell Kylie to keep an eye on his coffee for him. I don't know why it needed to be watched it was just the three of us on board. So to teach him a lesson, I chugged his entire cup of coffee. I didn't care if it was piping hot, that guy needs to learn to respect his pilot in command—ME! I burned my tongue something fierce, but it was totally worth it, because I'm amazing. When Raphael came back to the plane he accused me of drinking his coffee. You know what I said to that? You're welcome. Kylie said she'd make him another cup, and I told her to make it two, I needed to get the taste of failure flavored coffee out of my mouth. Raphael asked her not to make his coffee extra frothy like she does mine, and then he winked at her. That must be his way of trying to pick her up, which isn't going to work because she's totally into me.

During boarding I told Kylie to stand behind me in the galley so I could greet my loyal fans at the boarding door. She told me that they weren't fans, they were passengers, and that they weren't there to see me, they were there to fly to Charleston. I beg to differ. I shook every man woman and child's hand that boarded that plane and told each one of them how great it is to have such loyal fans. I made Raphael fly this leg because he's a loser and I had work to do. I asked Kylie to send up fifty napkins to the cock pit, so that I could personally autograph each one for my fans in the back of the plane. That only took two and a half minutes, so I spent the rest of the flight reading a copy of Hustler. I only read it because of the articles. And by articles, I mean the pictures of naked chicks. When we landed in CHS, I pushed Kylie out of the way and handed out my autographs to the deplaning passengers. Some of them laughed. They must know I'm working on my act to be the world's greatest comedian/pilot/terrorist hunter. Most of them were confused. Probably because they've never had a celebrity of my status give them his autograph so willfully without charging them seven-hundred and fifty-two dollars for it.

On the van ride to the hotel I asked Kylie and Raphael what they were doing for dinner. They said they were just going to stay in their rooms tonight like a couple of slam-clickers. When we got to the hotel I took off my wings and tie and sat down at the hotel bar to have a beer. I drank twelve beers in twenty minutes waiting to see if any hotties would come by. Having my uniform and luggage beside me at the bar makes me a total chick magnet. They didn't, so I went back to my room to change. The bar tender stopped me and said that I needed to pay my tab, so I told him to charge it to my room. Then I told him my name was Raphael and gave his room number instead.

I changed clothes and came back downstairs just in time to spot Kylie and Raphael leaving the hotel together. I guess they changed their minds about eating dinner. I caught up to them and suggested we go to South Carolina's premier strip club because I have the hookup there. They said they'd rather go to outback steak house instead. Borrrrrring. We went to their stupid steak house where I told them I wanted a lobster. They said they didn't have lobster, so I ordered seven of the biggest steaks they had instead. My co-workers got mad because I didn't leave a tip, but I told them I'm not tipping any women unless they're taking their clothes off and dancing for me. Raphael asked me what my problem was. I told him global warming was my problem and that everyone was to blame for it but me, but I am working on the solution. Wind powered air planes.

When we got back to the hotel I asked Kylie if she wanted to come to my room for a little loving. I'm going to have to work that into my comedy act, because she found it really funny and laughed at me. Whatever, I'm sure tomorrow will be just as amazing as today was. That's because every day is amazing when you're me.

Captain A.

Therapy to a holding pattern

December 23rd 2009

It's nearly eight at night
and the plane
circles above Virginia-
caught in a holding pattern.

Most passengers are asleep,
waiting to land
as I sit in my jump seat.
Quietly
sipping my coffee.

It's been a long day,
we should have been done
hours ago.
My bones ache
just as much
as my heart does.

Every time we circle
to the left again,
I can see hundreds
of tiny houses below
start to light up
from the window
of my commissary door
like tiny stars
on the world below.

I like to think
that she's in
one of those houses below.
Turning on the light for me,
waiting
for my delayed flight
to land
even if she's not.
It's almost therapeutic.

Flight delay games

March 15th 2010

3:00PM-
We are all set to go to Philadelphia from DC. The flight is full. After my announcements, I take my jump seat.

3:10-
We are still on the ground. Still not taking off.

3:23-
The air craft engines turn off.

3:24-
My pilot comes on the PA:
"Well folks, we're all set to go to Philadelphia . . . unfortunately air traffic control has just informed us that due to heavy thunderstorms in the area, we are currently in a ground stop because no planes are allowed to land or leave the airport. We should have an up—date in the next half hour or so."

3:25-
Everyone grunts and groans in anger. I smile.

3:26-
At least three call buttons light up. My smile goes away.

3:27-
"Yes sir?"

"I have a connecting flight at 6:00! Will I make it?"

"Yes. When a ground hold occurs, nothing happens at all, and everything is pushed back for the amount of time we hold."

3:28-
I repeat myself to the next two passengers that ask the exact same question.

3:30-
I explain over the PA what I just explained to the last three passengers.

3:35-
I decide now is a good a time as any to play my flight delay games and announce over the PA:
"Alright, since we're all sitting on the ground doing nothing anyway . . . we are going to play a little game. Here's the way it will work. I will ask you a question. If you think you know the answer to the question, just push that little call button above your head—like on a game show. I will then come to your seat and you will give me the answer to the question. If you get the answer to the question correct, you will win a prize. The prize will be something like a whole can of soda of your choice . . . two bags of spinzels . . . etc. However, if you have the answer to the question incorrect, you will win . . . nothing, and I will move on to the next passenger. So, now that we know how the game is played, I will begin with the first question."

3:38-
People are smiling again. At least they're happy.
"The first question of the day . . . how far can this airplane fly into the clouds? Once more . . . how far can this airplane fly into the clouds?"

3:39-
Ding (Call button lights up.)
"32,000!"
A passenger calls out.

"32,000 what?"
I ask.

"32,000 feet!"

"No, incorrect."

Ding! (Call button lights up.)
"34,000 feet!"

"No. Also incorrect. I'll give you a hint. It's not a number."

3:43-
Ding! (Call button lights up.)
"Half way."
A middle aged man in a polo shirt says.

"That's correct! Why half way?"
I ask, looking for an explanation to his answer.

"Because after that, the plane's flying *out* of the clouds."
He cleverly responds.

"Absolutely right. Everyone give a round of applause to passenger 6C for getting the question correct. What do you want to drink?"
I ask.

"Just a sprite please."

3:47-
"Alright, next question. Why do you not want to be on a plane going from Washington DC airport . . . to Fort Lauderdale airport? Again, why do you not want to be on a plane . . . from Washington Reagan to Fort Lauderdale?"

3:52-
"Because I want to be going to Philadelphia!"
A passenger shouts out.

"You didn't push your call button."
I say.

Ding (Call button lights up.)
"Because I want to go to Philadelphia!"
He repeats.

"No. Incorrect."

3:57-
Ding (Call button lights up.)
"Is it because there is no airport in Fort Lauderdale?"

"No, incorrect. In fact, there is an airport in Fort Lauderdale, and yes, UPside Airlines is beginning service there starting this fall."

4:04-
Ding (Call button lights up.)
". . . Because I'd rather be *in* the plane and not on it!"
An older woman says to me.

"Correct!"

4:05-
"All right, next question-"
I begin.

"I'd rather not! I'm trying to sleep!"
Some woman in 1F bitches at me.

I'm quiet for a moment. More shocked than anything.
"Sorry everyone, at this time, the game has been discontinued. Thank you for playing, we should have an update soon."
I sit down in my jump seat and begin to twiddle my thumbs.

Most of the plane makes booing noises at the woman, one passenger shouts:
"Throw her ass off!"
Everyone laughs. Bitchy woman ignores them, as she pretends to sleep.

4:07-
I continue to twiddle my thumbs. A large black woman in 1D looks at Bitchy woman next to her and then looks at me. She smiles and shakes her head. She is displeased with
bitchy woman.

4:09-
The pilot comes back on the PA.
"Alright folks, still no word on our release time yet . . . it shouldn't be too much longer. The reason why we don't want to take you back inside the airport is because we're already parked out here and next for take-off. So when we do get released we won't have to re-board and wait again, we can just leave."

4:11-
A baby starts crying in 4D.

4:14-
I start walking through the cabin offering a water service. Cute girl in 8C smiles at me. I smile back. Frat boy in 9A wants to know why I stopped playing the game, he was having fun and tells me I'm the coolest flight attendant he's ever met. I explain that my boss Mikey has told me I'm not really supposed to be doing that kind of stuff. And even though everyone else was enjoying it, and it was taking their minds off of having to sit on the ground, someone asked me to stop for the first (and only) time ever. So I had to stop. He admits with pride:
"I was the one that shouted to throw her ass off!"
I smile and give him a thumbs up.

4:26-
I go into the bathroom and take the empty tissue box, and replace it with a new one.

4:27-
I take the empty tissue box back to my jump seat and begin folding it in half and drawing on it.

4:30-
I've turned the empty tissue box into a hand puppet. I put it on my hand and show it to 1D. She chuckles loudly
"Honey, you some thin' else!"
Bitchy woman is becoming even more displeased with not only me, but the woman next to her now as well.

4:31-
I take the tissue box puppet back to the crying babies parents in 4D. The parents do that stupid baby voice as they talk to their child.
"Look! Looky what the nice man made for you!"
They put the puppet on their hand and begin using its mouth to bite the babies nose. The baby is wildly entertained by this.

5D looks at me and inaudibly says
"Thank you."
No one wanted to keep hearing that kid cry any way.

4:33-
I pour myself a cup of coffee.

4:34-
Ding (Call button lights up.)
I turn around from the galley and see Cute girl in 8C has pushed her call button. I look at her for a moment before picking up my inter phone.
"Sorry, the game is over, you can't answer any more questions."
I say over the PA. Everyone laughs but Bitchy woman in 1F.

4:35-
I walk back to Cute girl in 8C.
"I'm hot."
She says to me.

"You don't have to tell me twice."
I say, winking at her. She laughs hysterically and I tell her to wait one moment.

4:36-
I call my pilots
"Hey, it's getting hot back here."

"Alright, you can open the commissary door if you want to get some air flow into the plane, just make sure no one tries to make a run for it, or light up a cigarette there. Believe me, it happens."

"Any word on leaving yet?"
I ask.

"Dude, it's Philly. You know how it goes. A little bit of rain and that whole airport goes into snail mode. We could be here a while."

4:37-
I open the commissary door and a rush of cool air comes into the plane. I love the smell in the air when it rains on the pavement.

4:38-
I sit back in my jump seat with my coffee.

4:46-
The captain comes back on the PA:
"Well folks, good news, we've been released to go to Philadelphia now and we'll be taking off shortly. Flight attendant, prepare the cabin for takeoff."
Everybody claps.

Frat boy in 9A Shouts out:
"Hell yea!"
Everyone laughs again.

5:23-
We arrive in Philadelphia. Everyone is happy and thanks me tremendously for keeping them entertained during our two hours on the ground with the exception of Bitchy woman. Two passengers give me 'Up and away' certificates, which is really just something passengers on

STRATA Airlines frequent flier program can give to me to rub in Mikey's face and prove to her that I'm doing a good job after all.

5:36-
Everyone has deplaned. I still have four more flights to work before I'm done. And I'm still smiling.

Work together, never together

June 24th 2010

I dangle my feet
over the side of the bed
in this hotel room
in Norfolk.

No more than an hour ago,
I was going through
my yearly recurrent training
with Kylie, Corazon,
and an instructor . . .
quite a flirtatious guy.

I convinced Corazon
to let me come back
to her room
to 'study.'

We crack open two
mini bottles of wine
and make a toast.
Here's to our first year
in the airline.
Here's to best friends.

We crack open two wounds
to make conversation.
Open them up wide enough
and we shouldn't be able
to feel them anymore.

She's still trying
to make her marriage work
for her kids sake,
which isn't turning out so good.
I don't agree with her,
but it's not my decision to make.
That's why
we stayed friends.

Bite my tongue.
Live with
what we've done.

Mistakes we knew we made . . .
we can recover from them.

We're a year older
than we were in Chicago,
so I should just
let the past
lie where it is.

"I'm sorry I kissed you."
I admit.
"Well . . . I kissed you back."
She says.

This will never work.
No matter how much
I want it to,
it's not the way
it's supposed to be.
And I know it will take time,
but I will come to accept it.
I'll come to move on.
After all, I won't live forever.

And we slept beside each other
and I lied to myself
and pretended everything was fine.

Move over.
Move over.
Move over.
Move over.
Move over.
~~Move over.~~
~~Move over.~~
~~Move over.~~
~~Move over.~~
~~Move over.~~
~~Move over.~~
~~Move over.~~
~~Move over.~~
~~Move over.~~
Lie down.
This is all for the best.

Chuck Norris and my first enemy

January 16th 2010

Surprising as it may sound, not everyone in my company likes me, and I found this out the hard way in mid-January. I was called out on reserve to do a trip that over nighted in Syracuse on a Thursday night. When I made my way out to the plane I introduced myself to the pilots in the flight deck.

The captains name was John, who would ultimately become one of my favorite pilots to fly with. Much like me, John also enjoyed playing a guitar and singing. But he played an older type of rock that reminded me more of Bruce Springsteen. He was an all-around nice guy from Billings, Montana, and one of the first things that he told me was that he had been in our company so long that he really didn't care about much of anything there anymore. He explained to me that it didn't take a genius to fly the plane and that he was only there to have a good time and make an honest living.

And have a good time we did.

>>>>>>>>>>>>>>>>>>>>>>>>>

A few months following, he and I had an overnight in White plains. The hotel had three old bikes they would let us borrow and ride out into the town. So John, our FO on that trip, and I rode these busted up bikes down to the nearest gas station at midnight where John bought us a case of beer.

We went back to the hotel and drank the night away while we compared notes about music and songs . . . that night turned out to be one of my better overnights that I still look back on with fondness.

<<<<<<<<<<<<<<<<<<<<<<<<<

I wish I could have said the same about this trip though. While John happened to be one of my favorite Pilots to fly with, the First officer Aaron turned out to be one of the worst. After the pilots introduced themselves, I proceeded to introduce myself as well, to which John responded: "Chuck Jenni . . . hey man, is that any relation to Chuck Norris?" He asked me in his country accent. I couldn't help but laugh because fortunately for me, Chuck Norris was the biggest star to make fun of at the time, and unfortunately for Aaron, I happened to be the biggest jerk in the company at the time.

"You know, Chuck Norris once got into a knife fight . . . and the knife lost." I said. Both pilots were quiet for a moment before John burst into laughter. He laughed as though this was the funniest thing anyone had ever said to him in his life. And that was my cue to keep them coming. "Chuck Norris can run around the earth so fast . . .

he can punch himself in the back of the head!" I said as John continued laughing. This was not so much the case with Aaron, who looked at me like I was nuts.

Our bus of passengers pulled up to the plane, I gave the thumbs up to board, and on with the day I went. When everything was secure on the plane, I called up to the flight deck. "This is Chuck Norris, the cabin is secure." I said into the inter phone. I could hear John burst into laughter from the other side of the door again and I knew at that moment I was going to like flying with that guy.

We had a two hour sit in Pittsburgh, where we decided to grab some lunch. "Hey man, why don't you tell me some more of these Chuck Norris facts?" John asked me.

"I'd rather not hear that . . ." Aaron said.

"The dinosaurs aren't really extinct. You know they're all just hiding from Chuck Norris." I said. Aaron did not find this amusing and he walked off and ahead of us.

"Don't worry about that guy, he's no fun at all." John said to me.

When we arrived at the hotel that night, we figured a beer would be in order. But it was too cold outside to walk anywhere, so we decided to just meet downstairs at the hotel bar. We all pulled up stools. John was to my right, and Aaron to the right of him. We ordered beers. The bartender was younger and pretty cute, and since there was no one else in the bar, she decided to chat with us a bit. "So what are you guys doing here?" She asked.

"Business." John replied as he raised his glass to drink.

"We're pilots. We fly airplanes." Aaron blurted out. ". . . Except for him at the end . . . . He's the flight attendant." He said, pointing toward me, real condescendingly.

She looked at him with a weird face as I shook my head. "No . . . I am not the flight attendant. The politically correct term is 'Stewardess', thank you." I said raising my glass for a drink. The bar tender giggled and turned around to go back in the direction of the kitchen.

"Don't think you're being funny. That won't work with her." Aaron said to me in an unfriendly tone.

"Work . . . what with her, what are you talking about?" I asked while looking at John who merely shrugged.

"You've been making those stupid Chuck Norris jokes all day. They're not funny. And you're not funny!" He said.

"I'm not trying to be funny . . . Chuck Norris really *can* slam a revolving door!" I said. John snorted as he laughed.

The bartender returned to find John laughing and asked: "What's so funny?"

"Oh, I was just telling my coworker here that there is no theory of evolution. Just a list of animals Chuck Norris allows to live." I said.

She lowered the glass that she was cleaning, cracked a smile, and said: "Well I heard that Chuck Norris has counted to infinity. Twice."

John lost it at that. He nearly had beer coming out of his nose, he was laughing so hard now, realizing that I wasn't the only person that had heard of these before. She turned back around to go into the kitchen again.

Aaron leaned across John and over to me. "One more Chuck Norris fact . . . and I swear you're going to regret it." He said in a threatening tone.

I could tell he was serious, and thought that maybe he meant enough was enough. I should probably quit while I was ahead. "All right . . . I'm sorry. Hey, did you guys see that special on the discovery channel last night? You know, they said that Chuck Norris' tears can cure cancer . . . too bad Chuck Norris has never cried before. Ever!" And at that, Aaron reached over across John to where I was sitting, and picked up my half glass of beer. He then proceeded to chug it until it was empty, and slammed it back down in front of me. I couldn't believe what had just happened as I stared at John in amazement, who seemed just as surprised as me.

You don't chug another man's beer. It's the rule. The rule of the universe.

Rule number 23:

You don't chug another man's beer.

I wondered if I should hit him over the back with a bar stool or something. That's how it always worked in the movies. Although, that would probably lose me my job. Those that know me, know that I am not a confrontational person whatsoever, so what I did next, still surprises me (And makes me laugh) to this day. Without thinking, I reached over to his beer, picked it up, and began drinking from it. Everything seemed to slow down.

What the hell am I doing?

This is not good, I changed my mind.

I don't want to drink his beer, to stoop to his level.

So I spit the beer back into the glass and placed the glass back down in front of him. And still as it was happening, in slow motion, I realized that this was probably even worse than what he did. He stood up, knocking his bar stool over like he was going to start a fight with me.

"Oh man, this is it." I thought. "I knew I'd piss someone off here and get the crap beat outta me sooner or later. Always thought it would be a passenger to be honest."

Suddenly John stood up intervening between us like a ref in a boxing match. "All right boys . . . let's call it a night." He said, looking sternly at Aaron.

We paid our tabs and walked back to our hotel rooms in silence. There was such tension. I said nothing as I went into my room and sat down on my bed. I thought a minute before I picked up the phone and called John's room. "Hey John . . . it's Chuck." I said.

"Hey man, what's up?" He asked.

"I just wanted to say . . . about earlier . . . you know I didn't mean to be out of line or anything. I should have stopped with those jokes when he asked me to-"

John cut me off right there. "Hey man, it's cool don't worry about it. The first thing he did when we started flying together was gloat about how mommy and daddy paid his way through flight school and how unhappy he is here. Meanwhile guys like me are up to my eyes in debt, trying to pay off student loans from flight school . . . well into my forties . . . That guy's a prick. If he tries to say anything to management or anyone, I've got your back. Don't worry."

I let out a sigh of relief. "Thanks John. You're a good guy." I said.

"Hey, no problem. Like I told you before, I'm just here to have a good time and make an honest living. If Aaron doesn't want to have a good time with us, that's his problem." He said. I said goodnight and hung up the phone.

Aaron didn't speak to me the rest of the trip, but every time I called the flight deck from the cabin, John was always the one to answer phone. And when he did, I was always ready to make him laugh with a new Chuck Norris fact.

How to pack your suitcase-flight attendant style!

I tend to get this question a lot now that I travel for a living: "Hey Chuck, what exactly do you pack in your suitcase for a four day trip around the globe?" Well, first of all I'm not going around the globe, I'm only going up and down the east coast, a little out west, and to parts of Canada. But that's still a very valuable question. I hope the following will shed some light on the topic and help people realize that they don't exactly need all that much to get by.

Size does matter (When it comes to suitcases.)

I see passengers get on board with 72 inch suitcases. Two of them. No joke! What the hell are you packing in there, an entertainment system? A mo ped? A forty two volume encyclopedia? Or is it you just don't want to pay the extra money for your three year old child to have a seat? Just kidding (Or am I?)

Passengers lug these suitcases on board and then become baffled when I tell them they're going to have to check their bags plane side. I would just like to state for the record that you saw what the plane looked like from the outside. You knew it was one of those 'little planes' (For more info read: *"Take that! . . . Bitch."*) But you still decided to bring on a suitcase made for Andre the giant. Quit trying to stuff it in the overhead, it's not going to fit. If you just let us gate check it, it *should* be at the gate when we arrive at your destination. Don't make a spectacle and let's all get on with our lives.

On a side note: Most airlines will charge you to check your suitcase at the ticket counter. If you plan on checking it any way, carry it to the gate instead. It's a bit of a hassle to carry it through security, but if you're cheap like me, you can have it checked at the gate to your final destination before boarding without having to pay for it.

Now, for a four day trip, I fly with a 22 inch suitcase which expands into a 24 inch. You may be wondering "But Chuck, how is that possible?! A 24 inch suitcase for just four days?!" To which I reply: Shut up and read on to find out!

Socks, underwear, and under shirts

These are probably the most important part of what's in my bag. I tend to keep six pairs of each for a four day trip. Why you may ask? Because as long as you have a clean pair to wear every day, it doesn't really matter what's over top of it, so long as you don't plan on running through the mud.

Six pairs are more than enough to last a four day trip, and then some. I once made the mistake of only bringing two pairs of each for a trip I *assumed* was just going to last two days. The pair I was wearing and a pair in my carry-on bag (I didn't even bother to bring my suitcase for that trip.) And lo and behold, what happened? A trip that was only supposed to last two days, turned into five. There's a moment in life when you find yourself standing naked in a hotel bathroom feverishly scrubbing your undergarments in the sink with a bar of hotel soap that you look in the mirror and tell yourself "Well . . . I won't be making *that* mistake again."

Pants

One pair of jeans, one pair of nice dress pants, one pair of shorts. As I said before, I'm going to be staying in hotels for three nights, not roughing it in the great outdoors. I don't expect I will be doing that much to put my one pair of jeans in jeopardy. But, should I manage to dirty them up/forget them in the room when I leave/have them ripped off by a wild pack of super models, I still have two backups.

The nice dress pants can be anything from a pair of khakis, to gray press slacks. These are critical for two reasons. When paired with my nice shirt, they're my ticket to sneaking into events the hotel may be hosting, worn if my crew decides to go to a nice restaurant for dinner, or worn if I'm in a city with a club that requires a certain dress code. The second reason is should something happen to my only pair of jeans I can still get away with wearing these pants with just a white undershirt pulling off a look that says 'simple, yet classy' (I swear, I did not steal that from a GQ magazine.)

The shorts usually tend to be a pair of basketball shorts. These serve several purposes as well. They're great for just laying around my hotel room when I'm flying with a group of slam clickers. I can wear them during my five trips I make to the gym a year (This is usually in the spring, when I tell myself I'm going to get in shape for the summer, and then get lazy and stop going.) These shorts also serve as a swim suit when the hotel has a nice enough pool. That doesn't happen very often, which is why I don't carry an actual bathing suit.

Shirts

I bring one tee shirt, one sweater, and one dress shirt. The dress shirt as I have said before is reserved for the dress pants and usually worn somewhere nice. Now, because I may be in Canada one day where it's freezing cold, and then in Florida the next day where it's sweltering hot, I also need a sweater.

The time of year and where I'm at depends on what I'll wear. I'm obviously going to wear the sweater where it's cold, but the tee shirt is my first choice. If something happens to it, I can wear the sweater where it's warm and just roll the sleeves up. If it's the other way around and something happens to the sweater, like I forget it in the hotel, I'm out of luck when I get somewhere cold.

Jackets

I'm more of a hoodie guy. I pack one in my suitcase, rolled tightly like the rest of my clothes. It fits just fine and takes up about as much room as my sweater or a pair of jeans. If it's cold outside I wear my sweater under the hoodie, I'm never outside walking in the cold all that long before I reach whatever place I'm venturing out of my hotel to find. Should I decide to scale a mountain on an overnight one day, I'll consider bringing an actual coat, but they're just so bulky and take up so much space in the suitcase that they're not really worth it.

For the ladies

I would like to state that all of this is of course written from the perspective of a male flight attendant. Women obviously dress different, so I've included a short list of the following things that I've seen Corazon pull out of her seemingly bottomless 22 inch suitcase on a four day trip:

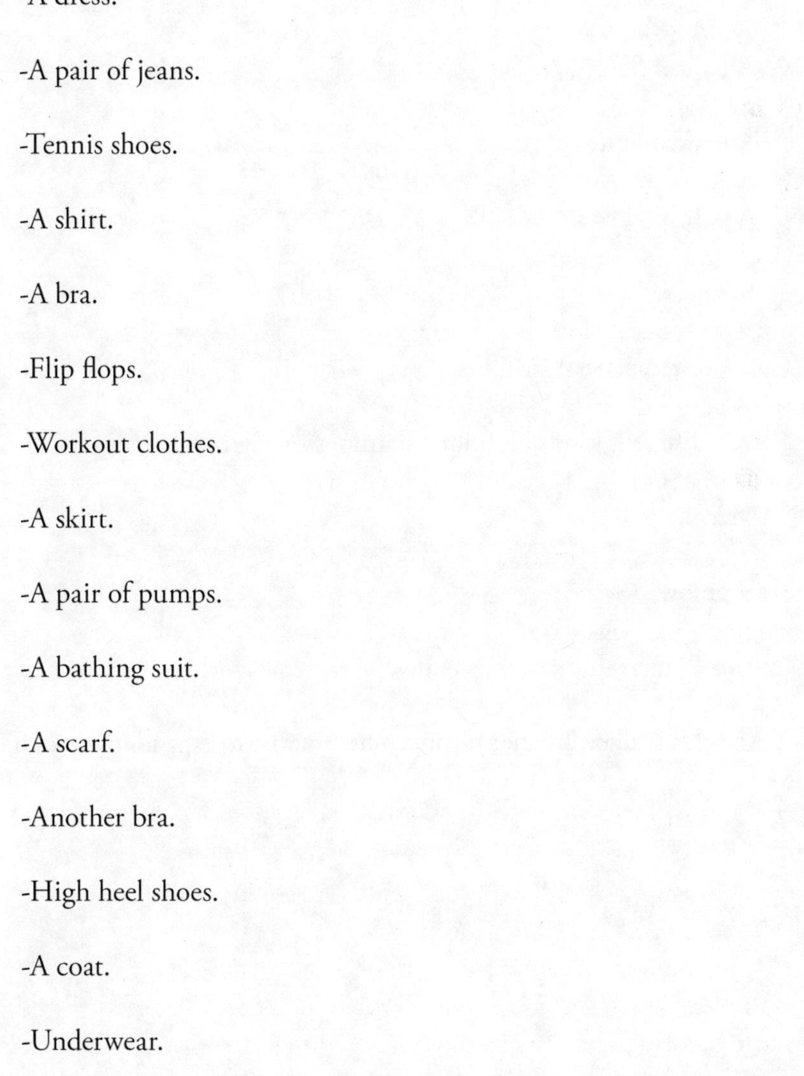

-A dress.

-A pair of jeans.

-Tennis shoes.

-A shirt.

-A bra.

-Flip flops.

-Workout clothes.

-A skirt.

-A pair of pumps.

-A bathing suit.

-A scarf.

-Another bra.

-High heel shoes.

-A coat.

-Underwear.

-A sweater.

-A pair of boots.

-A sexy bra.

-Pajamas.

-A hat.

-A pair of flats.

-A makeup kit.

-A pair of gloves.

-Slippers.

-Six different Shakira CDs.

-Ten different kinds of lotions/shampoos/shower gels/hair products.

-Mace.

-A pillow.

-Some entertainment magazines.

And this is all before she's unzipped her suitcase to expand into a 24 inch.

What I will be thinking should my plane unfortunately plummet from the sky. (Not to be taken as more than a joke.)

We've all had that fear before (Well, at least those of us that have been on an airplane). Terrible turbulence, a sudden drop in altitude, and God forbid the oxygen masks deploy. It's got to be a crappy way to go, but I figured, why not lighten the mood? If you know you're going down, why not crack a joke and enjoy it? The following is a list I have compiled of what I will be thinking should my plane unfortunately plummet from the sky.

30,000 Feet—Hmm . . . this isn't normal.

29,724 Feet—Yup. We're definitely going down.

28,735 Feet— . . . Did I remember to turn the oven off?

26,495 Feet—Well, for once I'm on a plane
and *not* thinking 'Are we there yet?'

24,482 Feet—Don't those people know they're supposed to
remain *in* their seats while the seat belt sign is illuminated?

23,211 Feet—Will somebody PLEASE shut that baby up!

22,746 Feet—Maybe if I had been a better person in life,
we would be plummeting up instead of down.

20,683 Feet—I should say something in German to
someone that doesn't speak it. That way, like Albert
Einstein, my last words will never be known.

18,842 Feet—I wish I had more time to learn German.

17,211 Feet—At least I can say I made it through life having never seen a single episode of 'Jersey shore'. And I'm pretty damn proud of that.

16,179 Feet—Now I'll never know how LOST ends.

14,730 Feet—Maybe this will be just like LOST and I'll crash land on a mysterious desert island with Evangeline Lilly instead of these fatties from the mid-west.

12,926 Feet—That passenger looks a lot like Ashton Kutcher.

10,624 Feet—Alright Ashton, you can jump up and tell me I've been 'Punk'd' any moment now.

9,384 Feet—Huh. Guess it's not him after all.

8,152 feet—If my dad let's my sister drive my car after I'm gone, I'm gonna be pissed. That's why I don't leave a spare set of keys with them.

7,361 Feet—Oh crap, where are my keys?

6,969 Feet—HAHAHAHAHA

4,263 Feet—Those pilots scream like a couple of pansies.

3,372 Feet—That passenger could try out for a hard rock metal band with that kind of scream.

2,193 Feet—I think somebody just wet my pants.

1,583 Feet—Dammit, I just spilled my coffee EVERYWHERE.

312 Feet—Well, at least I'll die doing what I love—ignoring complaining passengers.

First date

June 16th 2010

Around mid-June,
after about a year
of working at UPside Air,
I was on a flight
from DC to White Plains.

It was maybe half full.
And that's where
I met Sarah.
She was in seat 5D,
which meant
I had something pretty
to look at for the next
forty-six minutes.

Despite all the smiling
and flirting
she was doing,
when I made the announcement
that drinks would be offered
upon request only,
she didn't request one.

I was pretty disappointed
until we were preparing
to land.

All of the sudden,
the passenger call button
lit up.

Now normally,
if it had been just
any other passenger
pushing that button
during landing,
I would ignore it.
Unless they were dying
or having a heart attack
or something of the sort.

But a hot girl however,
well . . . that's a different story.

She said she wanted
a cup of coffee.
So I hurried her
a cup
and napkin
before landing.

I returned to my
jump seat and watched her.

She was downing
the piping hot coffee
quite fast.
I began thinking
she didn't particularly
want the cup.

She stuffed the Styrofoam cup
into the seat back pocket
(a huge no-no for me on the plane)
and asked the person
next to her for a pen.
She inconspicuously
wrote something
on the napkin
and folded it into a tiny triangle.

As she was deplaning,
she handed me
the folded up napkin
and thanked me.

I tossed the napkin aside
onto my galley counter
as if I didn't care
and said thanks.

It may sound like
it was a stupid thing to do,
however,
this wasn't the first time
I had been in *that* scenario.

<<<<<<<<<<<<<<<<<<<<<<<<
A few months prior,
I was working a flight
with a girl on board
who was really
flirting with me.

It's got to be the suit.
I look really good in it,
so I'm starting to think
I should start wearing it
more often when I fly.

She asked me
if all flight attendants
were as cute as I was
when she boarded the plane.
I said no,
I was the best looking one.

She asked what she had to do
to get a free drink from me.
I told her anything
she wants.

She called me to her seat
and asked where she could find
her gate information
for her connecting flight
on her ticket,
taking my hand
when I pointed to it
on a map of the terminal
in the back of our inflight magazine.

So when she left the plane,
she handed me
a folded up napkin
and winked giving me a
"Thanks!"

"No, thank *you*!"
I said
like a complete idiot.

John, who I was flying with,
had come out
from the flight deck
to say goodbye to passengers.
So when he saw this
little transaction,
he began nudging me
with his elbow,
and widening his eyes
"Good job man!"

You should have seen me.
I was ecstatic
as Ralphie on Christmas morning
when he got that be-be gun.

Until
I opened
the napkin.

Nothing but a chewed
piece of gum inside.
I suddenly felt
like Ralphie on Christmas morning
when he shot himself in the eye.

John began laughing at me,
and then made some reference
about how Chuck Norris
would have got her phone number
that I really didn't
want to hear.
(He hasn't stopped with them
since we first flew together.)

What's even worse
was that not everyone
was done deplaning yet,
so the few frat boys
that were left on board
had seen this
and laughed
as well.
>>>>>>>>>>>>>>>>>>>>>>>

So this time,
I made sure
that everyone
was gone first
before opening
the napkin.

Sure enough I had received
my first phone number
from a passenger
with an X chromosome.

When I texted her
it went something
along the lines of:

Chuck:
"Hey, you know you forgot
your number on the plane."

Sarah:
"Oh did I?
Well I'm lucky
it was YOU that found it
and not some creepy
old business man."

Chuck:
"So do you live
in New York, or DC?"

Sarah:
"Neither, from Ohio originally,
going to college in Texas.
I'm just interning
at a company in White Plains
for the summer,
so I was only passing
through DC.
I'm glad I did though,
I had a really
cute flight attendant."

Bingo.

After that, Sarah and I
were on the phone
with each other
pretty often.
Although, the more
I got to know her,
the more I started realizing
that it probably
wouldn't go anywhere
relationship wise.

She invited me to White planes
for dinner a few weeks later,
but I suggested
lunch instead.

The reason I did this
was simple.

I basically figured
that if I did jump seat
up to White plains
and realized
that I didn't like this girl
whatsoever,
and wanted nothing more
to do with her,
at least I could still
get out of there
while there was time
to catch the last flight
home to DC.

The more we talked,
I was able to come
to a few conclusions.

First:
She was a nice girl overall,
but I think that
I was just so thrilled
at the idea of a passenger
(who wasn't a guy)
giving me a phone number,
that I didn't really care
if we had anything
in common or not
when we started talking.

Second:
After spending the afternoon
with her, I realized
that she really didn't have
a whole lot to talk about with me
in person and I couldn't wait
to get on that plane
and fly back home.

Third:
She did *not* think
that Chuck Norris facts
were funny.

And last:
I came to the realization,
that even after almost a year,
I was still in love
with Corazon.

Chicago in the morning

August 20th 2009

It's the beginning
of a new day
in Chicago
as the light
slowly makes its way
into the room
after a long night.

I stand up
and swing open
the hotel curtains
to find
the cities rusty gears
starting to turn.

And it won't be long now
before it's all clogged up again.
It almost makes me
depressed enough to jump,
to join the rest of the robots
in their machine.

Dammit, who am I trying to fool?
My plan to live
like the rest of you below
is nothing more now
than just
a childhood memory.

Corazon stirs in the bed
behind me
as I focus hard enough
outside to remember:
I told her
that we were
born to run
like there's no tomorrow.

As I stared
into my eyes
in the reflection
of the sixth floor hotel window,
I suddenly
came to the conclusion
no one ever told me
that I was so afraid
of running away
to understand what it is
that I'm running towards.

"I'm going to have myself
in pieces-" she said
"before this even begins."

I held her tightly and whispered:
"Everything is going to be
OK in the end.
If it's not OK-
it's not the end."

Part II

Flying with eyes closed

For a good cup of coffee in Toronto, Canada

June 9th 2011

The alarm blares.
Wake up. *Wake up.*
The sun is peeking
through the curtains
and into my eyes.

What time is it?
Ten in the morning?
I roll over and shake Mary.
"Hey . . . hey, come on.
Wake up.
We've got to be out of here
in an hour."

She makes an in distinctive
grunting noise,
gives me an evil eye,
and then rolls back over,
burying her face
in the pillow.

"Are you still mad
about the bra thing last night?"
I ask.

She makes the same noise,
and pulls the blankets
over her head.

"Alright . . . I'll be back."
I say.

I toss on
my white tee-shirt
from yesterday.
Black hoodie.
Dirty jeans
I've worn
since leaving Pittsburgh.

I put on my tennis shoes,
zip up my hoodie,
shuffle my feet
out of the hotel room
(Key in the back pocket),
and down the hall
like a man on a mission.

Coffee, coffee, coffee, coffee, coffee, coffee, coffee . . .

It's chilly in Toronto
for early June.
The city looks different
in the day light
than when we arrived last night,
but it could be
just the hangover talking.

The streets are busy,
and I can see
my breath in the air.

There's too many people,
and it makes me feel like
I'm overwhelmed sometimes.
Maybe I should
hold my breath
to keep myself
from drowning in it all.

Who am I?
I'm usually the guy you see
strolling around,
hoodie zipped up,
listening to my iPod . . .
just a ghost to you
in this city
where no one knows my name,
and it's sad
that there's a certain comfort
to be found in that.

I make my way
into the nearest coffee shop.
I can't recall if it was
a local owned place
or another chain of
corporate owned shops,
offering health insurance benefits
and minimum wages
to mid-twenties
college dropouts.

As I wait in line for my coffee,
between the Robots
and the blue collared working class,
I imagined my life
working at a coffee shop.

~~~~~~~~~~~~~~~~~~~~~~~~

There I'd be,
wearing my apron,
standing behind a counter.
Smiling as my regulars approached.
~~~~~~~~~~~~~~~~~~~~~~~~

"Good morning
Mr. Insert-regulars-name-here!
The usual:
medium, double vanilla
sugar-pump steam milk
coffee this morning?"
I'd ask cheerfully.

"Make it a large . . .
I've got that business presentation
to give today!"

"That's right,
I forgot about that!
Good luck, and say hello
to the Missus for me!
See you tomorrow!"

And then we'd laugh
as I'd hand him his coffee
and greet the next
regular customer
I was so used to seeing
morning
after morning
after morning
after morning . . .

Yea, that would be me,
and I'd even write a book about it:
'Bad barista'.
No wait-
'Good barista'.

~~~~~~~~~~~~~~~~~~~~~~~~
~~~~~~~~~~~~~~~~~~~~~~~~

I approach the counter
and order two cups of coffee
and two blueberry muffins.
I make my concoction
at the side of the counter:
Two creams,
three sugars,
a stir stick inside,
and the lid back on.

As I make my way for the exit,
a Robot in her late twenties
approaches the door
to come inside.

We do that move
where we both reach
for the door handle
at the same time
and then pause-
who will make the first move?

I open the door to allow her
access to the coffee shop
as she smiles warmly at me
and says
"Thank you."

This one was different
than the normal robots
I had on my day to day flights.

Maybe it was
that she had not yet
had the life sucked out of her
by the daily grind
of the corporate world.

Maybe it was
the tight pant suit
that complimented
her attractive figure.

As I stood there,
holding the door,
I imagined my life
as a Robot
in the corporate world.

~~~~~~~~~~~~~~~~~~~~~~~~~

There I'd be,
wearing my expensive suit
sitting at my cubicle
on the 37th floor
of ConglomoCorp.

I'd stand up from my rolling chair,
walk over to the water cooler
and pour myself
a paper cup of water.
Smiling as my co-worker approached.

"Good morning,
Insert-working-class-single-female-living-in-the-cities-name-here!
Did you catch last night's
episode of
'pointless-reality-TV-show-we-talk-about-every-day'?"
I'd ask cheerfully.

"I did! I can't believe
that twist that everyone saw
coming happened!
Don't forget it's
Overweight-accountants
surprise birthday party
in the break room at three pm!"
~~~~~~~~~~~~~~~~~~~~~~~~~

"That's right, I almost forgot
about that
pointless-reason-to-celebrate-all-the-time-party!
I'll have to sign the card
with a funny inside joke of ours!"

And then we'd laugh
as I'd return to my cubicle
I'd sit in day
after day
after day
after day . . .

Yea, that would be me.
And I'd even write a book about it:
'Bad working class robot'.
No wait-
'Good working class robot'.
~~~~~~~~~~~~~~~~~~~~~~~~

I leave the coffee shop
and return to the streets
of Toronto
and walk back
in the direction of my hotel.

The streets are busy now,
full of people heading
in their own directions,
with their own lives.

I contemplate the decisions
I've made up to that point.
I think about my time
in the airline.
~~~~~~~~~~~~~~~~~~~~~~~~

I wonder what it would be like
to live a normal daily life
as a coffee shop worker.
As a business robot.
As a normal person.

And despite the fact
that I know where my hotel is,
I don't seem to know
where I'm going.

As I return to the hotel room,
I find Mary fixing her hair
in the mirror.

I set the cups of coffee
and muffins
on the computer desk
and stare out the window.

I think
"That could be me down there,
living life as . . ."
When suddenly,
Mary interrupts my thoughts.

"Good morning, Chuck!
That was a good time
at the Loose Moose last night.
Did you check
the passenger loads
to see if we'll be able
to get on a flight
out of here today?"
She asks cheerfully.

I turn away from the window
"No, not yet.
But if they are full to D.C.,
we'll just have to connect
through another city,
and if they're full there . . .
we'll just have to
stay the night
wherever we wind up."

"That's right,
I forgot that could happen . . .
that could be another
fun adventure though!
Oh, did you get us
those muffins?
Thanks, you didn't
have to do that!"
she laughs, and begins
gathering her suitcase
back together again.

I turn back
to look out the window again.

The streets are busy,
full of people heading
in their own directions,
with their own lives.

There are too many people,
and it makes me feel like
I'm overwhelmed sometimes.
And when I contemplate
holding my breath
to keep myself
from drowning in it all,
I remember that I have
a friend like Mary
to take my hand
and pull me back up
out of it all.

To remind me
that of all the lives
we could have chosen
to live below,
we were living ours
up there.

The business end of a loaded shot glass (Mary's philosophy on life)

June 7th 2011

"Come on Mary; just give me your bra! We're running out of time!" I demanded. I was at the loose moose bar in Toronto, Canada sitting next to Mary. Above our heads was a metal rod extending from one end of the bar to the other, completely covered in bras.

"That's right ladies, all you have to do is throw your bra up onto this bar, and you can win free drinks for the rest of the evening! Come on, come on, come on! Step riiiiiiiight up!" The low paid, middle aged DJ kept screaming repeatedly over an extremely loud sound system to a nearly empty bar. I smiled at the sight of a patron covering his ears and nodding disapprovingly at the DJ in the same manner that passengers do to me when my P.A. is turned up too loud.

I kept smiling at Mary, who was biting her lip and raising her eyebrows at me.

<<<<<<<<<<<<<<<<<<<<<<<<<

The first time I met Mary was in Rochester, New York. It was the last overnight I had with Lizzie after a month of flying together. I wasn't in much of a mood to go downstairs and have a drink, but in the end she convinced me since we might not be flying together again for a while.

We were staying at the old Strathallan hotel, where there wasn't really anyone else in the bar with the exception of Mary. She was seated at the other end; drinking some kind of girly martini and making small talk with two older men that I assumed she had arrived with. As Lizzie and I recounted one of the craziest overnights we had ever had involving a run in with a Satanist, one of the men that was with Mary asked us if we had a lighter. Lizzie went outside to smoke with the two men, leaving me alone with Mary to strike up a conversation. I moved over to the stool beside her.

"So what are you doing in Rochester?" She asked.

To which I replied: "Business." It's kind of a rule that I have with myself to never immediately reveal what it is that I'm really doing there.

The men returned with Lizzie a few moments later, and formal introductions were exchanged. I don't particularly remember the names of the men, or pay much more attention to them because:

1: They were the same Robots I have to deal with on my flights on a daily basis.

2: They were not there with Mary after all, which meant if I had a choice between getting to know those losers or the pretty little brunette . . . I'm probably going to choose the latter option.

They were the typical older business guys at the bar that are quick to try and impress the ladies by throwing around money and buy drinks for everyone else, which I have become particularly keen in taking advantage of. After all, I've always said that a tequila and tonic always tastes best when it's free.

I quickly made it clear that Lizzie was nothing more than a co-worker, so when they offered up a round of shots, I made sure to jump right in there with them making the 'Hey, remember I showed up with the lady.' Look on my face, earning me my free shot as well. If you're gonna try and pick up my pilot, you're gonna have to go through me first, buddy.

Sadly, it wasn't long before I was on my fourth drink, and in full on Chuck-story-mode. ". . . So there was Lizzie and I in Ottawa, trying to ditch this crazy Satanist . . . !"

Mary suddenly cut me off. "You guys sure do travel a lot for work . . . what exactly is it that you do?" She asked.

I took a deep breath and looked at Lizzie, giving her the 'We might as well tell her' look. Lizzie rolled her eyes and nodded disapprovingly at me, as she stated: "I need to stop drinking with you." She thinks she's hot stuff just because she can hold her liquor better than me.

"Well, we . . . work for the airline." I said.

Mary's face lit up as if she just spotted a friend she hadn't seen in years. "Oh, which one?!" She asked excitedly.

". . . It's a regional express carrier of STRATA Air." I replied.

". . . Alright . . . but which one?" She asked.

Now I knew that she knew more about the airline industry than she initially lead us to believe. People that don't fly normally just leave it at that when I drop the big airlines name since they don't tend to know the difference between a mainline carrier and a regional express carrier. Not this girl though. I knew I'd be breaking my own rule of not revealing what airline I worked for, but it didn't stop me. Well, the tequila didn't stop me.

". . . UPside Airlines." I said hesitantly.

"Really?! I work there too! What do you do there?" she asked.

"I'm . . . a flight attendant."

"No way! Me too! What airport are you based out of?" She was getting almost as loud as I had been.

". . . Washington Regan."

"Oh! . . . Me toooo!" She said excitedly. She was clapping her hands together and laughing like a loon on *Sesame Street*.

From there on out, we talked as if we were the only two left in the bar. She had only been hired a month prior, so she had plenty of questions. And I had plenty to tell her about, being the big senior flight attendant.

Note: I really only had a year and five months under my belt by that point . . . still long passed the life expectancy of a flight attendant in our company.

I talked with her about Mikey, crazy passengers, and of course my now infamous juice can race story. She shared with me her stories of training, passengers, and most importantly, her philosophy on life.

Lizzie got tired of talking to the business-bots and left shortly after to go to bed, and since I was talking to the only girl left in the bar, the other two losers left. Mary and I closed down the bar, exchanged numbers and went back up to our rooms. It was well past 3 am when we left. That was the start of how I met my best friend at UPside Air.

>>>>>>>>>>>>>>>>>>>>>>>>

We kept in touch every so often, but our first real 'adventure' was nearly seven months later in June. I was finishing a trip on a Tuesday evening when I randomly ran into Mary at the airport as I was getting ready to leave.

"Oh, Hey! What are you doing right now?" She asked me.

"I just finished my last flight of the trip . . . so absolutely nothing."

"Come to Ohio with me! The flight leaves in an hour!" She just blurted out. It was one of the most random invitations I had ever received.

". . . I don't know. What for?" I asked.

"My old college friend is having a party! When do you work again?" She asked.

"Saturday."

"So do I! We'll be back by then! Come on, be my travel partner! . . . remember my life philosophy?" She asked. Boy did I.

"Only all too well . . ."

"Ok, so you'll come?"

Apparently that was all the convincing I needed, as I found myself on a plane to Ohio with her shortly thereafter. An old college friend of hers named Dobin was having a party at his house about forty-five minutes from the airport, so her brother Jiffy picked us up to take us there. When we arrived, Dobin came out of his house, brandishing a bottle full of liquor and singing at the top of his lungs: "I love you baaaaaby, and if it's quite alright, I love you baaaaaby la-da-da-da-da-da . . . !" as he lifted Mary up in a bear hug, followed by me, in the exact same manner. I knew that I was going to like partying with this guy.

I woke up sometime around noon the next day on a green deflated air mattress in the living room. I'm not really sure if it was inflated when I passed out on it, but I don't think it would have helped with my hangover in the least bit. It felt like there was a party in my mouth and everyone was hung over.

Jiffy took Mary and I back to the airport later that day. I was sure that we would be flying back to DC from there until Mary passed by the gate with a flight departing for Chicago. "Oh! We have to go! The Tossers are playing in Chicago tonight! They're my favorite Irish punk band! Come on, let's go, let's go, let's go!" I had to think about it for a minute. I was already pretty beat from the previous night, and I kind of wanted to go home since I hadn't packed enough clothes to be gallivanting around the country for much longer. I wasn't exactly sure that jumping on an airplane and going to Chicago to see an Irish rock band would be the smartest idea by that point. Luckily there was still a trump card to be played.

"Ok . . . let's go check to see if it's a full flight." I suggested.

We waited for a while by the gate for the flight to Chicago until we found out that all the seats had been sold, and we wouldn't be able to make it on. Mary was pretty upset. I said I was too, although I was secretly relieved.

Since we still had a bit of time before our flight to DC, we decided to go to one of the airport bars and have a drink. When we left, Mary was still pretty down about not being able to go to Chicago. That changed quickly when we passed by a gate with a flight that was going to Toronto. I knew I was going to regret the next decision I made. I took a deep breath and suggested: "Hey . . . want to go to Canada tonight?" Her face lit up once more when hearing this. "You're my new travel partner . . . so, let's travel." I said.

"Do you mean it?" She asked.

"Absolutely. And by travel, I mean drink ourselves silly in cities around the world." I said laughing.

Two more drinks later, and we were on a Dash 8 well on our way, without a plan, to Toronto. The conversation with customs there went a little something like this:

Customs agent: What are you doing in Canada?

Chuck: Getting drunk.

Customs agent: Where are you staying?

Chuck: We don't know. We're just gonna jump in a cab and ask for a hotel downtown.

Customs agent: When are you leaving?

Chuck: No idea.

Customs agent: What do you two do for a living?

Chuck: We're flight attendants.

Customs agent: Welcome to Canada!

We took a cab to some cheap hotel and soon found ourselves wandering the streets until we came to the first decent looking bar we saw called "The Loose Moose." I said that it looked good enough for us, although I really just wanted to get out of the cold. I studied the semi-empty bar and its interior as Mary ordered us weird mixed drinks with names such as 'The Moosetini'. There was an awful DJ at the end of the bar that kept making moose references by saying things like: "Hey all you Mooses and Moosettes, don't forget it's Moose hour every day from six to seven PM! That means half prices on all Moose-tails and Moosetinis!" I shouted out that those deals were mooseing crazy. There was a table of rowdy college students at the far back of the bar screaming for their local hockey team to win. But the most notable part of the Loose Moose was a metal rod above our heads extending from one end of the bar to the other.

Covered completely in bras.

Becoming more and more intoxicated, I couldn't help but inquire about this unusual decoration. According to the bartender, if you stand on the bar, take your shirt off, and toss your bra up on the rod, you'll win free drinks for the rest of the night.

This was all I needed to hear to turn a decent night at a dive bar in Toronto into an awesomely decent night at a dive bar in Toronto.

"Mary, you have to do it. No questions asked. Free alcohol is at stake here!"

"No, I'm embarrassed, I don't want to do that!" she pleaded.

I thought for a few minutes. "Hey, all he said was that the bra had to be donated. He didn't say from whom! So all you have to do is go into the bathroom, put your bra into your purse, and bring it back to me. Then I'll go into the bathroom, put the bra on, jump onto the bar and throw it up there!"

"I don't think that's how it works." She said.

"Even if we don't win the free drinks, it'll still be funny as hell! I'll even buy you a new bra!"

"But I really like this one though!" she detested.

"Mary . . . I went to Ohio . . . then I jumped on a plane with you to randomly go to Canada . . . all because of *your* philosophy on life! Have you forgotten your own philosophy?" I asked her.

She knew it all too well.

<<<<<<<<<<<<<<<<<<<<<<<<

Nearly seven months prior in November, we were sitting at the hotel bar in Rochester, New York. Lizzie had just left to go to sleep, followed shortly by the two business men. I was drunkenly laughing and rambling about passengers demanding a whole can of soda, when Mary just cut me off and said out of nowhere: "You know, I really don't want to die old. I'd prefer to die young."

"Ok . . . craaaazyyyy . . ." I teased her.

"No, hear me out! Not literally die young, but my philosophy on life is if I look at things that way, it makes it easier to live like every day is my last. You know, like the whole no regrets thing. It made it that much easier to leave school and all my friends in Ohio and come out here to be a flight attendant. So it makes it that much easier to just jump on a plane on a whim and go wherever I feel like!"

I thought that philosophy was a little silly at first, but she did have a valid point. The bartender then announced last call, and even though we'd had enough, I still ordered one more round of shots. I probably shouldn't have, since I'd reached my limit by that point, but I realized that Mary was right. There may not be a tomorrow, I won't live forever. And it was at that bar in Rochester that I decided to start living by Mary's little philosophy of life as well. I raised the shot and made a toast to her.

"Alright then, here's to new friends . . . and living life like there's no tomorrow."

The best crew VS. the Satanist

October 7th 2010

The thing about working for the airline
is that there's always
good overnights
and bad overnights.
But then there are overnights
that I've come to refer to
as 'One of those nights.'

What exactly is it
that makes
'one of those nights?'
For me it's the crew
that you're with.

The location doesn't matter.
The fact of the matter is,
the city is probably the least
contributing factor.

Of course we stay the night
in awesome cities
and towns;
Rochester, NY;
Ft. Lauderdale, FL;
Wilmington, NC . . .
but those overnights
mean nothing
if you don't like the people
you're flying there with.

The first time I experienced
'one of those nights'
was in Ottawa, Canada.

It was my first time flying
with ElHeffey
and Lizzie.

ElHeffey was without a doubt
Chris Farley reincarnate.
He is a somewhat larger guy
in his late thirties
from Wisconsin.
He used to drive a school bus
in his younger days,
and when he'd tell stories of it,
he'd really get into it.
He'd flail his arms around
and use this really funny,
scratchy low-voiced character
for almost everyone
in his stories.

Lizzie was the first pilot I met
that claimed that UPside Air
has a reputation
for only hiring attractive female FO's,
which, one look at Lizzie,
would agree
is accurate.
She's slightly taller than I am,
with that little bit
of Puerto Rican ancestry in her
to give her an extra push
of attractiveness.

She was about ten years older,
with that sweet, protective older sister
attitude towards me
(She's cut me off
at a bar in Binghamton before
when I said I was perfectly fine,
and then took care of me all night
while I hugged the toilet
and apologized
for not listening to her earlier.)

But the thing I liked most about her
is that she used to work
for STRATA Airlines
as a flight attendant,
and after a few years of that,
she decided to become a pilot instead.
So she is one of the few pilots
that can actually relate to me
as a flight attendant.

The first time we all flew together,
ElHeffey pointed out to me
that Lizzie had accidentally
tucked the back of her shirt
into her underwear.
We let her go on
like that for about three flights
before finally pointing it out to her
and then proceeding to taunt her
mercilessly for it.

I knew I was going to like this crew.

Ottawa made it
all the more better.
We arrived at about noon
in a hotel
that was located right in the middle
of downtown.

We changed
out of our monkey suits
and decided our first stop of the day
would be a restaurant/bar
down the street from our hotel
called Minglewoods.

This is where all of our other
crew members told us
to start off at,
and for good reasons.

It was decorated
like a giant old log tavern.
The food there is terrific
(I always ordered
the chicken tenders
and poutine).
There's a foosball table
that stands in the corner.
The waitress that's always working
during the day there
is extremely attractive
(although, in my opinion,
most of the women
in the Ottawa area we stay in are),
and the Canadian beer on tap is cheap.

But my favorite part
about Minglewoods
is a giant,
wooden carved beaver
outside of the bar that is
holding a sign telling you
what the special of the day is.

We ate and drank beers,
as ElHeffey regaled us
with hilarious stories
of his days as a bus driver.

I suggested
that he should publish a book
about his days as a bus driver
and told him
that I had began
writing about my experiences
as a flight attendant for my website,
but he said he was too busy
having a life to do that.

After finishing the afternoon
drinking and playing foosball,
we left Minglewoods,
and reached the turning point
of the evening.
We could go back to the hotel
and call it a night,
or we could continue on
to the next bar.

I was prepared to call it a night
until ElHeffey called me out.
(In his scratchy voice)
"*Come on you wuss!*
You're going to bitch out now?
Lizzie's drinking more than you
and she's a girl!
Are you going to let a girl
show you up?!
You're going to come
have another drink with us,
or I'm going to call up Mikey
and tell her you've been
a bad flight attendant again!"

He shouted this
in the middle of the streets
of Ottawa making
a big hilarious scene.
Of course Lizzie and I
knew he was joking
since that's the way he is,
and needless to say,
I went along with it.

"Alright ElHeffey . . .
if it'll keep you
from getting me in trouble . . .
I have no choice but to drink!"

Lizzie laughed
and stated that she needed
to stop drinking with us.

We carried on to our next stop,
a Scottish themed bar,
and continued our night
of drinking together.
Lizzie told us stories
about her days
as a flight attendant
working for a mainline carrier,
and this
was where the trouble started.

Two men came in
and sat at the table
next to us,
a large bald man,
and a smaller man.

Both of these guys
were creepy looking.
They were dressed fully in black
and looked like
they had just rolled out
of a death metal
rock show.

They had piercings and tattoos
covering up whatever skin
looked like it hadn't been
in a bar fight.

As Lizzie and I laughed
and rambled on about passengers
and their insane demands
of wanting two bags of spinzels,
the two men
who had been eaves dropping
and eying Lizzie
figured out
that we were employees of the airline,
and decided
that they needed to be a part
of our conversation as well.

"Which airline do you work for?"
The larger one asked
from the table next to us.
I may have been drunk,
but even I knew
that this would not lead
anywhere good.

I glanced at ElHeffey
who kind of shook his head
and frowned in a
'Please don't tell them' look,
as I swallowed deeply and answered
"Soma air."
The last thing we needed
were for these lunatics to know
what airline we really flew for.

Lizzie asked
if someone had a lighter
she could borrow,
and excused herself
to step outside and smoke,
obviously trying to escape.

The big one handed her
a lighter from his pocket,
as the little one said:
"Oh, I'll join you."
With a look in his eyes
that really meant to say:
"Oh, I'll rape you."

Lizzie got a kind of
'don't leave me alone with this freak'
look on her face
as ElHeffey stood up and said
"I think I'll join you as well."

I looked at the fat one
and got the same
'don't leave *me* alone with this freak'
look on my face,
but no one seemed to notice.

"So . . . what do you do for a living?"
I asked the Penguin.

"I work in a piercing and tattoo shop."
He replied creepily.

Surprise, surprise.

"Must be scary working for the airline?
All those terrorists and all."
He said.

"Um . . . no, I try not to think
about that sort of stuff . . ."
I said reaching for my beer,
slightly trembling.

"There's a lot of Muslims
runnin' around up here.
Makes me sick."
He said, leaning in closer to me,
talking in almost a whisper.

I started looking around the room
for an exit, an escape,
anything
to get me away from this lunatic.

The look in his eyes
made me feel
like I was on fire.
"I'd like to take them all out.
Kill all those bastards."
He said quietly to me.

Terrific.
He's crazy,
and a racist.

He placed his hand on my shoulder
"You know what I would do
if one of them
ever came into *my* tattoo parlor?"
He was right in my face,
reeking of alcohol and cigarettes.

I was getting really nervous.
And scared.
That was a bad combination,
considering I was inches away
from this monster
with me in his death grip.

I knew there was only
one way out of this mess.
Pull yourself together man.
Take a breath.
Just agree
with every last word he says.
Don't say anything
to cause him to go berserk
and rip your head off.

"God help them
if they ever wander
into your parlor."
I said nervously,
forcing a laugh
and a fake smile
across my face.

"God? I don't worship God.
I'm a Satanist."
He said smiling.

My smile went away.

ElHeffey suddenly patted me on the back,
startling me so bad
I could have pissed my pants.

"Hey, I just settled
our tab at the bar,
so we're going
to get out of here now."
He said.

I stood up from the seat,
breaking the cement blocks
that felt like
they were holding my legs down.

I don't really remember
leaving the bar, or what I said
to that monster as I escaped,
probably something like:
"Nice meeting you."
or some shit like that.

As soon as we were
a safe enough distance away though,
I do remember trying
to recount what just happened
and yelling at my pilots.

"Why the hell did you leave me alone
with that Satanist?!"
I asked, still trembling.

"Oh, so I see the other guys friend
was a practitioner of
the black arts as well?
Mwa ha ha!"
ElHeffey laughed
in an evil voice.
I didn't find it funny.
At all.

By the time
we got back to our hotel,
I had calmed
down a bit
and we were actually joking
about it now.
It didn't even seem like
it had really happened.

We rode the elevator up
to the 16th floor
where our rooms were.

I suppose that my room key
had got too close
to my cell phone
and been demagnetized,
because I was the only one
that couldn't get into my room.

I said good night
to ElHeffey and Lizzie
and returned to the lobby
once more to get a new key.

After I had it,
I turned around,
and couldn't
believe my eyes.

There was the Satanist himself,
standing outside
of our hotel!

"What the hell?
Did we tell him
where we were staying,
or did he follow us?"
I wondered.

I tried not
to make eye contact with him,
as I hurried around the corner
to where the elevators were.

Go away.
Please go away.

I heard the lobby doors slide open,
and his monstrous footsteps
moving in my direction.
"Hey, Chuck!"
I heard him call out.
I was hoping there was
someone else in the room
with the same name as me.

I began hitting
the elevator button furiously.

He was moving closer.
I hit it more furiously.
I looked up to see
that the elevator was parked
on the 10th floor
and was now slowly
making its way down.

I looked back
to see that three hundred pound monster,
standing behind me.

"Oh, Hey.
How's it going?"
I asked casually,
trying not to piss my pants.

My eyes shot up to see
how close the elevator was.

9th floor.

"Not bad. You all left
in such a hurry . . ."

Oh no, he's come to kill me.

8th floor.

". . . Lizzie got away with my lighter,
so I came to get it back."
Oh no, he's come to kill Lizzie.

7th floor.

I took a deep breath and said
"Oh. Well I'm just on my way up
to my room now.
I'll get the lighter for you
and bring it back down
in a minute."

He crinkled his eyebrow and replied:
"I was just going to get it from her myself."

6th floor.

"But . . . you don't know what room she's in."
I said trying to protect her.

"It's ok, you can take me there."
He suggested.

5th floor.

"Yea . . . I don't remember
what room she's in . . ."
I said.

A confused look washed across his face
"But . . . you just said
you'd get it from her
and bring it back down to me.
How can you do that
if you don't know what room she's in?"
he asked.

Oh man, I'm a horrible liar.

4th floor.

"Well, I was going to call
the front desk and have them
connect me to her room.
Then I was going to ask her
to bring the lighter to me.
To bring down to you."
I said nervously.
I was starting to lose it.

3rd floor.

I began devising a plan
of what I would do
if he got into the elevator with me.
I would ride it up to the 12th floor,
and then once we were in the halls . . .
I'd run like hell to the stair well
and dash up to the 16th floor.
There's no way
that tyrannosaurus
could keep up with me.
I'd lose him for sure.

"Well, why don't you just ask Lizzie
to bring the lighter down to the lobby?
That would save you
the trouble of coming back down."
He suggested.
I'm sure
what he really meant to say was:
call the lobby
and alert the police.

2nd floor.

"Even better."
I said, smiling as the elevator
reached the first floor
and the doors opened up.

I stepped inside
and pushed the button
for the 16th floor.
The doors didn't close,
and there was the Satanist,
standing before me,
ready to murder the first foreigner
to give him the wrong look.

It took all my will power
not to frantically
hit that elevator button rapidly
until the doors shut.
Oh God, please close.
Oh God, please close.
Oh God, Please close.
Oh God, Please close.

Yep. Just another
'one of those nights.'

24 hours in Ft. Lauderdale

April 18th 2011

12:36 PM-
I land in Ft. Lauderdale with our Captain: The King, and our first officer: Krista. We have off for the next 24 hours overnighting in Ft. Lauderdale, Florida. I am ecstatic, because not only am I flying with Krista (one of UPside Air's most attractive FO's), but she tells me her younger sister will be flying down to meet us as well on Krista's flight benefits. In addition, since Kylie is friends with both Krista and I, she will also be joining us for this overnight. We wait in the airport for the two of them to arrive.

12:58-
Krista's sister and Kylie arrive on a STRATA Air flight.

1:25-
The five of us pile into the hotel van. The drivers English is horrible.

1:57-
We arrive at the Sheraton Yankee clipper on route one. The hotel is literally across from the beach. I almost wet myself in happiness. My happiness grows even more when Krista tells us that another friend of hers that just got hired as a pilot at UPside air named Jess is on the way. I figure the more women, the better.

2:07-
We get our room keys. We agree to meet in the lobby at 6 PM to go out. I decide a nap is in order since I had to be at the airport at 6 in the morning and I have a long night ahead of me.

2:10-
My room is terrific. And it has nice view of the beach from my patio balcony. I think about going to the beach.

2:12-
I lie down and fall asleep on my bed.

4:15-
I wake up, afraid I may be late meeting everyone else. I look at the clock and am relieved. I set the alarm on it for 5:30 PM.

4:17-
I lie in bed a moment and seriously contemplate going to the beach in hopes of seeing Krista in her bathing suit.

4:18-
I fall back asleep.

5:30-
My alarm clock blares. I get up, make some coffee and put on my favorite shirt, lucky boxers, and dirty jeans.

5:47-
I drink my coffee on my balcony and finish getting ready.

6:03-
I meet The King, Krista, Krista's Sister, Kylie, and Krista's friend Jess in the lobby. Krista introduces me to Jess. Jess isn't as attractive as Krista. It doesn't stop me from innocuously flirting with her.

6:05-
We walk around to the back of the hotel and to where the board walk begins. Every building on the board walk is a bar. Every other building on the board walk is a tattoo parlor.

6:29-
We decide dinner is in order before drinking is. We find a decent looking restaurant on the second floor. Of a bar.

6:40-
The menu is expensive. I order the cheapest bowl of pasta and a tequila and tonic. I figure if I'm going to be spending a lot of money on alcohol, I may as well do it in style.

7:05-
The food isn't worth its price. I eat it anyway. Kylie begins grilling me about what's going on between Corazon and I. She swears she saw me go into Corazon's room the night that we were in recurrent training together back in June. I tell her to shut up and eat her dinner.

7:42-
We settle our bill and go back to the board walk. Everyone is ready to drink. I smile to myself, knowing damn well it's about to turn into 'One of those nights'.

7:51-
We arrive at our first bar 'Bier Garden'. German beer a plenty. The King orders us a round. Krista and Jess try to refuse his offer, but he orders them beers anyway. Kylie and I have no problem with this, as we are poor flight attendants. I make a toast to him, since this is the way airline captains should be.

7:59-
I try to strike up a conversation with Krista's sister who hasn't said much that evening. All I really get out of her is that she's younger than Krista (Krista was about twenty eight, and her sister about twenty six) and that she was upset about something.

8:01-
The King brings me another beer.

8:02-
Jess begins looking more attractive than she did earlier.

8:03-
I get bored talking with Krista's sister, and decide to talk to Jess instead. Jess tells me that she met Krista in flight school, and that's where they became friends. Two weeks ago, Krista helped Jess get hired at UPside Air. I tell Jess that Krista didn't have anything to do with it, we just have a reputation for hiring attractive female first officers and she fit the bill. Jess likes hearing this.

8:13-
We leave to go to our second bar. The girls walk slightly ahead of The King and I. The King tells me I should have come to the beach earlier that afternoon; I missed seeing Krista in her bathing suit. I immediately regret my decision to nap the afternoon away.

8:20-
We go to our second bar and drink.

9:53-
We go to our third bar.

10:26-
We leave our third bar. I am tipsy. Krista's Sister is not having a good time at all. She decides to leave us and go back to the hotel. I boo her. Krista says that her sister's not having a good day. I ask if it's because she's on her period. Krista says no. I tell her I had to know if it was really a bad day or not.

10:33-
We pass by street musicians outside a bar. Kylie does a little dance in the street.

10:41-
Fourth bar. I sit next to Kylie on a bar stool. The King is catty corner to us with Krista and Jess. Kylie and I start that serious talk about being flight attendants and how crappy we get treated by everyone. Kylie tells me that she wants to become a pilot. I tell her people become pilots because they love flying and it's what they're born to do. I tell her a lot of flight attendants become pilots because it's what they love to do (Lizzie and Krista were both flight attendants before becoming pilots). I ask her if she wants to fly air crafts because it's what she loves doing, or because she doesn't know what else to do with her life.

"No one wants to be at a shitty regional carrier like UPside Air forever. I think this is just a stepping stone to wherever we're going in life career wise. But do you want to become a pilot because flying is what you love to do, or do you want to become a pilot because you don't know what

else to do and think that it's just the next step up from being a flight attendant?"
I ask.

Kylie begins to tear up.
"I don't know what I'm doing with my life. I just thought this was temporary, and now I've been here almost three years with no idea what I'm doing! I don't want to do this forever, but I don't know what else to do."

I tell Kylie I'm just as lost as she is, but at least I know it. Krista comforts Kylie by giving her a hug and tells her not to worry, she'll figure things out.

10:50-
The King tells us to stop being buzz kills, slams shots down in front of us, and demands we take them.

1:49 AM-
We stumble out of the bar drunk. I consider getting a tattoo. But it's only because I'm drunk. All the tattoo parlors are closed.

1:57-
The hotel is farther than I remember. I tell Jess never to upgrade to Captain. While all of UPside Airs female First officers have a reputation for being good looking, all of our female Captains aren't anything to brag about. Jess asks if I think she's good looking.
I tell her she wouldn't have been hired if she wasn't. She likes hearing this. She puts her arm around my shoulder and tells me she needs help keeping her balance.

2:01-
Jess tells me she thinks I'm cute. I tell her I didn't hear what she just said and ask her if she can repeat that loud enough for everyone else to hear. She laughs and repeats herself.

2:21-
We arrive back at our hotel.

2:23-
Kylie and I realize that we left our credit cards at the last bar we were at. We say goodnight to everyone else and decide to walk back and get them.

2:29-
Kylie is staggering in a zigzag, rather than walking in a straight line and laughing to herself about something I don't understand.

2:37-
Kylie is walking too slowly. I tell her to give me her driver's license so that I can get her credit card for her, and to go back to the hotel.

2:38-
I hurry back to the bar before it closes.

2:55-
The bar was farther than I remember, but since we were drunk when we covered most ground throughout the course of the night, it didn't seem so far at the time.

3:02-
I find the bar and show our IDs to the bartender. I get our credit cards back and begin slowly walking back to the hotel.

3:07-
Two frat boys with popped collars aren't far behind me holding each other up. They are the college types I hate.

3:10-
They begin shouting at me
"Hey! Can we get a few bucks to get a cab back to our place?"

"Sorry, I don't have any money."
I reply, and continue walking.

"Come on! Just a few bucks!"
They shout again, laughing. I ignore them.

3:12-
They continue shouting at me. I continue ignoring them.

3:14-
"Come on man! We just need a few dollars! Don't ignore me, what's your problem?!"
One of them begins shouting even more aggressively. I hear them coming up behind me faster. I walk faster. I can hear one of them right over my shoulder. Out of nowhere, he gives me a hard shove. I stumble forward, tripping over my over my own two feet. I fall head first into a palm tree. Hard.

3:15-
I'm dizzy for a moment. I know there's a bruise on my forehead, and I know I'm slightly bleeding. However, I also know I'm outnumbered by two frat boy douche bags that are twice my size and drunk. I do the only logical thing I can think of, and begin running as fast as possible. I don't even bother looking back to see if I'm being followed or not.

3:36-
I am back outside of my hotel. I am sweating profusely and out of breath. I look over my shoulder to see that I wasn't followed. I go to Krista's room where all the girls are staying at and knock on the door. Krista flips out when she sees my bruise. Kylie is still drunk. Jess has her head in the toilet.

3:41-
I arrive back in my room. I look in the mirror to see how bad of a mess I am. My face is red, my nose is running, and my forehead is bruised. It doesn't look as bad as it feels. I splash my face with cold water.

3:43-
The phone rings. It's The King. He is still slightly drunk, but wants to make sure I am alright. I tell him not to worry. He tells me that he can call crew scheduling and have me taken off the trip if I want, but I tell him not to do that. The reason being is that we've only been overnighting in Ft. Lauderdale for a few weeks. And if the company catches wind of my little incident, that hotel area would be deemed 'unsafe' and we'd be out of that fantastic location and into another lame airport hotel so fast that no one would ever want to do that over night again. Also, it was technically my fault for walking the streets alone at three AM, knowing all the drunks were out, so I was kind of an easy target any way. I tell him not to worry, it was just a little bruise.

3:52-
I pass out on my bed with the balcony door open.

11:03 AM-
I wake up in a daze. I make myself coffee and get ready for work.

11:52-
I meet The King and Krista in the lobby. Krista says she feels bad for me and asks if there's anything she can do. I moan and tell her my head hurts so bad that maybe a back rub will make me feel better. She laughs and tells me that she's glad a little bump on the head hasn't affected my sense of humor.

11:58-
We board the hotel shuttle to go to the airport.

Despite my little run in with those jerks at the end of the night, this was definitely one of the best overnights I had ever been on. I got to drink myself silly, hang out with some cool co-workers, and save an awesome overnight from turning into a lame one by not getting taken off the trip. The only downside is that I have done that Ft. Lauderdale trip many times following, but they always end up disappointing and anti-climactic following that first great one.

Second date (Must've run all night)

September 17th 2010

"Carrie! Oh God,
please wake up!"
I screamed,
shaking the motionless girl.
But nothing.
She began convulsing again.

I wondered
how this would look
if her friends burst into the room.
Carrie lying on the bed,
twisting like that possessed girl
in the Exorcist,
and me,
standing over her
twisted body.

They had to have known
about her epilepsy condition.
She couldn't drive
and had to have
a friend pick us up
from the hotel.

I had a million thoughts
bursting out of my skull
all at once.
I was seeing stars.

I kept thinking
that this wasn't my fault.
I should have gone for help.
I should have shouted
for her friends.

What I did next,
still shocks
even myself to this day.
And the only justifiable reason
I could even have
for doing what I did,
was that none of this
was really happening.

I took off running
from that room.
Telling myself
I should have never
followed her in there.

I ran from the room.
Past her friends
in the living room
that were drinking.
Burst through the front door
of that large,
beautiful blue house.
Past her friends
in the front yard
that were smoking.

My legs were trembling.
Wet spaghetti noodles.
My mind felt separated
from my body.

Running
in
slow
motion.

Practically floating
down the side walk.

Trying to recall the events
that lead to that point.
Trying to make some sense
out of a story I would stick to
when and if the cops showed up
at my hotel room
looking for me.

Keep running.
Keep running.
Run.
Run boy.
Run.

<<<<<<<<<<<<<<<<<<<<<<<<
Carrie was a passenger
on my flight to Rochester
going home from college.
I gave her a few drinks.
No-
I *sold* her a few drinks.
She was twenty two.
It was legal.

She wanted to come
hang out at my hotel.
She arrived.
We had a drink.
She told me
that she had to be careful
with her alcohol intake
and what she does to herself
because she has a disease
and could have a seizure
without warning . . .
>>>>>>>>>>>>>>>>>>>>>>>>

I was at the end of the street.
I could hear her friends
behind me shouting,
but it all sounded jumbled.

Maybe they were asking
where I was going
in such a hurry.
Or maybe they were asking
what I had done to her.
Shit, I don't know,
I was so out of it.

I didn't want their words
to catch me.
I didn't want *them* to catch me.
I remembered
the exact way back to the hotel.

End of the street,
then a left.
End of that street,
then another left.
And then straight ahead.
Maybe two miles,
maybe ten.
I don't know,
I just kept running,
replaying the nights events
over
and
over.

<<<<<<<<<<<<<<<<<<<<<<<<<
We had a drink at the hotel.
She said that a friend of hers
was having
a mid-term college party.
She wanted me to go with her.

Her friend picked us up
from the Strathallen
and drove us.
Down the street from my hotel.
Maybe two miles,
maybe ten.
Then a right turn
and all the way down.
Then another right turn.
It was a large,
beautiful blue house.

Her friends all thought
it was romantic
that we met on a plane.
Like out of a movie
or something.

She started drinking.
Much more than I.
I only had two.
Maybe three . . .
>>>>>>>>>>>>>>>>>>>>>>>

I stopped running for a moment.
I placed my hands
on my knees and bent over.
Cars were blowing by me
at what seemed like
a thousand miles an hour.
The street lights blurred.
Sweat poured
from my forehead.
I thought for sure
I was going to vomit.

I caught my breath
and then took off running
towards the hotel again.

—Back to what
I could piece together
from the party . . .

<<<<<<<<<<<<<<<<<<<<<<<<
I was talking to her friends
telling stories
and making them laugh.
Every time I saw Carrie
She was smoking.
Or drinking.
Doing all the things
she told me back at the hotel
that she shouldn't be doing
quite so heavily.
And she was going hard.

She came over to me,
and seductively whispered
into my ear:
"My friend said
we can go to her room
to be alone . . ."
She took my hand,
and I followed.

Oh God,
why did I follow?

I should have taken off running.
I'd be exactly right where I am now,
minus the one part
of the story
that I was still
trying to convince myself
hadn't happened.

I followed her into the room.
Closed the door.
We kissed for a few moments,
and she lay down on the bed.

Just as I was about
to lay down next to her,
it happened.

I thought she was kidding at first,
but I knew better.
She began shaking.
Slow at first,
but then much more violently.

"Carrie?"
and she twitched
and convulsed.
Then she stopped.

"Carrie! Oh God,
please wake up!"
I screamed . . .
>>>>>>>>>>>>>>>>>>>>>>>>

I was panting,
clasping my chest,
trying to keep my heart
from exploding
out of it.

I was passing land marks
in Rochester
that I was familiar with,
approaching the Strathallen hotel.

I was beginning to come back
to reality.
My brain
reconnected
with my body.
My legs
reconnected
with the ground.

I began to argue with myself.
Why didn't I just get help?
Why did I leave her
lying there,
trembling like a leaf
in a hurricane?

I tried turning it around,
making myself angry with her.
Why would she invite me out
and then dive head first
into something that would cause
her own condition?

I tried making sense
of everything.
Nothing.

I shuffled my feet
past the front desk
I was so familiar with,
eyes fixated heavily
on the floor.

Into the elevator,
and up to my room.
My heartbeat
was pulsing in my eyes.
I opened the door,
shut it behind me,
and bolted it
into the locked position.

Panting, coughing, sweating.
I didn't bother
to take my clothes off,
just my shoes.
I crawled into bed
and lay there a long time.
Waiting.

Waiting for the police to show up,
waiting for her,
or one of her friends to call.
Waiting for terrible dreams
to creep into my head
and fill my sleep.
To begin replaying
those events
over and over.
None of them came.

That was the last that I heard
of the epileptic college girl.

But the memory
that still stands out in my mind
the most to this day,
wasn't leaving her
shaking on that bed
like a coward.

No,
what stands out
the most to this day
was the horrific run
all the way back
to the hotel
that stays burned into my mind
and I just can't seem
to get it out.

El Parakeet

May 24th 2011

I like to sleep
with the balcony door
open in Ft. Lauderdale.
It's soothing
to pass out with the smell
of the ocean breeze,
the sound of waves
filling the room.

If I can wake myself up
early enough,
I like to sit on the balcony
and drink a cup of coffee
before I have to start
getting ready for work.

I awoke this morning
to find a parakeet
sitting on the chair
beside the sliding glass door
staring at me.

He had to have flown
in the room through
the open door
(I know this
because I don't give my room
keys out
to strange birds I don't know.)

He stared at me a moment
before saying:
"Buenos dias! Como estas?"

I stared back at him
before replying:
". . . No habla espagnole."

The bird lowered his head
in disappointment
before saying:
"Oh . . . ok. Adios."
and waved his wing
goodbye
before flying back out
the same way
that he had come in.

I think now
that perhaps I should have
tried communicating
with the bird.

I could have called Corazon
and asked her to interpret
between the bird and I,
but as she has told me before,
she's not my personal translator
and I need to learn Spanish
'the correct way'
(Not through Dora the explorer.)

Maybe the bird needed help.
What if he needed
a place to stay,
or a good meal to eat?
And all I did
was shoo him away.
Now I feel bad.

On the other hand,
he could have flown
into the country illegally
from Cuba
and needed a place
to hide out from the INS.

And the last thing I need
is to be caught
housing an illegal
Cuban parakeet
in my hotel room.

Now I don't feel so bad.
I suppose that if I was
put in that situation again,
I would react differently.
Maybe I would try and find
out what the bird wanted
before shunning him.

However I'm glad he left
peacefully the same way
he had arrived.
Anyone that's ever had a bird
fly into the room before
knows that they can cause
quite a mess
before leaving again.

The complete flight attendants guide to: Cooking on an airplane

When it comes down to it, it's pretty hard to eat healthy when you work for the airline. Working for an express carrier like UPside Air is of course no exception. On a typical day, I'll do anywhere between three and five flights with only a half hour break in between legs if I'm lucky. That leaves very little time to grab any food. It seems like as soon as we've landed at the airport and deplaned, the gate agents are right there at the front of the galley:

"You ready to board yet? You want to board them up now?"

No. I don't want to board them up. Send them away. The general 'Ok to board' sign is a thumbs up if you're ready, thumbs down if you're not. After the fourth flight of the day with nothing to eat, I tend to be cranky and give a middle finger instead. So with no time to grab food in what can normally be a ten to twelve hour non-stop day on the plane, I've had to find other ways to improvise.

Keep in mind, I fly on a fifty seater aircraft. It's not that big. There are no microwaves, no ovens, nothing of that sort. This really pisses me off, because sometimes passengers ask me when the cookies will be done. I guess our main carrier, STRATA Airlines, bakes cookies for our passengers, but not at UPside Air. We're an airline. Not a bakery. There was a rumor going around for a while when we went from having two coffee makers on board down to one that it was to make room to install an oven, but I doubted we'd ever have one on board. Not all of our flight attendants are the brightest, and to be perfectly honest, I wouldn't trust them to be shoving their hands in and out of a 400 degree oven.

So with that said, I take what's available to me on the plane and use it to my advantage. The most useful object at my disposal is hot water. There's really only one kind of water that comes out of the tap, and that's the most vile, disgusting, germ infested water imaginable. There's no way of cleaning the tanks that hold the water, so after years and years of water passing through them, you can probably imagine that it's pretty algae infested in there. I'm pretty sure it's where Swamp Thing lives.

That water's only meant to wash hands. This is why when passengers ask for a glass of water, we serve it out of a bottle. However, for hot tea and coffee, we take the same water, and send it through a super-heated tap to boil all the germs away, thus making it safe and drinkable. We're talking lava water here. This is the kind that's scalding and will burn your taste buds off, but it's the only way to make that water drinkable.

This is perfect when it comes to oat meal and a cup of noodles. This is by far not a meal in the least bit, and after a few days of non-stop ramen, I'm pissing noodles. I've tried adding tuna to my ramen noodles, because it's cheap and doesn't need to be kept refrigerated, but I hate fish, and whenever I try adding it to my soup, all it does is upset my stomach and make the front of the plane smell like a fish market.

Fruit and trail mix make for good snacking, but the only problem with that is it takes up too much room in my suitcase and after I eat it, I'm still hungry. So that's usually a no go as well.

What I've found pretty helpful on the road are prepackaged freeze dried meals. These are sealed in plastic all the way around, making them super air tight. So what I do is fill up two small, plastic white trash bags with the boiling water and drop in the meal. The hot water heats it to the point of being edible. It doesn't need to be refrigerated which is great, but the only problem I have with these meals is because of that the sodium is through the roof. A few of those, I start feeling way too out of shape. And this is bad, considering I'm out of shape to begin with.

When we do have extremely long sits in between flights however, that's my time to pig out, since the next time I get to eat may not be until we finish for the day at our hotel. The only problem is that most food places in the airport are not healthy in the least bit. Subway is usually the best bet if I'm trying to eat 'healthy', but I usually finish a flight of angry passengers in an upset mood, so I decide to take my aggression out on my body by eating whatever the hell I feel like. McDonalds, pizza hut, whatever I can get my grubby little hands on. Asian food usually does the trick, but I can eat it until I feel sick to my stomach and then be hungry an hour or so later.

The main problem with airport food is that airports tend to overcharge the prices of everything, and don't have value menus. They get away with charging three dollars for a cheeseburger because cheeseburgers are so rare in those parts of the country. But the sad truth of the matter is, America's so overweight, passengers think they will just die if they don't get some food in them at the airport. So the food joints have figured out that if you're going to pay a crap load of money to sit in a tiny seat for 3 hours, why not pay a crap load of money for a tiny cheeseburger you can get outside the airport at half the price?

Having a good decent meal usually only happens at a sit down restaurant in the airport with a long two or three hour wait in between flights or after we get to the hotel and go to whatever decent restaurant is close to where we're staying. The problem with that is, it can get pretty expensive. One meal can equal upwards to almost ten dollars, not including drinks and tips, and doing that twice a day, for three days nonstop can get pretty pricey.

So ultimately when people ask me:

How do I survive when it comes to eating in the airline?

I tell them:

I don't. Ramen noodles and freeze dried meals for breakfast. Airport fast food for lunch. Some diner or restaurant for dinner. I can come back from a trip feeling terrible and I'm sure my heart will agree with me. But the hell with it, I'm only 22 and It's for this reason that I'm always joking and telling people

"I don't expect to live well past the age of thirty."

With eating habits like these, who needs healthy living?

When I still had the original website up and running, here were a few of my favorite comments/responses to this story:

> Babie vigo
>
> The only reason I am alive today: miso soup, instant mashed potatoes, instant noodle bowls (not in english but the pictures look appetizing), instant oatmeal and anything else you can re-hydrate on a plane.

But the best meal ever has to be canned ravioli or any other canned food. Make sure it has a pull tab though. Just take the label off and put it on a warmer while you do your service. Finish up, shake the can, pop the top, and instant pseudo meal!

=^.^=

<u>Kimberly</u>
Oh my yes, I've learned a lot of tricks of the trade along the way, too. Here are a few of my favorites.

*Instant mashed potatoes are the best. Fill up half a cup of hot water, some potato flakes, about 4 coffee creams (milk substitute), salt and pepper, and I'm in business.
*Canned soups and veggies are great. Just empty the contents into a zip lock bag, put the bag in an empty coffee pot and brew, let sit in hot water for 10-15 minutes. A can of green beans, corn, and the instant mashed potatoes is actually quite filling! :-)
*Sometimes I'll cook a big meal before a trip if my hotels will have fridges. I may cook some chicken wings and macaroni & cheese and wrap everything into individual servings in aluminum foil. When I'm ready to eat, I'll set the foil wrapped food on the coffee pot hot plate and flip 2-3 times over 15-20 minutes. This works AMAZINGLY well!

<u>Susan</u>
Ah yes, I remember those days well. The joys of working for an express airline just can't be adequately described to someone who has never experienced it, but you did pretty well.

There were days when ALL I ate were either pretzels or peanuts . . . depending on which one we were cycling through at the moment. The times we were transitioning from one to the other, we always felt like we were feasting like kings and queens . . . 'peanuts AND pretzels!'

One of my favorite overnights was actually Wichita, of all places. Not that there was time to do anything, and certainly not that

I liked staying at Holiday Inns. We arrived around midnight with about 8 hours until our next showtime. As you know, that doesn't leave much time to go find food, if you can even find a "convenience" store open that late. But that particular hotel always had boxed lunches waiting for the crew. The food wasn't special, but when you're ravenous and over did it on the honey roasted peanuts throughout the day, it was a glorious feast. The only problem was when I forgot to stash a couple bottles of water in my flight bag before leaving the plane.

And of course, Double Trees always have a cookie waiting for you, which was usually the best thing I ate all day. People who have never experienced living as an underpaid, overworked flight attendant (or pilot for that matter) simply don't understand how great little things like a soggy sandwich and chips, or a fresh baked cookie at the end of a long stressful day can bring so much happiness.

Once I had to do a two week TDY stint on the other side of the country (IAD). I spent all day every day sitting ready reserve at the airport, so when I went back to my hotel at night, I was able to go eat at a sit down restaurant. I spent all of my per diem on real food . . . and it was worth every penny. =o)

I'm actually beginning to feel nostalgic . . . some days I wish I could go back to flying. Maybe when the kids are grown.

Valentine's day

February 14th 2011

You're so damn beautiful.
Sometimes it still
gives me heart ache
to be around you.
You're (were) everything to me.
And it's easy to make
"The best attempt at being best friends."
Easier said than done.

A conversation
with Corazon
on a February morning
by the Chicken place
inside the DCA airport:
". . . I'm not a good person.
I don't think I've done a good thing
in a long time."

And the horrible truth
of the matter is . . .
I may still only be here
because you're here.

It's not that I'm dependent on you . . .
but I'm not so sure
how I'd get along
without you here.

This is what we get
for playing with fate.
This is what I get
for playing with Karma.

It's another Valentine's Day.
And I'm alone . . .
you're alone . . .
And still the fact of the matter burns:
"What happened between us
is in the past."
And the question leaves
that horrible ringing in my ears:
"Would you ever
want to date that girl Mary?"
Corazon asks.

"No."
I respond.

"Why?"
"Because she's my friend."
"Aren't we friends also?"
She states.
Dammit. You got me there.
But the difference between
Mary and Corazon is:
that I was never
in love with one of them.

I think I took those days
in Chicago for granted.
And I would have given anything
to have them back again,
if only for a moment.
But she's right.
What happened between us
is in the past.

I hate this stupid holiday.
I pass by a million people
in the airport every day.
Tons of single, beautiful girls.
And I still want you.
I want you to use me.
I want you
to
ruin
me.

The pain of you being
my last thought before sleeping.
My first thought after waking.
My first thought before sleeping.
My last thought after waking.
In slow motion.

It's another Valentine's Day.
And I'm alone.

"And what are you supposed to be for Halloween?"

October 31st 2010

I guess I've never experienced a 'scary Halloween' before I started flying. I always enjoyed horror movies, but it takes quite a lot to scare me. I was working a trip with ElHeffey the first time I flew with Tyler. He was in his late twenties, not much taller than I was. It was at a French bakery in Canada where we really connected. After a few drinks we left Minglewoods and Tyler kept complaining that he wanted authentic French bread. Unfortunately, there were only a few places in Ottawa where that could be found, but after exploring the French speaking side of town for a good half hour, we discovered exactly what he was looking for.

ElHeffey excused himself to the bathroom, while Tyler pressed his face against a display case looking at all the different types of bread like kid in a candy shop.

The highlight of this little excursion came when the French Canadian baker approached Tyler. The transaction proceeded to go a little something like this:

La baker: "Ah . . . hello. Is there . . . somezing you . . . you want?"

Tyler: "Alright . . . I need . . . three baguettes."

La baker: "Ok . . . and you want zem in . . . bag?"

Tyler: "Uh . . . yea sure. And I also want . . . four croissants."

La baker: "Ok . . . and where do you . . . want zem?"

Tyler: (With a dumb stare on his face) ". . . In my mouth. Stuuuuuuupid!"

I was practically in tears at that unexpected outburst, and the best part was when ElHeffey joined us a few moments later from the bathroom. He didn't even need to know what I was laughing at, he just started cracking up along with me.

>>>>>>>>>>>>>>>>>>>>>>>>

A few weeks later I flew with Tyler again on a trip that went right through Halloween. We woke up in Greeneville, SC on Tuesday morning. It was an early show time, and since the hotel was in the middle of nowhere, we had to take a cab to get to the airport. It was a yellow checkered cab, kind of like the ones you see in movies. But it was what happened inside the cab that ultimately frightened me.

The cab driver opened the trunk from the inside of the cab for us to put our suitcases in, immediately giving our captain the incentive to make the 'No help, no tip' face. We tossed our suitcases in the trunk and climbed into the cab. I called shotgun, a decision that I would soon come to regret. Tyler and the Captain climbed in to the back of the cab, and I climbed in the front. The cab driver was an older Native American man, totally stereotypical. Long dark hair that went all the way down to his shoulders, a dream catcher hanging from his rear view mirror. He wore an old tore up leather jacket that smelled like smoke.

Just above his dashboard he had taped a picture of a motorcycle. He was one of those cab drivers that liked to have conversations with his passengers. The captain and I weren't really morning people, and kept to ourselves, but Tyler didn't seem to mind talking with the man.

"So . . . where you guys going today?" Asked the cabbie.

"A lot of places. Ultimately Rochester." Replied Tyler.

"Oh, that sounds nice."

The cab was silent for a brief moment before Tyler leaned over the seat and pointed at the picture of the motorcycle. "Hey, do you ride that bike?" Tyler asked.

"Oh yea. That's the motorcycle I'm trying to build. I used to ride all the time. That was before my accident though . . ." He replied, trailing off. I guess he was waiting for someone to ask him what happened, but no one did. It didn't stop him from proceeding with his story anyway. "I was riding my bike one day after having a few drinks, and when I was passing by the liquor store, a woman in a green pick-up truck backed out and ran me over. She must have been going about a hundred miles an hour. No kidding. She ran over my leg and crushed my bike. She crushed my bike like she crushed my leg!"

He said redundantly.

I didn't have to look back at Tyler or our captain to know they had the same confused facial expression as I did. He continued with his story: "I didn't see her license plate number or anything, but all I remembered was a green pick-up truck. So I went to the hospital and they said they couldn't save my leg. They would have to cut it off."

I looked down at his leg. He was wearing a dirty pair of jeans, so I had no idea if he was lying or not. I had hoped that because it was Halloween he was just joking with us, but I started to think that maybe this story was true. Maybe that's why he didn't open the trunk and help us with our bags. I imagined how it possibly went:

~~~~~~~~~~~~~~~~~~~~~~~~~

The hospital,
an old dingy tent.
Dark red marks
splattered all over the wall.

The cabbie would be
lying there with some
insane doctor
standing over him,
wearing a butchers apron
with a clowns mask
over his face.

With one foul swoop,
doctor insane-o
brings a butchers knife down
on the old cabbies leg,
making a crackling noise
as it splits open.
Two more swings
and the limbs detach,
bringing a waterfall
of blood with it.
~~~~~~~~~~~~~~~~~~~~~~~~~

As he begins
to scream in agony,
the doctor grabs
a welding iron
from a tray of
rusty scrapers,
needles,
tools . . .
he begins to torch
salvaged motorcycle parts
on to the cabbies leg . . .
~~~~~~~~~~~~~~~~~~~~~~~~

I was starting to freak myself out thinking about it. I had to stop, but I couldn't help but looking at his leg from the corner of my eye. I kept picturing a mechanical monstrosity of motorcycle parts welded together underneath. His story didn't end there either. "So I was in the hospital for probably about eight months or so recovering. During this time I hired someone to track down the woman in the green pick-up truck. And then, after several weeks, he found her."

By now, his story was getting out of control. I failed to see how any of this was true. But I certainly wasn't going to interrupt him to ask.

"So a month later I got out of the hospital and went to the house where she lived with my shotgun. I kicked open the door and started screaming for the woman to come out. But as it turned out, she no longer lived there. Lucky thing for the man I was threatening. It took some convincing that she had moved away a month prior. I had almost blown his head off. So that's why I'm working on fixing up my new bike." I couldn't believe what I was hearing. This was insane.

We stopped at the airport and he began to reach over to the glove compartment. I was sure that he would open it up, and pull out what was left of his leg. Or his shotgun. Or even worse, the butchers knife that took his leg off that he now carried around with him to exact his revenge on the world. Maybe he thought the woman that ran him over was a flight attendant?!

He opened the glove box and pushed a yellow button, inside of it, popping open the trunk. He then turned to me and said: "There you go. You folks have a happy and safe Halloween!"
~~~~~~~~~~~~~~~~~~~~~~~~

Bare facts

November 11th 2010

Damien was smearing
mashed potatoes
all over her left breast,
laughing maniacally,
like some kind of mad scientist,
and then demanding
for me
to pour gravy
all over her right.

Wait-
I guess
I should back up
and start this story over.

<<<<<<<<<<<<<<<<<<<<<<<<
Damien replaced Lizzie
when she got pulled
from a trip that she,
ElHeffey, and I
were doing in November.

He was in his late twenties
and loved two things:
drinking,
and women.

Everything else
came third to that
(including flying airplanes
which is ok,
because airplanes
bore me also.)

He was disappointed
that I wasn't a hot flight attendant,
but was happy
that I was a straight one.
He had never flown
with one before,
so this new phenomenon
seemed to boggle his mind.

When I counted
my passengers
for weight and balance,
I wrote down
how many hot girls
were on board
and what zone
of the plane they were in.

He thought this was funny,
and started making me do it
on every flight from then on.

Mary had become
his new obsession,
so you can imagine
his jealously
when I told him
that she and I
had been hanging out together.

He decided that since the three of us
were flying together
and Ottawa was always a good time,
our overnight
would be designated as
'guys night out.'
He didn't care if it was
two in the afternoon
when we arrived,
and we had to leave
at five the following morning.

The three of us hit up Minglewoods
after checking in
and changing,
where Damien told me
to 'watch a pro at work'.

He ordered us
a pitcher of beer
and then began flirting
innocuously
with the waitress.
And when she didn't reciprocate,
he just ordered more beer.

After seeing that he was getting nowhere
with his 'little maple leaf'
(as he called her),
we hit the streets
to find some dinner.

Damien said he knew
the perfect place,
and dragged us to a strip club
by the name of 'Bare facts'.

ElHeffey said
it was time for him
to call it a night,
so Damien
called him a bitch
and told him to leave,
although I think it was just
the beer talking.

As we entered the club,
I quickly understood why
Damien brought us there.

For ten Canadian dollars,
we each got a pitcher of beer . . .
and a ticket
for an all you can eat
dinner buffet in the corner.

We filled our plates
with roast beef,
mashed potatoes,
green beans,
and then topped it off
with gravy
and took a seat at a table.

As soon as we began eating,
a stripper
(not so good looking)
approached our table.
"Hey boys . . .
How about a lap dance?"
She asked.

Damien looked at her
as if she had just spit
in his potatoes
and scolded her
"What are you nuts?
I'm tryin' to keep my food down,
get the hell outta here!"

I laughed at this
between bites of roast beef.

Not even ten minutes later
another stripper
(good looking)
took a seat at our table.
"Either of you want
a private dance?
Maybe a little more . . . ?"
She asked seductively.

Damien dropped his fork
on his plate in disgust,
making an audible clanking noise.
"What the hell?!
I just told Shrek over there
to leave me alone,
can't you see we're trying
to eat here!"

I almost spit out
my mashed potatoes at that,
as the unphased stripper
got up and left our table.

"Hey, that one was good looking,
why didn't you take her offer?"
I asked him.

He raised his eyebrows
and looked at me
before responding:
"I make about two thousand dollars
more than you do a year,
and most of that goes
to payin' off my damn
flight school bills.
I aint got no money man!
I came here to get a good
cheap meal
and pitcher of beer.
Not get harassed by naked beggars."

I understood his wisdom in this
and continued eating.
No sooner than he had said that,
the most monstrous
of all the strippers
sat down beside him.
"Hey boys . . .
what can I do for you tonight?"

Damien's eyes lit up.
I thought for sure
he was going to jab her
with his fork.

Instead,
he calmly sat back in his seat,
wiped his mouth
with his napkin
and asked
"How much for you
to come back to our hotel
with the both of us?"

I almost choked
on my green beans.

She leaned toward us,
and whispered
". . . Four hundred.
For one of you."

Damien loudly replied
"Four hundred
for the both of us!"

". . . Six hundred
for the both of you."

"Three hundred
for the both of us!
And you let me
beat you around
like a rag doll!"
he hollered.

". . . Five hundred
for the both of you."

". . . How much for you
to take us out back
and give us a handie?"
he asked.

". . . Two hundred
for each of you."
she quietly answered.

"Two hundred
for the both of us!"
he shouted, pounding his fist
on the table.

". . . Seventy for each of you."

". . . Seventy for the both of us!
. . . And you let me
slap you around like a rag doll!"
I had no idea if he was joking or not.

She sat back and folded her arms.
I thought for sure
she was going to have us kicked out,
or even worse,
have us roughed up
in the back alley
by a bouncer.

Damien leaned forward and asked
"Alright, how about this . . .
for fifty dollars . . .
you let me
and my friend here . . .
smother some food
on your tits."

That was it.
I thought for sure
that would have sent her away,
got us kicked out,
or worse.

Instead, she rolled her eyes
for a moment and finally said
"Deal."

Damien clapped his hands,
and shouting "Hot damn!",
pulled out a crisp,
fifty dollar Canadian bill
and slapped it down
on the table.

So—as I said before,
Damien smeared
mashed potatoes
all over her left breast,
and then demanded for me
to pour gravy
all over her right.

Airport delay games

May 10th 2011

2:59 PM-
I land in Nantucket with B-rye and Raphael.

3:36-
After cleaning the air craft and taking care of my duties, the gate agent asks if I'm ready to board. We have to make it quick, because a storm is quickly approaching.

3:37-
Lightning and thunder is heard outside the aircraft. *BOOM!* B-rye calls from the flight deck:
"Start the clock!"
I laugh, and give the gate agent the thumbs down for boarding. She rolls her eyes and drags her feet up the jet bridge to tell our passengers the flight is delayed until further notice (it's like watching someone walk death row.)

3:39-
B-rye and Raphael tell me they want to get lunch (We had a late start, and had just been snacking on spinzels all day, so we were pretty hungry by this point).

3:40-
We open the door to the terminal to hear the gate agent finishing her announcement
". . . we will update you with more information as the weather passes."
Everyone at the gate groans and complains. A long line of passengers approach the ticket counter. I laugh to myself, thinking that I certainly wouldn't want to be the gate agent right now. A few evil glares are made in our direction. B-rye puts his hands up and slowly makes his way through the crowd stating:
"Not my fault . . . I don't control the weather . . ."
Raphael and I laugh.

3:43-
We get to the terminal restaurant. The special of the day is written on a chalk board: lobster bisque for seventeen dollars. We ask to see a menu. The prices are insane. We split the cost of a large cheese pizza for fifteen dollars. The hostess tells us it will be done in twenty minutes. I ask B-rye if we have enough time to wait.

3:47-
The sound of lightning and thunder is heard again. *BOOM!* B-rye states
"Start the clock!"

3:48-
We return to the gate. The line of complaining passengers is down to ten people now. The gate agent asks for an update. B-rye looks out the giant glass window at a pitch black sky outside. He then looks back at the gate agent, frowns and declares:
"Houston . . . we have a problem."
A lame line from an old movie, I know, but surprisingly it gets a laugh out of at least two passengers.

3:50-
Lightning and thunder strike *BOOM!* and B-rye states
"Start the clock!"
Raphael laughs and asks him if he's going to declare this every time it happens. Almost as if on cue, *BOOM!*, and B-rye quietly says:
"Start the clock."

3:53-
A casually dressed rich guy that has been standing by the counter appearing amused by our banter asks:
"What's this 'start the clock' thing?"
B-rye explains that every time we hear thunder, the outside ramp needs to be closed and ground operations halted for at least ten minutes, because we can't have the workers outside with the chance of being struck by lightning. B-rye makes sure to state this loud enough for other passengers standing in line to hear as well. They nod in understanding.

3:59-
BOOM!
"Ladies and gentleman . . . start the clock!"
B-rye calls out. A little girl standing close by with her parents looks up at them and laughs in amusement by this.

4:00-
The gate agent says that she likes it when a pilot has a sense of humor. I tell her
"You think he's funny? You haven't seen me in action yet; I'm not going to let B-rye . . . steal my thunder! Zing!"
This gets more laughter from passengers in the area.

4:05:
BOOM! B-rye calls out
"Start the clock!"
and this time, the little girl laughs and repeats him as well.

4:06-
B-rye leaves to get our pizza.

4:07-
I ask the gate agent if I can use the phone at her counter. She tells me it's supposed to be for only calling other phones in the airport. I tell her that's what I intend to do, and ask her if she can connect me with the luggage department office. She smiles, dials an extension number on the phone, and then hands it to me. I put it on speaker phone.
"Nantucket baggage office, this is Kelly."

"Hi Kelly, this is Rodney . . . I just flew in on the UPside Air flight from JFK and . . . when I got my suitcase off of the conveyer belt I opened it up to make sure everything was alright inside and . . . oh boy . . . there was a dead rat in my suitcase."

"I'm . . . I'm sorry sir? Did you say . . . ?"

"Yea . . . A dead rat."

"Oh. Oh my. Now are you sure the rat is dead?"

The gate agent begins giggling.

"Um . . . yea. I'm pretty sure. I mean I'm standing here at the ticket counter with my bag open and a dead rat inside . . . I didn't know what to do. I went to the ticket counter and they didn't know what to do either, so they connected me to you guys. My little kid's standing here, asking why there's a mouse sleeping in daddy's suitcase."

By this point, a group of ten passengers have gathered around me to watch me in action.

"Oh dear . . . now is this a half a rat, or is the whole rat intact?"
(I'll admit, this caught *me* off guard). By this point, the gate agent has her hands over her mouth to keep the luggage rep from hearing her laugh.

"What? Half of a rat? Has this sort of thing happened before? How many rat halves do you guys have showing up in passengers suitcases? And where are the other halves of them? Are these standard questions you ask for this situation?"

Before she can answer, *BOOM!* and the little girl that decided to join in with B-rye previously calls out:
"Start the clock!"

"What . . . who was that?"
The luggage rep asks.

"That was . . . my daughter. She's playing this . . . game . . ."

B-rye has now approached with our pizza, and has a gigantic smile on his face when he sees this spectacle.

"Alright sir, I'm going to need you to come down to my office and fill out our dead rat form . . ."

The passengers around us can be heard chuckling. Even I'm starting to laugh.
"What . . . ? Are you serious?"

". . . Are *you* serious? . . . Gate number four?"
she asks. Everyone bursts into laughter and I hang up the phone.

4:12-
B-rye sets the pizza on the counter and wants in on the action.
"Oh, me next! Me next!"

The gate agent calls the ticket counter and puts B-rye on speaker phone.

"STRATA Airlines ticketing, this is Michelle."

"Hi Michelle, this is . . . Tom . . . Zuckerberg . . . over in the IT department. Are all of your computers running properly?"

"One moment . . . yes, they're all working fine."

"Yea, but are they . . . running fast?"

"Not . . . really. They've always been kind of slow, especially with this weather."

B-rye looks like she's ruined his punch line.
"Oh. Well . . . you better go get them, before they start running fast and then you can't get them, because they ran away!"

". . . What?"

B-rye hangs up the phone and looks at the passengers for approval. They just kind of shrug and return to their seats. Raphael pats him on the back and says
"Nice try, man. You did your best, and that's all that matters."

4:14-
We take the pizza behind the counter and sit in the wheel chairs. We eat the pizza and watch the darkened sky.

4:16-
BOOM! before B-rye can say it with a mouth full of pizza, the little girl calls out:
"Start the clock!"

B-rye gives her a thumbs up
"Hey, she's learning!"

4:25-
We finish our pizza. I roll the wheel chair over to the trash can and put the pizza box in it.

4:27-
When I roll back to my pilots, B-rye calls out
"Let's race to the restaurant! Go!"
Before I can say anything, he takes off in the wheel chair. I assume he devised this race while I was gone. I take off after him.

4:30-
He beats me to the restaurant, but only because he had a head start.

4:35-
We return to the gate. B-rye looks outside.
"We haven't heard anything for a while . . . we should get back to the plane and load up."
Passengers cheer when hearing this.

4:37-
The second we open the door to the jet bridge *BOOM!* (This one was distant, but still audible) everyone laughs as B-rye looks at the little girl and they both shout out:
"Start the clock!"

4:39-
Casually dressed rich guy asks:
"How about another wheel chair race!"
B-rye says he doesn't want to lose his title as the winner, but is convinced anyway when several other passengers start encouraging us. We jump in the chairs and bolt for the restaurant again. Passengers cheer. B-rye wins again, but only because it's an uphill race, and I have no upper body strength.

4:44-
The airport security guard (who had to have been pushing a hundred years old), approaches us and says that those chairs are for the handicapped only. B-rye says there aren't any handicapped passengers around. The old security guard tells us that we still have to get out of the chairs. I say this is an outrage, stand up, and pretend to limp back to the gate.

4:50-
The gate agent says that she got a call from tower and was told we should be good to go. Everyone in the gate area applauds.

4:56-
We load the plane with smiling passengers who stop to thank us for making the delay in the airport enjoyable.

Not every delay I've ever had has been like this. Most of the time, I just listen to my iPod and take a nap. But those delays aren't really worth writing about. Looking back now, it was the fun delays like that that manage to stand out in my mind more than the bad ones, and made my job interacting with passengers much more enjoyable.

Princess and the pickup truck

April 6th 2011

She's one of the friendliest,
sweetest FO's
that I ever had the pleasure
of flying with.

In my time at UPside Air,
she was always willing
to get a cup of coffee
from the Chicken place
inside the DCA airport
in between our flights,
or a glass of wine with me
after a long day
even if it was
only down at the hotel bar.

I don't know what it's like
on the other side
of the flight deck door,
but for whatever reason,
a lot of Captains
don't like the way
she operates the Air craft
and complain about her
when she's not around.

It causes issues
between them up there,
and it's for that reason
her and I usually
end up hanging out together
alone when we fly our trips.

I've personally
never had any issues with her,
and she's one of the few
that make the job
all that much more enjoyable.

The first time
we flew together,
our Captain
had recently got married.

After every flight
he was on the phone
to his wife,
talking the way
that newlyweds do,
saying things like
"Hi Princess!
. . . How's your day been Princess?"

She confessed to me
that she was becoming annoyed
having to hear this repeatedly.

So every time
I called the flight deck
and she answered,
I would talk to her
jokingly in the same manner,
saying things like:
"Hello Princess!
Passengers are complaining
about the temperature back here,
could you warm it up
for me Princess?"

She thought it was funny,
and the nickname
kind of stuck after that,
so I began calling her
Princess
from there on out.

I haven't forgotten
her real name,
but it doesn't mean
I have to tell you
what it was.

>>>>>>>>>>>>>>>>>>>>>>>
It was a windy,
rainy day
in April
that we were flying together.

It was one of those days
when nothing
seemed to be going right.

We were about four hours
behind schedule.
Our plane was sitting in DCA,
broken
and on maintenance.
And even if it was fixed,
we wouldn't be leaving
anytime soon,
due to the lightning storm
that was illuminating
the sky
every ten minutes.

We were parked
as far away from the airport
as we could possibly get,
sitting on an empty plane,
passing the time by
reading celebrity gossip magazines
and making puppets
out of empty tissue boxes.

Princess asked me
if I wanted to go inside the airport
and grab a cup of coffee
from the Chicken place.

I knew that being parked
so far away from the airport
meant a good ten minute walk
in the pouring rain
and stinging winds
to get inside
while hoping for a passenger bus
to pass by
and pick us up
if we were lucky.

We made make shift ponchos
out of giant trash bags
by poking two holes
out of the sides for arms,
and a hole in the top
to stick our heads through.

Just as we were getting ready
to brave the elements,
Portly mechanic
who had been working
on the aircraft asked us
if we wanted to drive
his pickup truck to the airport,
since he wouldn't be
going anywhere
any time soon.

He told me
as long as we were careful with it,
didn't tell anyone about it,
didn't mess with the tool box
in the bed of the truck,
and drove straight
to the terminal
and back,
it would be alright.

I'm sure
had I not been
with such a cute FO,
about to walk to the terminal
dressed like a homeless person
in a trash bag,
he wouldn't have loaned it to us.

But I seized the opportunity
and took the keys.

I climbed into the driver side,
and Princess
took the passenger side.

I've never driven
on a tarmac before,
but the minute long ride
was one of the most exhilarating
experiences
I've ever had at an airport.

And it wasn't enough.

When we were halfway
to the terminal,
in an empty part of the airport
where the planes park,
I turned to her and said
"Hey Princess, want to make this
even more fun?"

Before she could answer me,
I whipped the wheel
of the truck,
as hard as I could,
and began driving in circles.

Slow at first,
but then picking up speed.
Going in circles,
and then in figure eights.
She was screaming in fear.
Laughing in excitement.

And at that moment
we weren't a pair
of Airline employees,
dressed in giant trash bags,
driving a pickup truck
to an airport
on a rainy,
miserable day.

For a brief moment,
I was a brave knight.
Riding my horse towards a castle.
And that was our land we ruled,
our kingdom.
I was a brave knight,
and she
was the Princess.

Side note to this heartwarming story: Portly mechanic ended up being written up and getting in trouble for giving the mechanics truck to crew members who were not qualified to be joy riding company property around on the tarmac.

The Kansas City teachers convention

November 20th 2010

Kansas City to Philadelphia is one of the longest flights that we operate. Whether or not the winds are in our favor (they're generally not) determines just how long it takes to get from one city to the next. Usually it's about a two and a half to three hour flight from point A to point B. The three hours will usually tend to go a little something like this:

00:00-
Close door, read safety announcements, safety walk through.

00:11-
Sit down in jump seat, wait to take off.

00:19-
Set up beverage cart, begin service.

00:43-
finish beverage service, collect trash.

00:50-
walk through cabin.

01:00-
Walk through cabin again.

01:01-
Sit in jump seat.

01:10-
walk through cabin.

01:11-
sit in jump seat, twiddle thumbs.

01:20-
Walk through cabin. Again.

01:21-
Sit in jump seat, drink a coffee.

01:30-
Walk through cabin with coffee.

01:31-
Stand by jump seat with coffee.

01:40-
Walk through cabin with trash bag.

01:41-
Count the ratio of the number of passengers awake to the number of passengers asleep.

01:46-
Count the ratio of the number of passengers asleep to the number of passengers snoring.

01:50-
Walk through the cabin twiddling thumbs.

01:55-
Call pilots and ask how much longer until we get there.

01:56-
Groan at the general answer, another 30-60 minutes.

02:00-
repeat hour 01:00-01:50 until landing.

This is how the normal flight between Philadelphia and Kansas City goes, and then once more going back. Most people sleep, so I get bored because there's nothing to do. The only memorable flight from Kansas

City to Philadelphia was when I had the Kansas City teachers convention on board. I didn't know it was them at first and the thirty six or so that were on board pretty much took up the whole flight.

No matter who's on board, I'm generally going to try my best to impress them and put a smile on their face, so this was no exception. I went on with my safety announcements, and much to my surprise, they were all pretty much laughing by the middle of my routine, and clapping by the end. That's always my first indication that it's going to be a good flight. As I was doing my beverage service, one of the first few passengers I served told me they were all from Kansas City, and were on their way out east for some kind of national teachers convention.

They all told me it was very refreshing to have such a nice young man that was enjoying what it was he was doing and all that other good stuff you would expect from your guidance counselor. I told them about some of my more memorable teachers I've had in my days as a student, and how they really can shape the minds of young people.

My Captain called to use the bathroom, so I went up to the flight deck and did the old switcheroo. When I came back out, I returned to the group of teachers that seemed the most interested in talking to me, and continued on with our conversation.

"So when the pilot comes out to use the bathroom, who flies the plane?" One of them asked.

"Oh, I do that." I said with a serious look on my face, even though it was a total lie.

"What? Really? Is that hard?" One of them asked.

"Not at all. I just have to make sure that the auto pilot button is on, and the crash landing button is off." I joked. They laughed like it was the funniest thing they had ever heard in their lives, but most of them were kind of older, and I remembered older teachers I had with a sense of humor always laughing at the stupidest comments I made.

There was a particularly cute young teacher that was probably in her mid-twenties, sitting with another teacher that was a few years older. They asked for some wine, and I pulled the old 'Sorry I can't serve to minors' line. They laughed as I went to the front of the plane and returned shortly with two bottles. I told them that I over nighted in Kansas City sometimes, and asked if there were any good bars or clubs worth checking out. They told me the name of some place, although the main problem was that our hotel was in the middle of nowhere, and a cab ride to the city was about twenty dollars each way, so it wouldn't really be worth it. I was really just making small talk with the cute one.

I returned to the other teachers in the middle of the plane who asked me about life in the airline industry and wanted to hear some of my stories. At this time, I had just began writing stories on my website, and was lucky if I got even ten page visits a day, so the fact that people were interested in what I had to say felt terrific, even if it was a story directly from me, and not my website. I told them my famous juice race story, and they all loved it. They begged and pleaded for me to re-enact that great race, but I had made a promise to Mikey to never let orange juice have its rematch against apple, and I am a man of my word.

At the end of the flight, they all shook my hand and thanked me for a wonderful two hour and forty three minute flight. The teacher that had been sitting with the younger one handed me a folded napkin as she was deplaning and said to me "Here's your report card." With a smile. When I opened the paper it read the following:

Chuck the steward
(Pretzel guy)
Report card—November 20, 2010

Sense of Humor A+
Quality of interaction A+
Pretzel stewardship/ distribution A+
Story teller A+
Substitute pilot A+
Friendliness & personality A+
Rolling cans (apple & orange) F
(You really need to try harder-
failure to demonstrate what you know)
Next time we expect to see it!
Custodial duties C-

We enjoyed having you in class/
our flight! Best of luck to you on
your next flight! (-: Teachers from Kansas

Another entry from Captain Amazings diary

May 27th 2010

05/27/2010:

Dear Diary,

Today sure was freakin' sweet! It got off to a rough start, but by the end of the night . . . boooooo doggy! I woke up 9 AM in Kansas city. I thought about washing and ironing my uniform because it smelled like strippers, but then I realized there was no need, because the second I put it on, it straightened itself out and made me look super ultra-hot.

I went down to the breakfast area and met with my crew—and get this, not only are they both women . . . they're both super smokin' hot women also! The only downside? Corazon speaks English as a second language (foreign English is her first), and Princess isn't all that great of a pilot. I can forgive her though, because after me, the second best pilot on earth was God. They were sitting at a table for two people, so I pulled a chair up. This gave me a chance to demonstrate my awesome strength by lifting the chair up over my head when I asked them if I could join them. They must have just finished breakfast because they stood up and said I could have the table. This gave me the chance to demonstrate my weightlifting abilities even farther by raising the table up over my head. Unfortunately, they were already gone by then, but that's fine. I needed to get my workout in for the day anyway. I ate every strip of bacon in the warming pan and then balanced it out with some lipitor. I also ate a hard boiled egg but I threw away the yolk (the doctor said I need to watch what I put into my body), before getting on the hotel van.

I told the girls that they missed an awesome time at the strip club last night (neither of them could make it when I invited them, because they both had to wash their hair at the exact same time.) They didn't respond, so I told them how all the strippers were all over me because I was the best looking guy in the club, and strippers dig pilots. Princess asked me how the strippers knew I was a pilot, and I told her that was a stupid question, I obviously wore my uniform to the strip club. I told them I only spent $14,867.42 and a buffalo nickel last night, and when Corazon asked how I could afford that much, I told her it's because I became a gazillionaire after beating President Obama in a game of poker. So why am I spending so much at the strip club? Hey, I've got to stimulate the economy somehow!

I got to the airport and prepped the plane by making Princess do all the work. I needed a nap after my hard night of partying! I told her I would work the flight from MCO-PHL. During the flight I took another nap though. How did I pull this off? I have a pair of glasses with the eyes painted on them! These puppies have come in handy so many times, especially during our boring HR meetings I'm forced to sit in. I guess Princess caught on though, because she woke me up and said I was snoring so loud Corazon could hear me from the other side of the flight deck door. I'll be the first to admit, I have been told that I snore before. By Playboy playmates. When they slept with me. In my bed (And there wasn't a whole lot of sleeping going on, if you know what I mean!)

When we arrived in Philadelphia I went to the crew room to check my V-file. I couldn't believe my eyes, inside was a love letter. For me! It must have been from one of our hot, new, eighteen year old flight attendants because it was written on a Justin Bieber happy birthday card, and the second I opened it, it started playing his song super loud. ElHeffey and Damien were sitting in some nearby chairs watching this happen and started laughing their asses off. It was laughter of envy; I could tell they're totally jealous.

When I got back to the pane, I overheard Corazon talking to Princess about her marital problems she was having. This was the perfect in I needed. I didn't have any flowers or chocolate to woo her with, so I quickly etched out 'from a secret admirer' from the card I had got and wrote 'from the man of your dreams' in its place with my phone number below. I handed her the card and told her if she ever needed anyone to talk to . . . I was there for her. She looked at Princess with a confused look. Probably because I didn't write my hotel room number in there also, but that's because we weren't at the hotel yet!

The day had been pretty awesome . . . until we arrived in DC . . . Our chief Pilot, David Friendly, was waiting at the aircraft for me. And he did not look too happy. He told me that he needed to have a word with me in his office. At first I thought I was finally getting promoted to CEO of UPside Air, but then I was worried that he had heard about that homeless guy I beat up on my New York City over night and I was going to get written up. Luckily it wasn't anything nearly as severe. He just droned on about some allegations being brought against me for safety and security and then he told me that I was on thin ice with the FAA. HA! I eat thin ice for breakfast. Then he said it was serious and that the FAA had me under investigation, and he was only trying to help me. I told him that if he wanted to help me, he should start by fixing the model aircraft on his desk. Then when he asked what was wrong with it, I picked it up off of his desk, threw it on the floor and stomped on it. Then I told him to get out of the way, I had a plane full of passengers to fly to Cleveland.

I was so mad when I left his office—because he had made me miss my lunch! So I went to the Chicken place inside the DCA airport, but since the line was super long, I just marched up to the counter and took the first takeaway bag I saw and left. I got back to the aircraft and told Princess how some jerk had turned me into Captain Friendly. Her response to that was "I can't imagine why." At least I know if I ever get in trouble, she's got my back. I ate my lunch while she prepped the aircraft again, and then we flew to Cleveland. During the flight, I personally autographed napkins for all my passengers, and when Princess asked what I was doing, I winked at her, picked up the PA, and made an announcement to everyone that they had a celebrity on board today (me), and that I'd be handing out autographs at the end of the flight. I told Princess when you're as famous as I am, you have to sign the boobies and kiss the babies. And sometimes you have to sign the babies and kiss the boobies.

When we arrived in Cleveland, I told Corazon to rob the liquor cabinet. She said she wasn't doing that because it would be stealing from the company. I told her if I really wanted her to steal from the company, I'd ask her to siphon jet fuel out of the back of the plane. Then I'd sell that fuel to the terrorists. And when they bought it, they'd lead me to Osama Bin Laden. And then I'd have him right where I wanted him and karate chop him to death. And then I'd take the fuel back and ask him what he's learned. Of course by the time I was done explaining this, Corazon and Princess were halfway up the jet bridge, leaving to go to the hotel. And since Corazon locked the liquor cabinet, I had no choice but to leave my precious booze behind.

We rode the hotel shuttle to our hotel, and I told the ladies dinner and drinks were on me tonight. What I didn't tell them was that I would 'accidentally' leave my wallet in my hotel room so that I wouldn't have to pay for dinner. After all, I'm a pilot, not a gazillionaire! That plan backfired, because when I got down to the hotel bar, the girls weren't there. So I ordered a T-bone steak and a bottle of their finest vodka. The bartender said I couldn't order the whole bottle, only mix drinks or shots. So I told him to line up fifty shots of vodka. THEN the bartender said I could only order one at a time. So I ordered my shot and ate my well done steak. I told the bartender I left my wallet in my room and asked if I could charge it to room 402 (Not my room number). But the bartender asked for my name and said he needed to consult the front desk if that was really my room or not. Well, I had been in that situation before and knew where it was heading. So the second he was gone, I leaped over the bar, grabbed the bottle of Vodka and bolted like hell out of there.

And what perfect timing! As I darted down the hall, I passed by the workout room and spotted Corazon and Princess on the treadmills! So I stepped in to join them. I asked if they wanted some of my top shelf vodka, but they declined. Good, more for me! I jumped on the stationary bike and pedaled 20 miles in 20 minutes, a new personal record for me! I celebrated each mile with a shot of vodka. I guess the steak I ate was undercooked, because I immediately threw up afterward. I rinsed my mouth out with another swig of vodka and told the girls that the party was in my room tonight. They told me they'd meet me there shortly, and to get the party started. It must have been one hell of a party, because I don't remember anything after opening the door to my room, and woke up face first on the floor in the morning. I'm just going to assume that the girls showed up, and we had a threesome, because that's probably what happened. Just another awesome day being me!

Captain A.

Post card from an airplane (don't write back)

December 20th, 2010

Dear (You know who),

How's the weather where you are?
Above the clouds
it's always sunny.
Sometimes it's cloudy
under my feet,
but most days
I can see
the world below.

It's moving,
although to be honest,
I'm not really sure
if I'm moving
along with it.

I get to share that
with a group of strangers
that are on their way to
business meetings,
vacations,
families . . .
they're just as much
a group of strangers to me
as I am to them,
but that's only because
I'm such a damn good liar.

I only lie about
who I really am.
I use a smile as a disguise.
I use a smile as a bullet.

>>>>>>>>>>>>>>>>>>>>>>>
Two more days-
My suitcase will be back home
(Hopefully with me
attached to it.)

And I expect to have
a letter waiting for
me when I get home
that I sent to myself yesterday
asking: “Is everything alright?”
I’ll write back
when I have an answer.

Wish you were (anywhere but) here,

Chuck

Chuck makes a fool of himself in front of a Victoria's secret model

March 17th 2011

I spotted her coming down the jet bridge from almost a mile away. This girl was incredible. And since it was a nearly full flight, passengers were taking their sweet time boarding, giving me plenty of time to eye her up and down. Long thin legs, dark shoulder length hair, beautiful green eyes, light olive skin complexion . . . this girl was unbelievable. I tried casually sipping my coffee and leaning against the galley, trying to look cool as she boarded. The line of passengers stopped moving once more. And she was stopped in front of me. Oh yes. She brushed her hair back and smiled at me. "Um . . . Is this New York?" She asked in the loveliest sounding Australian accent I'd ever heard.

I smiled in return "No . . . this is . . . Philadelphia. But we're going to New York." I replied smiling.

She moved her eyes upwards for a moment calculating what I had just said before smiling back. "No—I mean . . . oh, haha! Good one." She said laughing. I know it's a good one. From my hilarious brain, to your beautiful face.

Everyone boarded and took their seats. I passed through the aisle counting how many passengers I had on board, while keeping an eye out for Aphrodite. There she was in the back, seat 12A by herself. "Damn it, out of sight distance." I thought. We smiled at each other as I passed by.

Before I returned to the front of the cabin, she stopped me. "Excuse me, the overhead locker's a little full, I can't seem to get my bag to fit. Can you . . . ?" She asked. Alright, now's my time to shine.

"Absolutely." I replied. I lifted her pink duffel bag up and played a game of overhead tetris with some of the other bags before attempting to shut it. It was still too full. I pushed the bags behind hers back a little harder and put some force into it before finally getting it closed. I smiled and then jokingly said: "Hit it 'til you fit it! That's my motto." She began laughing again. I was suddenly glad I hadn't called in sick for the trip, having just got over a head cold.

As I walked hastily through the aisle to the front of the plane some business robot in seat 4F stopped me "Excuse me, could you put my briefcase-?"

"Yea, I'll be right back." I said as I hurried up into the flight deck.

Note: 'I'll be right back' is how a flight attendant says 'F-you.'

I entered the flight deck "How many hot chicks are on board, and where are they sitting?" Damien asked me.

"That's not important." I said handing him my passenger count. "There's this . . . goddess . . . sitting in 12A. She blows every other woman I've ever seen out of the water. Ten times hotter than Corazon. She has to be a model or something."

"What? No way." Damien replied.

"I swear. 12A." I told him.

Damien looked over at John, who was our captain that day.

". . . I'm going to use the bathroom. I have to get a look at this girl." he said, climbing out of his seat.

"What? You have a girlfriend." John replied.

"Calm down . . . I said I just need to get a look at her. Not grope her. I'm allowed to look at her . . . . And then maybe grope her." He said laughing as he climbed out of the right seat.

As we were waiting for Damien to come back, John looked up at me and stated: "Hey, you know they say that Chuck Norris can kick a fifty yard field goal from the New York Giants stadium to the Dallas Cowboys stadium!" And then began laughing hysterically. I don't care how many years go by, I'm always going to keep laughing at those jokes, as long as John keeps telling them.

Damien came back in a matter of minutes. "Dude, she's got to be a model. No doubt about it."

"Really?" John asked.

"Gorgeous. She's got some like . . . British accent." He replied.

"British?" I asked.

"Or Spanish! Hell, I don't know. She's hot!" Damien exclaimed.

I breathed onto my knuckles and polished them on my shirt.

"Well, I'd love to stay and hang out with you guys . . . in the flight deck . . . where there's nothing nice to look at . . . but I've got a job to do in the back there with a gorgeous passenger, so you boys have fun up here . . . alone . . . doing whatever it is you do . . . up here." I gloated.

"Whatever man, you're acting like you're going to get her phone number or something!" Damien said.

"So what . . . maybe I am." I replied.

"Shut up man. John told me that you thought you got some girls phone number once, and it ended up being nothing but a piece of chewed gum inside of a napkin!" He laughed.

I looked at John disappointingly. "You told him that?"

"Hey man, I thought it was funny! You never told me *not* to tell that story!" John said defending himself.

"Yea, well . . . this time it's going to be different." I declared.

"Oh yea? Five bucks says you end up empty handed by the end of the flight." Damien said condescendingly. I bit my lip and looked at John who was entering our passenger zone count into some screen.

"Whatever bet you two want to make is between you . . . I hear nothing . . ." he said.

I smiled and shook Damien's hand "Alright. You're on." I said.

I closed the passenger entry door to the plane. "See you in forty minutes . . . with a phone number!" I said smiling at Damien as we shut the door to the flight deck.

The clock began.

I did a brief service, hastily walking through the aisle with a few bags of spinzels, throwing them at whoever wanted some like those guys you see at baseball games. I'm pretty sure one hit a passenger in the face, but I couldn't stop to check, I had a number to obtain! I took out a roll of toilet paper from the front overhead bin and made my way to the bathroom. I needed to look like I was keeping busy and needed a reason to go to the aft of the air raft. I opened the bathroom door and tossed the roll aside somewhere, before closing the lavatory door and approaching the girl again.

"Hey, do want anything to drink or . . . ?" I asked.

"Yea, actually do you have any white wine?" She asked.

"Oh . . . I'm sorry, I can't serve to minors." I said smiling. She laughed and showed me her ID. I forensically studied it. California license. Mandi. Her name was Mandi. She was a year younger than I. I had actually guessed that she was a little older. Either way, I always pull the 'can't serve to minors' line on attractive women. It makes them feel young, and makes me look funny.

As I walked to the front of the plane, 4F stopped me. "Can I get another bag of pretzels-"

"One per person. This isn't the queen Marriott. You're not special."

I pulled a bottle of wine out of the liquor cabinet, placed it in a plastic cup, put ice in the cup around it, and twisted a napkin to sit on the top of the bottle in the shape of a flower. I returned to the angel in 12A with the wine. She began to take out money when I shook my head no and waved my hand. "Don't worry . . . it's on the house." I said winking. She smiled.

"I'm Mandi." She said, as if I hadn't just scanned her information off of her license into my brain. "Do you do this route often?" She asked.

"You know . . . as often as it needs to be done." The second I said that, I replayed it in my mind, and it sounded bad. "What the hell? That had to have been the lamest thing I've ever said. Why did I say that? Get it together man." I thought.

"I used to want to be a cabin attendant and travel the world when I was a little girl." She said.

"Oh, really? So did I. Wait—I don't mean when I was a little girl. Also . . . not the flight attendant part. Just the . . . traveling part."

She laughed. I hadn't been this nervous in quite a while. I realized that I would have never been able to get this girls number any way, but I think if I didn't have five dollars at stake, I wouldn't have been bumbling around like an idiot trying so hard either.

"So what do you do for a living now?" I asked her, pouring the wine into the cup.

"Oh, I model." She said.

"I *knew* it!" I thought.

"I mostly do Victoria's secret magazine. That's what I'm going to New York for, there's a fashion show going on." She said. I almost spilled the wine. I'm pretty sure my face was turning red, trying to keep my eyes leveled with her, while trying not to picture her in lingerie. Before I could say another word, the call button lit up from the flight deck.

"I'll . . . be back. Duty calls!" I said in a sort of super heroes voice. She giggled even though it was probably even lamer sounding than the last joke I had just made.

I hurried to the inter phone and picked it up. "This had better be a damn emergency." I said.

Damien laughed. "How's it goin' back there Casanova? Any numbers yet?"

"What? You called to ask that? You're distracting me! That's against the rules. I'm back there, working my magic on Mandi, and you call to take me away from her. I thought this was airplane related!" I said unhappily.

"Ooooooh, Mandi. Very good, you finally got a name! You learn anything else about her?" He asked sarcastically.

"Yea. She's a Victoria's secret model. Anything else?"

"Bull. Prove it." He said in disbelief.

"I don't have time for this! You're keeping me from doing my job. I gotta get back to work . . . . Dick."

"Wait, can you find out if she has a friend for-" I hung up the phone before he could finish and turned back around. I needed to come up with another reason to go back to the aft of the plane again. I grabbed a few bags of spinzels and began walking to the back. The plane started to begin it's slow descent, I had less than fifteen minutes to bag this bird.

I tossed the pretzels in 4F's lap as I passed by.

"Thanks. About how much longer until we arrive?" He asked.

"Yea, I'll get right on that." I said passing by. I had no time to stop for frivolous banter! I was a man on a mission.

"Hey did you want another . . . ?" I asked, pointing to her wine.

"Oh my goodness! Your nose . . . !" Mandi exclaimed, pointing at my face. I wiped my nose with my hand. Blood. My blood. I had a damn bloody nose.

"Excuse me." I said with my hand covering my nose, as I turned around and went back into the bathroom. I kicked the roll of toilet paper that was sitting on the floor out the way as I shut the door behind me. I looked at my face in the mirror. It wasn't that bad. I knew I should have called out sick with that head cold. What a perfect time to get a bloody nose. I began vigorously splashing water on my face, but it wasn't coming out of the tiny faucet fast enough. I started cupping it in my hand and splashing it upwards, not caring where it landed. I could hear time ticking away in my head. I looked in the mirror. My face was fine again. A bit wet, but clean of blood. I took a deep breath and sighed, as I opened the bathroom door.

I walked back to where Mandi was seated.

"Sorry about that-" I began. She cut me off when she started laughing, loudly, as she covered her mouth with one hand and pointed at my pants with the other. I looked down. Sure enough, there was a big wet spot in the center of my pants running down my legs, making it look as though I had just wet myself. "Wow. This . . . probably looks bad. I can assure you it's just water. From the sink. I was . . . splashing my face to clean it and I guess I just got some on my pants . . ." I said embarrassed.

"Flight attendant prepare for landing." John announced over the PA.

Mandi continued laughing, as I pointed to the front of the plane

"I should . . . probably . . ." I slowly shuffled my feet up to my jump seat, picked up the inter phone, and called the flight deck. ". . . I'm sending the five under the door." I said to Damien and hung up.

Conversation with a gay flight attendant

November 25th 2010

I met James while in training. He was a few years older than me, and a super nice guy. There was also a constant rumor going around that he was gay. I failed to see how this was possible. I had no previous experience interacting with the gays before becoming a flight attendant—but from what I had seen in television and movies, he certainly did not fit the stereotype that Hollywood portrays. He wasn't flamboyantly open, marching down the streets, waving a rainbow flag in a pair of ass-less chaps. He was just a normal dude in my class. I wondered if it could be because of his previous work experience, or the tell-tale signs that other class mates pointed out, but that couldn't be it. There are plenty of straight, male nurses and flight attendants that own cats. And so what if he has 'sleepovers' with a girl in our class named Chrissie? I had 'sleepovers' with Corazon all the time in training (We were also dating at the time as well). But one day I decided to set the record straight.

We all had just piled in to a cab after a night of partying in Chicago during training. Chrissie was in the front seat. James, Corazon, and I were in the back. James had been rambling on all night about this love triangle that he was caught up in that went a little something like this:

James: . . . So yea, I don't know what to, I mean, I really like this—uh, person. But they're involved with this other . . . person. But I really feel a connection and know that we have feelings for each other! I just don't want to be the one to ruin . . . their relationship.

Chuck: . . . Dude, are you gay?

Corazon: Mono! How rude!

James: No it's ok . . . . Yea, I am.

Chuck: Ok, I was just getting really confused by all the third person references you were making. But now that that's out in the open, can you explain the situation like a normal person now?

James: So, I really like this guy Christian . . .

I know it was uncool for me to just blurt that out in the open like that, but I was drunk, and he was really just confusing the hell out of me. After that, he told us his problems without talking in some kind of secret code, and we gave him our advice like drunken friends that know what's best for everyone. I apologized many times the next day, but he brushed it off and told me it was fine, and we all moved on. He was based in Philadelphia, and every time I had a flight through there I called him and we met up if he was around. One afternoon I had a two hour sit in the airport the same time he did, so we met up for a cup of coffee. The following, is the conversation that took place between us that afternoon.

James: So, what's been new?

Chuck: Same old, same old . . . I can't complain.

James: Are you and Corazon still together?

Chuck: Well, I can always complain about that. No, she's trying to make her marriage work again for her daughter, but I think they're going to get divorced soon. What about you and Christian?

James: Yea . . . I don't think that's really going to work either.

Chuck: How come?

James: I think I love how he *treats me* more than how I love *him*.

Chuck: So what's the problem there?

James: What I meant to say is how he treats me . . . to whatever I want. With his money.

Chuck: Oh, yea I forgot. Isn't he like, a lawyer or something?

James: More of a legal consultant. He makes really good money though.

Chuck: Damn, we're in the wrong industry. You know, I can't even say that. I should stay in this industry and just find me my own sugar daddy. What's the female version of a sugar daddy?

James: A Cougar?

Chuck: No, that's like, an older attractive woman with a younger man, but I don't think a cougar necessarily has a lot of money.

James: A Sugar cougar?

Chuck: Hahaha that sounds like a desert at the cheesecake factory. 'Try our newest cake, the Sugar Cougar!' No, I think it would just be sugar momma. That's what I need. A sugar momma.

James: I still like the term 'Sugar Cougar' more. I'm trade marking that. Besides, there aren't a lot of rich, single, twenty year olds running around. And if there is, they're all spending daddy's money, not their ex's. Keep your eyes out on the flights man, especially to like, Cape Cod, and Nantucket, and ritzy islands like that. I'm sure there's plenty of single attractive Sugar Cougars going there.

Chuck: Yea, the problem is, I can flirt like crazy with girls on the plane, and I still get stereo typed as being gay, just because I'm a flight attendant.

James: So? I get stereotyped as gay just because I'm a male flight attendant.

Chuck: Yea, but you *are* gay. This girl came up to the front of the plane once and was like: "Hey, my friend in the back that I'm sitting beside thinks you're really cute and was wondering if you want to exchange numbers?" And I was like: "Oh really? Which one is your friend?"

James: See, that's something at least!

Chuck: She pointed to the back and said "That's him there!"

James: BWAHAHAHAHA!

Chuck: Dude, stop laughing, it's not funny!

James: HAHAHAHA Yes, it is! HAHAHAHA!

Chuck: Ha. Well, I guess it is a little funny.

James: That took guts. Or in this case, it took balls. I would never just straight up ask a guy for a number. Unless I was drunk and flirting.

Chuck: Yea, but he didn't ask. He sent the girl to.

James: That's true. You know, that's because women make the best wing men.

Chuck: This is also true. I felt bad for the guy though, I could tell he was embarrassed, and I still had an hour left in flight.

James: Did you say anything to him?

Chuck: Yea, I had to ask him what he wanted to drink.

James: I've had a guy just slide me his number on a piece of paper before while deplaning.

Chuck: See, I've thought about doing that on a flight as well. Find a cute girl, flirt with her for an hour and a half, and then give her my number as she's deplaning.

James: Why don't you?

Chuck: Ehh . . . I'm worried she'd come back at the company and claim it was harassment or some shit like that. And the last thing I need is Mikey writing me up for that.

James: So? If Mikey says anything, you could just deny it.

Chuck: The only problem is that the company has my phone number on file, so it's kind of hard to deny that it's *not* my number, when it's written in *my* hand writing.

James: Yea, I guess that makes sense. What if it was like my situation, would you take the number if it was just given to you?

Chuck: Well, that's a different story, but you didn't ask that question.

James: Hey is it true that some girl gave you a number on a plane once and when you opened the napkin there was just a chewed piece of gum inside?

Chuck: What? . . . No. Who told you that?

James: John did.

Chuck: Dammit, I wish he'd quit telling that story, it wasn't that funny.

James: I think it's pretty funny.

Chuck: Well, maybe a little funny.

James: You've got numbers on the plane before though, I remember you telling me about that.

Chuck: Yea, it didn't work out though. We didn't have a whole lot of things in common.

James: You mean things like . . . you still being head over heels for Corazon?

Chuck: Yea, little details like that. Let me ask you something, you've been with girls before. Isn't dating much easier as a gay man?

James: I was with girls in high school. And being gay doesn't make *dating* any easier. Especially when you're as picky as I am about who you date. And relying on a 'gaydar' to pick guys out isn't always reliable either. You know, I thought you were gay when I met you.

Chuck: Yea, I tend to get that. I have a lot of feminine qualities. So what is it you don't like about women?

James: I didn't say I don't like women. Don't get me wrong, I love women. Especially their boobs.

Chuck: HAHA you should get those breast cancer support bands. Do you know which ones I'm talking about? They're like the Lance Armstrong cancer bands, only they say 'I heart boobies'. How funny would that be?

James: The irony itself is pretty funny.

Chuck: So what was it that turned you away from women?

James: Nothing really 'turned' me away from women. I think I just always knew in the back of my mind that I was gay. Growing up in rural Pennsylvania though didn't give me a whole lot of options to explore that route. At least until I got to college.

Chuck: Then what happened?

James: Like I said, I always kind of had the feeling I was gay, so I figured; guess I wouldn't know unless I tried it.

Chuck: See, I disagree there. For example: I don't like brussel sprouts. I've never tried them, but it's just one of those things that I can just look at and think ". . . Nah. Not for me." However, if *you* like brussel sprouts, that's cool. I'd even come out to the Sprout pride parade to support my brussel sprout friends. But they're not my thing.

James: Wow. Way to go overboard with the analogy.

Chuck: Yea, I'm thinking of writing a book. I'm trying to come up with as many ideas and analogies as possible.

James: Well, let me know how that goes. What time is it?

Chuck: Almost two.

James: Damn, I gotta get back to the plane. Hit me up when you're back in Philly again.

Chuck: Alright, later GAYtor.

James: Keep working on that one.

Flying is for losers, and baby I was born to lose

December 22nd 2010

Would you like something to drink?
Would you like some pretzels?
Would you like something to drink?
Pretzels? Would you like a drink?
Would you like pretzels with that?

"Would you like something
to drink ma'am?"
I ask.

"Yes, I'll take an apple juice please.
So how long
have you been flying for?"
she asks.

"Let's see . . . about a year
and a half now.
Would you like pretzels?"

"No thank you. How old are you?"

"Twenty two."

"Oh, I see. So what else do you do?"
She asks.

"What do you mean?"
I reply.

"I mean other than flying. What else
do you do?"

What the hell
kind of question is that?
I drink,
I hang out with my friends,
and I hit on hot girls,
you old nosy bat.
What do you want me to say?

"I . . . play in a band back home."
I finally respond.

"Oh, is that all?
So what are you doing
with yourself?
You don't want to be
a flight attendant forever.
You should think
about something else."

What? What are you,
my damn
guidance counselor?
I like being a flight attendant,
so until I can figure out
where I'm going next in life,
piss off.

"Thanks, I'll consider that."
I smile.

Don't worry about it man.
Just brush it off.
A few more passengers
and I'll be done
with this service.

Then I can roll my cart back up
to the front of the plane.
Drink a nice cup of coffee.
Wait to land.
Deplane.
Board the next flight.
Repeat the same process again tomorrow.
And the next day.
And the next month.
And the next year.

Oh God, what am I doing?
I can't keep this up forever.
Is this where I want to be
in twenty years?
Working at a mid-size
regional airline branch
of STRATA Airlines?

A call to the flight deck:
"Hello Charles. What is it
you need now?
It's still another
hour and a half
until we get there,
so don't start pushing
my buttons now."
ElHeffey joked.

"No, it's this passenger
in the back here.
She started grilling me
about what I was doing
with my life and made my job
seem really miniscule and unimportant . . .
she was really condescending
towards me.
It just got me down is all."

"What? Is that it?
To hell with her.
You're good at your job.
Hell, you're great at your job
and you know it.
You keep passengers happy,
and you have a terrific sense of humor.
In the past year
look at all the countries
you've gone to in your off time:
Switzerland, Brazil, England, Mexico.
How many times do you think
that bitch has been to Brazil?
None? Would none be
a correct answer?"

"Yea you're right.
Thanks ElHeffey."
I said with a laugh.

"Don't worry about it.
We'll get to Portland tonight
and have some beers.
Forget all about it."
He assured me.

I hung up the phone,
made myself a cup of coffee,
and sat in my jump seat
as I sighed
and thought for a moment.

I'm young. I'm lost.
I don't know what I'm doing.
I don't know where I'm going.
I'm so confused.
I'm so heartbroken.

I'm poor.
I'm a mess.

I smiled to myself.
I don't care.
I'm not a failure.
I'm happy.

The complete flight attendants guide to: Picking up strangers at a hotel bar

March 23rd 2011

I can't really recall where I was, and I suppose it's kind of irrelevant to this story. After about a year and a half a lot of lame overnights tended to kind of just blend together. I know it wasn't one of our better locations, because if it had been, after the long day I had just finished, it would have been worth going out to have dinner and a drink. But it wasn't one of our better overnights and therefore, my pilots didn't want to do anything when we got to the hotel.

We checked in, got our room keys, and made our way for the elevator. My stomach growled on the way. I would normally change first and then head down to the hotel bar to order my dinner and a drink, but I was so hungry, I figured I would just go to the bar, order my food, and take it back to my room. There was no point in changing first if I wasn't going to have a beer and I hate drinking alone.

I said good bye to my pilots as they got into the elevator. I dragged my suitcase down the hall and into the hotel bar. As I expected, it was empty with the exception of one person. This person usually tends to be a middle aged robot drinking at the hotel bar alone on business, but this was a different case. A blonde girl that had to have been about my age sat alone quietly stirring her glass.

I thought: "Maybe I should try and strike up a conversation. Maybe she'll invite me to sit down with her. Maybe she's a classy business woman that's single and makes a ton of money and is looking for a funny, interesting guy."

The bar tender, a middle aged man that had probably been doing his job long enough to have more stories than I, took my order of chicken tenders and fries. He told me it would be about ten minutes for the food to arrive and then vanished back into the kitchen behind the bar. I stood with my hands in my pockets for a moment, glancing at the girl every now and again.

I thought: "She's cute. Not exactly model material, but that over all nice girl quality to her. I could see her being my type." She glanced over at me and smiled. Not exactly an invite, but I figured the hell with it; I'll go over and give it a shot. I approached her. "Is this seat taken?" I asked her smiling, as if we weren't the only two people in the bar. She said no. "Would you like some company?" I asked.

"Sure, that would be fine." She replied.

I sat down. My experience in the airline industry had helped me become a master craftsman at making conversations with total strangers. I introduced myself. I can't recall her name, but that doesn't matter, I would have changed it for this story anyway. So I'll say it was Samantha just for the sake of it.

"So are you here on business, or pleasure?" I asked.

"Neither, I was on my way home and my flight was canceled. And since it was the last flight of the night, the airline sent me here." She replied.

"Welcome to my world. The airline sends me to a hotel every night after the last flight."

She laughed.

Then she said nothing.

Not much on conversation I figured.

"So are you in school, or do you work, or . . . ?" I asked.

"Oh, I'm in school." She replied. And that was it.

"Dammit, this is going nowhere . . . . Yet." I thought. Time for plan B.

"I have to go up to my room and change before I can have a drink, were you planning on hanging out here for a while?" I asked.

"Well, I have an early flight home, so I wasn't going to stay down here for too long . . ." she replied.

"I'll tell you what. If you stay down here and keep me company, I'll buy you a drink." I offered. She agreed and I went up to my room on the fifth floor. I hurried and put on my nicest outfit and then sprayed some cologne on myself.

"Maybe this will turn into an interesting night after all." I thought.

I hurried back down to the bar. I sat beside her again, just as the bartender returned with my food. "Can I also get a tequila and tonic to drink? And for Samantha . . ." She ordered some girly drink. It was time to get this ball rolling. "So what is it you're studying?" I asked.

"International business." She replied. I could imagine her in one of those suits that complimented her figure. And in my imagination it looked good.

"So you like traveling then?" I asked.

"I do." She said.

"Something we have in common." I replied, taking a sip of my drink. She just nodded. I could tell that this was going to be one tough nut to crack. "So if you could go anywhere in the world . . . where would it be?" I asked.

"I would love to visit Greenland." She said.

Dammit, one country I knew absolutely nothing about. It was time to throw in a joke. "I would visit Jupiter. I hear it's lovely this time of year." I said smiling.

She laughed.

"Alright, now we're getting somewhere. Maybe after two more drinks we'll be laughing like old friends. And then after five drinks we'd be opening up with intimate details about our lives. And then after seven drinks we'll be leaving together."

I thought.

"How long have you been a flight attendant?" She asked. I was happy that she didn't mistake me for a pilot, and even happier she didn't call me a stewardess.

"About a year and a half."

"You must see a lot of places. Any interesting stories?" She asked.

"Oh, yea. I just came back from Paris (a lie). And tomorrow I fly to Australia (also a lie). As for funny stories . . . I just recently made a fool of myself in front of a Victoria's secret model (not a lie)." I proceeded to tell her about the model that I had embarrassed myself in front of, as it was the most recent funny thing that had happened to me. She found it funny, and covered her mouth with her hands every time she laughed.

The bartender came back and I ordered another drink. Samantha was still working on hers however. "That's alright, the night is young." I thought. She then suddenly asked the bartender for her check. "What the hell?" I thought.

"You ready to get out of here already?" I asked.

"Yea, like I said I have an early flight . . ." She replied.

"Yea, I suppose I should get out of here also." I said, asking for my check. Twenty seven dollars, and that wasn't even including tip. Way over my daily allowance for a dinner. I downed my drink and left the bar with her.

We walked to the elevator as I checked her out from the corner of my eye. "She's much better looking now that she's standing up. She has a nice bottom also. Maybe hooking up with her will fill that empty hole in my heart Corazon left. My pilots are going to be so proud of me tomorrow." I thought.

She pressed the elevator button for the third floor and the elevator started moving. Before I could say anything she turned and said to me: "I'm going to my room alone, you know."

". . . You bitch! I wasn't planning on going to your room. What did you think; we were going to hook up? HA! You're not my type. And your ass is too big. And I have feelings for another woman. Can't a guy just be nice and buy a girl in a bar a drink, without trying to pick her up?! What's the world coming to?!" . . . is what I was thinking.

Instead, what I said was:

"Of course not, my room's just on the same floor as yours."

(This was another lie.)

We got off the elevator. She said it was nice meeting me and went to her room as I walked toward the end of the hall as if it was where my room was. I heard her door close and audibly lock behind me. I stopped and stood in the hall for a moment feeling defeated. I let out a sigh. I opened the door to the stair well and climbed two floors up to my room alone and went to bed. Oh well, at least I tried.

Things only happen for a reason because we make them

July 19th 2011

I spent all night with Corazon
on the floor of our hotel room
in Raleigh-Durham
pouring over old papers,
notes,
stories . . .
the first year of my life
in the airline
chronicled on
wrinkled airplane napkins.

Laughing and drinking wine
as if we had known each other
since we were children.

Giving each character
silly little pseudonyms
and fake names.
Picking out the stories
that would make me 'famous'.

"Publishing a book
is gonna be my ticket
out of here."
I declared.
How right and wrong
I was at the same time.

She used to tell me
that we met for a reason.
I thought it was strange
how our two paths
seemed to intersect
and then run parallel
to each other.

I guess we did meet for a reason.
I could see it
in all of those stories about us,
now laid out
bare on the floor
before us.

Cutting our lives
open with a pen
and spilling
our stories
through ink
into the world.

God Damn,
time has a strange way
of sneaking up on you.

One jaeger, two jaeger, three jaeger, floor

March 30th 2011

3:49PM-
I arrive at our hotel in Milwaukee. My FO is an insanely tall pilot that has just transferred from Norfolk that I call Treetops. Our captain, B-rye is working his first trip since upgrading. There is literally nothing around our hotel, with the exception of other hotels, the airport, and a bar called Final approach. Since this is a crew of anything but slam clickers, we decide that Final approach will be the one (and only) place to spend the evening.

4:01-
We are changed and meet in the lobby of our hotel. We leave and walk to Final approach.

4:12-
Final approach is the literal meaning of a dive bar. There's a main bar when you first walk in, with raised tables to the right surrounded by bar stools. The whole bar is decorated with old airplane seats. There is a giant propeller hanging from the ceiling that looks like it's ready to collapse at any moment. The place is pretty much empty, with the exception of a few regulars that were all sitting at the bar. I assume they either drive trucks or farm for a living.

4:18-
Our waitress is a young Hispanic woman named Karina. She takes our orders of beer, which is dangerously only a dollar during happy hour. And since it was the fifteenth of the month, we had just been paid. It was about to become a VERY happy hour.

4:23-
We order our first beer from Karina.

4:34-
We order our second beer.

4:46-
Third beer.

4:56-
The moment Karina is gone, Treetops confesses to us that he's only twenty years old, making him the youngest pilot at UPside Air. He can't legally drink for another four weeks. We contemplate cutting him off.

5:09-
We order our fourth beer.

5:19-
Karina stops to talk to us for a moment. She shows us photos of her daughter at home. Treetops asks Karina her name again. She responds in a thick Spanish accent, rolling her R's. Treetops begins trying to say her name in the same manner.

5:29-
I go to the bathroom to break the seal. The bathroom is just as dirty as the rest of the bar.

5:33-
When I return to the table, Treetops is still trying to roll his R's.

5:34-
B-rye orders us all Jaeger bombs. I decline until he tells us they're on him.

5:40-
Treetops is becoming impatient waiting for his Jaeger bomb. He calls our waitress 'Chalupa girl' and tells her to hurry up with our drinks. Chalupa girl does not like being called Chalupa girl.

5:42-
Treetops leaves to go to the bathroom.

5:44-
Karina brings us our Jaeger bombs and apologizes for taking so long. I apologize for Treetops calling her Chalupa girl.

5:46-
Treetops returns. We make a toast to UPside airlines for doing something right (Pairing together this awesome trio), count to three, and throw back our Jaeger bombs.

5:47-
I clasp my chest and catch my breath for a minute. I say I think I need a break. B-rye thinks I need another drink.

5:52-
Fifth beer.

6:03-
I am slowing down. The drinks are setting in. Treetops calls me a pussy. I challenge him to chug our beers. No twenty year old is showing me up!

6:04-
Treetops and I chug our beers furiously while B-rye cheers us on. Chalupa girl watches from two tables back, laughing at the gringos.

6:06-
I beat Treetops in a chugging competition and remind him who has the higher employee number at UPside airlines (I had been in the company for almost two years, He was at one). B-rye orders another Jaeger bomb.

6:10-
Karina brings us our shots. B-rye asks why she won't do one with us. She says it's because she's on the clock. B-rye says she has his utmost respect, and toasts to Karina. Treetops toasts to Chalupa girl. We count to three and throw the shots back.

6:11-
I do not feel good in the least bit.

6:13-
I order a glass of water. That seems to be an immediate solution to all of my problems.

6:22-
I stumble to the bathroom. I am not sure if I am going to vomit or not. I stand over the toilet for a moment before taking a leak.

6:29-
I stand in front of a cigarette machine contemplating whether or not to spend five dollars on a pack of cigarettes (I only smoke when I am drunk).

6:31-
Karina approaches me and says that my tall friend is not being very nice. I tell her that's because my tall friend gets nervous around beautiful women. She smiles and says he had better be leaving a big tip.

6:33-
I return to the table to find another beer waiting for me. I tell Treetops what Chalupa girl just said. He replies:
"Oh, I got a BIG tip for her!"
B-rye laughs as though this is the funniest thing he's ever heard, although he is also probably a good three beers ahead of me.

7:02-
I am not even a quarter of the way through my beer. B-rye orders "One last Jaeger bomb" and gets our check.

7:05-
I make one last toast as I stand up and loudly declare:
"I have an announcement to make! I have an announcement to make! . . . I am drunk. That is all. Carry on."
B-rye is in hysterics again. I think it's funny that my captain is even more drunk than I am. And I am *drunk*.

7:13-
We stumble out of Final approach. Treetops says goodbye to Chalupa girl and apologizes for not remembering her name. B-rye laughs again. Karina is not amused in the least bit.

7:15-
As we stumble back to the hotel, B-rye sprints ahead of us and dives into a parking lot, ducking behind a car.

7:16-
B-rye leaps out at me and Treetops in an attempt to scare us, as if we hadn't just seen him run and hide.

7:20-
We are at the entrance to the hotel. B-rye tells us:
"Just act cool so the receptionist doesn't notice that the airline crew is drunk."
We walk into the hotel. Since the elevator is out of order, we must walk up a flight of steps just beyond the lobby. Treetops hurries past us and up the steps.

7:21-
B-rye and I are halfway up the stairs, crawling on our hands and feet, when he collapses. On the stairs. I shake him
"Come on buddy, let's get you up! Time to go to your room!"
I look back at the receptionist who is now leaning over the counter looking at us.

"Is he alright?"
She asks.

"Yea. He's just . . . really tired."
I reply.

7:22-
I scoop B-rye's arm over my back and lift him up. He is heavier than he looks. And I am drunker than I look.
"Don't worry. Everything's under control!"
I call back to the receptionist who is still watching.

7:23-
I carry B-rye to the top of the stairs and turn the corner. Treetops is sitting on the floor outside of his room. I ask him for a little help. He helps by pointing and laughing at me. I ask B-rye which room is his. He barely points and grunts at the room next to where Treetops is sitting. I carry B-rye to his room.
"You have to get your key out so we can open the door."
I say to him. B-rye fishes around in his pockets.

7:25-
B-rye informs me that he has lost his key by looking at me, shrugging his shoulders and laughing. I stand him up and ask Treetops to keep an eye on him while I go get another room key from the front desk. As I approach the stairs, I hear B-rye fall over, making a dull 'thud' noise on the floor. Treetops points and laughs.

7:26-
I return to the front desk and tell the receptionist that B-rye lost his key and that I need to get new one to let him in his room. She looks suspiciously at me and says that he has to be the one to come and get it. I remind her that he is the one that collapsed on the steps and I really don't have the energy to carry him back down the stairs, get his key, and then carry him back up again. She rolls her eyes and makes a new key card for me.

7: 29-
I unlock the door to B-rye's room. Treetops and I throw him on his bed and hand him a bottle of water.
"You guys . . . are awesome crew members! I love you guys!"
He mutters.

7:29-
His room phone rings. I look at Treetops who shakes his head not to answer it.
"It could be Captain Friendly! Answer it!"
B-rye demands. I fail to see why the chief pilot of UPside Air would be calling.

I answer the phone.
"Hello?"
I say.

There is a woman on the other end.
"Who is this?"
She asks.

"This is Chuck. Who's this?"
I reply.

There's a pause.
"I'm B-rye's fiancée."

"I'm B-rye's flight attendant."
I respond.

"I freakin' love you Chuck!"
B-rye shouts from the bed.

"What's going on? Will you put him on the phone!"
She demands.

"I'm not so sure he's . . . coherent right now."
I respond.

"What?! Why, what's going on?! Has he been drinking?!"
She shouts loud enough for everyone in the room that's not on the phone to hear her.

B-Rye shoots up from bed.
"Oh, damn it! Don't put me on!"
I hand the phone to him.
"Don't put me on! No, don't—Heeeeeeey honeyyyyyy! How are you? What? Nooooooo I'm not drunk!"

Treetops points and laughs.

7:36-
Treetops and I leave B-ryes room. I fiddle with my door and its key for a moment before getting it open. I turn off the light and collapse on my bed. The room feels like it is spinning. Furiously.

7:38-
I can't take it anymore. I turn back on the light to assure myself that the room is not spinning.

7:41-
I turn on a re-run of family guy and sit at the edge of my bed rocking back and forth, cradling a bottle of water. I feel terrible.

7:47-
I feel *really* bad. I stand up and stumble to the bathroom and stand over the toilet for a moment. I vomit Jaeger bombs and beer profusely.

7:52-
I curse B-rye's name for buying me jaeger bombs.

7:55-
I vomit some more.

8:00(?)-
I pass out on the toilet.

9:00(?)-
I regain consciousness.

9:01(?)-
I vomit some more.

9:11(?)-
I pass out again.

10:32-
I crawl from the bathroom to my bed. I curse B-rye's name again and then giggle to myself for no apparent reason. I lie across the foot of the bed shivering before passing out.

4:45 AM-
My alarm rings and I wake up. The lights and television are still on. My mouth tastes like death. I brush my teeth several times while preparing for work.

5:23-
I meet Treetops and B-rye in the lobby. We all just nod a hello to each other and climb in to the hotel van to go to the airport. We do not speak a word to each other.

5:29-
We pass through security. We still do not say a word to each other.

5:37-
We prep the airplane. In silence.

5:53-
I enter the flight deck and tell my pilots that my security checks are complete. No one says a word. Finally, Treetops turns to me and asks:
"So . . . was I calling our server 'Chalupa girl' all night?"
We are all in hysterics again.

As miserably hung over as the three of us were all day, we still made it through. We spent the rest of the day regaling each other with stories of things we may have forgotten from the previous nights events. B-rye didn't remember what happened between the time we took our last jaeger shot until his fiancée was yelling at him, and he told me that he took hell because I answered his phone. To this day Treetops and I still laugh about his first Wisconsin overnight and Chalupa girl.

Famous last words

August 27th 2011

There was a time in August
when Mary and I
had the same basic
flying schedule.
Starting and ending our trips
on the same day,
at just about
the same times.

We created a sort of
game to play.
Most people would say
this is a game
for the young and impulsive . . .
perfect for Mary and I.

After finishing
our last flight of the trip,
we would change
out of our uniforms
in the bathroom by the crew room.
We would then meet
at the airport bar
and have a few drinks
until we were tipsy.

Then with our suitcases still full,
not even two hours
after our last flight,
we'd pick a random city
off of the departure board,
hop on an airplane,
and fly to that city
to party for the night.

We woke up,
still tipsy on an airplane
in Rochester
and caught a ride
to the Strathallan hotel.
Went out for a night
in the city.

Three days off,
and we decided
that we'd spend them together
partying in Rochester.

Our lives don't revolve
around the airline.
But who else can just
pack up at the last second
and jump onto an airplane,
going to who only knows where,
for three days with you
when you're a flight attendant?

What do we care?
We're young and impulsive.
And besides,
that's what friends are for.
To raise a toast with you
in a bar with a pair of
school teachers that you just met.
That you'll never see again.

And we pretend to be
just as interested
in what they do for a living
as they are with us.
But the conversation
always goes the same way:
"You guys fly for a living?"

"Oh, that's nothing,
you teach for a living.
I once had a flight full
of teachers from Kansas city
on their way to a convention . . ."

We'll let you buy us drinks
and we'll repay you with stories
about how amazing
our lives are,
even though they're really not.
We're just doing our jobs.
Even when we're not working.

Keep your eyes open for us.
We're the strangers you see
in the middle of the night
tripping over our own two feet
because we're too intoxicated
to give each other
piggy back rides.

Getting into slapping contests
with each other
just for the thrill
(and laughs)
of it.

Singing songs
at the top of our lungs
to the stars
in the warm night sky
when we can't remember
the lyrics.
The tune.
The song.

Holding each other up
on the walk back to the hotel
because no one else
is there to.

No one else
is hundreds of miles
away from home
with a co-worker
on their days off
drinking just because
they're young and impulsive.

It almost . . .
just almost
makes me glad
I can't hold my liquor.

Washington D.C. in the morning

December 29th 2011

>>>>>>>>>>>>>>>>>>>>>>>
It's the beginning
of a new day
in Washington D.C.
as the light
slowly makes its way
through the windshield
of my car
after a long night.

I raise my car seat
back up to see the clear,
cold sky
over the Potomac River
as planes begin to take off
and land at the airport.

I can barely bring myself
to look into my tired eyes
in the rear view mirror
for a moment
before turning away.

It's not long
before a silver SUV
pulls up next to me
and Corazon steps out
in her uniform with her suitcase.

I meet her
in front of our cars
and nod a hello to her.
There's an awkward silence
between us momentarily.

"How's the fight going?"
She asks me.

"Slow . . . you know,
Sally said
these things take time.
So . . ."

"You're not giving up then?"
She asks.

I shake my head no
"I've been . . . flying a lot.
Las Vegas and
Ft. Lauderdale . . ."

"You need to stop flying around
and start working again.
You look awful.
You slept here last night?"
She asks.

"I couldn't very well . . .
drive home."
I reply.

"You were drinking again?"

"Yea, well . . ."
I lower my head.

". . . Why?"
She asks.

I look back up at her
"Come on, Corazon.
I'm an author aren't I?
. . . And I'm jobless . . ."
I say.
". . . I'm finding fewer
and fewer reasons . . .
to care anymore."

She bites her lip
"Stop talking like that . . ."
She says.

"Why? This is all my fault.
I've caused everyone
so much trouble.
I keep . . . hoping . . .
that the court trial
can set this right.
Make it the way it used to be."
My throat swells up
when I see tears
start to stream down her face.

"You can't keep regretting
what you did-"

I cut her off
"I didn't want it
to end this way though!
. . . Not like this."

She stands silently
staring at me for a moment
before starting
to move towards
the employee bus to the airport.
"I need to be leaving.
Mikey will write me up
if I'm late again-"

I take her by the hand
and pull her into my arms.
She embraces me
as I whisper
"I have to get my job back again.
I wasn't ready to stop flying yet."

She shakes her head
"But you needed to."
Her tears land on my shoulders
with nothing but the sound
of planes
taking off
and landing
all around us.

Part III

Re-routing of a flight path

If Harry Potter can make money doing it, why can't I?

This is all one big
damn popularity contest.
Over the course of working
for UPside Air
for two years,
I had stories to tell.

Some were believable.
Some were not.
Some were real.
Some were not.
But they were all just stories.

I'm not a writer,
I'm a flight attendant.
Flying just happened to give me
something to write about.
And after two years of flying,
I could tell you some stories.

The problem is-
you don't know me.
The real me.
You only know me
from the stories that I've told you.

When I first started flying
at UPside airlines,
I grew tired of telling people
the same stupid stories
over and over.

That's why I decided to start
writing these stories down.

I wanted my stories to go
from my head,
to my fingers,
to my computer,
to my internet
to your eyes,
to your brain.

None of what ultimately happened
was my intention
when I began writing
on my website.
I just needed somewhere
to put the stories
that I was tired of telling
over and over again
to everyone.

And that's where
my original website
www.badflightattendant.com
started.

At the time,
it was nothing more
than a crappy site
for my friends
to check out,
and for me to vent
my ramblings of my
everyday work life.

I changed names, dates,
locations, events . . .
this was all to protect myself
and the people I wrote about.

My friends thought
the website was great.
Friends outside
the airline industry-
as well as inside.

That was how it really took off.
Friends of mine at UPside Air
shared my website with friends
of theirs at other airlines.
They shared it with their friends
at mainline airlines,
little propeller airlines,
private charter airlines . . .
even our rival airline
Soma Air.

Flight attendants began
writing me emails, along with
gate agents, rampers,
ticket agents,
disgruntled passengers,
strangers in other cities.
They all began writing to me.

They enjoyed my stories.
They thought they were funny,
they thought they were sad.
They thought they were poetic.
They thought I should take
courses in writing.

I'm going to be pretty frank here,
I really gave a shit less
about what people thought
about my stories.
I only continued writing
as a means of escaping boredom
on lame layovers in lame cities
when flying with slam clickers.

This was until I began receiving
e-mails from people
that thought
I should publish these stories.
I had never thought about writing
before as a profession.

It was over the summer of 2011
I began to search for publishers.
I was rejected several times.
'No prior published works.'
'No writing experience' . . .
They were pretty brutal,
but what it came down to was this:
No popularity.

Who would want to buy a book
from some unknown kid
rambling about some
mid-size regional airline
that he works for?

Up until then,
I had thought
that the hundred some emails
that I received from people
(including the crazy ones),
meant that I had a million people
willing to buy a book from me.

Now; I want any one that is
considering going into
the publishing industry
for the first time and is reading
this to pay attention closely.
Having a couple hundred people
enjoy a few short stories
that you wrote,
doesn't necessarily mean
all those people
are ready to shell out
X amount of dollars
for a book you have published.

Whatever grandiose vision
you may have about publishing
your first book and becoming
rich and famous overnight,
you can just flush away now.
Unless you're Mr. Potter,
don't expect fame
and fortune all at once.
Thinking back on it now,
perhaps I should have
called up old Harry
and discussed the route
he went.

Toward the end of the summer,
and of my
second year in the airline,
I found my publishers on line.
Deals were made,
papers were signed,
and money was spent.
Plenty of my own money.

I'm sure that at the time
it was all a pretty big risk.
My target audience was
other airline employees
that could somewhat
relate to me.
Oh, they're out there.
It's just a matter of finding them,
and then convincing them
to buy a 132 page book
of my ramblings,
crummy plot holes,
and spelling and grammatical errors.

Oh, but the fun doesn't stop there.
Published books don't fall
out of the sky.
I spent what I considered
to be a fortune
to have my book made,
and that was the cheapest
package my publishers offered.

When I say 'made'
I mean
I had to pay for the graphic design,
I had to pay for the editing and formatting . . .
As I write this now,
I realize all the mistakes I made
the first time around,
that hopefully,
by the time you read this,
will have been ratified.

The end result of this all,
was a poorly published version
of the first quarter of the book you hold now
Part I: 'Bad flight attendant',
with a few stories added,
a few stories removed,
and the rest of the stories
drastically changed.
(My apologies to my readers
that already have a copy of 'Bad flight attendant'.)

The economics of publishing
aren't all that difficult
to figure out.
After all,
money makes the world
go round.

My publishers paid me
three dollars a copy
per book sold.
They sold it for ten
to the book stores
and media outlets,
making them
seven dollars per copy.
Book stores and media outlets
then in turn sold it
for twelve to fifteen dollars.

I'm pretty sure
that you can do the math
and figure out
who makes what,
and at three dollars per copy,
I'm not exactly rolling
in swimming pools of money
cartoon style.

Why you may ask?
It all goes back to popularity.
If you have the money,
publishers will really
publish anything
you have to say.
It's just a matter
of whether or not
people will buy it-
which ultimately determines
whether or not
you will ever see
the money again
that you paid to have it
published in the first place.

I slowly discovered these things
as I chiseled my way into
a cut throat industry
of reading and writing.

But I had a story to tell.
And despite the fact that
it ultimately led
to my downfall as a flight attendant,
a huge battle
between my airline and I,
and sent me into the most
alcohol induced state of depression
that I had ever been in
in my life,
(You'll read about that soon)
the day that a shit load
of promotional copies of my book
arrived at my door step
I had only one goal.

At that moment,
I didn't care about
selling copies.
I didn't care about
book signings,
or the amount of money
I would make back
out of all the trouble
I went through to have
my writing published.

All I cared about,
was the smile on the face
of Corazon,
when I placed a copy
in her hands
and said in the simplest way possible:
"I made something for you."

I'm through doing shit that will get me fired. And this time, I mean it!

September 2nd 2011

I used to think that I was one of the craziest flight attendants our company had to offer. Don't get me wrong, we're all a little crazy (Otherwise we wouldn't be doing this job), but some are just a little crazier than others. I may have thought that I was about as wild as they came, but that was before I met Ne-ne. Ne-ne has got to be borderline certifiably mental. Ok, maybe that's pushing it a little too far, as she is still a close friend of mine to this day. But after the events of the first night we spent together, I can say that she was definitely a wild child, and by the end of this story you'll know why.

I first met Ne-ne through Mary around September, three months into my third year of flying at UPside Air. Mary and I had begun frequenting the Irish pub outside of DCA when we weren't out gallivanting around the country on our off days. Ne-ne was new to UPside airlines and smoking hot, which meant one thing: I had to corrupt her before anyone else could. At the time, I liked to think of myself as a sort of welcome wagon to our airline. Of course at the age of twenty three, I had that wagon full of alcohol and good times a plenty.

Note: My welcome wagons did not apply to anyone other than hot girls.

She was very quiet and reserved the first night that I met her, but it didn't stop me from regaling her with stories of trips Mary and I had been taking together as of lately and flirting with her like crazy.

"I'm going to be over nighting in Rochester tomorrow night. Since you and Mary are always talking about how much you love that place, you should come with me!" She suggested.

I looked at Mary and smiled. "We *should* go with you! It'll be good times!" I exclaimed, after discovering from Mary that our new found coworker was very much single. And so the plans for a night I wouldn't soon forget were made.

Since Mary had to do a turnaround flight in the morning out of DCA, she decided she would catch a later flight into Rochester at 8 that night. I had just gone into my off days from flying for the next few days, so I took the afternoon flight from DCA-ROC which I figured would give me a good four hours of alone time with Ne-ne before Mary jump seated in.

When I arrived at the Strathallan hotel, I called Ne-ne. She was already out at a bar around the corner having a drink and had left keys to her room for Mary and I at the front desk. I was beginning to like this girl more and more. I dropped my bags off in her room and hurried down the road into town to find the bar that she was at.

She was sitting at a table outside, wearing dark sunglasses and a tight, white button up shirt. It was early September, so the weather wasn't unbearably hot outside. Her frosty glass of beer was resting on a coaster. She had her cell phone in one hand, and a cigarette in the other. She looked so chic. It made me feel as though we were meeting in Europe somewhere. It took all of my will power not to stare a hole through her shirt as I approached the table. She lowered her glasses and gave me one of the most seductive looks that had ever been shot in my direction. I took a seat beside her at the table.

"Where are your pilots?" I asked.

"They're being boring and staying at the hotel. I hate those . . . what do you all call them? Slam clickers? So I'm glad you and Mary decided you'd come, or else this town would be so lame tonight."

Now, I've been on some pretty crazy over nights in the lamest cities, but I know for a fact that even if you're alone, Rochester can be a fun town to go out in. I made small talk over our drinks. "So what do you do for fun on your off days?" I asked.

"I usually just hang around DC, go out with my friends to see bands, smoke a little, go out to bars and stuff . . ." She said raising her cigarette to her lips and inhaling. I was confused for a moment.

"Wait, you mean smoke like . . . get high?" I asked.

"Oh yea, all the time." She said, exhaling in to the air. I didn't say anything else about it, I just assumed that she had quit getting high when she started flying since there was a chance of us getting randomly drug tested.

"That reminds me I have to see Jimmy, I'm almost out." She said. This caused me to raise an eyebrow, but rather than talk about the subject anymore, we went inside and ordered two shots of tequila with limes and salt.

"Let's make a toast. The first night I met Mary, she told me about this philosophy she has on life . . . well, it's not really a philosophy, it's more of just trying to live life like there's no tomorrow . . . So here's to living life like there's no tomorrow!" I toasted.

". . . To wild nights." She said winking at me.

After two more shots of tequila, I was feeling good. I was making her laugh with stories about crazy passengers and overnights and telling her how much I loved my job and what I was doing at the moment, no matter how crappy it could be sometimes.

She looked at her watch "Oh, we should go to the Attic bar, I want to see if Jimmy's around tonight."

"What? Why, we don't need to have more guys than girls with us tonight!" I protested, not even remembering her mentioning this Jimmy fellow earlier.

She smiled "Aw, don't worry baby boy, you're still my number one." She said, giving me a peck on the cheek. This was all convincing I needed to follow her into a dark back alley that I had never been down before and into a shady looking dive bar.

In a room to the right of the entrance of the Attic bar was a dirty pool table in front of the bathrooms. To the left was a flight of stairs leading up to a bar and a deck that overlooked the alley. We went up and ordered some drinks.

"Since you made me drink that tequila at the last bar, it's my turn to pick a shot for us to do here." She said. She ordered us a pair of flaming Dr. Peppers. Now, if you're unsure of what this drink is, it's essentially a shot of amaretto, topped off with Bacardi 151. That shot is then lit on fire, dropped into half a glass of beer, and then chugged furiously. Let me warn you: It tastes exactly like Dr. Pepper, and it can get you drunk *very* quick. The bartender made the shots, lit them on fire, and dropped them into our drinks. Ne-ne downed hers like a champ. Halfway through mine, I choked a little and coughed, but before I could lower my glass,

Ne-ne shot her hand up to the bottom of it, forcing it back to my lips and commanded: "Drink! Drink! Drink! No tomorrow!"

I choked down the last of the drink as Ne-ne took me by the hand and led me to a table outside. I wiped the tears away from my eyes, caused by the shot that had asphyxiated me. I was feeling nice and toasty as I took a seat in the metal chair. She looked around for a moment.

"I didn't see Jimmy here anywhere . . . I'll be right back." She said, and walked inside. By this point the drinks had set in, and I found myself leaning back in the chair, holding a conversation with the stars in the sky above my head.

"Oh, hey stars. Nice evening we're having isn't it? Have you seen Mary up there? She's supposed to be flying in soon-"

Clang!

Ne-ne slammed another half glass of beer, and a shot in front of me.

"Who were you talking to?" She asked.

I said nothing, as a large grin wiped across my face and I pointed to the stars above. I was in la-la land. Ne-ne sat down and pinched my cheek as she took out a lighter, lit the shots, dropped them into the beer and made another toast to something ridiculous. We were flirting like crazy as I alternated between using one hand to hold my beer, and the other hand to keep my balance on the table. Ne-ne started asking me things like: "Do you think I'm cute?"

To which I'd reply with remarks like "If I had a choice between making out with Eva Longoria or you . . . you would be disappointed. With me. Because I'm a terrible kisser."

"Oh, are you? Maybe we should find out." She said leaning in towards me. Her lips fell on to mine, hook line and sinker. And it was at that unfortunate moment that all the tequila, and beer, and Flaming Dr. Peppers decided to make their grand reappearance. I stopped kissing her a moment and stood up. I knew this was not leading anywhere good. Ne-ne apparently thought that I was playing hard to get as she stood up as well, smiling at me. I forced a smile back. I thought that maybe I just needed to stand up to feel better. She pushed me back down into my seat and climbed on top of my lap. She started kissing me again, and as I shut my eyes, I realized it was time to pay the doctors bill. I pushed her off of me and bolted for the balcony like the roof was on fire. I began vomiting violently over the edge and on to the streets of Rochester below as if I were trying to send out a distress signal. For a moment I thought Ne-ne was rushing over to my aid, but I was wrong when she leaned over the side of the rail and immediately began joining me.

As soon as I was mobile again, I wiped my mouth, wrapped her arm over my shoulder and carried her down the stairs to the bathroom. We both went into our separate bathrooms to wash off our faces. I looked like I had been smacked across the face with a two liter bottle of Dr. Pepper. I took a few moments to splash my face with water, shake my head at myself and lie to the mirror stating the same old "I Won't make *that* mistake again."

I walked back upstairs to find Ne-ne at the bar with another beer in her hand. She hugged some long hair hippie and waved in my direction. I approached her, as he passed by, giving me the 'what's up' nod.

"Thanks Jimmy!" She said, waving good bye to him as he left the bar. "Hey, I just got some weed, you want to go back to the hotel and smoke?" She asked.

"What the hell? What are you crazy, you could get drug tested. Are you trying to lose your job?" I asked.

"So what, I could also get hit by a bus tomorrow and be dead. Just like I *could* get drug tested, but I don't give a shit! No tomorrow, remember? Come on, let's go back to the hotel!"

I failed to see the logic behind her reasoning, but I decided to play along with her anyway. Now, don't get me wrong, I had no intention of smoking with this girl. But I had figured that after a fifteen minute walk back to the hotel Mary would be arriving by that time and Ne-ne would forget all about wanting to smoke.

She chugged her beer and I paid our tab as Ne-ne headed for the steps. Just as I turned around, I heard a loud crashing noise. I didn't even have to think twice in order to process what had just happened. I rushed to the top of the stairs to find Ne-ne, lying at the bottom. My mind, as you can imagine, was in a frenzy.

Oh shit.
I killed her.
Now we're not going to hook up for sure!

She suddenly stood up and began laughing. It was one of the most unbelievable things I could have ever seen. I flew down the stairs as fast as I could.

"Ne-ne! Are you alright?!"

"Yea, I'm fine! These things happen all the time!" She said, brushing her shoulders and shrugging off the fact she had just somersaulted down a hundred year old flight of wooden stairs. I wrapped her arm around my shoulder and began making our way back to the hotel. She was having trouble keeping her balance by this point.

"Chuck, I'm so sorry . . . I'm so sorry." She kept repeating.

"It's alright; I think you just need to lie down for the rest of the evening." I said. I had the feeling she certainly wouldn't want to get high by this point.

It was about ten PM when we arrived back at the hotel. When we got in the elevator, I leaned her against the wall and pushed the button for our floor while taking the key out of my pocket.

"Thank you so much for helping me, I'm so sorry . . ." She kept repeating.

"It's alright, really." I said. I had no idea why she was apologizing. I opened the door to the room and carried her to the bed. I laid her on top of the comforter and took off her shoes.

"Let's go smoke . . ." She suggested, sitting up suddenly.

"No, I think you need to lie down and sleep." I said, turning off the light.

"Yea, I think you're right . . . can you at least come lay with me." She said, crawling toward the edge of the bed.

"How can you sleep when you're moving towards the edge of the bed like that?" I asked.

"Because . . . I said I want to lie down. Not sleep." She replied, seductively unbuttoning the top two buttons of her shirt. She grabbed me by my black hoodie and threw me down on the bed. She climbed on top of me and began kissing me again. She tasted like vomit and bad decisions. I didn't care though. She tore open the rest of her shirt, pelting me in the face with one of her buttons. I nearly lost it. I flipped her over on her back and began kissing her like the rapture was coming. Just as her hands were reaching for my belt, the door opened up, and in came Mary. Ne-ne pushed me off of her and tried closing her shirt over her white lace bra. I sat up and kind of waved at Mary who was dragging her suitcase into the room behind her.

"Mary . . . you made the flight I see." I said, clearing my throat. I wondered if she had seen anything in the dark. She stopped in her tracks, took one look at us, and smiled. It didn't take a genius to figure out what was going on here.

"Yea, I just got in . . . I was just going to drop off my bags and head downstairs to the hotel bar. You guys can join me . . . if you're not too busy." She said with the biggest grin on her face. She saw something.

"I think I'm going to stay here . . ." Ne-ne said, casually running her fingers through her hair. Mary smiled at us and left the room.

"Wait here." I said to Ne-ne. I met Mary in the hall, waiting for the elevator.

"Well, I see you two are getting along well." Mary said smiling.

"That wasn't what it looked like . . ." I'm not exactly sure why I said that. It was exactly what it looked like.

Mary laughed. "It looked like you were about to get laid . . . . It's fine! Go! I wouldn't want you blocking me. Do I have to remind you of my life's philosophy?"

"Yea, yea, I know. The 'no tomorrow' thing." I said, raising my hands.

"I'm just going down to the hotel bar to have a few drinks. I'll be back in an hour or so. You two have fun, and I'll make sure to knock next time." She said laughing as she got into the elevator.

I returned to the room. Ne-ne wasn't in bed. I looked in the bathroom to see if she was puking again. She was nowhere to be found. I wondered if she had imploded on herself. I suddenly noticed the long curtains lightly blowing in the evening breeze. I pushed them aside to find Ne-ne standing out on the balcony. And I knew exactly why she was there. I stepped outside to a smell that I hadn't recognized since my college days, and stood beside her. Sure enough, she was lit and smoking up. She only had the top two buttons of her shirt done. I took off my hoodie and wrapped it around her.

"This was one of my favorite shirts . . ." She laughed. "Was Mary upset?" She asked.

"No. Her and I are just friends." I said. "So . . . you're getting high, huh?" I asked after a minute.

"I don't see what the big deal is. I'm not getting high and then getting on the plane, am I? This is just my way of winding down." She said. I had no response. She handed it to me. I grinned and took it nervously. It probably sounds stupid, but I guess it was the peer pressure that made me take it from her. I really didn't want to be in that position. I had probably smoked three times in my life, in college, and they were all horrible experiences. I was trembling, about to raise it to my lips, when suddenly I stopped.

It was almost like I had just had an epiphany.

What the hell am I doing? Ne-ne may not care about her job, but I do. I like my job. Shit, I realized at that moment that I loved my job. This wasn't worth losing it over. I had no intention of leaving anytime soon. If UPside Air was a sinking ship, I planned on staying aboard until I either went down with them, or jumped overboard of my own decision. But I didn't want to do anything that would cause me to get thrown overboard at the time.

The decision was made. I handed it back to Ne-ne.

"No thanks . . ." I said. "I think I'll stick to being a bad flight attendant for now . . . just not bad enough to lose my job."

Seat back pocket

November 13th 2011

Sometimes,
when there's nothing else
to do on the plane,
I like to stand
at the front of my galley
with a cup of coffee
and eaves drop
on passengers conversations.

I'm carefully attentive
to each person
sitting in their own seat,
next to another stranger,
thinking whatever random shit
goes through their own little minds.

Most of them
have never met before
and will probably
never meet again.

It's the oddest thing to think
that just for about an hour or two,
fifty strangers
are all facing the same direction,
blasting through the air
in a thin metal tube,
at the exact same time-
but I digress.

Watching strangers
who have never met each other before
interacting for the first time
gives me a little entertainment
in an otherwise boring,
normal day.
It's almost like getting
my own personal short film
on every flight,
and it's always
something different.

Watching a business man
talking to a high school student . . . .
Watching military personnel
converse with an elderly woman . . .

People don't always want
to have a conversation
with the person
they're forced to sit next to,
but sometimes there's no choice.

They talk to one another out of courtesy.
They talk to one another because they're bored.
But in my mind,
I really like to think
that they're talking to each other
about their own different lives
just for me
and my twisted amusement.

I listen to them come up
with the most random
conversations,
stories,
lies . . .
what does it matter?

They're never going
to see each other again.
And I'm the only one
that gets to witness
this short, unedited interaction
that goes on
between two complete strangers.

This little hobby of mine
(although by now
it's become
more of an obsession.)
started a couple of months back.

On the sixth and final leg
of a long day of flying,
all that was left was to go
from Norfolk to DC
and I would be done with my trip.

I made myself
one last cup of coffee
and went through
my whole safety dance
before taking my jump seat.

There was a couple on the plane
sitting in the front row:
seats 1A and 1C.
They had to have
been in their late twenties.

I had been in and out
of my jump seat all day,
going back and forth
on our short turns
from DCA-PHL.
PHL-DCA.

DCA-ORF . . .
I had a terrible headache,
and by this point in the afternoon,
I wasn't feeling very sociable.

Instead, I had been watching
all the passengers
that had cycled in and out
of those particular seats
throughout the day.
1A and 1C.
Some boring,
some interesting . . .
but this couple
took the award
for the most entertaining.

As I sat in my seat
sipping coffee my coffee,
I watched the two of them,
while intently listening in
on their conversation:

". . . So why won't you just tell me
what Jonathan said then?"
Asked the man.

"Because it's none of your business."
Replied the woman.

"I don't care. After everything
that's happened . . .
after you left New York-"

"See, I knew you would bring that up
again. That was a year ago."

"Did you just think
that would be something
I was just going to drop?"
Asked the man.

They were trying to keep quiet.
Oh, this was getting good.
I couldn't wait to see where
this would head next.
The woman ignored the man,
as she reached in
to the seat back pocket
for our inflight magazine.

If only I had been quicker,
or able to warn her ahead of time
what it was that she would find,
when plunging her hand into that
unknown pouch,
hanging on the bulk head wall
in front of her seat.

But I didn't stop her.
I sat there and watched
for my own amusement.
And that
was the defining moment
of what made this little side show
that I loved watching
flight after flight so worth it.

It was the moment
when two different stories
from two different flights
crossed paths,
intersecting with each other.

Her eyes widened
and a look of horror and disgust
washed across her face.

The man that she was with
saw the look
before she could react.
"What is it?"
he asked.

She began to shriek,
catching the attention
of the entire plane
and for a brief moment
before I had to get up
from my comfortable seat
and attend to her,
I smiled to myself.

Five flights worth
of passengers
had been in and out
of that seat throughout
the course of an entire day.
Five flights worth
of passengers
before this couple
had passed through
that I heard say things.
Watch do things
when they thought
no one was paying attention.
When they thought
no one was watching.
But I was.

Only I knew the stories
of the five flights worth
of passengers
that had occupied those two seats
before that couple did.

And only I knew
what it was
that was in that seat back pocket.

The story I swore I would never write

September 15th 2011

I can't exactly say
I'm proud of every decision
I've made over the course
of my time at UPside Air.

This story was particularly
hard to write about,
but I've recently
decided to include it.
It was mid-September, three months
before my book went live
when I met Jazzy.

I had just flown back into Baltimore
after another meeting
with my publishers
since it was closer to where I was
living at the time than DC was.

Jazzy was a gate agent for
STRATA Airlines, and had seen me
in my uniform the few times
I flew out to Indiana.
I had been using my flight benefits
to get back and forth
which meant I had to fly around
in my uniform,
so she knew
I was a flight attendant.

I made her laugh
when I read her name tag
and asked if that was her stripper name.
I didn't believe it was real.
She told me it was short for Jasmine
and asked if I was a commuter.
I told her why I was going to Indie
and about my book
and all the meetings
I had to have with my publishers
and what not.

I was so excited at the time about
having a book come out,
about doing something artistic
that I thought
would make me famous,
that I told everyone about it
with a pair of ears
with the exception of Mikey.

I wasn't all that attracted to Jazzy,
but I exchanged numbers with her
just for the hell of it
when she asked me
if I wanted to get together
for drinks sometime.

She texted me all throughout
my next four day trip constantly,
so I could tell
that she kind of liked me.

Toward the end of the trip
on Friday afternoon,
Corazon texted me
to tell me
that she'd be going
to the Irish pub outside of DCA
with some of our other coworkers.

I of course agreed to join,
having still been
in love with her
at the time.

As the evening drew closer,
I got a call from Corazon.
She told me that she didn't
think it would be
such a good idea
for me to come out
since her husband would be there.

I argued with her back and forth
for a bit, but in the end
she really thought
it would be for the best
if I didn't come with them.

I was pissed to say the least.
So what did I do?
Did I just call it a night
and end it there?
That would have been
the sane thing to do.
So I of course
did the complete opposite.

I called up Jazzy
and told her
that I wanted to take her out that night.
Of course she agreed,
but was a bit confused
when I suggested
that we go out in DC
rather than Baltimore,
which was much closer.

I told her
that I liked the night life
in DC better,
which was a total lie,
considering my theory
that every city is really the same
once you're drunk in it.

I can't justify my actions.
I came up with a plan
for Corazon to see me
out with Jazzy
and try to make her jealous.
It was immature, I'll admit,
but at the time
I was too blinded by my feelings
to make rational decisions.

We went to the Irish pub outside of DCA
and ordered some drinks at the bar.
I pretended to listen to her
talk about being a gate agent
while pounding down
my tequila and tonic water
as I combed the room
with my eyes for Corazon.

After a few moments
of searching through
the crowded room,
I spotted her over Jazzy's shoulder.
She was sitting at a table full of martini glasses
near the corner of the room
with her husband
and some other people I didn't recognize.

My heart started pounding
and I started sweating.
I kept trying
to pretend to be focused
on what Jazzy was saying
while looking past her.

When I saw Corazon stand up,
I grabbed Jazzy
as she was in mid-sentence
and kissed her.
My eyes opened to find
Corazon gone.

I sat there disappointed,
realizing that she must have left
without having seeing me
with my date for the night.

Jazzy was smiling,
despite the fact
that I clearly wasn't.
I ordered another
tequila and tonic
and excused myself
to the bathroom.

I took my drink
and locked the door
to the tiny one toilet bathroom
behind me.
I downed the last of it
and splashed my face
with cold water from the sink
as I sighed,
staring in the mirror.

I began arguing with myself.
What the hell was I doing?
I had to quit chasing
after this married woman
whom I had somehow
convinced myself
that I was going to wind up with.

I opened the bathroom door
to find Jazzy,
standing in front of me
with the same look on her face
that the lonely housewife
gets before pummeling
the cable man in porn.

She pushed me
back into the bathroom
and against the wall,
locking the door behind her.
I was startled as she began kissing me.

Images of Corazon
began flashing through my mind.
I had been drinking,
and I had been heart broken,
and at that point I couldn't care less.
I felt like
I was taking revenge on Corazon,
even if she'd have never known
what happened that night.

My right hand slid
down to her waist,
pulling her closer towards me.
She turned around
placing one hand
against the dirty wall of the bathroom,
hiking up her black dress with the other.
I pushed into her from behind
covering her mouth
when she let out a yelp.

I didn't make love to her.
I didn't have sex with her.
I used her.

I should have just cut my ties
with Jazzy that night,
but apparently
sex in the dirty bathroom of a bar
was some kind of indication
that we were together now.

This became
an unhealthy situation
that carried on
for the next month:

Corazon would get
into a heavy argument with her husband
and call me crying about it afterward,
because I was her only true friend
that she had.
I would get upset
that she wouldn't take my advice
that she deserved
to be treated better;
secretly hoping
that she'd leave him for me.

This would lead to me
immediately calling up Jazzy
and having sex with her
as a way of taking out my aggression
over the fact
that there was nothing I could do
about the situation.
I was miserable over the fact
that she was miserable,
trying to make her marriage work
for the sake of her kid.

The worst part is that every time
I would hook up with Jazzy,
it was Corazon
that was always on my mind.

It was a Wednesday night
in mid-October
when I got a call from Corazon.
Through all of her tears,
she told me
that she had left her husband
for good
after he had laid his hands on her.

She took her daughter
and went back
to her mother's house
in northern Virginia,
and that was the end of that.

I asked her
if there was anything I could do for her,
but she said
that she had already contacted the police
and that she felt safe now.

She apologized
for not having listened to me sooner
and asked
if I would meet her
to talk the next day.

After hanging up,
I felt terrible.
Somehow in my twisted mind
I was really happy
that she was no longer
together with him,
but at the same time,
I wished
it had been
under different circumstances.

I was supposed to pick up Jazzy
from the airport
after she got off work
since her car was in the shop.
I decided
that would be the night
that I would end it.

She was smiling,
and kissed me
when she got into my car.
I felt awful
for what I was about to do,
but before I could say anything,
she said that she had something
to tell me.

She told me
that she wanted to transfer
out of Baltimore
to work as a gate agent in DC
so that she could see me
more often.
I felt even worse,
but she said there was something else
that I needed to know as well.

She told me that she was already
in a relationship with someone else
and had been for nearly a year now.
She told me how unhappy she was
and that the night I took her out,
her only intention was to use me
because she had caught him
cheating on her before.

But as time went on,
and the more time
we spent together,
she came to realize
that she really was
developing feelings for me.

I was shocked.
Pale as a ghost.
This was my chance
to tell her about Corazon.
This was the opportunity I needed
to come clean
about the fact
that I had been using her also.

Instead
I freaked out.

I began yelling at her,
asking how the hell
she could do this to me.

The worst part is,
I had been using her as well,
and yet somehow
I felt as though I was the one
that had been betrayed.
She did that comforting thing,
by placing her hand on my arm.
I continued shouting at her,
calling her a slut,
and told her to get out of my car.
I really let her have it,
when ultimately it should have been
the other way around.

Looking back on the situation now
I handled it pretty bad.
I had a really nice,
cute girl, who genuinely liked me.
I had the chance to start
a real relationship
rather than continuing to chase
after someone that I couldn't have.

Instead, I was so enamored
with Corazon
that I had convinced myself
that if I couldn't have her,
then I didn't want anyone at all.

I didn't speak to Jazzy again
for a long time
after I drove away from her
that day.
I ignored all her calls,
and needless to say,
she didn't transfer to DCA.

>>>>>>>>>>>>>>>>>>>>>>>>
It was almost a year later
when I called her
and asked her out to lunch.
I finally explained
everything to her
that had really happened
and apologized for acting
the way that I did.

I think that I treated her
the way I did
because it was myself
that I was really upset with.

She had dumped the guy
that she had been dating
and was seeing someone new
that she was
really happy with.

We haven't spoken much since then
which is alright,
because ultimately,
I think that I really wanted her
to forgive me
for what I did
so that I could forgive myself.

24 hours to Ft. Lauderdale

September 20th 2011

12:00PM-
I awake to a text message from Treetops. He tells me that he just jump seated into DCA and wants to party. I tell him it's too early to party. He tells me it's 5 PM Zulu time, therefore, he wins this argument. Stupid pilot time.

12:15-
I get out of bed and begin to get ready.

1:00 PM-
I head towards DC.

1:47-
I meet Treetops outside of the passenger pick up zone. He throws his suitcase into my trunk. He is still in his uniform. I tell him he needs to change. He takes off his wings. This does not mean he's changed; now it just means he can drink.

1:55-
I drive back up to the passenger drop off so that he can change inside.

2:17-
Treetops comes back in normal clothes. I decide to take him to the Irish pub outside of DCA, being the new hotspot for crew members.

2:26-
I park my car in the employee lot for two reasons. One is because it's free parking in DC. The other is because if I get too drunk, I won't have to worry about leaving my car in some random garage overnight and returning to find it with a huge fine, a boot on the wheel, or worse.

2:38-
We are walking to the Irish pub outside of DCA. I tell Treetops that I have a trip at 6:30 AM the following morning, so I won't be drinking past 8:30 PM. He tells me this just means we're going to have to drink harder and earlier.

3:03-
We arrive in the Irish pub outside of DCA. Treetops immediately orders us some beers. I tell him no Jaeger bombs after our fiasco in Milwaukee. He laughs as we try and recall stories about that night and Chalupa girl.

3:20-
Second beer.

3:37-
Third beer.

3:56-
I can quickly see where this is heading. I decide to slow down.

4:02-
fourth beer.

4:15-
I get up to break the seal. Treetops calls me a wuss for not being able to hold my alcohol. Well, maybe if I was seven feet tall, it would take me a decade to pass alcohol through my system also.

4:18-
Kylie calls me as I am going to the bathroom. She tells me her trip ends in DC at 5:30, and she wants to do something tonight. I tell her Treetops is with me and we'd be happy to do something. She asks me if I am in a bathroom. I say no and then flush the toilet.

4:21-
I tell Treetops Kylie will be finished with her trip in about an hour and wants to hang out. He wants to go to the airport immediately to meet

her. I tell him we still have plenty of time, but he wants to get a head start.

4:32-
We pay our tab and leave the Irish pub outside of DCA. We make our way back to the airport again, only now we are tipsy.

4:55-
We arrive back in the airport, only this time, neither of us are in uniform. We feel strangely naked. I tell Treetops we shouldn't have left so early.

5:03-
We go to the bar inside the airport that Mary and I always go to before traveling on our days off and order shots. Treetops tells me he's flying with B-Rye tomorrow afternoon. I tell him about my wheel chair races that we had. He loves a good airport delay story.

5:10-
Treetops now wants to race wheelchairs. Everything seems like a good idea after we've been drinking.

5:13-
We go to the section of the airport where ten million wheel chairs are kept for the handicapped. We take two.

5:15-
We begin racing our wheel chairs through the airport. We figure since we are not in uniform, we can't get in trouble.

5:19-
We slow down when we pass our chief pilot, Captain Friendly. He does a double take, trying to figure out if he knows us from somewhere, and then begins clapping his hands together and laughing to himself. I always liked that guy.

5:21-
Airport security tells us to get out of the wheel chairs or we'll be escorted of the premises. Treetops gets out of his chair and limps away mumbling that he fought for our country in World war one and this is an outrage.

5:28-
We wait for Kylie outside of security.

5:43-
Treetops is getting impatient waiting and suggests we get more to drink. I tell him I don't think that would be a good idea at the moment.

5:51-
Kylie comes through security with two old pilots. We give her huge hugs, spinning her around and making a scene. She asks if we have been drinking. We both lie and then laugh.

6:00-
She goes to get changed in the airport bathroom.

6:04-
Treetops wonders aloud whether or not Kylie looks good with her clothes off. I chuckle to myself.

6:11-
Kylie comes back out ready to party. I tell her I only have until 8:30 before my cut off time since I have a trip in the morning.

6:17-
The three of us catch the bus to the employee parking lot.

6:30-
Since Treetops and I have already been drinking, we decide to take Kylie's car. I call shotgun. Treetops mumbles how he is a war hero that fought for our country in World war one and that this is an outrage. I laugh when his knees go practically above his head in the backseat.

6:42-
Kylie drives through the streets of Washington DC like a lunatic. It takes all of my will power not to vomit, although looking back on it now; I owe her one for the first night we hung out in Toronto.

6:48-
We arrive at one of Kylie's favorite bars, The hipster bar. A bunch of artistic people are being original by dressing accordingly to the latest fashion in Europe. I'm waiting for a poetry reading to break out. I hate the bar and everyone in it. I point these observations out to Treetops who points and laughs as he orders the three of us beers.

7:14-
Treetops and Kylie are drinking much more furiously than I am so that Kylie can catch up. I decide it's time to slow down, since I have to stop drinking in forty-five minutes. Treetops calls me a wuss again and tells me to chug. That does not work on me this time, as I am beginning to sober up.

7:55-
I finish my beer as Treetops and Kylie continue their epic drinking battle against one another.

8:00-
A semi-decent cover band begins playing Primus covers. I spend the rest of the evening judgingly watching the band play while trying to flush the alcohol out of my system by drinking as much water as possible. Kylie and Treetops continue their new drinking game, which seems to only have one rule: drink until you win.

11:02-
We leave hipster bar and walk to Kylies car. Kylie and Treetops stumble about, laughing at the fact that Treetops has only recently turned twenty one, yet has drank on many overnights prior to that.

11:07-
I take Kylies keys from her. She wants to continue the party at her house. I have no problem with this, other than the fact that I can't continue to drink. And I have to be at the airport at 5:15 in the morning to work. And I live forty-five minutes away. Kylie tells me to stop bitching or she'll report me to Mikey for God only knows what. Treetops points and laughs at me.

11:17-
I am driving Kylies car through the streets of DC. Kylie is in the front seat squinting her eyes at every street sign we pass. Treetops is in the back seat, nodding his head that eventually passes out on the window.

11:27-
Kylie realizes we made a wrong turn.

11:36-
Kylie has me make another wrong turn.

11:44-
Kylie is unfamiliar with the residential area we are driving through and is not even sure if we are on the right street, right city, right state, or right country.

11:45-
Kylie tells me to stop the car. I'm afraid she is going to puke her guts out. She tells me we are in front of her house. Treetops springs to life, bumping his head on the ceiling.

11:47-
We are in the living room of Kylie's small, two bedroom town house. She has a giant flat screen plasma television. She tells us excitedly that in fifty two more monthly payments it'll be hers!

11:52-
Treetops and I take a seat on her couch as Kylie grabs three beers from her fridge. I remind her that I can't drink anymore because I have to be at

work in about five hours. She tells me that the other beer is for Treetops. Treetops cheers at this fact.

12:02 AM-
Kylie turns on her television to an alternative music channel. I slump back onto her couch.

12:15-
I'm getting bored and tired of watching the two of them drink.

12:27-
I'm beginning to get sleepy, as I check my watch and realize I am *not* going to have
a pleasant day at work when the sun comes up.

12:49-
Treetops gets up to use the bathroom. I can tell it must be urgent by how quickly he leaves the room.

12:50-
Kylie can see that I'm obviously bored and tired and asks if I'm having a good time.
I reply that I am, although that's a total lie. Kylie stands up and walks towards me sexily, wiggling her hips as she moves. She sits on my lap facing me and asks
"Are you sure you're not having a good time yet?"
in a very seductive voice. I'm awake now. She leaps off of me when she hears Treetops' monstrous footsteps coming back down the stairs and into the living room again.

(I have never told him this part of the story, and can't wait until he reads this. Thanks, Jolly green giant.)

1:08-
I am getting drowsy again. I set the alarm on my phone for 4:30 AM just in case I fall asleep.

1:16-
I fall asleep.

4:30-
The alarm on my phone startles me awake. I feel worse than I did before closing my eyes. Kylie is lying face down on the couch opposite to me. Treetops is sprawled out on the floor, with a blanket barely covering his torso, and a beer close by. I shake the both of them awake and tell them I have to get to the airport. They take their time getting up.

4:39-
We all climb back into Kylie's car. She says she is alright to drive, despite the fact that she looks like hell.

4:52-
We arrive in the employee parking lot of the airport. I'm dropped off at my car and pull my uniform and suitcase out of my trunk. It's because of situations like this that I'm always prepared.

5:09-
I arrive in the UPside Air crew room. John is asleep on the couch. That guy always spends the night in our crew room. I throw on my uniform in the bathroom next to the crew room and re-emerge to find John waking up to catch his flight to commute home. He laughs when he sees me and feels obliged to tell me:
"You know; Chuck Norris doesn't sleep. He waits."

5:14-
I etch my name into the sign in book to see that I'm flying with The King and Jess (See: 24 hours in Ft. Lauderdale.) I am excited to have a good crew, and upset that I am beyond exhausted. It's easier to tell myself that this is everyone's fault but mine. I make my way out to the plane.

5:24-
I arrive at the plane. The King and Jess are happy to see me since this is the first time I've seen either of them since our last adventure together in Ft. Lauderdale. I tell them not to expect too much out of me and recall

the events of the previous night. They laugh and say as long as I keep a pot of coffee going, they'll be happy. I tell them I'm already on it.

5:26-
I do my security checks on the airplane.

5:42-
The bus of passengers arrives at the plane. I give the thumbs down not to board the flight.

5:45-
I finish my security checks and pour myself a cup of coffee.

5:46-
I take a deep breath and then give the thumbs up to the bus to board the flight. About thirty seven passengers board. Two are hot Florida chicks, and yet, I am too exhausted to even pretend to flirt with them.

5:54-
I give my pilots my passenger count, close the door, and do my safety demo. I'm not sure if people are laughing at my jokes because they're funny, or because I'm saying them as if I'm about to pass out from exhaustion. Probably both.

6:03-
Our flight takes off. I am struggling to stay awake.

6:25-
I do a brief service because everyone is sleeping. Everyone but me. It makes me jealous.

6:42-
I am pacing up and down the aisle of the plane to stay awake.

6:49-
I call the flight deck. The king asks how I'm doing. I tell him everyone is sleeping. Everyone but me. And it sucks. He laughs, although I don't find

it funny. He says there's only about an hour left of flight time and I groan in agony.

7:50-
The plane lands in Orlando. Everyone deplanes.

8:14-
I curl up in the back of the plane and shut my eyes while The king and Jess go inside the airport for breakfast. Everything goes black.

9:30-
I am pulled from a deep sleep when The king tells me over the PA passengers are going to be boarding in a few moments. That short nap was just what I needed, although I am still pretty tired. A few passengers laugh at the sleep lines on my face. I just shrug my shoulders.

9:50-
I do my demo, make everyone laugh and take my jump seat. It's only a forty five minute flight, but it's always the most relaxing one from Orlando to Key West to Ft. Lauderdale, as my passengers are nothing but old people, Jimmy Buffett fans and alcoholic chicks from the south.

10:32-
We land and deplane in Key West.

10:42-
I am literally slapping myself in the face to stay awake. I just have one last leg to go. I want to die.

11:10-
We take off for Ft. Lauderdale. The King promises me that he's flying the plane as fast as possibly allowed, although I'm so tired, it feels as though the plane's moving in reverse.

11:42-
We land in Ft. Lauderdale. Every passenger that deplanes tells me to get some sleep.

That was the first and last time I ever worked a flight after pulling an all-niter. Once we got to the hotel I crashed hard and slept through the whole over-night, missing out on one of the best places we got to fly to. This means not only did I sleep away one of our best over nights, but I also missed getting to see Jess in a bathing suit drinking beers on the beach by our hotel. I should probably plan ahead more carefully when I know I have a flight to Florida.

A chapter from my soon to be published, not yet titled action novel!

Chapter 23:
A struggle in the sky! There can be only one winner.

Ka-churn!

Went the sound of the aircraft, as it shook violently, launching Chuck from the floor of the cargo bay to the ceiling. He smacked his head as it happened, landing face first back on the floor. He picked himself back up, wiping the blood from his forehead, blindly feeling around in the dark for his walkie-talkie. He grabbed it, and radioed back up to the flight deck above.

"ElHeffey! What the hell is going on up there?! Over."

ElHeffey picked up the radio and chimed back: "I don't got a lot of time to talk right now, kid! We're flying through some kind of electrical storm that I aint never seen before! The instruments are all going hay wire! We're getting tossed around worse than an oiled up lamp at a German flea market!" He tossed the walkie aside and turned to Lizzie. "Liz-doll! Have you finished hacking into the terrorists main computer network yet?!"

Lizzie sat beside him in her FO seat, pounding away feverishly on the keyboard of her super computer. "Not yet, Heff! They're using some kind of binary reverse code, the likes of which I've never seen before! I need ten more minutes!"

"Dammit Lizzie, we don't have ten more minutes! I'll give you nine and a half more, but after that, we're gonna be spinnin' outta control faster than a dradel at a government Kwanza party!" He picked back up the walkie. "Chuck! Did you find the wired box yet? Over."

Indeed he had, at that moment, through the darkness, and over the mountains of tossed suitcases, he had stumbled upon the electrical panel he was searching for that he had stowed away in the aircraft cargo to access at this precise moment. He pried it open, only to be left with a shocked look of disbelief on his handsome face.

"ElHeffey, I've got a problem . . . over." He said into his walkie

"You think you got a problem? Lizzie's got seven minutes left to hack into the terrorists network, and I'm sweating like a camel in Alaska wrapped in thirty seven mink coats! Just cut the red wire and retrieve 'HoneyPot'! Over."

"That's the problem . . ." Chuck replied, wiping the blood and sweat from his masculine brow. ". . . They're all red wires!!! Over."

Meanwhile, in the cabin of flight 939, chaos ensued. Passengers were running up and down the aisles, screaming at the horror they were in the middle of. Corazon stayed quietly hidden in the last row of seats alongside Mary. The two of them peered over the seats cautiously.

"Do you think that's him? Could that be the leader?" Mary asked, looking back at Corazon.

"It's hard to tell . . . he certainly is the largest of the others. I'm going to charge him, while you make a diversion." Corazon replied.

"Charge him? Are you crazy?" Mary asked.

"I took an oath to protect my passengers, no matter what!" Corazon explained.

"Alright . . . I'm with you. But what kind of diversion did you have in mind?" Asked Mary. Corazon held up a two liter bottle of soda and a packet of pop-rocks.

"On my word, you're going to mix the two together. And when you do . . . it'll be crazier than the Halloween of 2010."

"You're absolutely insane . . ." Said Mary "But you're also the bravest flight attendant I've ever known. Let's go!"

Back in the flight deck, Lizzie continued to punch away feverishly on her keyboard as ElHeffey tried his best to maintain the air crafts flight pattern through the electrical storm.

"Dammit, Liz-doll you got five minutes left, you better start working faster than a taxi driver in a herd of buffalo!"

"I just need more time!" She replied, frustrated.

"We don't have any time! Chuck! You need to cut the wire, NOW! Over." ElHeffey shouted into the walkie.

Chuck was standing in front of the electrical panel holding the red wires in his hand, faced with the decision that would either save them, or doom them all. "Red wire or red wire . . . red wire or red wire . . ." He mumbled repeatedly. "I got it! The *red* wire!" He exclaimed, yanking the red wire out. There was a sigh of relief, as the safe attached to the electrical panel unlocked, opening up. Oh, did I mention there was a safe attached to the electrical panel? Because there was. Chuck let out a sigh of relief as he radioed back up to ElHeffey "ElHeffey! I did it, I've retrieved 'HoneyPot' from the cargo! Over."

"Not a moment too soon, kid! Liz-doll just cracked the reverse binary code at the last second. We're gonna be safer than a hamburger at a sushi joint! Over."

"Not safe yet . . ." Chuck said aloud, lowering his walkie-talkie. He began wondering how he would save his passengers now that he had what the terrorists wanted in his possession. He began rummaging through suitcases looking for anything that would help him, when suddenly he spotted exactly what he needed.

Within moments, Chuck punched through the ceiling of the cargo hold, emerging in the middle of the aisle of flight 939, and to an aircraft of startled passengers.

"Fear not, over paying frequent flyers! I have arrived." He announced.

Just then, Mary sprang up from behind the last row of seats "Chuck, watch out! It's a trap!" Before he could react, Benjamin the brown bear emerged from behind the galley with Corazon in his paws.

"Benjamin the brown bear . . . I should have known it was you all along."

"Did you really think the New York City zoo could contain me?! You're too late, stewardess! Now hand over 'HoneyPot slowly, or the girl gets mauled!" He snarled.

"Don't do it!" Corazon pleaded.

"I don't have a choice . . . you just have to trust me." Chuck replied, tossing HoneyPot to Benjamin the brown bear. He released Corazon, catching HoneyPot, as Corazon rushed over to Chuck.

"Chuck . . . what have you done?" She asked.

"Precisely what I intended to do . . . outsmart the bears." He replied.

As Benjamin the brown bear reached into HoneyPot, he suddenly let out a howl. He pulled his paw out, revealing a large steel bear trap clamped down tightly at the end of it. "Oh no! My only weakness! A bear trap hidden in HoneyPot! I should have known!" He howled tossing HoneyPot into the air, flailing his paws wildly.

Chuck leaped forward, catching HoneyPot in the nick of time before it shattered on the floor. Then, with his mighty right leg, Chuck kicked the door to the aircraft open. The pressure of the altitude sucked Benjamin the brown bear out along with all of his other bear lackeys. Then, with his even mightier right arm, Chuck shut the door to the aircraft before any innocent victims were pulled out.

All of the passengers applauded as Corazon threw her arms around Chuck and announced "My hero!"

"All in a days work!" He replied.

Chuck called up to the flight deck. "ElHeffey! HoneyPot has been retrieved! The day is saved."

"I wouldn't celebrate just yet, kid! The landing gear is stuck, and we got a flock of angry pterodactyls on our tail! We're in hotter water than a mummy in a witches cauldron!"

Chuck hung up the phone with a worried look on his face.

"What's wrong?" Asked Mary.

"We're not out of the woods yet . . . Corazon, grab me fifty rolls of toilet paper from the supply cabinet! Mary, I'm gonna need all the seat belt extenders on the aircraft! . . . We're going pterodactyl hunting . . ."

The last Thanksgiving I ever worked

November 17th 2011

There wasn't anything
particularly special
about my last trip at UPside Air.
It was just like any other trip.

I remember arriving
in Fayetteville, North Carolina
with my pilots early in the afternoon.
It was Thanksgiving Day
and the flight was relatively empty.
Everyone was already
where they wanted to be
for the holiday.

I can't even remember
who the last two pilots
I flew with were.

I do however remember
that whether they were
slam clickers or not,
none of us wanted
to be alone on Thanksgiving Day
and decided to get together
for dinner.

I remember there was
nothing special about our hotel;
it was in a business district,
surrounded by other hotels
and gas stations,
some business offices,
and a few restaurant chains
not worth mentioning
even if I could remember
them all.

I remember meeting them
in the lobby
at around five in the evening
and deciding to go
to Cracker barrel
for our big Thanksgiving meal.

We stopped at a gas station
on the way to buy
twelve bottles of cheap beer.
The plan was to sit outside
and drink the beers before dinner.
Or maybe after dinner.
I can't remember
that particular detail.

I can, however, remember
that when we sat
in those rocking chairs
beside a giant barrel
that had been fashioned
into a checker board,
we realized we had no means
of opening the bottles.

I remember making
a ten dollar bet with the captain
that I could find a way
to open the bottles within ten minutes.

I remember taking the twelve pack
and running
as fast as my legs could carry me
all the way back to the hotel
to ask the receptionist
for a bottle opener,
and telling her
that it was an emergency.
I must have looked crazy.

I remember returning victorious
to my ten dollar bill
and three well-earned cold beers.
I remember sitting
in those rocking chairs
outside the restaurant
drinking beers
and playing checkers
with the pilots
as the sun
slowly drowned in the trees.

I remember the FO
telling me he was a fan
of my website
and had heard that I was
getting ready to publish those stories.
He told me his favorite story
was "Chuck Norris and my first enemy".
He asked if our Thanksgiving together
would become a story.
I laughed and told him no,
because it honestly

wasn't all that memorable
and that not every trip I flew
ended in some kind of
crazy story worth writing about.

I wish so bad
that I could remember who
that pilot was
and tell him
that last trip of mine
became a story after all.
I wish I had been
in a favorite city of mine.

I wish I had flown with pilots
that I always had
great times with
on that last trip.
I wish that my other
flight attendant friends
had jump seated
out to meet me
and that we had one last
crazy overnight together.

I wish I had known
that it would be my last trip
at UPside Air
and that I had done something
special on it.
But I didn't know.

There wasn't anything
particularly special
about my last trip
at UPside air.
It was just like any other trip.

Another Halloween for the record

October 31st 2011

I don't know what it is about my Halloweens in the airline industry. It could just be my bad luck, or it could just be that the crazies only come out on this particular night, but I digress . . .

It was the last flight of the trip and it happened to be on Halloween night. It was a flight from New York's LaGuardia to DCA that departed at around ten at night. Passengers walked down the stairs of the jet bridge, on to the tarmac, and back up the stairs onto our plane. And my first interaction with every passenger that boarded the flight went a little something like this:

Chuck: And what are you supposed to be for Halloween?

Un-memorable passenger: . . . I didn't dress up this year. (As if I hadn't noticed).

Chuck: And what are you supposed to be for Halloween?

Family man with wife and baby: (Kind of laughs. But more of a pity laugh.)

Chuck: And what are you supposed to be for Halloween?

Creepy looking guy: Huh? What?

Chuck: . . . And what are you supposed to be for Halloween?

Creepy looking guy: (Makes an indiscernible grunting noise before shuffling down the aisle to his seat.)

Chuck: And what are you supposed to be for Halloween?

Business Robot: I was supposed to be home four hours ago, but your . . . damn airline screwed up my booking! (He must have been grumpy smurf that year.)

Despite my barrage of uninteresting passengers that didn't find my witty banter amusing, I still maintained a smile on my face, knowing that I would be meeting a recently single Corazon that night for drinks after the flight. We were five minutes from closing the door, when the last two passengers arrived. The first was a short, over-weight girl that looked like she was on her way back to her trailer park for a quiet evening of Mountain dew and Nascar races. The woman behind her could not have been more completely opposite. She was a tall Asian with blonde highlights in her hair. She wore a pair of black stiletto heels, and her short, tight white dress left nothing to the imagination, including her obviously large, fake breasts.

Chuck: . . . And what are you supposed to be for Halloween?

Stripperella: Oh I can be anything you want me to be, handsome. *Anything.* (She repeats this seductively quiet, while licking her lips.)

I immediately felt all of the blood in my body rush to my beet red face, amongst other places. Trailer park girl turned around halfway down the aisle and demanded: "Gianna! Come on!" The Asian woman made her way to her seat beside her mismatched friend, causing every head on the plane to follow her as she went.

I wrote down what part of the air craft the seven passengers and one lap child were sitting in, and delivered it to my pilots in the flight deck. I said nothing about my interaction with the woman, as they handed me their paperwork and told me I was good to close the door. I turned around to find the two women had moved up to seats 1A and 1C. I stood there, staring at them for a moment.

"Is it ok if we sit up here?" Gianna asked.

I nodded.

"Yea . . . sure, that's fine."

I handed my paper work out to the Ramper and pulled the door to the plane shut. I went through my announcements, making my normal jokes that Gianna found to be hilarious. I took my jump seat facing Gianna and the white tissue wrapped around her that she claimed to be a dress. She smiled at me, reached up, and pushed the call button.

". . . You don't need to press that. I'm right here." I said.

She laughed that dumb girly laugh and asked: "So when do I get my wine?"

"After take-off." I replied "So . . . what were you doing in New York?" I asked.

She looked at her troll of a friend and they both kind of laughed.

"I guess you could call it business." She replied. I couldn't help but wonder if she was in the business of taking off her clothes for money. "I mostly work in DC though . . . Hey have you ever been to the Crystal City Sports Bar?" She asked. I had indeed been there. And it certainly wasn't a sports bar. The very misleading name was in fact a strip club. I laughed and nodded.

"Yea . . . yea, I've been there. Kind of a random question. Why do you ask?"

"Just wanted to know what team you played for . . ."

"Gianna . . . behave." Her friend scolded her.

We were taxiing towards the long line that we always had to wait in at New York before taking off. I had a thousand scenarios as to what this woman did for a living running through my mind, none of which were very family friendly.

"And you? What were you doing in New York?" I asked her portly friend, trying not to focus all of my attention on Gianna.

She smiled "I guess you could say I'm Gianna's . . . manager."

I wondered if manager was another word for pimp. The plane began to pick up speed to take off.

"So . . . do you live in DC?" Gianna asked.

"Yea. Just a little north-"

Before I could finish my sentence, at the exact moment we were taking off, the creepy looking guy stood up from his seat, stormed into the aisle and shouted at the top of his lungs: "Why the hell aren't we taking off yet?!"

My heart leaped into my throat. I wasn't sure if he was crazy, planning on doing something crazy, or both. "Sir, we're taking off, you need to take your seat NOW before you hurt yourself or someone else!!" I shouted. He looked out the window to see we were indeed taking off and flopped down in an empty seat. My eyes were as wide as everyone elses on the plane. It was silent with the exception of the engines and the normal noises of the plane carrying us up into the pitch black sky. That's when the baby started to cry. Loudly. Gianna turned back around and looked at me with a 'What the hell' look on her face. The call light chimed from the flight deck. But not just any light. The emergency call light.

"Is everything alright back there? We heard shouting." The captain asked.

"Yea . . . I think so. I'm going to check on this passenger, he just kind of freaked out as we were taking off and asked why we hadn't left yet, so I had to get stern and tell him to sit down. I'll call you back in a minute." I said, hanging up the phone.

We passed above the altitude where it was safe for me to get up. I cautiously stood up and made my way down the aisle towards the creepy looking guy, the whole way thinking to myself: "*Please don't do anything crazy. Please don't do anything crazy.*"

I approached his seat. He was slumped against the window. And he reeked of alcohol. "Is everything alright sir . . . ?" I asked.

"Yea . . . I was just getting frustrated waiting to take off. I didn't mean to scare that baby or anything."

I'm sure what he meant to say was "I'm drunk, sorry I caused a spectacle."

"It's alright, it's no problem at all." I said. I felt bad for the guy. I turned around and returned to the front.

As I passed her chair, Gianna took me by the hand.

"Is everything ok?" She asked.

"Yea, nothing to worry about." I replied.

"Can I get that red wine now?" She asked.

"Sure, just a moment." I said. I picked up the phone and called the flight deck. "Hey, it's Chuck. Ok, I went back and checked on that guy. He reeks of alcohol, so I can see why he had an outburst. He's slouched in his seat, generally embarrassed. I've dealt with drunks before, he's probably just gonna pass out now." I assumed that would be the end of that problem, but I was far from right on that assumption.

"No, that's unacceptable! He's a hazard to himself and the other passengers, and I'm calling this in! When we arrive in DC the police are going to be waiting for this guy." The captain said. I couldn't believe what I was hearing. My eyes went wide.

"That's . . . not really necessary. I mean, he's fine now." I turned back and looked at Gianna who was smiling at me. But just behind her, a couple of rows back, I saw the drunken passenger, peering over his seat, coldly staring at me. I smiled at Gianna, hoping that loon hadn't seen me make eye contact with him. I'm sure everyone knew what I was discussing on the phone. "Really, it's ok now, there's no need-"

"No! I'm making this call and it's a call to the airport authorities. This was a verbal attack and I'm not letting it escalate! We'll be on the ground in twenty six minutes." The captain said. I hung up the phone.

"How about that wine?" Gianna asked.

My heart was beating, hard. I reached into the liquor kit and pulled out a bottle of red wine. I dropped it into a plastic cup, and wrapped a napkin around it. I handed it to her and sat back in my jump seat. The man was still peering at me with his wild eyes. I tried ignoring him, as my focus shifted back to Gianna, who was reaching into her purse.

"It's on the house." I said, shaking my head.

"Because of that man that went crazy and startled everyone?" she asked.

"What? No." I said, although that's what I would ultimately write on the liquor form under the explanation as to why I compensated the drink.

"How sweet of you . . ." She said, seductively caressing the top on the bottle. My heart began beating rapidly, when suddenly a call button lit up from a passenger seat. And when I saw who that passenger was, my heart went into overdrive. "I'll be back . . ." I said, standing up from my seat, walking back towards the drunken passenger once more. "*Please don't do anything crazy. Please don't do anything crazy.*" I repeated in my head, as I approached the man.

"I didn't mean to scare anyone! Really, I didn't!" He pleaded. He sounded like an innocent man on death row.

". . . It's fine. I know." I replied.

"I can't get arrested!" His tone of voice changed. He sounded less like an innocent man on death row and more like a lunatic on death row. And the fact that he said 'I *can't* get arrested' as opposed to 'I don't *want* to get arrested' concerned me even more.

"It's fine, no one is going to arrest you." I said, blatantly lying through my teeth.

He stared at me with an off centered eye, making him look even nuttier. I slowly turned around and returned to the front of the plane. I took my seat.

"Do you have a girlfriend?" Gianna asked out of nowhere, sipping the wine through her glittering, glossy lips.

"Yes. I mean—no. Not at the moment . . . but there's a girl I think I'm going to get back together with soon." I said, referring to Corazon who had recently left her husband for good.

"It's alright if you do, I don't mind. A lot of my . . . . clients . . . have wives." Gianna said.

I looked over the seats at the man who was still staring at me. He had to have known I lied. Everyone on the plane must have known what I called the pilots about.

"Flight attendant, prepare for landing." The FO announced over the PA. I did my final security checks and took my jump seat.

"Is that guy going to get arrested?" Gianna asked.

I was caught off guard. "What? No. of course not."

"Are you sure? What if he's a terrorist?"

I couldn't believe my ears. "Please don't say that." I said.

"So . . . Can I have another wine?" She asked.

"We're landing now, I can't do that." I replied.

"Are you sure . . . ? I'll make it worth your while . . ." she said, running her index finger over her chest and down the center of her dress. Her friend playfully hit her in the arm and told her to stop being a tease.

My mind was firing in a million different directions. I could deal with this hussy flirting with me, and I could deal with the drunken passenger freaking out, I just didn't want to deal with the two of them on the same flight at the same time.

We landed in DC and I couldn't believe my eyes. Out of the commissary door I could see police cars waiting. But that wasn't all. There were also fire trucks, ambulances, maintenance trucks . . . every conceivable vehicle with flashing lights were all lined up. And they all had their flashing lights on at once.

"Oh no . . ." I said to myself.

Everyone was staring out of their windows with the exception of the man, who was staring at me. We parked, and the seat belt sign turned off. As everyone stood up, the man quickly made his way to the front of the plane. I braced myself for whatever was charging at me, almost certain he was ready to attack. He stopped in front of me. "Are all of those out there because of me?!" He demanded.

I nervously shook my head 'no'.

"Oh man, you smell like alcohol. He's going to get arrested, isn't he?" Gianna asked. I looked at her and shook my head no again with wide eyes.

"I can't get arrested again. I can't!" He shouted.

"So Chuck, what are you doing tonight? Do you want to party?" Gianna asked.

"They're here to arrest me, aren't they?!" The man said.

I shrugged my shoulders. There was a knock on the aircraft door. I opened it, lowering the stairs. The man took one look at me, one look out the door, and then bolted down the stairs. I stood at the entrance to the aircraft watching him in disbelief as he ran circles around the police on the tarmac for a moment, before being toppled to the ground by the authorities.

Gianna handed me her business card. I looked down at her job title: 'Private masseuse'. "Call me if you want to get together . . ." She said, brushing my arm and deplaning with her friend and the rest of the passengers trailing behind her.

When the last passenger was gone, I sat down in the first row of seats, trying to take in everything that had just happened. I took out my phone and called Corazon.

"Hello Mono! How was your flight?" She asked, just as the police were coming on board to take my statement.

". . . I think I'm going to be a little late meeting you for drinks tonight . . ." I said.

Lay together, Lie alone

November 14th 2011

I lay in bed beside Corazon
listening to her lightly breathing
as she slept.
I whispered her name,
but she didn't respond.

In the darkness
I could see her pink
silky nightwear
covering her chest
lightly rising
and lowering
with each breath.

I smiled to myself.
I was happy.
Because I was lying.
I was lying to her.
I was lying to myself.
I was lying there alone.

<<<<<<<<<<<<<<<<<<<<<<<<<<
Corazon invited me
on her overnight
to Raleigh
in mid-November.
I of course agreed
and jumped
on the first flight
from DCA-RDU
that morning.

I waited in the airport
for about an hour
for her to arrive
with her pilots.

She and I went to a restaurant
down the hill from our hotel
just outside
of the Duke campus.
I can't recall the name of it,
a local owned joint
with children's games set up
at each table to be played
while we waited for our food.

We laughed and drank wine
while trying to build
our jenga tower
higher and higher
only to have it
knocked down again.

And when she smiled at me,
I smiled back.
And oh,
how I wanted her
so bad.

We held hands
as we walked back
up the hill to the hotel
and to her room.
We lay in bed
and watched some terrible
black and white movie
from the fifties
that I really paid no mind to.

And then she got up,
turned the lights off
and climbed back into bed
next to me.

We held each other again.
I went to kiss her,
but she recoiled stopping me.
She made me promise
that we would take things slowly.
She didn't want
to make the same mistakes
we did two years ago.

I held my breath
and promised her we wouldn't,
because I cared about her
too much
to let things become
that bad between us again.

But she asked me
to make another promise.
She asked to remain
anonymous in my writings.
She didn't want anyone to know
that we were together
when we had met in training
while she was separated
from her husband.

She didn't want our business
to be put out there
for the world to know about.
I promised her
that while there were stories
about what happened between us,
she wouldn't be identified
and kept out of anything
that would happen as a result.

And I lied through my teeth.
I knew
that it would cause problems.

And I lied to myself.
In my mind
we weren't in Raleigh.
We were back
in Chicago again.
It was as if nothing bad
had ever happened.
I felt as if
we were right where
we were supposed to be.
Together.

And I knew these lies
could ruin any kind
of future we had together.
But at that moment
I didn't care.
I had her.
I had her right where I wanted her.

And she was happy
with the lies I told her.
And I was happy
with the lies I told myself.
And so we kissed
and made love
for the last time.
>>>>>>>>>>>>>>>>>>>>>>>

And my smile faded.
I felt alone,
though she was lying there
beside me.

And my suspicions
that we were not meant to be there
were confirmed
with the promises
that I had made and broke.
And it couldn't be
more of a mess.

It was time.
I had to separate
the truth from my lies.
I was awake,
and we were through.

Because I was lying.
I was lying to her.
I was lying to myself.
I was lying there
alone.

The beginning of the end

December 1st 2011

I arrived in DC and headed to the crew room as normal at the end of my trip on Thursday, the first day of December. Surprise, surprise . . . another email from my in-flight manager Mikey.

"Charles, we need to have another meeting on Monday to discuss an issue regarding your flight attendant manual . . . blah blah blah . . ."

God, what did I do this time? I've said it before, and this time felt no different. My life's like a freakin' television show. Every week there's some new problem or issue that arises. After two and a half years though, that kind of stuff no longer got me all worked up or worried:

"Shit, here we go again . . . I probably told a joke on the flight and someone from management didn't find it funny. And rather than address it with me directly like adults, they went running to my in-flight manager."

I used to always assume the worst, until I eventually realized it wasn't. It was never the end. It was always just another e-mail from Mikey for another meeting, for another mistake. That ended with another slap on the wrist, us laughing about it, and her telling me to get out of her office. I wondered what it could be.

But not this time.

This was different.

On Monday morning, the day before a scheduled Ft. Lauderdale overnight that I would be working with ElHeffey, I entered her office, but unlike all the other times, it wasn't just her and I. I recognized our Chief Pilot; David Friendly, but the other two people I wasn't so sure of. One was a middle aged, sweet looking flight attendant I had seen in passing. The other was a tall man in his mid-thirties, dressed in a sharp looking suit. They were all sitting down, and they all had serious looks in their faces. I stood there, stunned for a moment, before smiling and announcing:

"What is this, an intervention?!" Nobody laughed. "Oh boy . . ." I said quietly.

Mikey said to me "Charles, take a seat please. This is our Chief pilot, David Friendly . . ."

I shook his hand familiarly and warmly smiled a "Hi, nice to see you again."

". . . And this is your union representative Sally Blansberg, and your union lawyer Mark DeLong." I shook their hands as well. "Do you have your manual with you?" Mikey asked.

"Yea sure . . . what's this about?" I asked, nervously handing it to her. She said nothing as she began flipping through it. I'll admit there were a lot of scenarios running through my mind as to what was really going on there. Every joke I had made on the PA, every alcoholic beverage I had compensated, every wild overnight with my crews . . . Yet I couldn't understand what she wanted with my flight attendant manual. There were a lot of things I did that would be considered as gray areas in our companies policies, but the manual was a safety issue. And that was something I always kept current, up to date, and never messed around with. She finished briefly flipping through it and handed it back to me.

"Alright, it looks good . . ." She said. I sat back in the chair letting out a sigh of relief. "Now, onto the next issue that needs to be addressed . . ." She pulled out a vanilla folder. My heart beat sped up. "Are you publishing a book?" The look on my face suddenly fell somewhere between a deer in headlights and a skydiving deer that just realized his parachute wasn't opening.

"What's this?" I asked casually laughing. My mind went into a flashback of the hundreds of people that I had told: "I signed a contract with a publishing company, and I'm putting out a book about being a flight attendant!" and then immediately followed with: "But don't tell Mikey about it, she'd probably fire me if she found out!" I looked at Dave who was staring at me blankly. I looked at Sally who raised her eyebrows and bit her lip. I looked at Mark who kind of shook his head in a 'plead the fifth' manner. I looked at the 'Hang in there' poster on her wall with the kitten dangling on a rope, who I could have sworn shrugged its shoulders at me.

"Charles. Are you publishing a book?" She repeated.

". . . I don't know." I finally choked out.

Mikey stared coldly at me. She opened the folder and began to pull out numerous papers printed from www.badflightattendant.com. "Are you familiar with this website?" She asked. There they were. Print outs of stories of my trips that I had written. Comments from the readers. Links where you could pre-order the book. A picture of ElHeffey, Lizzie, and I beside the giant wooden beaver outside of Minglewoods. ". . . Oh shit." I said.

"This is you in the photo that came from this website. A website with links to pre-order a book published under your name. A book of stories that I assume are of the same subject manner as on the website. Is any of this correct?" she asked.

I had no idea what to do. So I began quietly mumbling an inaudible string of non-sense. Dave laughed. Mikey, however, was not amused.

"Charles! Stop playing games! This is your doing, isn't it?!"

I quietly replied ". . . Yes."

Mark shook his head and let out a sigh. Mikey cupped her hands over her mouth "Charles, I don't know what to say . . . of all the things you've done, this is by far . . ."

It was at this time that Sally intervened "Alright, wait just a minute. Charles doesn't once name our airline. In fact, he calls it UPside Air. None of the people in these stories even work here. From what I've seen, there's no proof that these stories are even remotely true!"

"The juice can races. That was true." Mikey said. I knew I should have left that one out.

"Alright, big deal. So Chuck wrote a funny story about the one time he's ever been in trouble here." Sally replied.

"Charles is in my office almost every other week for an issue!" Mikey snapped back.

"Show us the documentation." Mark chimed in. Mikey stared blankly. I suddenly realized that of all the times that I had been scolded; it always resulted in just a slap on the wrist. Not once had I ever been officially written up with the exception of the racing of the juice cans.

Mikey finally spoke "You've made yourself look bad, and you're making the company look bad. We're taking you off your next trip tomorrow. We're going to have you come back in three days while we investigate this further and we'll have a decision about what we plan to do with you."

I didn't know what to do. Finally, Sally and Mark stood up. "Let's go, Chuck." Sally said. We left Mikey's office. I was speechless.

As soon as we were in the terminal, they turned to me.

Mark said "You have nothing to worry about. If they terminate you, we can take this case to court."

I couldn't believe what I was hearing. ". . . If they terminate me?! You mean if they fire me! This is insane! All of this because of some book and website?!"

"They don't have a leg to stand on. There's no proof any of those stories are real." Sally chimed in.

"Most of them are real!" I shouted, placing my hands on my head. I felt like it was spinning in circles.

"I wouldn't . . . make that publicly known by shouting it in the middle of the airport . . ." Mark said looking around the terminal "you may also want to shut down the website for the time being."

"Calm down. This is all going to be alright." Sally said, placing her hand on my shoulder. I don't know why, but it felt motherly. I let out a sigh. "You're allowed to bring a witness to the meeting on Thursday." she said.

"A witness?" I asked.

"David Friendly was in the meeting as Mikeys witness. That way if anything is said or happens, they can appear in court should the case go to trial." Mark said. I couldn't speak. It was all too much to take in at once.

"Do you know who you'd like to be your witness?" Sally asked. I just nodded. "The meeting is set for Thursday at Three PM. Are you going to be alright?" I simply nodded again.

They left, but I still couldn't move. I took a seat facing the big glass window that you could see the planes out of. Out of nowhere, the chief pilot David Friendly approached me. "Meet me by baggage claim seven." He said quietly, and walked away. I wondered what this was about. It took me a moment to gather myself together and stand up.

I took the escalator down to the lower level of the airport and found the baggage claim. I walked to carousel seven, but Dave was nowhere to be found. The baggage carousel spun slowly around with one lonely bag on it. There was a whistle, and Dave motioned me over to the other side of the empty carousel when I spotted him. I felt like a secret agent. "This is off the record; technically I'm not even supposed to be talking to you. What I'm going to tell you has to stay between us." Dave said.

"It's alright. Whatever you say is between you and me." I replied.

"I'm sorry about all this. It has nothing to do with me; I was just forced to be in that meeting because Mikey needed a witness. I really didn't want to be there. To be honest, I like your website. I think it's all pretty funny."

I laughed "Well, I'm glad someone does. I wish Mikey felt the same way."

"I know this is hard for you to hear. But they are probably going to terminate you." He said. I shut my eyes and let out a deep sigh. "But they're going to give you two options when they do. They'll ask if you want to resign first. The reason for that is because if you resign and want to go on to another job, it looks better to say you resigned from here rather than saying you were terminated."

"I don't understand . . . why wouldn't I want that?" I asked.

"Because if you resign, you can't take the case to court to get your job back. But if you're terminated, you can. They can fire you for allegedly slandering the company, but I've read all these stories. You didn't slander anyone. You're going to take this case to court, and you're going to win. Because what it comes down to is freedom of speech." I couldn't believe the chief pilot of our company was standing up for me.

". . . Why are you telling me this?" I asked.

"I have my reasons . . . I'll see you Thursday." He said.

I rode the shuttle to the employee parking lot. It faced the Potomac River, where planes could be seen taking off and landing over. I sat in the driver's seat for a moment, before calling ElHeffey.

"Hello, Chuck. Aren't you a day early to be bothering me? What's wrong, your liver couldn't wait until tomorrow to be destroyed by me in Ft. Lauderdale?" He laughed. ". . . I have a bit of a problem." I said.

I proceeded to tell him about what had happened.

Over the course of the next three days I called my other friends at UPside to explain what was going on, and this was all of their reactions/advice/pearls of wisdom:

ElHeffey: This is bull! They can't fire you because of some stories, that's a violation of your freedom of speech! They don't have a leg to stand on! Sue them! Sue them poor! Take all their money and prove them wrong!

Ne-ne: Oh man, that sucks, I'm sorry baby boy! Do you want to go to the Irish pub outside of DCA and get drunk?

Kylie: Dude, you're screwed. You better start looking for another job now.

John: Chuck Norris has never been fired from a job. Because he sets his jobs on fire first.

Mary: Oh no! You can't get fired! I wanted you to come to Vegas with me in two weeks. I need someone to keep traveling with. Please don't get fired!

Lizzie: Take the website down. *Now*. Delete any incriminating evidence. Deny everything. And get a fake mustache. Fake mustaches are cool.

Damien: They can't fire you over this shit. Me and you have done way worse together and no one ever said 'boo' to that. Can you do me a favor though and change my name? I don't want my girlfriend to find out it's me in those stories.

>>>>>>>>>>>>>>>>>>>>>>>

Thursday afternoon came around and I found myself sitting outside of Mikeys office beside Mark and Sally. I was sweating and trembling, constantly checking my watch.

"Do you have a witness coming?" Sally asked.

"Yea. She's on the way." I replied.

Mikey opened the door to her office "Charles, I'm ready now." She said.

I looked at my watch. "Just five more minutes. Please." I said.

"Alright. Five minutes." She replied. Mark and Sally stepped inside. I looked at my watch again, starting to lose faith. Corazon suddenly came into the room out of breath "I'm so sorry Mono, there was traffic, and I came as fast as I could . . ."

"It's alright, you're here now." I said smiling, as I hugged her, kissing her on the cheek. I walked into Mikey's office with her. We sat down together in front of Mikey's desk.

"Is everyone here?" Mikey asked looking around. Dave was beside her. Corazon sat to my left. Sally and Mark to my right. Mark said that they were. "Alright . . ." Mikey said. She shuffled through some papers. I was shaking. "Charles, the company . . . has decided to terminate you . . ." Corazon took my hand under the table and let out a gasp. I couldn't believe this. It was so sudden. There was no discussing it, no beating around the bush. She just sat me down and cut to the chase. ". . . Now, there is another option. You can step down and resign instead. I'd be happy to write you a good recommendation letter for future jobs-"

"No." I said, cutting her off.

"What? Mono, no!" Corazon pleaded.

I looked at Dave, who inconspicuously nodded.

"Terminate me." I said.

Mikey looked more surprised than anyone else in the room. "Charles . . . I don't think you know what you're doing . . ." She said.

"Yes. I do." I said sternly. Corazon squeezed my hand.

Mikey stared coldly at me. "Alright . . . if that's your wish." She said, with an upset tone in her voice. She slid some papers over to me. I didn't read them, but I knew what they were about. I tried to keep my hand as steady as possible, signing my name each time. At the end of each signature was a smiley face that had x's in place of its eyes.

"Is that all? Are we done?" I asked. Mikey simply nodded. We all stood up.

"Charles-" she stopped me "I'd like to have a word with you alone. In private." She said, looking at the others.

"You don't have to do that, Chuck! Our business is done here. You don't have anything left to discuss, and if you do, you're still entitled to union representation and your witness!" Sally snapped.

Mikey stared blankly. "Just five minutes. I gave you the courtesy of five minutes to wait to start the meeting. It's the least you can do."

"It's alright. She's already fired me, the only thing left she could do is murder me, am I right?" I joked. Nobody laughed.

"We'll be waiting outside." Sally said.

The door was shut behind me. I sat back down. What happened next still baffles me to this day. Mikey stared at me for a moment, and then, in the most honest and heart wrenching way, began to cry. And through her tears, she said: "Charles, I'm so sorry. I want you to know that none of this was my decision! It came down from corporate, I just have to do my job, I'm so sorry! I'm begging you, please, if my name appears anywhere in this book, you have to take it out! My livelihood is at stake here. Think about what you're doing. You could be single handedly hurting a lot more people than you realize!" I couldn't believe what I was seeing. Here I was, the one that had just been fired, and I actually felt bad for her.

"I promise . . . your real name does not appear anywhere in the book. No ones does but my own. But I can't stop it. It's already been pressed and is on the way to its media outlets." She continued to cry. "Believe me, if I'd have known what was going to happen, I wouldn't have done it. I truly love my job more than anything. I never meant to hurt anyone." I felt like this was all going over her head.

"Then why? Why did you take the termination? If you love this industry why not step down, take the recommendation letter, and go to another airline?" She asked.

I thought about what Dave had told me about being able to take this case to court. ". . . Because I don't believe I'm wrong. And I'm going to prove it." I stood up and turned around ". . . Goodbye, Mikey." I closed the door to her office behind me. I never spoke of it or told anyone what had happened in that room between Mikey and I until now.

Sally was waiting outside of her office with Corazon and Mark. "What happened? What did she say?" Sally asked.

"It's not important. Mark, how soon do I need to let you know if I want to take this case to court?"

He smiled "I was hoping you would ask that. As soon as possible." He replied.

". . . Just give me a few weeks to think it over." I replied.

Vegas baby, Vegas!

December 20th 2011

I guess that I have Mary to thank
for helping me
find a loop hole
in the flight benefit system.
Two weeks after having lost my job
she invited me to come to Vegas
with her and her brother Jiffy.

Having been fired on December 8th,
I had my doubts
that I still even had flight benefits
with STRATA Airlines.
But Mary told me
she had heard a rumor
that if you leave the airline,
no matter the reason,
you still have the flight benefits
for a month
in case you lived
outside of your domicile base
and had to get back home.

I guess the airline industry's
not completely heartless.

So after sobering up long enough
to log onto the airline's website,
I discovered
that I still did have
my flight benefits after all.

I was nervous as hell
showing up at the airport
and jump seating on a flight.
I kept waiting-
expecting
some gate agent
to pull me aside and tell me
I wasn't supposed to be there,
that I wasn't even
an employee anymore.
But I soon found myself
on STRATA Airlines flight to Vegas.

I guess that Mary preferred
that I drank with her in Vegas
rather than at home by myself.
She always was
a true friend.

There's always something
happening in Vegas for the right price.
However,
on a Tuesday night,
we found ourselves
at the hotel bar
of Circus Circus
where we were staying.

I found my mind beginning
to wander
as I slowly stirred
my tequila and tonic.

I thought that I should have been out,
enjoying my first time in Vegas,
shooting dice at a table,
surrounded by people
screaming and cheering.

Champagne bottles
popping left and right,
and money being tossed up in the air,
raining back down on me
in slow motion
like in the movies.

Not sitting next to my
former co-workers brother,
distraught over having lost my job.
What a cruel joke
Hollywood portrays.
I'm pulled away
from my depressing thoughts
when my phone rings.

I step away from the bar,
leaving the bartender
to continue mercilessly taunting Jiffy,
because of the the girly drink
that he ordered
to answer my phone.

I took a deep breath
when I saw Corazon's name on the screen,
not having talked to her
since I had lost my job.

I answered it.
She was in tears
asking why I hadn't
been in touch
after what happened.
She was also upset
over a meeting
that Mikey had called her in for
earlier that day.

<<<<<<<<<<<<<<<<<<<<<<<<

It was a supposedly a meeting for Mikey to check that Corazon's flight attendant manual was current and up to date. I wish I had known, having been snared in *that* trap before. What it turned into was a barrage of questions—an interrogation against whom I made it clear in my writings was a girl that I was obviously head over heels for at the time. The conversation went somewhere along these lines:

Mikey: Were you aware that Chuck was publishing a book about his trips at UPside air?

Corazon: Um, not particularly.

Mikey: Well, surely you must have had some indication—some notice he would be doing this. If I were you, I'd be pretty upset about the whole thing. Putting your business out there like that.

Corazon: I have no idea what you're talking about.

Mikey: Well, it's pretty clear you are the one in his stories he refers to as 'Corazon'. You both are always together . . . you've been reported by crew members riding to hotels together on overnights.

Corazon: We're just friends . . . I didn't realize it was against the rules to invite a friend on an overnight with me.

Mikey: UPside Air pays for your hotel rooms on your overnights. For one person. Not for you and a guest. He pretty much all but says you were having an affair with him. Considering the stories he wrote involving you, I'm surprised you were at the meeting as his witness over this situation.

Corazon: What are you saying?

Mikey: You know that there's no chance of him winning if he decides to take this case to court. Any . . . information you can disclose to us would help us out a great deal.

Corazon: You can't be serious.

Mikey: I've been keeping an eye on the sign in book in the crew room. You've been a little late on your last couple of check in times to work. And I've been letting that slide. If you would be willing to testify against him should this go to court . . .

Corazon: What is this, bribery? I rat out Chuck, who has already been fired, in order to save my own skin?

Mikey: I'm just enforcing the rules that I've let . . . slide with you in the past. Corazon, I want you to think about it. He betrayed a lot of peoples trust when he decided to publish these stories. This goes deeper than you realize. He may have changed every ones name but his own, but we all know who is whom in this book, and we are *all* currently under investigation with the airline. These are people's livelihoods he is putting in jeopardy!

Corazon: This was a meeting about my manual. It's been checked. May I leave now?

Mikey: Of course. I just wanted you to think about your future in the company of this airline as well.

Corazon: . . . You and I both *know* there is no future at a regional airline like this.
>>>>>>>>>>>>>>>>>>>>>>>

I tried reassuring Corazon
that everything would be alright.

Mikey was just trying
to turn her against me.
But the part
that she was more upset over
was the fact
that I had promised her
she wouldn't
be dragged into
any of this mess
that I had created.
That she would remain anonymous
and kept out of anything
that would happen good or bad.

And now that Mikey knew
her identity,
that promise was broken.

Corazon screamed
and told me
that whatever fight was coming
between me,
and the union,
and the airline,
she wanted no part of.
She said that she had
a child to support,
on her own now,
and did not foresee
her career in the airline
lasting much more longer
because of this
before hanging up the phone.

I returned to the bar,
feeling even worse than before.

I should have been out
with Mary and Jiffy,
having the time of my life.
Winning money,
going to shows on the strip,
dancing the night away at a club . . .
Not sitting at our hotel bar,
depressed over the events
unfolding before me
that were beyond my control.

Corazon used to tell me
that everything happened
for a reason.
And I believed that,
I truly did.
But not this night.
Not anymore.
I felt like shit was happening
to me just to happen.

I put my phone away
as Mary approached me
from the casino end
of our hotel
with the largest smile
on her face
and a drink in each hand.

She asked me
what was wrong.
"Dammit.
I need another drink."

Conversation with ElHeffey

December 28th 2011

The third week after having lost my job, I flew to Ft. Lauderdale to hang out with Mary on her overnight since I still was able to use my flight benefits with STRATA Air. The plane that she brought in was supposed to be flown out by Kylie and her crew, but due to a mechanical issue, they canceled their outbound flight and returned to the hotel. I spent the evening drinking with the two of them, while dodging the burning question: What would I do now that I was jobless? To be honest I hadn't really thought much up to that point as to whether or not I would actually go to court to get my job back. After I was officially fired, I was too busy drinking away my savings and flying around with Mary like I still *had* a job to be concerned with that. While I was in Florida ElHeffey sent me a text asking if I wanted to get together when I returned to D.C. to catch up over some drinks on him. I of course agreed, not being one to turn up free booze.

When I arrived in D.C., I caught the employee bus to the first stop and walked to the Irish pub outside of DCA (it's only a twenty minute walk that way, as opposed to a twenty dollar cab ride from the airport). The following is the conversation that took place between ElHeffey and me that evening:
ElHeffey: Holy crap, have you let yourself go!

Chuck: Thanks Heff, it's nice to see you also.

ElHeffey: What have you been doing with yourself since they terminated you?

Chuck: I've been flying around with Mary. Drinking. Hey, did you know that even after you're fired you still retain your flight benefits with STRATA Air?

ElHeffey: Yea, but it's a glitch in the system. It only lasts until the first of the following month. So it's a good thing you got fired at the beginning of December and not at the end of the month, or you'd be shit outta luck.

Chuck: You're telling me. I don't even know if what I'm doing is legal.

ElHeffey: *Technically* yes. You're just flying standby. You get your ticket at the counter. And use your driver's license to get through security. There isn't anything *illegal* about it. If I were working at TSA though, I'd be mighty suspicious of you. You look like a terrorist with that beard. When was the last time you shaved?

Chuck: When was I fired?

ElHeffey: That's only after three weeks?! Were you scratched by a werewolf as a child?

Chuck: My facial hair just grows fast.

ElHeffey: I'll say, you've got more bush going on than the girls in an entire issue of Hustler back in the eighties!

Chuck: Good one, Heff.

ElHeffey: You look like Will Farrel in Anchorman after he lost *his* job.

Chuck: Alright, I get it.

ElHeffey: "*Milk was a bad choice!*"

Chuck: Are you done?!

Elheffey: Haha! Not yet!

Chuck: You know, Mikey used to scold me all the time for having a little stubble. So I'm on strike. I'm not shaving until I get my job back.

ElHeffey: So you're really going to court, Grizzly Adams?

Chuck: I haven't decided yet. I have to call Sally soon and let her know my decision if I actually want to fight this thing or not.

ElHeffey: You opted to get canned rather than voluntarily step down . . . you should fight it. Just make sure you shave before court. You'd look like you just escaped from the lunatic asylum if you showed up looking like that to plead a case in court.

Chuck: I don't look crazy.

ElHeffey: Who are you trying to convince, me, or the monsters? By the way, I bought ten copies of your book on Amazon.

Chuck: You're kidding? I wrote the damn thing, and I wouldn't buy ten copies of it.

ElHeffey: Well, I figured I'd help you out since it's your only source of income now . . . and I had gift cards and points on my account to spend. Seven of the copies were gifts though.

Chuck: What about the other three?

ElHeffey: Toilet paper.

Chuck: Very funny.

ElHeffey: Hey, you're lucky I even bought that many copies. I'm not mentioned in that damn thing!

Chuck: I thanked you in the credits.

ElHeffey: Yea, but there aren't any stories about me in there! Kylie's in the book. John's in the book. *John!*

Chuck: That's because it was only about the first year that I worked in the airline. I didn't meet you until my second year flying.

ElHeffey: That's true. At least after reading it I know why he's always telling those stupid Chuck Norris facts. That story was pretty funny by the way.

Chuck: Thanks, people really seem to like that one.

ElHeffey: What convinced you to take the termination instead of voluntarily resign anyway?

Chuck: . . . I had some convincing from an unexpected third party.

ElHeffey: Was it Corazon? I bet it was Corazon.

Chuck: What? No. What makes you think that?

ElHeffey: It's obvious you two have a thing going on.

Chuck: *Had* a thing going on. We haven't spoken much lately.

ElHeffey: Why? Because you wrote about you two getting it on while she was separated from her husband?

Chuck: . . . Something like that.

ElHeffey: Was it something like that, or was it that?

Chuck: I don't want to talk about that . . . I burned enough bridges with that book.

ElHeffey: So you told a few embarrassing stories about people you work with. Big whoop. The fact is this . . . The regional airline industry pays us shit. We get treated like shit. Overall, it's a pretty shitty situation. But every now and then, we get to fly together. We get some good trips together. And it's people like you that make this whole situation a lot less shitty. These aren't the 'glamor days' of flying anymore. I'm not walking through the airport with three attractive, mid-twenty stewardesses on each arm of mine, while passengers in three piece suits salute me. Those days are dead. Flying at a regional airline for a major airline is essentially like driving the city bus for a limo company. And you decided to write about that. Big deal. You put our regional airline on the spot—indirectly, and they fired you for that. So fight it. This is bigger than you realize.

Maybe it was the inspirational speech. Maybe it was the seven tequila and tonic waters I had consumed by then. The point is, I had never been so motivated to change the course of my future by someone's words in my life as I had been up to that point. As I stumbled back to the employee parking lot, I called Sally with my decision: I wanted to take this case to court. I was going to use our union Lawyer and fight for my job back. Not because I wanted it back. Hell, by that point I wasn't even sure if I ever wanted to even fly again. I just had a point to prove. That I wasn't wrong by publishing those stories. And I wouldn't stop until everyone knew it. And when my drunken thoughts began convincing me to fight back, there was no stopping me. I suddenly had a new mission. Sally was happy with my decision and told me it would take time, things wouldn't happen right away. But she was glad that I finally came around.

I made my way back to my car in the employee parking lot and sat on the hood. It was nearly Three AM. I stared at the Potomac River that the parking lot faced and considered throwing up in it for a moment. Instead, I climbed into my car. Everything was spinning. I looked down at my keys. They looked back up at me in a disapproving manner. I told them they made a convincing argument before tossing them in the back seat and lowering my car seat back to sleep. Before shutting my eyes, I reached into my pocket for my phone. I stared at Corazon's number for a moment before making the decision to call her.
Corazon: Mono . . . why are you calling so late? Is everything alright?

Chuck: Yea . . . yea, I just wanted to talk to you. After our last conversation . . .

Corazon: Can this wait until the morning? I have to be at the airport early. I have a Six AM show time.

Chuck: I'm already here. In the employee parking lot. I can wait a few hours for you. I just . . . I want to talk to you. Please.

Corazon: . . . Alright. I'll see you in the morning before my flight.

She hung up. I laid back in the driver's side seat and shut my eyes.

It's the beginning
of a new day
in Washington D.C.
as the light
slowly makes its way
through the windshield
of my car
after a long night . . .

There's no place like home

November 7th 2011

On a chilly Monday morning
in November
about four weeks
before I lost my job,
Jon wakes up
on the crew room couch
at 5:30 AM
as I quietly enter the room.

"Sorry man . . .
didn't mean to wake you.
Did you sleep here last night?"
I ask.

"It's alright;
it was time for me
to wake up anyway.

I got in around eleven,
so there was no use
in getting a hotel room,
I figured I'd just crash
on the couch.

There's no place like home right?
I just wish there was a way
to turn these damn lights
off in here."
He laughs and gets up.

He puts on his uniform
in the bathroom
beside the crew room,
writes his name
in the crew room sign in book
and greets our FO, Raphael.

He sends Raphael and I
to the plane
while he goes to
the Chicken place inside the DCA airport
and gets three cups of coffee for us.

He exhaustively flies
two of the four flights
the first day of our four day trip,
knowing there's
a comfortable hotel bed
waiting for him
at the end of the day in RDU.

The second day of the trip on Tuesday
is another early show time,
but he is more alive
and energetic.

Throughout the five flights that day,
he tells me all the new
Chuck Norris facts he's read,
makes funny announcements
on the PA
and plays me a demo
of a new guitar riff
he recorded on his computer.

The three of us end the day
late Tuesday evening,
and have dinner in ROC.

The third day of the trip on Wednesday
is another early show time,
but we only have two flights
to work that day
and arrive in CHS by noon.

We walk down the hill
to whatever chain style restaurant
is by our hotel for our late lunch.
Because we have
a late show time the next day,
we can take our time.

We eat,
laugh,
and drink our beers.

We talk about
where we're from
and about our airline.
John tells Raphael and I
about his insane commute home
on a bad day.

I ask him if he would ever
consider changing
airlines or even careers.

His response was this:
"Ten years ago when I started
and we had our Chicago base,
it was a much easier commute.
But when we closed that base
two years ago . . . everything changed.

By this point in the game though . . .
it's not even worth it to leave.
I have high enough seniority here
that I get the trips I want.
I can pay my mortgage,
my flight school loans,
and take care of my family.

So to go to another airline
and start at the bottom
all over again
at this point in my life . . .
it would be pointless.
So what if the commute sucks . . .
Like I always said,
I'm just here to have a good time
and make an honest living."

The next day is a late show time.
We work four flights and arrive
in DCA around 10 PM Thursday night.
Raphael and I leave
and John stakes out his spot
on the crew room couch
for a restless night's sleep.

He wakes up at 4:30 AM
on Friday morning
and puts his uniform back on
in the bathroom
next to the crew room.

He goes to the gate
for his commute home.
The 5:30 AM flight is full.
The 6:00 AM flight is full.
The 6:30 AM flight is oversold.

At 7:00 AM he catches the flight
from DCA-ORD.
He arrives in ORD at 8 AM.

The 9 AM flight to DEN is full.
He realizes it's going to be
a bad day to commute.
He has breakfast in the airport.

He catches the 3:23 PM to DEN
and arrives at 4:55 PM.

The 5:38 flight to BIL is full
and a STRATA Air captain
takes the jump seat
in the flight deck.
He has dinner in the airport.

He catches the 9:49 PM flight to BIL
and arrives at 11:21 PM.
He drives an hour to get home.

He spends Saturday
with his wife and children
and on Sunday morning,
he wakes up at 4 AM.

He drives an hour to the airport
and arrives at 6:30 AM.

The 7:30AM flight to DEN is full.
He has breakfast in the airport.

He catches the 10:18 AM flight to DEN
and arrives at 11:46 AM.

The next three flights are full.
He realizes it's going to be
another bad day to commute.
He eats a late lunch in the airport.

He catches 4pm to CLT
and arrives at 9:08 PM.

He catches the 10:11 PM flight to DCA
and arrives at 11:21 PM.

His show time is 5:30 AM
the following morning,
so he contemplates
getting a hotel room.

By the time
he would get to the hotel
and in bed,
it would be midnight.
That would give him
four hours of sleep
before waking up at 4 AM,
getting ready,
and being back to the airport
for a 5:30 AM show.

He decides it's not worth the trouble,
and stakes out his spot
on the crew room couch
for a restless night's sleep.

On a chilly Monday morning
in November
about three weeks
before I lost my job,
Jon wakes up
on the crew room couch
at 5:30 AM
when Mary quietly enters the room.

"I'm sorry, I didn't mean to wake you up.
Did you sleep here last night?"
She asks.

"It's alright;
it was time for me
to wake up anyway.

I got in around eleven,
so there was no use
in getting a hotel room,
I figured I'd just
crash on the couch.

There's no place like home right?
I just wish
there was a way
to turn these
damn lights off in here."
He laughs.

Part IV

Slow descent

After I left

January 5th 2012

It's been a month.
A month since I lost my job.
A month since I lost Corazon.
The shades have been pulled,
and it's dark in here.

The door has been shut
for far too long.
Sleeping all day.
Staying awake all night.
Fighting off my demons
disguised as mistakes.

I don't want to see
the outside world.
I just want to wait.

Six more months
before I can go to court.
Six more months
until I can win.
Six more months
until I can fly again.

I have to get it together.
I don't even recognize
the person staring back at me
in the mirror anymore.

Pull yourself together man.

I'm done.
I'm done blaming myself.
Stabbing myself
in the back with this.
I'm done being alone.

I shave my face.
Splash it with cold water.
Pull myself together.

I kick the empty bottles
out of the way
and make my way
to the blinds.

I pull them open
and let the sun shine in.
It's time.
It's time to move forward.
It's a new day.

Chuck's first book signing!

January 28th 2012

I learned the hard way very quickly that publishing a book did not automatically equal fame and success. This became quite apparent at my first book signing. After sobering up and pulling myself out of the depressing state I was in after having lost my job, I took some advice from ElHeffey and decided it was time to do some promoting for my second job: being a terrible writer.

I got a hold of my publishers and told them I wanted to set up a book signing and an in store appearance. They were more than thrilled, considering my sales hadn't exactly been sky rocketing since it hit the shelves. Whatever, I had my hands full with more pressing matters at the time.

They set me up at a major book store that shall remain nameless at a mall in Virginia the last weekend in January. I'm not going to lie; I was more than excited on the drive down at seven in the morning on a Saturday. I could just imagine:

~~~~~~~~~~~~~~~~~~~~~~~~

I'd show up at the store to a line of screaming fans, all of them holding their copies of 'Bad flight attendant'.

"There he is! It's Charles Jenni!" an attractive woman would scream, and the line of a hundred thousand people would all go berserk. I'd take my seat at a large, nice looking table. Maybe from Ikea or somewhere with all that modern looking furniture. Hundreds of copies of my book lay out in front of me. A cardboard cutout of me in my flight attendant uniform holding my book in one hand and giving a thumbs up with the other, standing on one side of me. A large body guard standing on the other side of me. Maybe someone like Michael Clarke Duncan.

Guys would approach the table and high five me, telling me a Chuck Norris fact, and how awesome they think I am. Attractive women will tell I could do so much better than Corazon and have me write my phone number in their books and sign their chests (which are all quite large). Gay guys will tell me I've broken a new mold in the genre of books about flight attendants as a straight male telling it like it is. Older women will
~~~~~~~~~~~~~~~~~~~~~~~~

tell me what an inspiration I am to those that have always wanted to fly. J.D. Salinger will want to take a photo with me and tell me Holden Caulfield's got nothing on me.

I'd sell a million copies, earning myself 3 million dollars and never have to work again. What a great day.

~~~~~~~~~~~~~~~~~~~~~~~~

Yea. That's exactly what it would be like. This delusion wasn't helped when I arrived at the mall and eight in the morning and headed straight to the book store. There was no line of screaming fans—which was to be expected, it was still early. There was however a poster in the window. A sixteen by twenty four inch poster with a large picture of my book on it, and under it was written in sharpie: 'Meet the author: Saturday Jan. 28th'. I patted myself on the back when seeing this. "Finally! I've made it!" I thought. I approached the closed gate and pushed on it. It rattled, but no one came. I tried knocking on it. The manager, Roy, a man in his mid-thirties with shaggy hair and a goatee approached the gate.

Roy: We're not open for another hour.

Chuck: It's me! Charles Jenni!

Roy: . . . Who?

I pointed at the poster in the window.

Chuck: The 'Bad flight attendant'! . . . I wrote that book there.

He looked at the poster, and then back at me.

Roy: Oh. You. Ok.

He unlocked the gate, pulled it up enough to allow me to duck under it, and then pulled it back closed again. He pointed at one of those plastic tables with the folding metal legs in the middle of the store.

Roy: There you go. I'll be back in a second with the books.
~~~~~~~~~~~~~~~~~~~~~~~~

He disappeared into the back of the store. I looked at the table, confused as hell. He returned with a cardboard box full of about fifty copies of my book. He set it on the floor beside the table, looked at me, told me to holler if I needed anything, and then went back to his pathetic life as a book store manager. He was obviously nervous having never dealt with a famous author in his crappy store before.

I unfolded the table and put the copies of the book on top of it. It looked sloppy. I rearranged them several times, standing a few copies up, only to have them fall back over. I finally stacked up five rows of five copies each.

At nine, Roy raised the gate to the store, opening it up to the general public. "This is it! Let the floods of screaming fans in!" I thought. One elderly woman slowly walked in to the store and approached me.

Old woman: Excuse me . . . can you tell me where I can find your cook books?

Chuck: What?

Old woman: Your books. For cooking.

Chuck: I . . . don't work here.

Old woman: Oh. Alright, sorry about that.

As she walked away, reality suddenly hit me like a ton of books. By noon, I couldn't have looked or felt more pathetic. I sat at the table with my hand against my cheek watching people walk by. The store was crowded, but no one seemed to care that they were in the presence of a celebrity. "This is bullshit." I said to myself.

The transaction between most customers and I went like this:

Chuck: Hey. Hey you. You like books?

Customer: What? Uh . . . yea, I guess so.

Chuck: Come here and check out this book I wrote.

The customer would then walk over to the table and pick up the book.

Customer: You wrote this?

Chuck: Yea, look. Charles Jenni. That's me!

Customer: Huh.

The customer would then flip through it briefly, maybe stopping on a page in the middle of the book.

Customer: Ha. That's funny.

The customer would then look at the back of the book, chuckle again, and then set the book back down on the table.

Customer: Well . . . see ya.

Chuck: . . . This is bullshit.

I started to get hungry and decided to go grab a bite to eat.

Roy: You can't leave your table unattended!

Chuck: I'd rather someone steal a copy than not get rid of any at all today!

I came back a half hour later after eating a sub to find all the copies of my book sitting right where I left them.

Chuck: What a shocker! No one wants it even when it's free!

I shouted this at Roy, who simply rolled his eyes. I was getting frustrated. I couldn't figure out what I was doing wrong. Then came the turning point. I finally sold a copy. A woman in her mid-thirties came by the table and picked up the book. I stared at her resentfully, expecting this transaction to go the same way as all the others. Instead:

Woman: Did you . . . write this?

Chuck: Yea. And it's a *big* hit as you can see by all of my screaming fans that are here to meet me.

Woman: Haha, that's pretty funny. So are you a flight attendant?

Chuck: I was. Until I wrote this book and got fired.

Woman: You're kidding! What airline did you work for?

Chuck: UPside Air. It's an express carrier of STRATA Airlines.

Woman: That's amazing! I always wanted to be a flight attendant! Will this book tell me how to get hired?

Chuck: Um . . . Yea. Of course it will.

Ok, so I totally lied to her, but I would have done anything to sell a copy at this point. I watched ecstatically as she carried it over to the counter and not only purchased it, but brought it back to me to have it autographed! I tried to think of a thousand clever things to write. I had signed plenty of copies up until that point, but all were for friends and family of mine, never for a stranger. Finally, I just wrote: "Tell fifty people to buy a copy. Then have them tell fifty more people to buy copies also. This is the only source of income I have at the moment." She laughed, thanked me, and left. I Jumped up out of my seat and pointed at the manager.

Chuck: In your face Roy! How many books have you sold today, you loser?!

Roy: A lot more than you have.

Chuck: None of which were written by YOU! Watch out Harry Potter, I'm coming for you!

I don't think Roy understood the statement and told me to quit making a scene, but I was on top of the world. Nothing could stop me now. Over the next four hours I heckled anybody that would walk by the table in order to try and sell a book. These were some sales pitches I tried using:

To a pregnant woman: If you don't want your baby to grow up and hate you, you'd buy a copy of my book and read to it every night!

To a customer with a stack of six books: One more isn't gonna break your back! Come buy this!

To an attractive girl: If you buy this book from me, I will accept your invitation to dinner.

To a bald guy: This book makes a great hairpiece!

To a girl holding a copy of 'He's just not that into you': You don't need a book to tell you he's just not that in to you! I could have told you that! Spend your money on something awesome instead!

To a guy in a Vietnam veteran hat: If you don't buy my book . . . the terrorists win!

None of these exactly went over very well, and Roy told me that if I didn't stop being rude to his customers, I would have to leave. I did manage to sell three more copies however.

The first two were to a gay couple. How do I know this? Because they both had a hand in the back pocket of the others jeans when they passed by my table. And one was being lazy about it by only having the index finger hooked in the others back pocket. All or nothing buddy, do it right or don't do it at all. Neither noticed me or my book, so I had to think fast to get their attention.

Chuck: Support equal rights opportunities with each copy purchased!

They both stopped and turned towards me and then walked over.

Gay guy 1: What do you mean by 'equal rights opportunities"?

Chuck: . . . The right to share your money with me in exchange for my stories about being a flight attendant.

Gay guy 2: That doesn't make any sense.

Chuck: It does if you think about it.

Alright, so maybe it didn't make any sense, and Gay guy 2 seemed a little more skeptical. I noticed he was holding a copy of Chelsea Handlers book, so I pointed at it and told him that she was a huge influence on me, even though I hated her and and everything that she wrote. Gay guy1 told me that he was interested in becoming a flight attendant (shocker, I know), so I lied to him as well and told him my book would help him get into the airline industry. I feel bad about it, but at the time I was desperate to sell books, I figured the ends justified the means. They asked me to tell them about the book, so I told them "You didn't say the magic word." They both found it funny, and with a little more flirting, I convinced them both to buy a copy. I was on top of the world again.
The next customer to buy a copy was a really cute younger girl.
Girl: Oh my God, you wrote this book?

Chuck: Yep.

Girl: I can't believe it! I've never met a celebrity! I can't believe I'm actually meeting you!

Chuck: . . . You should have been in here earlier; it was packed when people knew I was here.

Girl: I'm glad I made it before you left!

Now, what happened next really took the cake. She looked at the book, read my name and then said to me:

Girl: I still can't believe I'm meeting Charles Jenni. I've been meaning to pick up your last book, all my friends loved it! They're going to be so jealous that I met you!

Keep in mind, no one calls me 'Charles' except my mother and Mikey, and they only did it when they were angry with me. This was the first time I had ever published something, which meant she was either lying to me because she thought I was a famous author, or had me confused with another writer all together, but I didn't care. If she thought I was famous, I was going to milk it.

Chuck: I'll sign a copy for you if you'd like. I normally have some extra copies laying around on the tour bus, but I gave away the last of the free copies yesterday at the store in North Carolina. These copies are all the stores, but if you buy one, I'll sign that for you.

She bought a copy, and then handed her phone to Roy and pointed at me. She came over and asked me for a picture. I told her that she could have one and use it to make all of her friends jealous for meeting a famous author. I told her to hold up her middle finger and on the count of three say: "Bad flight attendants!" The finger was more directed at Roy as an F-you to 'the man'. He rolled his eyes and took the photo.

I signed her book and wrote something like 'Thanks for being the greatest fan in the world'. After that interaction I knew my day wouldn't get any better, and by then it was five in the evening, so I decided it was time to leave.

Sure I had only sold four copies, and I wouldn't see that twelve dollars from the publishers until April. And sure I had spent more money in gas to drive down to Virginia, buy that sub, and drive back, but it was the principle of the matter and an important lesson that I learned that day: everyone's got to start somewhere.

If those four people that bought my first book manage to find their way to this one, I would like to apologize to them for lying; I hope you can forgive me for that. I would also like to tell them that their three dollars didn't mean as much to me as the interaction of people genuinely interested in the fact that I wrote a book, no matter how crappy it was.

I would also like to apologize to Roy for causing a scene in his book store and stealing the promotional poster of my book from the window on the way out as a memento of my first in store appearance.

Just kidding, that guy was a dick.

The complete flight attendants guide to: Getting hired at an airline

February 9th 2012

In February I heard that the mainline carrier STRATA Airlines was hiring up in New Jersey. Don't get me wrong, I still was going to go to court with UPside air, and I still wanted to go back to fly for them again, but I needed a backup plan in case that didn't work out. And since I wanted to be a flight attendant again, I figured this was this perfect opportunity. Sally told me I was more than welcome to go to the interview and use her as a reference. Apparently when you apply at a job, companies are only allowed to ask your last employer:

"Did the employee work there from (certain date) to (certain date)?'" They're not allowed to ask if you were fired. I have heard they're allowed to ask 'would you hire them back?' I knew the answer to that, but I figured I'd cross that bridge when I got to it.

The interview was set for eight in the morning on a Thursday at the Radisson outside of Newark airport. There was only one problem: Wednesday night a huge snow storm was expected to find its way over the East coast. It was a three hour drive to the hotel according to my GPS, but I wasn't going to risk it. I figured I would leave at Eight in the evening on Wednesday night, get a room at the hotel so I would be awake and ready to go in time for the interview.

8:00PM-
I put on my suit, throw a pair of pajamas in an overnight bag, jump into my tiny mustang, and leave my house to begin my drive to New Jersey.

8:42-
I am not even out of Maryland yet and it begins to snow. Hard. I hate driving in the snow, and it's not helping that I have to drive up to Jersey in it.

8:59-
I can barely see the road in front of me. I am driving 15 MPH on a 60 MPH road.

9:06-
A jeep equipped to drive in the snow passes me.

9:10-
A smaller car not equipped to drive in the snow passes me. I consider speeding up.

9:11-
The smaller car spins in circles and ends up off the road in the grass. I decide that 15 MPH is just fine.

10:13-
I am stressed. My hands are glued to the wheel. I am listening to classical music to try and calm my nerves.

11:03-
I arrive at the Jersey turnpike. I collect my ticket and get on the turnpike. I tell myself I am nearly there.

11:34-
I wonder where the hell I am. The estimated time of arrival on my GPS keeps rising.

11:42-
I get off the turnpike at the exit for the airport and pay the toll. The man in the booth tells me to drive carefully. It's reassuring.

11:57-
My GPS is going nuts. It keeps telling me to make a U turn when possible and then recalculates itself. I curse at the GPS and ignore it. I decide I know how airports work and don't need the help of a machine. I drive toward Newark airport.

12:13 AM-
I arrive at the airport. People don't know how to drive at the airport. Combine that with people that don't know how to drive in the snow, and you've got a recipe for bumper cars. I find the airport exit quickly and follow the signs for the hotel district.

12:32-
I am seeing signs for every hotel with the exception of the Radisson, and I am starting to run low on fuel.

12:40-
I find the Radisson and breathe a sigh of relief.

12:42-
I step out of the car and plunge my left foot into a puddle of melted snow/slush/dirty water. I bite my lip to keep myself from screaming. I march through the snow with my overnight bag into the hotel.

12:44-
I tell the front desk I need a room. They tell me they are all full. I ask how that's possible on a Wednesday night. They tell me flights canceled because of the snow storm and the hotel filled up. But there's a holiday inn next door I'm welcome to try.

12:48-
I trudge through the snow next door to the holiday inn. My left leg is getting colder.

12:52-
The holiday inn gives me the same story. I bite my lip once more to keep myself from screaming. I look at my options. The interview is in seven hours. That means I only have about six hours of sleep left to get before I have to wake up and make myself presentable. All the hotels are full. It looks like I'll be sleeping in my car.

12:56-
I slowly make my way back to the car, pull a blanket out of my trunk, and climb in the back seat. I take off my dress pants and place them over the dashboard heater and crank it on high. There's a certain moment in life when you're sitting in the back of your car in a snow storm in your underwear wrapped in a blanket waiting for an interview and you can't help but want to laugh. Oh, sorry did I say laugh? I meant cry. I put my pajamas on and wrap the blanket tighter around me.

1:14-
I doze off.

2:02-
I wake up. I turn the heat and the engine off and go back to sleep.

3:34-
I wake up again freezing. I put my dress shirt, and suit jacket on over my pajamas, the blanket back on me, and turn the engine on. I crank the heat up again once more. I sit shivering in the back seat before passing out again.

4:15-
I wake up once more and turn the engine off.

6:19-
I wake up freezing cold and decide there's no use trying to sleep anymore.

6:23-
I put my suit back on, step out of the car, right back into the same puddle I forgot I stepped in the night before. I bite my lip again.

6:29-
I trudge in the snow back over to the Radisson again.

6:35-
I go into the bathroom by the lobby, take my pants off, and hold them under the hand dryer. A business robot walks in, and stops to look at me. I tell him "It's exactly what it looks like." And go back to drying the leg of my pants.

6:53-
I buy a cup of coffee at a kiosk and take a seat outside of the doors of the meeting room where the interview will be held.

7:30-
The area is crowded with at least fifty hopefuls of future flight attendants. There are about nine other men, and they are all dressed much sharper than I am. I consider just leaving.

7:50-
The doors to the interview open. I enter the room and take a seat. I try putting my happy face on, despite the fact that I am miserable.

8:00-
A woman thanks us all for coming to the interview and divides us into five groups of ten.

8:10-
I go into another room with eight other women, a nicely dressed man in his mid-fifties and an older woman that is giving the interview. The woman asks us individually to stand up and talk about ourselves. The women all have different backgrounds and things to say about themselves, the things they've accomplished in life up to that point, the different languages they speak, etc. It was the man I was concerned about making me look bad. He tells us he was a flight attendant for another airline for twenty years, and he has a degree in hospitality and all this other crap that made me look like a bum under a bridge. I considered just bowing out gracefully and leaving, but at that point I was so tired, I didn't care. So when it got to my turn to speak, I stood up and apologized for looking like I slept in my car the night before, and then told everyone my journey to get to the interview. I told them about driving in the snow, stepping in the puddle, finding out the hotel was full, sleeping in my car, stepping in the puddle again, and drying my pants on the hand warmer in the bathroom. Everyone laughed and applauded for me, but I was sure it wasn't going to land me the job. Then I talked a little about UPside Air and told them that I worked for them for two and a half years and decided to try a mainline carrier.

9:30-
The woman tells us to go to the waiting area and that in twenty minutes she would put a piece of paper with our names on the door. If your name

was on the paper to come back inside for a second interview, and if it wasn't not to take it personal.

9:36-
While waiting, several of the women that were in the interview ask me if I made up the story of how I got there. I told them to look at the bags under my eyes and tell me if they thought those were made up. I was so exhausted, all I wanted was a bed.

9:39-
I go to the front desk and ask if they have any rooms available. They tell me they do. I pay for a room and go back to the interview area.

9:48-
The woman posts a piece of paper on the door. There are only ten names on it, and mine is one of them. I let out a sigh and wonder if there's some kind of way to re-schedule the interview. All I want is a bed.

9:50-
I go back into the conference room. I am the only male in the room. They congratulate us for making it to the second interview and have us go to another room for a one on one interview.

10:13-
I wait in a chair outside of another conference room. I look like hell and am struggling to stay awake.

10:24-
They call me into the room. I sit at a table with the woman that gave me the first interview, another woman, and an older man. They ask me to tell them about my work history. I tell them I worked at a video rental store for two years, then worked at an express carrier of theirs called UPside air. They ask me why I left and I tell them to pursue a career in writing (Technically I *was* currently employed by my publishers since I was being paid by them every 4 months.) Then I told them I missed the airline industry and wanted to fly again. They asked me the same questions as they did when I was hired at UPside, and I gave them the same answers I knew they wanted to hear:

"Why do you want to fly for our airline?"
"Because of your reputation of being a great airline to not only work for, but also to fly on as a passenger."
(Because I need a job. Duh.)

"What would you do in an emergency on the aircraft?"
"Put all my skills and training to use the best way possible to ratify the problem in the safest way possible."
(The level of the emergency depends on the level of freaking out I will do.)

"How would you rate your customer service skills?"
"On a scale of one to ten? A thousand."
(Just kidding. It's a seven. On a good day.)

I was a little nervous to be honest, I kind of wanted to experience flying for a major airline and figured maybe it was time to quit running around like Charlie Sheen and get my shit together.

10:34-
They all shake my hand and tell me they would be in touch. I was unsure how the interview went, but I only had one thing on my mind at that point.

10:39—I get my hotel key from the front desk, take it to my room and sleep for the next twelve hours before driving home.

Several days later, I received this email from STRATA Airlines and took it as a sign that it wasn't where I was meant to be:

> admin@strataairlines.intersourcing.com 2/13/12
> Add to contacts To Jenni_Chuck@email.com
> Please do not reply to this message as the email address is not monitored.
> Charles,
> The May class is full and we have halted all further training classes until further notice due to the recent increase in fuel

prices. We will be in touch regarding the next STRATA Airlines f/a training class.

Thanks.

Candice M. Thompson
STRATA Airlines recruitment dept.

Bad suit salesman

April 16th 2012

Four months after losing my job, the money was running out. I had spent just about every dime from the first check I had received from my publishers and I needed a job to hold me over until the court case settled and I could go back to flying again. In a moment of desperation I found myself at the mall applying to every store I passed by. The last one I would have expected to find myself in was a place called SuitStore. But I figured: "I wore suits on the plane. I look good in a suit. Why not give it a whirl?" The manager working was a fellow named Marlon. He had to have been a year or two older than me, and there were only two things he loved: Suits, and women (In that particular order). My hiring process went a little something like this:

Chuck: I saw your help wanted sign in the window. I'm looking for a job.

Marlon: You like suits?

Chuck: Sure.

Marlon: . . . Step into my office.

We proceeded to walk to a bench outside of the store in the mall and sat down.

Marlon: What have you been doing before this?

Chuck: I was a flight attendant for two and a half years. Then I wrote a book about it. Then they fired me for that. And here I am.

Marlon: No way, really? You wrote a book?

Chuck: Yea.

Marlon: What was it about?

Chuck: Funny things that happened on the flights and on over nights and stuff like that.

Marlon: What was being a flight attendant like?

Chuck: It's ok. All I had to do was hand out sodas. And pretzels. And pretend to like people. And I didn't even do that all the time.

Marlon: I like you. You're hired.

I couldn't believe it. Just like that, he hired me. Maybe it was my honesty or personality, I don't know. I wasn't even taking it all that serious, so it didn't really matter to me if I got a job at *that* particular store or not. He didn't even ask me what I knew about suits, which is good considering all I knew was how to put them on. And as it turned out I hadn't even been doing that right. Did you know that suit jacket lengths are S (Short), R (Regular), and T (Tall)? Yea, well neither did I until I worked at SuitStore. But Marlon taught me everything I needed to know and then some.

It wasn't a bad job, but I had a few qualms about working there.

I worked Monday-Friday. 9AM-5PM. You may think this is a perfect schedule, but I hadn't been up at that hour in the morning to drive to work since before I became a flight attendant. And one thing I forgot about was traffic. To *and* from work. What was normally a fifteen minute drive to the mall, became a thirty minute journey to the north.

But the worse part about the job was probably the customers. Who was our biggest clientele? In case you hadn't guessed, it was my old nemesis: The Business Robot. I can't quite seem to figure out when these guys work, unless their job is to pester me. If it's not on the plane, it's in a suit store. It was two in the afternoon and people were BUYING TIES. Shouldn't you be at work?! Because we worked off of commission, we had to be on the customer's back the second they walked in the store even if they were 'just looking around'.

Our store was across from the Nike woman's outlet, so when it was quiet in the store, Marlon would be across the way, flirting with the manager there. This wasn't really a problem, because that's when I was left alone in the store front to restock ties or suits or whatever. Instead I would be on my phone texting my co-workers from UPside Air to ask them about their flights, or any funny stories they had to share with me, etc.

I wasn't happy and being paid less than minimum wage didn't help. Two weeks after I started working there on a Friday, Ne-ne invited me to a party at her place in D.C. It was some kind of golf pros and tennis hos costume party that would start around seven in the evening. I told her I would probably be late because by the time I got off work, sat in traffic to get home, changed, and sat in more traffic to get to her place in D.C., it would be well after seven. While Marlon was across the hall flirting with the Nike girl, I was sitting on a table in the back texting, when the tailor Glenn came out from the back office. In his Jamaican accent he asked me:

Glenn: 'Ey mon. Wots da matter?

Chuck: Kinda bummed. I'm not happy here. I'm just working this job until I go to court and start flying again.

Glenn: You know, in da old countree, I was a tailor.

Chuck: Yes. I know.

Glenn: But dere wasn't no work. So I come to America. And Marlon give me a job.

Chuck: Yea, but this store sucks. We don't get paid anything here.

Glenn: That's not important to me. In da old countree, I want to be a tailor. But there was no tailor jobs so I come to America. I be a tailor here. Would I love to work for . . . da Perry Ellis? Or da Tommy 'ilfiger? Of course. But if I have work at SuitStore forever, so be it. Because I am happy as long as I am a tailor. You? You not happy here. I see dat. You got to do what make you happy. You probably not rich as a cabin attendant. But were you happy?

Chuck: Yea.

Glenn: Then that's what you gotta do.

Glenn only worked until three in the afternoon, so he was always gone by the time the afternoon rush came in. That was the last time I ever saw him, but his words stuck with me.

I was with a Business robot and his wife that were looking at a pair of shoes, and I couldn't have had a deader look on my face. They were holding up the shoes discussing which would look better with what outfit. I was only standing there to take the commission when I rang them up. They made their decision and took the shoes to the counter. Marlon took the shoes and said "I got this, you put this shoe horn back out on the floor." I suddenly realized that he was going to take my customers, along with my commission. Before I could say anything, I looked down and froze when seeing the name on the box I was holding: "Rochester shoe horn".

I suddenly had a flood of memories wash over me from all of my overnights in Rochester. Memories of another time when I was much happier. Memories of Mary and I stumbling from the bars on our nights off there. Of the epileptic girl that I went to a party with there. Of Ne-ne and I kissing on the deck of the roof top bar. Of Tyler and I laughing at dinner in the hotel restaurant Halloween night about our insane cab driver that morning. And then Glenn's words echoed in my mind once more: "You not happy here. I see dat. You got to do what make you happy." I calmly placed the shoe horn back on the counter and turned around. I began running.

And as I ran out of the store Marlon shouted: "Hey! Hey, where are you going?" But I didn't stop. I ran all the way through the mall. I ran to my car. I got in it, and I drove towards D.C. Marlon called my cell phone, but I didn't answer. I just kept running.

And when I arrived at Ne-ne's apartment, she had a surprised look in her face. "Wow, you're a half hour early! I thought you were going to be late! What happened? Why are you in that suit?" She asked, handing me a beer. I cracked it open and without saying a word, chugged the entire can. She asked if everything was alright.

"I quit my job at SuitStore." I said.

"What? Why did you do that?" She asked.

"I had an epiphany there. I'm not a suit salesman. I'm a flight attendant. I wasn't happy there. And I don't think I will be happy anywhere until I come back."

When I finally get around to running my own airline, this is what it will be like.

Once my court case has been settled, and my book becomes a number one best seller for eight hundred straight weeks in a row, I will probably have a ton of cash to throw around. I've been thinking of ways to spend my fortune: driving a dump truck full of money off of the empire state building. Filling an Olympic size swimming pool full of gold coins and diving into it duck tales style. Flying to the moon on the weekends to hit golf balls around with President Obama . . . I'm sure the possibilities will be endless, but there is one particular goal of mine I hope to accomplish; and that is running my own airline.

This might prove to be a bit difficult since my education is limited, and I know nothing about the fields of business management, economics, aeronautics, catering, or customer service. Just kidding about that last one. (Or am I?)

I am however qualified in the following fields: Being awesome, cooking and eating pizza (So long as it is frozen first), being a flight attendant, getting drunk, flying a toy airplane around the room, being a more awesome flight attendant, writing this book, and flying a toy airplane around the room while eating pizza (drunk). I also know what I like and what I'd like to see in an airline, therefore, I know it is what everyone else will want out of my airline. So with that said, when I finally get around to running my own airline, this is what it will be like:

The flight attendants that fly for my airline-

Probably not the best place to begin when building an airline from the ground up, but I figured it is the one field I know the most about in the airline industry, so I may as well start there.

The hiring process will be simple. The interview will be held at the most pristine hotel in every city around the United States. It will be more popular than an American Idol try out. Hopefuls will be lined up for miles for the chance to interview with my airline. When they come into the room, it will be a one on one interview. I will simply be seated at a nice oak table, wearing a nice suit. The name plate on the table will read:

~~'Chuck Jenni'~~
~~'Chuck Jenni, CEO'~~
'Handsome Chuck Jenni, CEO'.

The girl interviewing will come in to the room, and sit down in front of me. I will coldly stare at her, before reaching into a drawer in the desk, and pulling out a seventy year old bottle of scotch and two shot glasses. I will pour two shots. One for me, and one for her. I will then slide the shot across the table to her in a very cool bartender type manner.

Now before I continue, I want you to ask yourself: Who do you think I would want to hire in this scenario? The girl that takes the shot, or the girl that doesn't? If you said the girl that doesn't take the shot, I'm sorry you are wrong. This is a shot of seventy year old scotch I'm offering here! Not taking a shot that someone has offered you is the same as throwing it back in their face and that's just downright rude. How dare you. Now, if your answer was 'take the shot', I'm sorry, but you are also wrong. Drinking in an interview?! What the hell is wrong with you, I don't need a bunch of alcoholics working for my airline! So which girl gets the job? That's easy. The girl that's more attractive.

Now, for those of you wondering: "What about the guys that interview for you airline?" Sorry, but none of them get hired. How do I get around the equal rights laws? Simple, I will hire only two male flight attendants. My gay friend James, and I. That's right, I'm not only the CEO, I'm also an employee. Take a moment to let that sink in; I'm sure I just blew your mind.

Once hired, my flight attendants will not be called 'Flight attendants'. They won't be 'stewardesses', 'trolly dolly's' or any other stupid term people have come up with over the years. They will be known as 'Chuck's Angels'. Except for James. He will be called 'Bosley'.

There will be no set uniform for 'Chuck's angels' either. They can wear whatever they want. If they want to fly in a summer dress and flip flops, that's fine. If they want to come to work in their pajamas, more power to them. This is because attractive girls can put on almost anything, claim "Oh, I look terrible in this!" and still look good in it. This also goes back to the reason why I hired the attractive ones to begin with. I will continue to wear my suit however, because as I have said before, I look good in it.

The Pilots that fly for my airline-

This is a no brainer. Obviously every pilot I've written about in previous stories of mine are awesome enough to be mentioned, and therefore are automatically qualified to fly for my airline. Starting with ElHeffey. I'm making him my chief pilot, no question about it. He is hands down my favorite pilot to fly with and if I have to be a flight attendant myself in order to keep the equal rights lawyers off of my back, I'm going to be flying my trips with him.

There will be no need for a pilot union, because I will pay the pilots any amount of money that they want to fly for my airline, and give them whatever they need. Days off. Long overnights. Benefits for them and their families. Their own private jets to fly home. Whatever they want, it's theirs.

You are probably thinking: "Won't this bankrupt you?" Not at all. I have a full proof plan of how I will continue to acquire and grow my vast wealth (legally) which you will read about shortly.

There is one catch to being a pilot for my airline though. The uniform is a tuxedo. But a really classy, turn of the century type tuxedo complete with a cummerbund, a top hat, a cane, and a monocle. Think Mr. Peanut, if he were a pilot. Also the monocle is a spring loaded novelty monocle. That way every time I say something funny, the pilots will press a button and make it pop out.

For my female pilots? Every woman that I have ever met who is a pilot is always complaining how much she hates wearing the same uniform as the male pilots, and how unflattering it is. I have a simple solution to this: Playboy bunny outfits.

Catering-

If I ever eat another spinzel again in my life, I will freakin' lose it. These are the pretzel snacks that UPside Airlines made me hand out. Miniature salted pretzels, twisted around that my pilots and I were forced to eat as nourishment on long days when there wasn't enough time to run in to the airport in between our half hour turns. But no more!

Snoop Dogg has a personal chef travel around with him to make him fried chicken whenever he wants. I will have a chef do this for me, however my airline will serve only pizza, since that is my favorite food.

People always look at me like I'm crazy when I say that, considering how many other great foods there are out there, but I blame the Ninja turtles. From a young age they taught me it was the best food to have ever been invented, and to this day I still strive to achieve their level of being the greatest 'party dude' on earth.

I have also learned throughout the years in my travels that it can be cheap, expensive, made right, or wrong. But it's always great. Anyone who disagrees gets turned into the airport police under suspicion of supporting terrorism.

The beverages will be dispensed out of a fountain machine in the back of the aircraft. All beverages: soda, juice, water, beer, wine, champagne, spirits, coffee, and tea. It may sound a bit trashy, but to counterbalance this, all beverages will also be drunk out of champagne glasses. *All beverages*. No exceptions. That should even things out and make it a bit classier.

Also you have to get the beverages yourself. Your legs aren't broken, and I'm not having my flight attendants push a cart full of cans up and down the aisle. You know who pushes carts full of cans? Homeless people.

The aircraft interior-

Now I'm no interior designer, so I'm hiring the Swedes on this one. They seem to know what they're doing with the furniture from Ikea. The only downside to this is they'll probably make me assemble everything myself. I'm fine with that, because then I can proudly declare "I built this aircraft with my own two hands!"

The back of every seat will have a TV in it that will play every episode of LOST because that is my favorite show and I will need something to watch when I'm bored. If you don't feel like watching that show, every seat back pocket will have a copy of my book in it. You can read that instead, but you probably won't understand what everyone is talking about at the end of each episode when I open the floor up for a detailed discussion about what went on in that episode over the PA.

The routes we fly-

This will of course be an international airline so that I can live out my childhood dream of traveling the world. We will fly anywhere our customers want us to, however we will only fly east. Never west. I don't care if we're in Washington D.C. and we need to fly down to Florida. Florida is south. Not east. Therefore, we will fly east all the way around the globe until reaching Florida.

The reason for this is simple: when you cross the international dateline going west, you gain a day. But when you cross it again to go back east, you will lose a day. Therefore, I have figured out that if my airline only flies west and constantly circumnavigates the globe over and over again we will continuously gain days, ultimately sending us back in time. This leads me to my master plan of why I am starting this airline.

Time travel and how I will continue to grow and acquire my wealth-

Most pilots will tell you that airplanes can only fly up, down, left, and right. But they cannot fly backwards or through time. However now that I have discovered the secret to time travel by crossing the international date line in one direction repeatedly, I will continuously fly until I end up in 1998. This seems like the year that I should have been investing stock in everything that is popular now, and I'm kicking myself for not having done it when I had the chance, even if I was only ten years old at the time.

Unfortunately there are all these time travel rules about not changing the past or stepping on dinosaurs or whatever, so I will have to buy stock under my alias name: Rodney Danger (this is the name I always drop when I am in trouble).

I will then begin flying only west until I arrive back in the present and come home to find my stocks and net worth grown exponentially.

This may seem like a lot of work and trouble for running an airline-

I haven't even thought about how baggage will be handled. But that's the least of my concerns now that I've discovered the secret of time travel and have figured out how to become richer than I already will be. But my airline's not going to fly itself, and chances are it will probably hemorrhage money. But the important thing is that I will have the money to take care of everyone from UPside airlines that had my back and deserves to fly for an airline where they will be much happier. So I guess that's the real reason I will start my own airline.

Identity crisis

June 20th 2012

The night before
flying to Chicago
for my court trial
I went to
the Irish pub outside of DCA
to meet Ne-ne, Kylie,
and Raphael for drinks.

It was crazy to think
that I would be going
back to Chicago the next day
to go to court
over something
that would ultimately
decide my future.

I can't say that I wasn't nervous
about what would happen.
Too many
tequila and tonic waters
lead me running in circles
with my friends.

Sure, I was more than positive
I was going to win
and get my job back,
but what would happen if I didn't?

I had been hired three years ago
at the age of twenty one
as a flight attendant.
I didn't have
any other job skills.

No college education.
This was all I had left,
and I was throwing
all of my eggs
into one basket.

I had tried applying
at another airline,
that didn't work out.
I had tried working
at that suit store,
that didn't work out.

No, this-
this airline
was my future.
It was where
I was supposed to be,
it was where
I was meant to be.
And when I was fired,
that was taken away from me.
And I was determined
to get it back.

Ne-ne laughed and put me
back in my place.
I was talking
like I was at the end of my road,
as if there was nothing else
left for me
that I could accomplish
in my lifetime.

And then she told me
that she herself
had just quit UPside Air.
I was shocked.
She just didn't
want to do it anymore.
She had no solid job lined up,
only an offer to apply
at some office in D.C.
filing paperwork.
But it was an opportunity,
an opening,
a window out.

And she wasn't the only one.
Raphael had been applying
at other airlines as well.
He was tired of working
for a regional airline
and wanted to move up
to a major carrier
while he was still
in his late twenties.

It would be more worth it
for him to start
at the bottom there now,
working his way up
to retirement
for a larger carrier,
before he wound up
like one of our pilots
that had been flying
at our airline for fifteen years
and had nothing to show for it.

And within six months,
Kylie would leave
the airline as well.

It struck me at that moment,
that even if I did
come back to UPside Air,
it wouldn't be the same.
Nothing stays the same
for very long.

I wondered what
I was even fighting for anymore?
To get my job back?
To prove that I wasn't wrong
by publishing my book?
Hell, I didn't even know
at that point.

I told Ne-ne that she was right.
It was time to grow up.

Because even if I came back,
there wouldn't be
much for me to come back to.

I wasn't restricted
to just being a flight attendant
for the rest of my life
at that terrible regional airline
that didn't even want me anymore.

For the last six months
I had been holding on
to something
that I should have let go
at the time I lost it.

It was over,
and this was the end
of my story at UPside Air.
But before it was finished,

I still had one last thing
left to do
before closing
that part of my life.
I still had to prove
that I was right
and they were wrong.

"And once you've done that-"
Ne-ne asked me,
raising her beer to her lips
". . . once you've finished all of this?
What then?"

The court trial

June 21st 2012

Part One
Planes, trains, and automobiles
(The journey there)

On a Thursday in June, the day before the court trial, I was set to fly from Baltimore, to JFK, to Chicago. Everything was set, arranged and paid for by my union. The transportation, the hotel, nothing was coming out of my pocket (Which was good because I had no money left by this point.) I left for the airport at 8 AM. The following was the journey I underwent to get to Chicago.

8:00 AM-
I leave my house in the pouring rain, get into my car and immediately hit traffic. This is no big deal because my flight is not until 10:30 AM, and I have plenty of time to get there.

8:11 AM-
Sally calls. She says because of the weather in the area, my flight to New York has been canceled. I ask her how she knows this. She says just because I no longer have access to flight information, doesn't mean that she doesn't. I ask her what I should do. She tells me to keep heading towards the airport. I do so.

8:30-
I have an idea. I call Sally and tell her I still have my parking pass for DCA. I ask if it would be better for me to drive down to DCA instead and fly from there to JFK. She tells me that wouldn't change anything, it's bad all over my area. She tells me to keep heading to the airport though; they're working on a plan.

8:44-
Sally calls me back. She says they have arranged for me to take a train from BWI to LGA at 10:00, to just go to the train station in the airport instead of the STRATA Airlines ticket counter. From LGA I'll have ground transportation to JFK and fly from there.

9:04-
I am starting to worry, I'm only half way to the airport and neither the rain, nor the traffic is letting up.

9:10-
I blow the horn and curse at no one in particular.

9:22-
I am starting to freak out. I am sure I am going to miss my train.

9:34-
I arrive at the airport and park my car. I run with my suitcase towards where I assume the train station is in the airport.

9:44-
I cannot find the train station in the airport. I go to the information desk. The old woman behind the desk points me in the right direction.

9:52-
I check my watch again as I run towards what I hope is the train station. I freak out once more.

9:56-
I find the train station. I get my ticket and board the train. I let out a sigh of relief as I take my seat at a table by the window.

10:13-
The train takes off late due to weather.

10:56-
I have not been on a train since I was a small child. The ride is not as magical as I remember.

11:14-
I get up and go to the snack stand for a cup of coffee. I talk to the woman that makes me my coffee.
"How long until we arrive in New York?" I ask.
"About another three hours." She responds.
"That long?" I ask.
". . . What do you want? It's a train. Not a rocket ship."
I tell her she would make a good flight attendant, take my coffee, and return to my seat.

11:54-
As we pass through the Pennsylvania country side, the sun emerges from the clouds, warming my left arm by the window. I'm reminded of the Russian girl Mel that passed away what seemed like an eternity ago. I close my eyes and smile.

12:32 PM-
An attractive girl boards the train and sits across from me.

12:41-
The sun disappears behind the clouds again.
"Crazy weather we're having, huh?" I say to the girl.
She looks from the window to me frowns and just replies with an "I guess" And looks back out the window again.

12:45-
"So . . . Where are you headed?" I ask her.
She looks from the window back to me and answers "New York" And turns back to the window once more. Alright bitch, I was just making conversation. I'll let you get back to staring at all the exciting trees we're passing by.

1:11-
She gets off the train at the first stop in New York.

1:31-
The conductor announces the next stop is JFK airport. I begin wondering if I should get off since that is where I am flying out of.

1:33-
I try calling Sally. I get no reception. I try again. Nothing.

1:36-
We arrive at the JFK stop. I am sweating, faced with the decision if I should get off the train or not. I decide against it and remain in my seat.

2:05-
We arrive at LGA airport. The second I step off of the train, my phone rings. It's Sally. She says that she's been trying to call me, but wasn't getting through. I tell her I was trying to call because the train stopped at JFK and I wanted to know if I could have got off the train there. She says I could have, but there's no point now, to just find my transportation to JFK. I sigh and drag my bags from one end of the airport to the other.

2:16-
My ride is nowhere to be found. I call Sally back. She says that I should be looking for Princess limo service.

2:22-
I find my ground transportation when I spot an older Hispanic man holding a sign with my name on it beside a black town car. He puts my bags into the trunk and I climb into the back seat.

2:29-
I make small talk with the driver: "It's kind of ironic, there's a pilot at my airline that I call 'Princess'. And that's the name of your transportation service."
He looks in the rear view mirror at me and replies with a: "Huh. How about that." And looks back to the road.
"I should say my former airline. I'm actually on the way to Chicago to go to court with them." I say. I waited for him to ask what for or respond. Instead, he looks back in the mirror at me, says nothing, and then back at the road again. I lean back in the seat. I didn't realize it was national 'ignore the crap out of Chuck' day.

3:06-
I arrive at JFK and make my way to the check in counter. The computerized STRATA Airlines ticketing machine says that I have missed my 3:30 flight. I press the 'help' button. No one comes to my aid. I push it again. Again, no one comes.

3:10-
A ticket agent comes over and asks me if I need help.
"Yea, I'm not checking any bags, I just want to go straight to the flight. This machine says I missed my 3:30 flight." I say.
"Yes, check in for that flight was at 3:00 PM. That was ten minutes ago." He says.
"I was only six minutes late. You added the other four when you kept me waiting for you." I say.
"I'm so sorry, sir. I can book you on the next flight." He says.
"Look, I was a flight attendant for UPside for two and a half years. I know how it works. The gate doesn't close until ten minutes before departure. I can make it there."
"That's in seven minutes sir."
"That's because you've kept me here going back and forth with you for the last three!"
". . . Sir, do you want me to book you on the next flight or not?" He asks.
I sigh. I've been in this battle before, on the other side. The winning side. And I knew that as a passenger that wasn't the side I was on. I tell him he would make a good flight attendant, take my ticket for the next flight and leave.

3:14-
I call Sally and tell her I missed my flight and was booked on the next one that would put me in Chicago around seven.

3:20-
I go through security and decide that I deserve a well-earned drink.

3:22-
I find an empty bar in the airport and take a seat. I order a tequila and tonic water. It is nine dollars. I ask the bar tender if they give an airline employee discount. He says that they do, and asks to see my badge. I tell

him I don't have it because I was fired from my airline for writing a book about being a flight attendant, and that I was on my way to Chicago to go to court because of it. After explaining all of this to him, he laughs and tells me he'll give me the discount.

3:34-
He asks me about the book. I tell him the 'Chuck Norris and my first enemy' story and 'The now infamous juice can races' because those stories always get the best reception.

3:40-
I have another tequila and tonic water. This one is stronger than the last. He asks to hear another story. I tell him 'Mile high club' and 'You didn't say the magic word'. He asks what he has to do to publish a book about being a bar tender. I tell him he needs to have an audience that will read it, and he has to be willing to lose his job and burn as many bridges as possible. He laughs at this.

4:01-
He makes me another tequila and tonic. The bar is getting a bit more crowded now.

4:10-
A group of business men come in. The bartender looks at them, looks at me, and then does the robot dance, referencing my nick name for them. I laugh and tell him that's a good one.

4:21-
I get my tab. It's $24. I only got a dollar off of each drink with my 'employee discount', and because he was nice to me and gave me the discount anyway, I am forced to leave him a really good tip. I am tipsy, so I don't care.

4:32-
I stumble over to my gate. There are at least four good looking girls in the gate area.

4:35-
I text Damien (verbatim): "4 hot chix in gate area to ORD. Time for Chuck to shine!"
Damien texts back (verbatim): "LOL Ten $ says you're gonna be next to a Robot on the flight."

4:44-
They begin boarding my flight to Chicago.

4:59-
I take my middle seat with an old business man sitting on my left.

5:03-
I watch three of the four hot girls pass by my seat before another business man sits to my right. I text Damien back (verbatim): "U suck."

5:15-
The flight takes off. I pass out.

5:57-
I wake up. I need water. I go to the aft of the aircraft and ask a flight attendant that had to have been at least a hundred years old for a glass of water. I ask her how long she has been flying for. She says forty-two years. I cannot imagine having worked as a flight attendant for that long. I say nothing about the reason I'm there and return to my middle seat.

6:58-
The flight lands.

7:23-
Sally picks me up outside of the airport and takes me to my hotel, laughing when she asks me how my trip was.

Part Two
Freight train derailing
(The night before the trial)

My hotel was in downtown Chicago.
After checking in at 8,
I dropped my bags off
in my room
and went downstairs
into a conference room
to meet Sally and Mark.

They spent the next two hours
telling me all of the things
to expect at the trial
the next day,
what I should say,
and what I shouldn't say.
(There was more
of that than anything.)

They told me
to get a good nights sleep
when retiring
to our separate rooms,
but even after
having traveled all day
to get to Chicago,
I wasn't tired.

I rode the elevator up
to the eleventh floor
where the bar was.
It was pretty empty
for a Thursday night.

I ordered a tequila and tonic water,
and took it out
on to a balcony
that overlooked the city.

I leaned against the railing,
staring in the direction
of the airport.
The direction of the hotel
I lived in for two months
with Corazon.

I tried not to let my thoughts
get the best of me.
I tried not to think about
the girl I had lost.

As I sipped my drink,
the chief pilot David Friendly
approached me from the bar.
He asked if he could join me.
I told him he could.

I asked him
what he was doing in Chicago,
but he just laughed
and said that I already knew
the answer to that.
Then I asked him why
he helped me
the day that I was fired.

He took a drink
from his own glass
of whiskey and coke
and told me
that he was hired
by UPside airlines as a pilot
twenty years ago
at the age of twenty one.

He had seen a lot of co-workers
come and go.
A lot of good people,
a lot of bad people.
He saw the airline change,
and he got into management
five years ago
to try and make a difference
in the company.

But he told me that in the end,
the company
was like a freight train.

And it didn't matter
if you throw a pebble
at the train,
or a rock.
It's hard to make a change
in something
that you can't stop
from progressing.

Over the last five years
as chief pilot,
he had tried so hard
to make a change
in the company for the better.
But in the end,
it didn't matter
if he was on board
the train or not.

Everyone's got a boss
to answer to.
And no matter what he did,
the conductor of the train
was the person
who had the final word
in the fate of that train.

So when someone like me
comes along
and starts pulling on
bells
and whistles
and causing a scene,
it's the conductors job
to see to it
that that person is removed.

I told him that I thought
it was funny someone
in the airline industry
was making such a
large analogy about trains,
but I still didn't understand
what he was getting at.

He laughed and told me
that he was only in Chicago
because he had to be.
None of this
had anything to do with him.

He was only there
to testify
to what happened
in the meeting
the day I was fired.

He then told me
that he didn't like
the direction
that the train
was heading in anymore.

He was done trying
to change it's course,
and that he would be
getting off at the next stop
before it derailed.
And no matter the outcome
of the trial the next day,
he suggested
that I do the same.

He told me that he saw
somewhat of himself in me,
that I reminded him
of what he was like
when he began working
in the airline industry.

He did not believe
the companies decision
or the way they handled
the situation was right.
But he had no say in the matter,
he was management,
and therefore,
had to do what he was told.

I told him I would make
no mention of our conversation
at the trial the next day,
thanked him,
and returned to my room.

As I lay in bed,
staring at the ceiling,
I let our conversation sink in.
He was right.
Even if I did win,
there was no reason
to come back.

Even if I did win,
I wouldn't come back.
And I understood
how he and I were alike.

I was there to prove
I was right and they were wrong.
I was there for one last party.
I was there to waste
their time and their money.
I wasn't there
to get my job back anymore.
I was there
for revenge.

Part Three
The fisherman and the snake
(The court trial)

They say that when you're in a horrific situation, time speeds up, that everything happens so fast. I'm not going to be over dramatic here and say that the court court trial was was some kind of traumatic event, quite the opposite. It was actually more funny than anything. But it did all happen quite fast, and piecing together every detail has been challenging, but I will do my best. This is how it happened:

We entered the room at 9 am. There was no jury. Just a seating area behind us. Our table was on the left. I sat in between Sally and Mark. Mikey came into the room with a lawyer and another man and sat at a table to our right. She did not make eye contact.

People filtered into the room and took the seats behind us. Some I didn't recognize. Some, I did. David Friendly was there, of course, but amongst him were other co-workers that I did not expect to see. ElHeffey was there along with Lizzie, Mary, Damien (Who made it a point to sit beside Mary), Krista, B-rye, Raphael, Treetops (Who lived in Chicago), and James. I realized that I was not in this alone. It no longer felt like a trial, suddenly it was a goodbye party. There was one empty seat however that I kept looking at, hoping that Corazon would show up to take. She never did.

We all rose for the Honorable Judge to enter the room. He looked exactly like Dr. Drew. Mark told me to keep that to myself when I told him.

Mark stood up along with the UPside Air lawyer. They both began spewing some legal talk. Most of what was said that day was legal talk that I didn't understand. Mark sat down. Their lawyer began talking about how I had slandered the company. Made myself and everyone else there look bad, and should have publication of my book stopped before it did any more damage to our companies 'sterling reputation'. B-rye stood up and shouted "I object!" causing a few people to laugh, and then was told to sit down by the judge, who said if anyone else made an outburst like that, they would be escorted out of the room.

Mikey was called to the stand. She was asked to show the print outs from my website she had the day I was fired. The judge rifled through the papers and stopped at one particular page. I'm not sure which one, I couldn't remember everything that was printed out and used against me when I was fired. But he stared at it a little closer than the others, and then looked at me. I wasn't sure what to do, so I gave him a thumbs up and smiled. He did not smile back. Mark told me to take this seriously. Their lawyer began asking Mikey how this affected the company as a whole. She began saying the same things that I had been hearing over and over again since the day I was fired: slandering the company, making everyone look bad, etc. etc. She sat down.

I was asked to take the stand. I answered every question exactly the way Mark had told me to the night before.

I was asked if it was I in the photograph of me, Lizzy, and ElHeffey that was taken outside of Minglewoods. Mark had told me to be honest if asked that question. I said it was not only I, but also two of my favorite co-workers and pointed them out, who waved back at me.

I was asked if I could see how my website could hurt the reputation of the company, and I said I did not see how. That was just a photo of us standing in front of a large wooden beaver.

I was then asked if any of the stories were true. Mark had told me that because I had taken down the website, there was no proof of telling the stories were real, with the exception of the juice can race. So I said that they were all written from ideas I had come up with and none of them were really true.

Their lawyer then read aloud parts from 'The now infamous juice can races' (with no emotion, by the way) and then read the write up I received for the incident. Both were handed to the judge, and I was asked that if the stories were not true, how could I explain the connection between the two. I said that first of all, he was reading my story all wrong, and that if anyone was going to read from my book it should be me since I was the author. This caused more laughter, and was not the answer Mark had told me to give. I then said that the report that had been written by Mikey was only a brief summary of an incident that occurred when I had first started flying three years ago that never happened again. I merely took that brief summary and dreamed up a totally wild story, changing everyone's names as well as the airlines to make it even more fictional. That was the answer I was told to give.

I was then asked one final question: If I had changed everyone else name, why not my own? Mark did not cover this question with me, but I had been asked it so many times, I decided to give the same answer I always do: If I *had* changed my own name, I could never use that to impress beautiful women. Marks eyes grew wide when hearing this. I don't think it was the answer he wanted to hear. I returned to my seat.

The Chief pilot, David Friendly, was then asked to take the stand.

He was asked if he was aware or had seen my website or book. He said that he knew about it, but had no idea who I was, or that I even worked for UPside Airlines. He said that he was a little too preoccupied trying to manage a fleet of air crafts than to go on a witch hunt because of some website with a bunch of funny stories on it.

He was asked if he had seen the photos of me with pilots of ours on the website. He said that he had never seen any photos until the day before I was terminated, and when he went back to the website the next day, it was no longer working.

He was then asked to describe what happened the day I was terminated. He gave a brief recap and said that it was nothing out of the ordinary compared to any other meetings he had to sit in as a witness, with one strange exception. He said that at the end of the meeting, Mikey was asked to have a word with me alone, and he found that strange, since it had never happened before. This caused some whispers behind us, and when I looked across the room at Mikey, I could see that she was caught off guard. Their lawyer had no further questions. He sat down.

Mark stood up to present my case.

Mikey was called to the stand. She was asked apart from the juice can races, was there any other proof that any of these stories were real. She said no.

She was asked if I had been reprimanded for anything else since that incident. She said yes, I had been into her office many times since then to be scolded for breaking various other rules.

She was asked if she had any documentation or proof of these incidents. She said no, they were just verbal warnings.

She was asked why, if there was no proof of these stories being real, was my punishment was so harsh. She said that the decision was made from above and that even if those stories weren't real, I had written them. She said that because they were in my head and presented to the mass public, there was a chance that I could make them come true.

Mark asked her if she thought my punishment for writing fictional stories that never actually occurred was fitting punishment for a crime I hadn't yet committed. It took her a long time, but she finally responded yes.

She was then asked one final question: Why was everyone else asked to leave the room but her and I after I was terminated? She was obviously not expecting this question and it took her several more moments to respond. She merely answered that it was to say goodbye personally. Mark had no further questions for her and she sat down.

Mark then asked Captain Friendly to take the stand.

He asked him if he thought my termination was justifiable. He said no, and it's unfortunate that he had no say in the matter, because the inflight department has nothing to do with the pilot side, other than flying together.

He was then asked if he thought my book or website would hurt the company in any kind of way. He answered on the contrary. If anything, he believed it should have been embraced. To be used as a marketing stunt for publicity, or at the very least, have me start writing for their inflight magazine. To just terminating me was less than justifiable, and above all else, it was a violation of my freedom of speech. This caused more whispers behind us and was certainly not the answer I'm sure that UPside Air wanted to hear from their chief pilot. He was asked to take his seat. He sat down.

Much to my surprise, Mark called me to the stand. At the practice run the night before he told me that he wouldn't have any questions for me at the trial. In fact, he told me it would be best to not say anything at all. I took the stand, and he asked me one question: What did Mikey say to me the day I was terminated after she asked everyone else to leave the office? I responded that it was nothing important, she just wanted to say goodbye and thank me for my time working there.

He asked if I was sure, if there was anything else we discussed. I looked at Mikey. She did not make eye contact. She did not move. She just stared down at the table. I said no, that was all.

The judge told us we would break for a short recess before returning for his decision.

In the waiting room Mark asked what was wrong with me, and if I even wanted my job back. I said yes, even though it was a lie.

My friends that had come to show their support told me that after the chief pilot stepped up for me, there was no way I could lose. Damien said we needed to celebrate that night by drinking ourselves crazy. Treetops said he knew some good spots in downtown Chicago for us to go to.

Mary asked to speak to me alone for a moment. She and I went into a corner. She said that she talked to Ne-ne two nights ago, who said it didn't sound like I even wanted to come back to UPside Air if I won the case and got my job back. I told her that was true. She then asked why. Why was I going through all of this trouble? Why waste everyone's time to prove a point that I was right and they were wrong? I told her: they should have seen this coming. After all, the book wasn't called 'Good flight attendant.'

We were called back into the court room. The judge asked the UPside Airlines lawyer if he had anything left to present. He said no. He asked Mark if he had anything else. Before he could answer I stood up and said I would like to say something. I could tell by the look in Marks eyes that he did not approve of this, but I didn't care. I took a moment before saying:

"There once was a fisherman that lived alone in a shack by the river. He was poor, but he was happy, and he kept himself alive by fishing. One day, in the winter time, he found a poisonous snake washed up on the river bank. The snake said: 'Help me Fisherman! Please! You have to help me, I'm freezing and dying!' But the fisherman said: 'You can't fool me snake, I know your plan! You will bite me and poison me!' But the snake said: 'No, please! Find it in your heart to help me!' So out of the kindness of his heart, the fisherman helped the snake. He brought the snake back to his shack and all winter long, he shared his fish with the snake and nursed it back to health. And then in the spring time, the snake was healthy again. And the fisherman said: 'You are healthy again snake, you can go now.' And the snake thanked the fisherman. And as he was leaving, the snake turned around and bit the fisherman, poisoning him. And the Fisherman asked: 'Why snake?! Why did you bite me, why did you poison me after everything I've done for you?!' and the snake replied: ' . . . You knew what I was when you brought me in. And you knew what I was capable of.' . . . I can't say I'm sorry for what I've done and the decisions I've made. Because it is who I am. I don't regret anything I've done up to this point. It's because of this airline that I've made so many wonderful friends. I found and lost love. I've been to places I never expected to go, and had experiences I never thought I would have had. But above all, it gave me a story to tell. And that's all that matters in the end."

I don't think anyone really understood what I was talking about except for Mary and David Friendly. The judge rolled his eyes and asked if I had anything else to add. I said no, and sat down. I looked back at the empty seat once more, hoping to see Corazon. The judge said that he had made his decision regarding my future with UPside Air.

No answer he could have gave me that day would have made a difference, because the truth was, I had no future there. That airline was no longer who I was. It was who I had been, and it was time to move on. My story at UPside Air was over.

I never told you what I do for a living

June 23rd 2012

My last flight coming back from the court trial was from PHL to BWI on a Soma Air flight. Their air crafts were also fifty seater regional jets, designed identically to ours, being so that they were another STRATA Airlines express carrier. My seat was 12F, the last seat by the window on aircraft right before the bathroom.

I took my seat, put my carry on bag under the seat in front of me, and pulled the inflight magazine out of the seat back pocket. A beautiful looking blonde girl took the seat beside me. She smiled at me. I smiled back. The flight attendant, a woman in her mid forties, did her compliance checks, and took her jump seat. We taxied out, circled the runway a few times and then came to a stop. The captain came on the PA.

Captain: Sorry folks, but there's a bit of weather in the area . . . air traffic control has us holding here for the time being. Shouldn't be too long before we have an update . . . thanks for your patience.

Everyone groans but me.

Blondie: This is bull shit. This is the worst airline ever, this happens every time! I swear I'm never flying on this again!

Chuck: Sorry, were you . . . talking to me?

Blondie: Huh? Well . . . I was just making a general statement.

Chuck: Oh. Ok. When you say the worst airline . . . do you mean STRATA Airlines? Or Soma Air?

Blondie: What's Soma Air?

Chuck: It's an express carrier of STRATA Airlines.

Blondie: What's an express carrier?

Chuck: . . . Never mind.

I return to my magazine. Blondie looks out my window.

Blondie: It's not even raining outside!

Chuck: It doesn't have to be raining. It could be lightning and thunder storms. We can't fly the plane through a lightning storm.

Blondie: There's not a cloud in the sky!

Chuck: . . . Did you think that maybe the weather isn't over Philadelphia? That it's on the route we're flying?

Blondie: . . . What are you like a pilot or something?

Chuck: No.

Blondie: So what? You're like, a frequent flier or something like that?

Chuck: Yea. Something like that.

I go back to my magazine. After ten more minutes, Blondie is obviously getting restless.
She stands up and opens the overhead. The flight attendant gets on the PA.

Flight attendant: Ma'am, you need to remain seated please! The seat belt sign is still on, and we are on an active taxi way. We could begin moving any minute!

Blondie makes an audibly loud groaning noise and takes her seat. She crosses her arms and sighs again. She then reaches up and pushes the call button. The flight attendant approaches.

Blondie: I'm hot. Can I get something to drink?

Flight attendant: Of course, I'll bring you some water.

Blondie: I don't want water, I want a free drink for having to wait here. You're making me late.

Flight attendant: . . . I'm sorry, I can't serve anything else from the beverage cart until we're airborne.

Blondie: Fine, whatever.

Before leaving, the flight attendant stares at me momentarily before going back up to the galley. She returns and hands Blondie a cup of water. The flight attendant continues to stare at me as she hands Blondie the water.

Flight attendant: Do I . . . know you?

Chuck: I don't think so.

Blondie: Can I get some ice in this? It's hot in here!

The flight attendant gives her the same look I would have and I laugh. She leaves.

Blondie: What's so funny?

Chuck: Nothing you would understand.

The flight attendant returns seconds later without the water.

Flight attendant: Are you the one that wrote the book? With the website?

I laugh.

Chuck: How did you know?

Flight attendant: I love your site! I recognized you from the pictures on there. A friend of mine that works at UPside Air told me about it, so I checked it out. Your stories are great! What happened to the website, it went off line at the end of the year.

Chuck: Thank you, that means a lot to me, it really does. I got in a bit of trouble and had to take it down-

Blondie: Excuse me, can I get my water?!

The flight attendant looks at her, and then back at me. Then the flight attendant points at me.

Flight attendant: 'You didn't say the magic word'!

Chuck: Everyone loves that story.

We both laugh and she goes back up to the galley. Blondie is getting more frustrated.

Blondie: So what, you're some kind of writer?

Chuck: Far from it.

The flight attendant returns with a tray. She hands Blondie a cup of ice water from the tray, and then hands me a glass of ice, a can of tonic water, and two mini bottles of tequila.

Chuck: You don't have to do that . . .

Flight attendant: It's my pleasure. Come up to the galley during the flight, I want to talk to you more about the stories.

She returns back to her jump seat. Blondie is furious. I pour the tequila into the glass, add the tonic water to it, and stir it. I smile and raise my glass at Blondie and make a toast.

Chuck: . . . Here's to bad flight attendants everywhere.

. . . slowbacktohome.

June 23rd 2012

My time is up.
This is my chance
to tell you everything
I've wanted to,
even if it is too late.
My time is up.

"I'm selling my stories to the highest bidder!"
I've sold myself for less than you think.
But the jokes on you,
I have your three dollars now!

No one can do this better than me.
No one can replace me.
The first time around
was a God damn mess.
I learned my lesson.
I'm not ashamed.

And you held my hand
from the hotel
and underneath Chicago's crushing lights . . .

Now I've got you.
I've got you
right where I want you.
There's no stopping this.
Don't test me.

I won't apologize.
Beautiful eyes.
Chicago lies.

Pushed up
against a hotel wall
to kiss you goodbye.

Work up your nerves.
You have no where
to duck and take cover
from this.
There's no stopping me.
I'm calling you out.
I'm gutting out all
of (y)our secrets.
You know damn well
what I mean.

"The truth hurts more
than anything else."

Take it.
Don't flinch.
Move with me.
Move together
for a last dance
(Blood upon my hands).
We're both capable of the worst.
Your hands
are just as much of a mess
as mine are.

None of your crying can help.
Stand up
and wipe your eyes.
"Don't you dare compare
your pain
to the sympathetic look
in her eyes
when full of tears, boy."

'. . . And the two never met again'.
That's the real ending.
There isn't always a 'happily ever after',
Peruvian princess.
Tell Corazon I'm alone again.

"Aren't you proud of me?
The dust has settled
and I'm still standing."
Now watch me burn
as I ride this plane
one last time
into the sunset.

When the worst has ended,
the morning begins.
And as long as I never have to see you again,
in my mind
you'll always be the same.

. . . to the airport/ pack your
suitcase, take it to the
airport/ pack your suitcase, take
it to the airport/ pack
your suitcase, take it to
the airport/ pack your suitcase,
take it to the airport/
pack your suitcase, take it
to the airport/ I'm gone.

Acknowledgments:

First and foremost I have to thank **everyone I left behind at my express carrier** for the times we shared and giving me the experiences to write about. Whether they were good, bad, or just boring, they were an amazing three years together. It would take far too long to sit down and individually name all of you that worked there, and after all the trouble I got in by putting real names in the first book, I know better. But you know who you are.

My editor **Audrey Turner** (*http://audreykosher.blogspot.com*): You continue to inspire me to be a better writer. You are an amazing friend for reading through all of this non-sense and not only editing all of my awful mistakes, but giving me your input on what to change and alter in my stories (Some, I took to heart, and some I remained stubborn about and insisted I keep.) Thank you for all the work you did.

My graphic designer **Brian Snyder** (*http://briansnyderdesign.com*): I gave you several ideas and we turned those ideas into a reality. Then you took that reality and turned it into art. From my cover design to the airline logos to all the promotional pieces, you made an imaginary airline something real. Not only are you great at what you do, but you're able to make a living doing it, and that is something I have always felt is the key to real success.

My cover model **Tatevick Vardanyan**: Thank you for your patience as we photographed you 174 times. You were great as the *UPside Airlines* model flight attendant, but even better as a life long friend. Wherever we go in life, I know you'll always be just across the street.

About the Author

A.O Norris is not a writer. He's just a flight attendant that wanted to tell a story, and a book was the most logical, time consuming, frustrating way to do so. He has won the *"Most handsome flight attendant of the year award"* from 2005-2011 and again in 2013. He divides his time between flying and following artistic endeavors such as writing on his website *www.upsideairlines.com.* After selling one million copies of his book he plans on buying a really, really, really big house; marrying his supermodel girlfriend; and then starting his own airline (For more info read: *When I finally get around to running my own airline, this is what it will be like.)* None of his stories are true, and you can't prove otherwise.